"Miss?"

She brought her attention to his mouth, which also seemed quirked in amusement. That was irritating enough, but she found herself mesmerized like some dopey schoolgirl by the wide fullness of his lips and the white evenness of his teeth.

Her mouth went suddenly dry, and she licked her lips as she prepared to speak. For some reason, that made all traces of amusement in his face disappear, and his lips closed in a tight straight line matching the frown that etched his forehead. Lord, he was handsome.

"Clearly you have me at a disadvantage, sir. Would you please leave by whatever means you came . . ." She glanced around, looking for signs of transportation.

"Please come out of the water so I can explain," he coaxed softly. "You're beginning to turn quite blue, you know." This last came accompanied by that ravishing smile again.

Katrina considered her options. She could stay in the water, or she could climb out and take her chances with him. What if he was a thief . . . a kidnapper . . . or worse? Still, she stood a better chance of escaping on shore.

"Turn around," she ordered and was surprised when he obliged her immediately, even moving a few feet away to give her more room.

In a single movement she hoisted herself onto the rock and reached for her clothes.

"I wouldn't do that," he said quietly.

Oh, Lord, this was worse than she'd imagined . . .

TWILIGHT MIST

ANN JUSTICE

Supie —
Enjoy!
ANN
#5

B
BERKLEY BOOKS, NEW YORK

TWILIGHT MIST

A Berkley Book / published by arrangement with
the author

PRINTING HISTORY
Berkley edition / December 1992

ISBN: 0-425-13528-4

BERKLEY BOOK ® TM 757, 375
Berkley Books are published by The Berkley Publishing Group,
200 Madison Avenue, New York, New York 10016.
The name "BERKLEY" and the "B" logo
are trademarks belonging to Berkley Publishing Corporation.

PRINTED IN THE UNITED STATES OF AMERICA

10 9 8 7 6 5 4 3 2 1

Acknowledgments

No story that relies on historical fact can be accurately told without the help of those who work to preserve our history and keep it alive and available. I offer a salute to those who helped with this work:

To Bill O'Brien, who talks as easily about the nineteenth century beer industry as he does about today's weather. He got me started in the right direction.

To the local history room and Maritime Historical Collection of the Milwaukee Public Library, whose maps, photographs, and records were a godsend.

To the folks at the Chicago Historical Society and Milwaukee County Historical Society, who could not have been more supportive or helpful.

To the Fire Museum in Peshtigo, Wisconsin, where I was able to take an eerie walk back in time to that terrible day in 1871.

To the librarians of the microfilm collection at the Golda Meir Library of the University of Wisconsin-Milwaukee for their careful preservation of such accounts of routine life as *Peterson's Magazine,* the *Milwaukee Sentinel's* July 5, 1871, account of the Fourth of July festivities (including a reprint of the keynote address), and the eyewitness accounts of the Chicago Fire filed by reporters for the

Chicago Tribune and *The New York Times*.

To Larry Edgerton, who gave more tips for fine-tuning novels than he knew in his scriptwriting seminar.

To my agent, Jane Jordan Browne, and her great staff, who worked overtime to get this into print.

And most of all to Larry Schmidt, who is the best critic and supporter any writer could hope to have.

1

MILWAUKEE, WISCONSIN
JUNE, 1871

KATRINA BERGEMAN WAS having a bad day. First there was the altercation with Myron Hoffman over the delivery of the staves her father had ordered for the cooperage. They had beer to ship and no barrels to ship it in, she had announced to Hoffman. That was an exaggeration, of course, but she was making a point.

Then there was the weather—hot, muggy, the air at an absolute standstill. A man could remove his jacket and roll up his sleeves. He wouldn't be stifled by stockings, pantalets, three petticoats, a skirt, and, if one wanted to be truly in fashion, a bustle plus a draped apron over the skirt. And that list didn't even include the layers women wore from the waist up: camisole, corset, blouse—fastened to the neck, of course—and always a jacket if she was wearing a skirt in public.

The suit she wore was made from seventeen yards of percale, and in this heat it felt more like a hundred yards. Defiantly Katrina opened the top three buttons of her jacket and the top button of her blouse. She wished she could loosen the ties of her corset and breathed out hard, in hopes the tight strings might simply snap. But all she got for her trouble was a dizzy spell. No wonder women were always fainting in the novels and stories she read—the poor dears couldn't get any air!

At least she didn't have the added weight of a bustle. That wad of padding her sister Lulu would not be seen without, even inside the house, was just about the most frivolous and aggravating piece of nonsense Katrina had ever heard of. She had announced in no uncertain terms that she would not have such foolishness in her wardrobe. Mama had given in on that one, working with the dressmaker to give the illusion of a bustle without Katrina actually having to wear one.

"You are a member of an important family in this community," Sophie Bergeman had instructed her eldest daughter. "I will allow you only so much rebellion. You have to set an example. Whether you like it or not, my dear, people look to us."

Katrina had known there was no use arguing. For all her delicate beauty, Sophie Bergeman was not a woman one would willingly cross. While the Bergeman household was unorthodox in many ways, there were areas in which Sophie remained adamant. Maintaining a semblance of propriety appropriate for a family prominent in business and social circles was one of those areas.

So Katrina felt she had won a major victory when Mama agreed to let her forgo a bustle. Mama had even stood up for her with Lulu and Papa, although she had overheard Sophie tell Papa later that evening that Katrina was just going through a phase that would soon pass.

Well, Katrina didn't care. She would not wear a bustle *ever*, and she was not above leaving the despised corset behind on hot summer days like this one. The only reason she'd worn it today was that this morning there had been that wonderful cool breeze off Lake Michigan, fooling her into thinking the heat wave had broken.

But she worked for her father in the front office of the

family brewery and was expected to set an example for the other female employees. Still she had found ways to be as comfortable as possible, and had smiled when the other girls followed her example. Not one of them wore any of the draped and fringed layered dresses and skirts so much in fashion these days. And if she was any judge of fullness, she would guess they had only one petticoat under their skirts, as she did. There was little to be done, however, about the long sleeves and high necks that fashion dictated.

Of course, Papa was always urging her to take off early on such hot afternoons. "I don't know why you insist on coming in, *Liebchen,*" he would say fondly. But she knew it pleased him to have her there, and she would not allow him to show her any favoritism over the other employees. So she stayed, poring over the ledgers, filing bills and payments, and writing letters dictated by her father. All the while a small stream of perspiration coursed its way down her spinal column, and the hair at her nape and temples, which had escaped the twist of her chignon, lay damp and lifeless against her cheeks and neck.

Usually she enjoyed her work. Lately, though, it had been less satisfying than in those times when Papa had had to go off to war. Then he had left her and his chief assistant, Edward Mueller, in charge of everything. She had gotten used to working as Edward's equal—making decisions, solving problems . . .

Edward, she thought with a frown. The meeting earlier in the afternoon between her father, Edward, and the distribution managers from Chicago, Minneapolis, and Detroit had been the final annoyance in an already exasperating day. She attended the meeting to act as secretary, a role she filled willingly, preferring any part in the exciting world of business to the dull and oppressive world of society teas, club meetings, and meaningless gatherings that Lulu thrived on.

Father was grooming Edward Mueller to be his successor. On top of that, one day Edward and Lulu would probably wed. On top of that, he and Katrina had known each other forever—the man was practically a member of the family. Until this afternoon she had considered him a friend and confidant. Until he had betrayed her.

Oh, he would deny her accusations, of course. He would say she was making too much of the incident. But for Katrina it was just one more piece of evidence telling her that she was only fooling herself by hoping to make some meaningful contribution at the brewery.

The meeting had been going along just fine, the men all leaned back in their leather swivel chairs around the large walnut table August Bergeman used for such conferences. Katrina sat slightly behind her father, on a straight chair, carefully recording the minutes of their meeting, knowing full well what to include and what was off the record. The men usually forgot she was there, which was fine with her because then they behaved as they would have had there been no "lady present." They chomped on their cigars, hooked their thumbs in their vest pockets as they shared a laugh or bit of industry gossip, checked their gold pocket watches as the meeting droned on, and ran fingers under their tight starched collars as the heat of the day built. At least they had to wear those collars, Katrina reflected with a smile as she refilled their steins with the brewery's newest premium lager.

Katrina liked men. Rather, she liked their world—such incredible freedom they had! Such interesting topics peppered their conversations. Such wonderful possibilities to do something meaningful in life . . . something unexpected . . . different . . . with impact. She didn't want to *be* a man. She simply wished women had the same kind of freedom to choose and decide—and the freedom to be different. A man was often applauded for being a bit of a rebel. In a woman such behavior was unseemly, even shocking. Just look at the way everyone had reacted when Mama helped found the Women's Suffrage Association after the war.

One would think she had done something scandalous, run off with the town butcher or something. If a man organized a group for purposes of changing society, it was considered proper and fitting. But just let a woman . . .

"Are you getting this, Katrina?" Papa asked, as the managers reported the latest figures from their branches and depots around the region.

Katrina resumed her note-taking. She listened carefully as they made decisions about the coming sales season— how to advertise, what business deals to make, how to spread the word that Bergeman Beer of Milwaukee was the finest one would get in or out of Germany itself. The men discussed how best to introduce the new lager and how to mark the completion of their second decade. Ideas tumbled over one another in Katrina's own mind, and she itched to share her thoughts with these men who would make decisions that affected her family's future . . . her future.

Then Edward betrayed her. Oh, it was innocent enough, Edward had the aura of a choirboy. He had a thatch of straight blond hair that occasionally flopped over his forehead in a decidedly youthful way. His eyes were wide and blue, and his manner was one of constant amazement as he experienced the world around him. Edward was a joy to be with, but he was no fool. He knew full well that his position in Bergeman Brewing needed to be carefully tended. August Bergeman was not a man to simply surrender the top position in his business, even to his future son-in-law.

"Here's an idea," Edward said quietly, and even had the nerve to glance directly at Katrina before continuing. "What if we issued a commemorative stein . . . in celebration of our anniversary plus the introduction of our product to the east coast?" Then he looked at Katrina again, and this time he even winked.

The stein was her idea. She had told him about it just the week before as they sat together sharing lunch. She had moaned about how her father would never hear of such a thing, mocking his stern tone: "Too expensive,

Liebchen . . . matches . . . perhaps a tray, but a stein?" Then Papa would have laughed, his barrel chest shaking with merriment, his bushy eyebrows twitching with the deep rumble of his laughter. He probably would have patted her head and said, "You are a smart one, Katrina, but you must leave the business to the men."

She had told Edward all of her suggestions, and furthermore he had agreed with her. "A stein is a wonderful idea," he had assured her. "No one has ever done a commemorative stein before."

No, no one had. In fact, the Milwaukee breweries were innovators in the use of all sorts of souvenirs—matches, coasters, napkins . . . but never something so grand.

"A stein?" Each man at the table looked at Edward with alarm and then with some interest as the idea sank in.

"A stein," August Bergeman mumbled to himself. He got up and walked slowly around the luxurious office, the mark of his phenomenal success in a business where competition was tough. For a moment he paced the thick, geometrically patterned carpet, moving to the far end of the room, where his desk sat in front of a large arched window etched with the company logo.

"Nothing fancy," Edward hurried to add. "Simple . . . plain . . ." He looked over at Katrina as if he actually expected her to help him at this point. "Think how wonderful our lager looks in clear glass." He held up his own glass to illustrate his point. He also continued to glance nervously at Katrina, clearly expecting her to jump in and help him. "The clear golden color, capped with foam like a whitetop wave on the lake on a breezy summer's afternoon." He was quoting her own words.

The men at the table had turned their full attention to her father. It really did not matter whether they thought the idea a good one. The decision rested with August.

"A stein," he said again, his back to all of them. Then, glancing back at his daughter, he asked, "What do you think, Katrina?"

"It sounds expensive," Katrina said flatly with a malevolent glance at Edward.

Bergeman frowned. "Do you have figures, Edward?"

"Well, no, sir, not yet . . ." He looked from the father to the daughter, and his expression was one of pleading and confusion. *Help me,* his eyes begged. When he saw she would say nothing more, he added lamely, "It was just a thought, sir."

"And a good one," August boomed as he returned to the conference table and picked up his portfolio to indicate the meeting was over. "We will discuss it further on Friday. By then Edward will have a full report. Is that not right, Edward?" He draped an arm over the younger man's shoulders.

"Yes, sir," Edward replied quietly.

By the time the two men had bid the others good-bye and returned to the office, Katrina had tidied the conference room and moved into the outer office, to her own desk. She stood before the carved mahogany hall-tree mirror and speared her straw bonnet to her hair with a lethal-looking hatpin. She looked as if she might find a better use for the pin when Edward passed her and smiled uncertainly.

"Father? If you have nothing more for me to do this afternoon, I think I'll go home." Who was she kidding? She would never really be a part of the business. That was a man's world; she was tolerated, nothing more.

August turned and looked at his daughter with some surprise. She was almost as tall as he, stately and reed thin, but with a lovely face, her mother's full mouth, and eyes that could express volumes. At the moment those eyes were troubled.

"Are you ill, *Liebchen*?" He touched her shoulder and then felt her cheek with the back of his hand as he had seen his wife do any number of times.

She smiled. "Of course not. It's just that it's a lovely day, and I thought I might take the canoe out."

August walked to the window and looked longingly out

at the beautiful day. "You are right. We should all take the rest of the afternoon off . . . Alas, I have another meeting, but Edward . . ."

"Edward has a great deal to do, Father. After all, if you want details on a commemorative stein by Friday . . ." She let the comment hang, not looking at Edward.

"If you are sure," her father said, then shook his head. "You know, Katrina, you spend far too much time alone . . . and far too much time here. What chance have you to enjoy the pleasures a young girl should enjoy if you stay cooped up in an office all day and bury yourself in your novels at night?"

The translation of that statement was one Katrina knew well. What he was really asking was What chance was there that she would find a suitable young man and marry? She hugged her father and laughed. "I like my life, Papa. It suits me. Now don't be late for supper. You know how Mama hates that."

August smiled and kissed her forehead. "We will talk more," he warned her. "I know your life suits you, but it does not especially suit me. Do we understand?"

"We understand," Katrina replied solemnly, teasing him by mocking his serious tone. Then she kissed his cheek and picked up the basket she used in place of a purse. She had never understood how Lulu and other girls could make do with those ridiculous tiny pouches of beads and fabric they carried. "*Auf Wiedersehen*," she called as the double glassed doors closed behind her.

"Let one of the men drive you," Papa called after her.

"No. I'd rather walk."

Outside she dodged the traffic of the brewery—drays loaded for delivery pulled by teams of Clydesdales and Belgians. Papa did love horses—no oxen and mules for Bergeman Brewery, at least not for the public to see. Bergeman beer was delivered in freshly shined wagons, by uniformed workers driving matched teams of the finest horseflesh Papa could find. Oxen and mules were used in the inner workings of the brewery, to help in loading the freight cars on the railroad siding that ran next to the malthouse and cooperage or in moving inventory around the large yard.

Katrina raised her hand in greeting to several workers as she headed past the brewhouse and the noisy hissing of the steam engine that drove the machinery. Taking a shortcut through the brewhouse, she made her way along the clamorous obstacle course of men and vats and pipes and barrels and clutter that was the brewery.

Outside she was tempted to just hide out in one of the two large icehouses where the finished brew was stored. Lord, it was early in the summer to be so hot, she thought as she turned onto Juneau to walk the five blocks from the brewery to her home. The passing carriage traffic left clouds of white dust that clung to her clothes, and perspiration streaked her face as she climbed the slight incline. She probably should have accepted Papa's offer to have one of the men drive her. At least she would have arrived home less dust-covered and shopworn.

She frowned as she walked along. When Papa had first returned from the Civil War, it had taken some time before he showed much interest in returning to the brewery at all. Mama had been alarmed at his disinterest, and everyone had depended on Katrina and Edward to keep things running smoothly and to gradually encourage Papa to come back to managing the business, which he had built from a small neighborhood tavern and brewery to one of the most successful brands in the country.

Once he recovered, he took the reins of power firmly in hand, preferring to have all decisions go through him. To Katrina—used to some independence and decision-making power of her own—it had all come as something of a shock. The job that had filled her days with fresh challenges became routine. As time passed, her role became less one of a partner and more one of a secretary. Sometimes she felt less than that, more like some chirpy little volunteer, resembling the ladies of the hospital auxiliary.

She passed the women's college where both she and Lulu had gotten a college education at Papa's insistence. Education was important, he had told them, and Mama had added that one thing the war had taught women was that they could not always depend on a man to provide for them. So Katrina had studied to be a teacher, and Lulu had studied music, specifically the piano. Neither of them had put the training to use in the workplace for even one day, although Lu had come closer than Katrina. At least Lu sometimes substituted for the organist at Sunday services.

Maybe she should just leave the brewery, Katrina thought, get a teaching job, perhaps even move to another town. She certainly had few prospects here. It was clear that she would never be more than she was now at the brewery, and the young men who pursued her from time to time seemed hopelessly attached to some notion of womanhood as the devoted housekeeper and mother who knew enough to leave the room when men were talking seriously.

Katrina sighed, and then she smiled. If only some of those oafs knew how she and Lulu had giggled over them late at night as the girls talked in Katrina's room. She took a deep breath and allowed herself to enjoy the warmth of the sun. So it was hot. Soon enough the weather would be bone-chilling cold.

The closer she came to Lake Michigan, the better she felt. She was glad Papa had decided to build their house just north of the Lake Shore Promenade at Juneau Park. In some ways the park seemed an extension of their yard, where Mama prided herself on her formal gardens, with their beds of profusely blooming flowers, and the gazebo she had just last summer persuaded Papa to build in a hedge-guarded corner of the front yard.

Mama was used to living in the country. Her family still lived in northern Wisconsin, near the village of Peshtigo. Everyone who knew her understood that Sophie Bergeman was happiest in her garden. She missed the open spaces that had allowed her free rein to have everything from a vegetable garden, large enough to supply a small town, to a vineyard. Papa had tried to ease the stresses of life in the city by purchasing much of the block where their house was the focal point. This allowed enough space for at least a small kitchen and herb garden, as well as the hint of a vineyard in the arbor of Concord grapes that covered the path all along one side of the house. In addition, he had purchased a summer house and acreage on Lake Geneva, where the family joined cousins from Chicago for several weeks every summer.

In spite of her distaste for the other pastimes of home-making, Katrina shared her mother's enthusiasm for growing things. Often when she felt especially tired or depressed by the day's happenings, she would spend time in the herb and vegetable garden. There was something very soothing about the array of colors, scents, and textures of fresh tomato vines, surrounded by marigolds, dill, and mint. Even the root vegetables were a delight when they brought the damp exotic scent out of the earth with them.

By the time she reached the circular gravel drive that led to the large Italianate house, Katrina was in slightly better spirits. It was a fine house, sitting proudly across from the park, with an unobstructed view of Lake Michigan from almost every window. It was constructed of the unique cream brick for which Milwaukee was famous, and trimmed in limestone quoins, brackets, and decorative arched window hoods. The lawn and the flower gardens stretched to either side of the edifice, the nearest house being well over half a block away.

Katrina watched for a moment as her mother cut roses for the dining room centerpiece. No one sat down to a meal in the Bergeman house unless everything perfectly met Mama's specifications—the food, the wine, the flowers . . . Katrina wondered if such tasks would ever tempt her. Mama always told her that when the right man came along, she would discover a domestic streak possessed by every woman, but Katrina was skeptical.

"I'm taking the canoe," she called as she moved up the wide stone stairway to the entrance porch, which was shaded by the balustraded balcony outside her parents' bedroom.

Sophie looked up. "Katrina," she called when her daughter was about to move on into the house.

Katrina leaned over the decorative cast-iron railing, her foot poised on the top step, and looked back at her mother. "I'll be back in plenty of time for supper," she promised.

"We have company coming. Cousin Eloise from Chicago."

Katrina stifled a groan. Cousin Eloise was Papa's cousin, and she was in a constant panic that Katrina was not already married with at least two children.

"She's coming to spend the week," Mama continued. "In her letter she says she's quite anxious to get your ideas on the ball she's giving for Carlotta in October." Sophie continued cutting roses, pretending to be unaware of Katrina rolling her eyes in exasperation.

"I'm sure Lulu will be a big help to her," Katrina said, inching her way toward the door. "And I'll be nice," she assured her mother, "I promise."

"She's bringing someone with her," Sophie added as Katrina reached for the brass knob on the oak double doors.

"Not Carlotta," Katrina whispered to herself. The girl was only seventeen, but never had God created a more man-hungry female. She talked of nothing but beaus and kissing and the tricks she used to entice men. Lulu found her fascinating and amusing. Katrina found her irritating.

"A young man," Sophie added. "Not that he's staying the week. He has business in Milwaukee with your father and has graciously agreed to escort Eloise here. Isn't that nice?"

This time Katrina did groan aloud, and her mother actually laughed.

"Mother," she moaned. Again Sophie chuckled, walking into the house with her daughter and admonishing her for the dusty state of her clothing. "Couldn't your father have had one of the men drive you?"

"He offered. I wanted to walk."

"Well, don't stay out too long and do wear your hat. The sun is very hot today. Besides," Sophie added with a teasing grin, "you wouldn't want to give Eloise anything else to be upset about."

They both knew what was going on. Eloise was matchmaking. Ever since Edward and Lulu had become a steady twosome, Eloise had turned her full attention to Katrina. "After all, my dear, you are the elder daughter. It simply will not do for your sister to marry before you. Besides, you are already . . . what? Twenty?"

"Twenty-four," Katrina had blithely informed her. "And I may never marry, Cousin Eloise. I may decide I would rather have a career."

Eloise had clucked for several seconds over that and then wagged a finger in Katrina's face. "My dear, a career will not keep you warm on cold winter nights. A career will not escort you to the operas and dances you enjoy so much. A *career* will not keep you in the style to which you are already quite accustomed."

"Well, you'll have to forgive me, Cousin Eloise, but I refuse to marry at all if those are the primary benefits. What about love? What about a union of minds and spirits?" Her speech had earned her a reproachful look from her father, raised eyebrows from her mother, and a lengthy lecture from Eloise.

Katrina was simply not up to a visit from Cousin Eloise today, and she certainly was in no mood for being paraded before a man Eloise had selected as the proper match for her.

"Eloise has made it very clear in her letter that the young man in question is interested in Carlotta," Katrina's mother said. "However," she added with a dimpled smile, "she does note that he has many friends, and she is quite certain he can introduce you to any number of suitable escorts for the ball."

"Lovely," Katrina murmured wryly, earning a laugh from her mother. Just when the day had held some promise of turning out all right, her mood plummeted once again.

Upstairs Katrina walked down the long hall to her room. She closed the door behind her and moved immediately to the long, narrow windows that faced east and afforded her a view of the endless horizon of Lake Michigan. She loved this view. It changed every day. Today the lake was as blue as the Army uniform her father had worn in the war, and it stood in sharp contrast to the pastel color of the sky. If the war hadn't come along, Katrina might well be married by now. But the war had changed her life.

When Papa had joined the Army toward the end of the campaign, she had been eighteen and full of romantic notions of the rightness of the cause and the infallibility of President Lincoln. She had eagerly taken her place as Edward's assistant at the brewery. She wrote long letters to her beau, Abner Latham, and spent long evenings knitting scarfs and socks for the troops. But during the day her natural curiosity and inquisitiveness took over, and slowly she learned everything she could about every facet of the family business, often surprising Edward, not to mention the workers, with her savvy and acumen. By the time the war was over, Papa and Abner came home to a very different young woman. Papa delighted in her newfound enthusiasm; Abner was—to put it mildly—taken aback.

Katrina smiled ruefully at the memory. Pinpoints of white dotted the seascape; the masts of schooners and the smaller pleasure boats that plied the lake on any summer afternoon were comparable to the puffed clouds that moved across the sky. This would be a good day for playing cloud pictures, she thought as she hurried to change into her casual clothes. As children she and Lu and their older brother, Frederick, had lain on their backs in the side yard and created images out of the passing clouds.

Now Frederick was dead, she was no longer a child, and Lulu would soon be married to Edward with a home and children of her own. She frowned as she thought of Edward. What had he been thinking at the meeting today? It wasn't like him to hurt her deliberately. Still, her father had been displeased with him earlier in the week. She had heard Papa admonishing Edward about his penchant for frequently siding with the laborers. "You are sometimes far too understanding," Papa had roared when Edward defended himself by saying he was only trying to understand their point of view.

Was that it? Had he taken her idea so that he would seem more worthy in his employer's eyes? Katrina frowned and moved to the dresser to repin her hair.

"Hi."

Lulu stuck her head just inside the door and grinned. "Guess who's coming for a visit?"

"I heard," Katrina groaned around the hairpins she clenched between her lips.

Lulu laughed and moved into the room. She deposited herself in the middle of Katrina's bed and watched her sister try in vain to control the volumes of straight and fine red hair. "Here, I'll do it," she said, moving from the bed to stand behind her sister.

Expertly she twisted and flicked and secured the hair until it was perfectly arranged to stand the rigors of being out on the water. "She's bringing a young man," Katrina said as she jammed a derby of her father's which she used when riding or sailing, on top of the carefully arranged coiffure.

Lulu actually winced as she tried not to comment on the damage her sister was doing to the hairstyle. "I heard. He's supposed to be quite a catch," she teased. "Very high Chicago society, sister dear."

Katrina pulled on one shoe and then got down on her hands and knees to search for the other under her bed.

"But he's already spoken for by the ever demure Carlotta, sister dear," she teased back. "He's here as a broker. Eloise is becoming desperate and feels the need to have him look me over before choosing some one of his friends to woo me. On the other hand, Edward had better watch out. One look at those corn-silk curls and those limpid pools of blue you call eyes, and the fella's a sure goner."

Lulu's face lit up at the mention of Edward's name. "How is he today?" she asked dreamily. "What was he wearing? Do you think he'll come for supper with Papa?"

Katrina lay flat on her stomach so she could reach the errant shoe, then flipped over and sat on the floor to pull it on. "Of course he'll be here for supper. The man hasn't missed a meal in this house in weeks."

Lulu studied her sister carefully. "Are you angry at Edward? Did something happen?"

Katrina felt contrite. Lulu was not only her sister, she was her best friend. And on top of that she was in love with Edward, as Edward was besotted with her. She sighed. "We had a misunderstanding . . . business. It'll work out." Then with a grin she added, "I'm off with the canoe. Want to come?"

Lulu smiled back at her. "You look like a servant girl," she teased. "Here, wear your gloves . . . You don't want Eloise to criticize your hands."

Katrina laughed as she ran two floors down the back stairway to the kitchen. "Pauline, I'm going out on the lake for a bit," she called as she passed the cook, snatching a piece of radish as she went.

"You've got company coming for supper, young lady," Pauline warned. "Don't be spending all afternoon out there and leaving no time for getting properly dressed. You spend all day at that brewery and then go off like some tomboy, which you are too old to be—"

"I'll be back in plenty of time. Don't worry."

"Don't worry," Pauline muttered under her breath as she huffed her way over to the table, a bowl of freshly mixed strudel dough on one ample hip. "With that one all a body can do is worry."

In minutes Katrina had crossed Lake Avenue and followed the path down the bluff to the family's private dock. The canoe she and Lulu had used since childhood was tied there.

On most days she would have enjoyed paddling slowly up the coast, leisurely taking in the sights and sounds of the lake traffic. But today she had a destination, and with everyone so intense about Eloise's visit, she dared not tarry too long. Today she was thankful for the slight wind at her back that made paddling easier. She had the shore almost to herself except for the occasional fisherman. Later there would be more people out and about, trying to capture the coolness of the lake breeze on a hot summer night. But for now she was pretty much alone, which suited her purposes just fine.

2

KATRINA PADDLED NORTH to an area where the houses thinned out and the bluffs rose ever more steeply along the shore. Making sure there was no one to see, she tied the canoe to a tree jutting out from the bluff. Then she hitched her skirt through her legs, bringing it up in front to hook in her belt and form a sort of makeshift pair of pants. It took her no time at all to climb to the cluster of rocks that had split from the bluff after decades of bruising storms pounding the shore. The loosened rocks had tumbled into the shallows and formed a shelter that made her invisible from prying eyes on the bluff or the lake.

She reveled in the breeze that cooled the temperature to several degrees less than it was in town. Settling herself onto her favorite rock, she took off her shoes and stockings and dangled her feet into the pool formed between the larger boulders, water that had been warmed by its captivity between the rocks.

She took off her jacket, opened the top buttons of her shirtwaist, and pulled off the derby. Then she rested on her elbows and closed her eyes, letting the cool water work its magic on her feet and taking in the smells and sounds around her. Occasionally she could hear voices from the passing ships, workers on the barges and steamers that plied the lake from Green Bay to Chicago, from Milwaukee to Ludington. She envied those men and the places they had been, the things they might have seen.

She had never been farther than Marinette to the north or Chicago to the south, and she longed to travel. It wasn't that her family couldn't afford it. It was more a case of postponement. Papa was always promising a family trip, but the war and then the brewery had claimed all his attention. Mama was content to stay home. So nightly Katrina devoured books and the stories in *Peterson's Magazine* telling her of romantic places she could only dream about— New York, St. Louis, and of course Europe.

The wake of a passing steamer reached shore, kicking up waves that splashed over her knees and scattered against the rocks to tickle her face and neck. She remembered a spring day when as children she and Frederick and Lu had climbed down to these rocks and dared each other to go all the way into the water. Lu had adamantly refused, but Frederick had quickly shed his shoes, socks, and shirt and lowered himself into the cold water. He had paddled around for about a minute before his lips had turned blue and, having proved his point, he climbed back to the safety and warmth of the rocks.

Not to be outdone, Katrina had waited until he was safely back on shore and then slipped into the water herself, her skirts billowing around her as they filled with water, her breath almost taken away by the surprise of how cold the water was. When Lu pleaded and Frederick finally demanded she come out, she had shrugged and allowed them to pull her back to the rocks. That had been in late April. Frederick had died of cholera in August.

Now it was almost July and an unusually hot summer at that. Surely the water temperature was not so cold, and surely the heat would dry her clothes in no time. She was feeling dusty and disheveled. The lake promised refreshment. Washing away the frustrations of the day would make her better company tonight, she told herself. After all, Mama would expect her to be on her best behavior.

She was sorely tempted, and if she stayed behind the rocks, no one could see her. She stood up and took off her skirt and blouse. She had worn only one petticoat; her knickers and camisole formed a bathing costume. Of course, a real bathing costume would have been far less revealing, but again she checked, and there was no one to see.

She eased herself over the side until her feet reached the bottom and the water drenched her to her waist. She flinched in the cold water, but gradually her body temperature adapted. She closed her eyes and relished the cool, restorative force of the lake. Using her hands, she cupped water onto her shoulders and neck, but it was not enough. So she lowered herself until the water rose to her chin and then leaned her head down to blow bubbles on the surface, laughing delightedly at her own antics.

The toot of a tugboat brought her abruptly out of her revelry, and she scanned the horizon, ducking behind a sheltering rock to do so. But it was only a signal to another ship. No one could see her. No one was around. She hooked an arm around a rock to either side and allowed her feet to rise to the surface. Yes, her underthings would dry in no time, and no one would ever know she'd been swimming. She closed her eyes and drifted, not even minding when she felt the water lap at several strands of hair that had escaped Lu's careful pinning.

It was late afternoon by the time Ryan Sullivan finished his business at the grain exchange. It had been an exhilarating and profitable day, and he could not help smiling as he stepped onto the boardwalk outside the exchange building and observed the passing scenario.

Milwaukee . . . the Cream City of the Lakes. It was a long way from Chicago, even if it was only a hundred miles. Where Chicago was grimy, Milwaukee was almost pristine; where Chicago was bawdy, Milwaukee seemed undeniably virtuous; where Chicago was cramped and hulking, Milwaukee seemed quaint and rural. There was something so innocent about the place ... deceiving in a world Ryan Sullivan knew to be anything but innocent.

He frowned and flipped the cigar he'd been smoking into the street. A passing delivery dray left a trail of fine chalky dust that coated Ryan's polished boots and reminded him that his intention had been to quench his thirst. There was one thing a man could count on in Milwaukee—there was bound to be a tavern nearby.

He crossed the street and found a place at the bar of an establishment whose dark and cool interior contrasted sharply with the hot, sunny day outside. He glanced at the three other patrons and nodded as he ordered a Bergeman draft. He had an invitation for supper at the Bergeman house. He knew the brewer by reputation and thought it might be politic to have at least tried his beer. Besides, he had a good tip on some timberland the Bergemans owned up near Green Bay.

Scanning the saloon as he waited for the drink, Ryan was aware that the finely tailored cut of his clothes made him an oddity in this place. The other men were wary of him, but polite. Once he would have belonged here without question. These days he did not fit. He laid a coin on the bar and drained the stein the barkeeper had placed in front of him. It was good beer, better than some of the top brands. Bergeman had a decent product on his hands.

"Thanks," he said as he placed the empty glass on the counter.

"Another?"

"No, thanks. But could you tell me where I might rent a skiff? It seems to me to be a perfect day for getting out onto the water."

Following the barkeeper's instructions, Ryan found the river dock and the old man the barkeep had said might have something to rent. A deal was struck, and in minutes he was navigating his way along the river toward the lake.

The lake was his destination, but he noted with interest the thriving industry along the waterfront. There was money here . . . and money to be made. Milwaukee was already the center of the country's grain market—a bigger market than Chicago's—which was why he had come north for today's trading. The activity along the river spoke of a city on the verge of booming. In such a setting, someone willing to take a gamble could easily turn a small stake into a fortune.

Ryan removed his coat and rolled back his sleeves, and as he moved east, carefully steering the small craft among the larger steamers and schooners anchored along the riverfront, he relished the cool air that made its way up the river from the lake. The train ride to Milwaukee had been stifling.

He smiled as he recalled his conversation with his traveling companion, Mrs. Christian Hauptman, a Chicago society matron and a cousin of August Bergeman's. Ryan had had business dealings with Mr. Hauptman, and the family had been nice to him. Hauptman had been pleased when Ryan noted that he had business in Milwaukee and would be honored to escort Mrs. Hauptman to that city.

Their daughter, Carlotta, had a crush on him. In fact, Carlotta Hauptman promised to provide her parents with any number of adventures. The girl was a terrible flirt, and one day some man was going to take her flirtation seriously. Having listened to Mrs. Hauptman ramble on and on about the virtues of proper young women of good families, Ryan wondered what she would have said had he told her Carlotta had literally thrown herself into his arms and demanded a kiss just the evening before.

Not that he hadn't been tempted. The girl was seventeen going on twenty-five. She had a voluptuous body that would one day go to fat, but now was extremely enticing. Somewhere along the way she had read enough or experimented enough to know exactly how to get a man's attention without appearing brazen or cheap. But

Carlotta Hauptman was trouble, and Ryan Sullivan had no intention of being netted in her trap.

In the old days he would have taken anything a girl like Carlotta wanted to offer. In the neighborhood where he'd grown up, it was hardly news when a young girl found herself pregnant and abandoned after throwing herself too blatantly at a man. But Ryan had made his way in the world. He had worked hard to be where he was today, and Carlotta Hauptman was not a street girl from the old neighborhood. No, in the circles he moved in these days, there were stringent rules. If he messed with Carlotta Hauptman, it had better be for keeps, and Ryan Sullivan wanted more for himself. Beauty counted, but then beauty also faded. He wanted someone he could still stand to talk to in his old age.

He navigated through the channel where the Milwaukee River flowed into Lake Michigan. As he set his course north along the coast, he was glad to find the waters calm. He had had experience with the lake's moods and knew how to respect it. There was quite a bit of traffic. Several steam lines carried passengers up and down the coast and across to Michigan. A sidewheel paddler passed, and the sound of laughter and the chatter of excursionists drifted across the water to him. The workhorses of the waters— barges and cargo-hauling schooners—gave evidence of the thriving economy in the area. But even with all the traffic, the lake was a tranquil place to be.

Ryan frowned as he recalled another time when the lake had seemed as serene and imperturbable as it did today. Within hours it had turned an excursion of revelry into a nightmare of chaos, a sidewheel steamer into kindling. That night had been the turning point in Ryan's life. He had lost everything that night, and within a year he had joined the Army, ready to go wherever he was needed in a war he didn't understand and found incredibly hypocritical. All that had been a long time ago. Then he would never have imagined that at this stage of his life he would be hobnobbing with some of the richest men in the country . . .

Hell, on any given day, he *was* one of the richest men in the country. Of course, grain futures being what they were, there had as well been mornings when he awakened to find himself one of the poorest men.

Ryan grinned at the fickleness of his fortunes and banished the bad memories, turning his attention to the view along the shoreline. Closer to town the coast was graded and sloped, allowing for the commercial traffic that plied the waters of the lake and river. A promenade had been built in an area that bordered some of the more affluent neighborhoods. He could see the rooflines of several mansions as he made his way along the coast.

Now, north of the city, steep bluffs formed a basin for the deep blue waters, and at their base there were occasional outcroppings of rock formations, dropped into the water by erosion of the shore. Remembering his own boyhood and the misadventures his brothers and he had had, he could picture how the local kids delighted in these rocks that could become a fort or a castle with a little imagination. He shielded his eyes as he noticed a youngster, stripped to his underwear and poised on the edge of one large boulder. He hoped the kid wasn't planning on diving; there were too many hidden rocks for that. He was on the verge of calling out a warning when he saw the kid sit on the edge of the rock and slip into the water feet first.

Ryan was frankly jealous. On a day like this, what could be more refreshing than a dip in Lake Michigan? Of course, the kid would probably catch hell from his mom when he arrived home in wet underwear. On the other hand, the sun was warm enough that there was plenty of time for drying off before dressing and heading home.

Ryan found a place where the roots of a tree jutted out through the eroded soil and where he could tie the skiff, then climbed along the side of the bluff to have a better view. Sometimes success was not all it was cracked up to be, he thought ruefully. It demanded certain proprieties, especially when one was invited to the home of a very influential Milwaukeean for supper. Still, he could enjoy the kid's swim vicariously.

Ryan had removed his boots and socks and left them with his coat and hat in the skiff. Once he reached the open lake, he removed his waistcoat and pulled his shirttail free, impatiently tearing away the required stiff collar and four-in-hand tie and opening his shirt to allow the cool air full circulation. He made his way along the bluff now, his bare feet slipping on the dry, loose soil as errant pebbles and stones pricked his soles. *Tenderfoot,* he thought ruefully. *You used to be a lot tougher, Sullivan.* He crouched low to give himself better footing and to keep from startling the kid.

As he climbed over a fallen birch tree where the kid had tied up a canoe, he heard the soft splash of the water, and by the time he had a clear view again, he was close enough to draw in a shocked breath.

This was no boy. This was a woman, and she was wearing nothing but her pantalets and camisole, both of which were soaked. The sheer wet fabric revealed everything. She may as well have decided to bathe naked. Ryan almost lost his footing as he strained for a full view.

He was slightly behind and above her. She lay in the water, arms hooked around smaller rocks as she floated and hummed softly to herself. She had masses of reddish hair and seemed unconcerned that strands of it had spilled over her shoulder and into the water. Occasionally she tilted her head back, her eyes closed, her face turned to the sky and the breeze. She was smiling, a lazy contented smile. It was the kind of smile a woman might have after good sex, Ryan thought.

He was practically holding his breath so that she would not discover his presence. But his breathing took on a mind of its own as he allowed his eyes to slowly peruse the rest of her. Starting with the long slender neck and shoulders . . . a man could spend long moments getting to know those, especially if she accommodated by throwing her head back as she did now.

Of course, that action also added to the allure of her breasts . . . pressing the cleavage high above the lace trim of her camisole and the ruby nipples flush against the wet fabric. Ryan noted the ridiculous pink ribbons that decorated the front of the garment, holding it closed. His fingers fairly itched to loosen them and allow that bounty its freedom.

The rest of her was surprisingly athletic, almost boyish. She had a slim waist and firm flat tummy with little need for the corseting most women put themselves through to attain such a measurement. Her hips and legs appeared narrow and straight. She was tall, he judged.

Suddenly, like a trapped bird, she gasped and started. In a second her eyes flew open, and she glanced around.

Immediately Ryan saw the reason. In his zeal to move closer and see more, he had forgotten his shadow—the same shadow that now stretched long and damning across the rocks next to her.

Her eyes wide with alarm, she spun around and lost her balance, which sent her underwater for a heart-stopping second. Ryan was well aware that most girls could not really swim. If she had stepped off a rock into a deep pool . . .

Sputtering, she came to the surface and glared at him. In the brief moment it had taken her to determine that escape was impossible and that she certainly couldn't stay underwater, Katrina had decided a direct challenge was her only hope. "Who are you and why are you spying on me?" she shouted as soon as she surfaced.

He had moved closer. In fact he was standing—more like towering—over her. She was at a disadvantage looking up at him with the sun at his back. His features were in shadow. She knew only that he was very tall, very muscular, and wearing nothing but pants that seemed especially well fitted to his long legs and a shirt that hung open to reveal the only male chest she had ever seen in daylight, if she didn't count her father's and brother's.

"Well?" she challenged, inching her way closer to the next rock, ready to make her escape if possible. Perhaps if she grabbed one of his bare ankles, he would topple into the water, hit his head on a rock . . .

" . . . Sorry. If you'll forgive me, miss. Please let me help you out."

He had crouched now and was offering her his hand—a well-manicured hand, but one that had known some hard work, judging by the tanned skin and hardened palms. She squinted up again, ignoring his hand.

He was talking again, and for a moment she got lost in the inventory of his features. Now that he was leaning close, she could see him clearly. His hair was so black there were actually blue highlights where the sun hit it. She had really thought it was stretching the truth when heroes in her novels were described that way. Now she witnessed those handsome highlights for herself. Then there were his eyes . . . definitely blue and at the moment clearly trying hard not to crinkle with laughter. He did a lot of smiling and laughing, she surmised, for there were tiny lines at the edges, "laugh lines," her mother called them.

"Miss?"

She brought her attention to his mouth, which also seemed quirked in amusement. That was irritating enough, but she found herself mesmerized like some dopey schoolgirl by the wide fullness of his lips and the white evenness of his teeth.

Her mouth went suddenly dry, and she licked her lips as she prepared to speak. For some reason, that made all traces of amusement in his face disappear, and his lips closed in a tight straight line matching the frown that etched his forehead. Lord, he was handsome.

"Clearly you have me at a disadvantage, sir. Would you please leave by whatever means you came . . ." She glanced around, looking for signs of transportation.

"Please come out of the water so I can explain," he coaxed softly. "You're beginning to turn quite blue, you know." This last came accompanied by that ravishing smile again.

Katrina considered her options, of which there were two. She could stay in the water, which he had rightly surmised was uncomfortably cold, especially now that this particular piece of the coast was in shade, or she could climb out and take her chances with him. What if he was a thief . . . a kidnapper . . . or worse? Wouldn't he just love to know he had happened upon the daughter of one of the wealthiest men in the city? Still, she stood a better chance of escaping on shore.

"Turn around," she ordered and was surprised when he obliged her immediately, even moving a few feet away to give her more room.

In a single movement she hoisted herself onto the rock and reached for her clothes.

"I wouldn't do that," he said quietly.

Oh, Lord, this was worse than she'd imagined. She jumped as something brushed her shoulder. *His hand? His mouth?*

"Put this on at least until you dry off a bit."

His shirt!

She shrugged into it, noting the heady smell of cologne and tobacco that clung to it. She also noted the expensive fabric—cotton that felt more like fine silk.

"Thank you," she said and was surprised to see that he was still facing the bluff, not looking at her.

"Are you decent?" he asked, and she heard the slightest betrayal of mirth in his tone.

"You may turn around," she said and added firmly, "but stay over there." She moved farther away from him and studied him warily.

To her surprise, he grinned and stooped to his haunches. "Why don't you move over there," he suggested, indicating a large flat rock that was still bathed in sunlight. "If you face the lake, you can open the shirt and allow your . . . clothing to dry."

She did as he suggested, positioning herself carefully so that he was still in sight without actually being able to see her state of undress. His shirt formed a nice sort of curtain and she relaxed slightly. Of course, he had already seen her state of undress. She pulled the wet fabric away from her breasts and wondered how long he'd been standing behind her, watching her in the water, seeing . . . everything.

They sat in silence for several minutes. Hers was an uneasy silence, but he didn't seem to notice.

"I came by boat," he said suddenly as if in answer to a direct question. "Rented a little skiff from the old fisherman . . . Swanson? Swenson?"

"Sweeney," she supplied. Then after another pause, she ventured a question. "You're not from Milwaukee?"

He laughed at that, a sound of pure delight as if she had made a wonderful joke. "Is it that obvious? I guess it is. Not too many men in Milwaukee run around climbing barefoot along the bluffs and spying on beautiful women, I imagine."

She felt the heat of pleasure rise to her cheeks. No one had ever referred to her as beautiful, not even just to be polite. She was striking or pretty or attractive, but beauty was a word used to describe her mother and Lulu.

"How about you?" His voice was so very pleasant, low and lyrical. For some reason, she could imagine him reading poetry.

"Me?"

"Yes. How did you get here? The canoe?"

She nodded. "I . . . uh . . . live not too far away . . ." Although he seemed to be completely trustworthy, she could not risk giving him too much information.

"Your hair will dry faster if you take it down," he said softly.

He was right, of course—and how on earth would she explain why it was soaked when she got home, and how on earth would she get it dry in time for dinner even if she did let it down now?

"I have to go," she announced suddenly. "Please turn around."

"Here," he said and was so near that she started and involuntarily clutched the fronts of his shirt to her throat. She glanced up and saw that he was standing over her again, this time holding her clothes. "You can reach these better here," he noted, setting the garments on the rock next to her. Then he stepped away and after a moment said, "Okay. I'm turned away."

She dressed as quickly as she ever had on a freezing January morning, one eye on him the whole time. Actually her eyes were on his back, which was muscular and tanned with one jagged white scar that ran across one shoulder blade, pointing like an arrow to his narrow waist and hips. Katrina blushed. She had never considered the eroticism of a man's form from the rear before. Most of the time the men she knew were either covered by frock or morning coats or by baggy workpants or recreational clothing. This man stood before her, naked from the waist up, his suspenders hanging to the sides of the tailored pants that hugged his waist and hips in a manner she was certain bordered on sinfully taut.

"Are you done?" he asked, and her cheeks blazed because she wasn't certain whether he was asking about her state of undress or her close survey of his.

"Thank you," she said and took a step closer to hand him his shirt. She could not take her eyes off him as he shrugged into it. The black hair that framed his craggy face was repeated on his chest in a slightly curlier version. Katrina realized that she was having a great deal of trouble controlling her breathing as she watched him bend to pick up her derby.

"Here, let me help you. If we stuff all that hair into your hat, no one will be the wiser."

With a quick step he was in front of her, his hands gently poking her hair under the brim of the hat. She kept her eyes down but did not miss the steady rise and fall of his chest in rhythm with her own. When he had finished, he allowed his fingers to trail down her cheek to her collar.

"There," he said, almost in a whisper, but he did not move away.

If he had taken her into his embrace at that moment, God help her she would have let him. In all her life she had never met such a man. Lu told her she read too many novels and that she would never be satisfied with real flesh-and-blood human beings if she kept thinking she might meet one like the heroes in her books. But here he was . . .

"I also have to go," he said in the same husky tone, and she could feel him looking down at her, willing her to lift her eyes to his.

Instead she simply nodded.

"You'll be all right?"

Again she nodded.

His hands came up to cup her cheeks and lift her gaze to his. This time there was no amusement in the blue eyes that reflected her gaze. This time they were as fathomless and as mysterious as the lake behind her, full of secrets, full of possible danger.

He studied her for a long moment as if trying to decide something. Then he frowned slightly and kissed her softly on her forehead. "Don't do this anymore," he whispered against her cheek. "Promise. It's too dangerous."

She nodded. Was he talking about letting him kiss her, being in the lake, or taking her clothes off? She'd never know, because suddenly he was gone, moving nimbly around and over the shoreline to where he had left the skiff. By the time she got to the canoe and turned it south to head for home, she looked for him and saw the skiff well down the coast.

3

WHEN KATRINA GOT home, the sun was low in the western sky, its orange light flaming in the high arched windows of the house. Miraculously she was able to pass through the kitchen and up the back stairway without being seen. That was no easy task, because of the large staff in their home. But Pauline was giving instructions to the girl who'd been hired to help serve, and Heinrich, the butler, was probably in the dining room supervising the final table setting. Everyone else was busy preparing for the arrival of the Bergemans' guests.

Once she had safely reached her room, Katrina undressed quickly and hid her still-damp underwear in the bottom of the chifforobe, spreading it as best she could so it would dry completely before the laundress came to collect the laundry and found it.

Of course, hiding her underwear was decidedly easier than disguising the very damp masses of hair that fell heavily to her waist when she released the pins. Lu would know what to do, but Lu would also have a million questions. No, she would just have to come up with something on her own.

For the time being, she gathered the unruly locks, twisting them high and tight and around until the whole pile rested on the top of her head. She moved to her dresser, holding her hair with one hand while she searched for pins with the other. Stabbing pins in, she glanced up and saw her naked self in the mirror. The face, the body, the voice of the stranger came to her as vividly as if he had suddenly entered the room.

She closed her eyes and recalled his nearness, the way his whispered advice had brought his mouth tantalizingly close to her face. She opened her eyes and noted how her nipples had hardened to points, the same way they had when she had first entered the cold water . . . the same way they had when he touched her . . .

"Miss Katrina?"

With a start Katrina turned to the door. Then, realizing it was only the maid, Ernestine, she breathed easier. Ernestine would not walk in without her permission.

"I'm here," she called, reaching into the chifforobe to grab a wrapper to cover herself with.

"Your mother asked me to see if you needed anything."

"No, thank you, Ernestine. Please tell Mama I'll be down in a bit."

She heard the maid's retreating footsteps, then frowned. She would have to hurry if she was going to be presentable in time for dinner. In a frenzy of activity, she pulled out and donned fresh lingerie—the whole inventory from stockings to the hated corset, which she struggled to manage herself, not wanting to call Ernestine back to the room. Dressing properly was the least she could do to make amends for her misadventure of the afternoon. Of course, Mama knew nothing of where she'd gone or what she'd done . . . or whom she'd met. She felt the need to be on her best behavior, however, and make a good impression.

By the time she had put on all the layers, she was quite breathless, and her skin was covered with a fine sheen of perspiration. She rummaged through the jumble of ribbons, lace, and feathers that filled one small dressing table drawer until she unearthed a fan. Then with a sigh she closed her eyes, fanning herself furiously. She dreaded this dinner. Eloise would be sure to find a way to note that Katrina balanced precariously at the edge of spinsterhood. Her thinly veiled hints that this single state should be a cause of great concern to her parents had long been a source of amusement within the family. Katrina wondered what new material Lu would have to tease her with after tonight.

"My dear, we do move on," Eloise would say, and Lulu would later do a perfect imitation. This statement referred to the rather unfortunate episode four years ago when Katrina had finally accepted Abner Latham's proposal of marriage, only to have him dash off to help reconstruct the South and later marry a Southern woman whose plantation he had purchased in a land auction.

"There's been no one since?" Eloise would ask, her eyes filled with false sympathy. "Of course, it is tragic, my dear, but one must not allow the misery of one misfortune to color all of one's life."

"Especially when one is so young," Lu would add soberly, her eyes twinkling with teasing as she glanced at her sister across the table.

Katrina gave herself one last sweep of her fan and idly wondered what Eloise would have thought of the stranger this afternoon. She smiled and then glanced in the mirror and frowned. There was still the matter of her hair.

Occasionally there are days when Fate smiles on a woman's efforts to arrange the glory that crowns her into a presentable design on the first try; but this was not to be such a day for Katrina.

First, it took long, painfully agonizing minutes just to brush all the snarls and tangles out. Then, once it was brushed, the mop just sat there surrounding her face and shoulders like some kind of burning bush. What she wouldn't have given for the naturally curly, eternally manageable tresses of her sister.

She gathered and braided and twisted and unbraided and used combs and pins and barrettes to hold and anchor, but in the end it was hopeless. And that was the moment Ernestine reappeared to remind her it was growing increasingly late. "Mrs. Bergeman says to let you know the guests are arriving," she urged. "Do you need some help?"

"I'll be there," Katrina snapped. And then, realizing her tardiness was hardly the maid's fault, she opened the door a crack. "I'm sorry, Ernestine. I just have to put on my gown. I'll be right there."

Ernestine nodded, but she glanced at Katrina's hair, and her expression was doubtful. "I'll tell Mrs. Bergeman," she said.

Katrina put on her shoes and fumbled with the buttonhook until they were fastened. Why was it nothing went smoothly when she was in a hurry? And why was it that all this activity was conspiring to take away the pure pleasure of her afternoon's adventure?

She studied her face in the mirror once more. He had touched her hair, his fingers flickering over it as light as butterflies. He had wrapped one tendril slowly around his finger when he leaned in to whisper his warning. She felt warm just thinking of him . . . how his clothes had revealed the strength and power of his body . . . how his lips had seemed so expressively wide and inviting . . . how the late afternoon shadows had played hide and seek in the plains and valleys of his face . . . how his eyes had gone from teasing and mocking to serious and eventually sensual . . .

As if he were there, his hands moving through her hair with her, she shook it loose and began again. This time her hands moved with languid grace, lifting the masses to reveal the creamy length of her throat, twisting and braiding to catch the light of the late sun, anchoring until she felt the voluptuous weight of the doubled braid resting against her shoulder blades.

It would do . . . It would have to.

She spared only a moment to survey her gowns. With Eloise here, she knew her smartest move would be to wear the blue one Mama had just gotten for her. Its bustle was sewn in as a part of the dress, a feature Mama had quickly brought to her attention. "You won't even know it's there," she had promised. "It's not really a bustle at all."

It was a lovely gown, but a spirit of rebellion seemed never far from the surface when anyone attempted to mold Katrina Bergeman to an image of what was deemed "proper." Eloise was a master at such games, and Katrina could not resist the opportunity to goad her a little. She deliberately pushed aside the blue bustled gown and chose instead a three-year-old white organdy, made for her at the time fashion had not yet made up its mind what to do to follow the enormous hooped gowns of the sixties.

The body of the gown was hand-embroidered with blue-green flowers and then piped with aqua velvet around the neck, armholes, and wrists of the long fitted sleeves. Sixteen very small pearl buttons closed the tight-fitting bodice. Three tiers of lace-edged ruffles finished the skirt. Katrina hurried to fasten the five hooks and eyes that closed the skirt and then struggled to tie the wide aqua satin sash that accented her slim waist in front and formed a large bow with streamers that flowed all the way down the slight train in the back.

Katrina smiled. It was her favorite dress, not only because it was her most comfortable, but because it gave her confidence. She felt almost pretty in this dress, feminine and womanly. The stranger had called her beautiful. She fastened the high neck with the cameo her father had given her on her last birthday, dabbed on a bit of lilac water, and hastened down the hall.

After his charming encounter with the certainly unorthodox lady of the lake, Ryan Sullivan had returned to his hotel to change for his dinner engagement at the Bergeman home. Eloise Hauptman had told him that on hot summer evenings the Bergemans preferred an informal late supper to more formal dining. The way she had said it, he was certain she was waiting for him to disapprove. Clearly she did. In her social set in Chicago, such liberties with customs of entertaining would be frowned upon. There were rules, and regardless of how archaic or downright silly, rules were to be followed. It was only one of the components of belonging to the upper class that Ryan found stifling.

But after meeting August Bergeman and his handsome wife, Sophia, Ryan understood that toying with social custom was not born of ignorance in the Bergeman home. It spoke of the kind of confidence people would have in a family that had gained wealth and position through several generations. August and Sophia Bergeman had what they wanted and needed, and had no inclination to prove their position.

Ryan had been surprised at the house. It was handsome enough, but hardly the sort of mansion occupied by some of the New England Yankees who had held power in Milwaukee for many years. Actually it was a very livable place with inviting gardens that lined the drive to the portico, where one servant had taken Ryan's rented rig and another had led the way to the front entrance, where the Bergemans and Eloise Hauptman waited.

Now he stood with Bergeman in the spacious foyer, where a handsome hand-carved staircase curved its way to the second and third floors. Just as he was accepting a glass of Rhine wine from his host and complimenting him on the quality of his beer, the vivacious Miss Lucinda Bergeman entered the foyer on the arm of Edward Mueller. Mueller was introduced as Bergeman's chief associate; " . . . and probably future in-law," Bergeman added with a smile.

"Father," Lulu demurred.

She was a vision in yellow, from the gold moire ribbon that wound its way through her intricately cascading arrangment of curls to the summer gown she wore that showed off her figure to perfection and spoke of the absolute latest in women's fashion. Ryan liked her instantly and wondered that he was not attracted to her in a more dissolute way. Perhaps it was her childlike demeanor or the enchanting way she glanced up at Edward, her blue eyes clearly smitten as she gazed adoringly at him.

There had always been something slightly calculating in the women Ryan had known. Not that there hadn't been a number of them who had been equally adoring, but he had always known that his money played a role—at least in this stratum. The women who looked at him now would not have given him the time of day a few years ago.

"Miss Bergeman," he said in acknowledgment of the introduction, and then bowed to kiss her remarkably unblemished hand.

"Oh, Mr. Sullivan, we cannot be friends and be so formal. My name is Lucinda, but my friends call me Lu or Lulu." She had left her hand in his, suggesting to Ryan that she was a young woman with uncommon confidence when it came to interactions with the opposite sex. Perhaps it was because her love for Mueller was so secure.

Ryan bent a second time and kissed her hand. "And I am Ryan, Lu."

For some unaccountable reason, he was reminded of the girl's hand this afternoon. Where Miss Bergeman's hand was clearly unused to performing any task unless it was perfectly protected by gloves, his lady of the lake had had hands that were uncallused but also freckled and slightly tanned.

Ryan shook hands with Edward, and while the Bergemans moved to greet two other couples they had included as guests, the three young people chatted about the heat and the differences between Chicago and Milwaukee.

"Chicago is so incredibly exciting," Lulu enthused and then added with a slight pout, "whereas Milwaukee can be a bit staid. Don't you think so, Ryan?"

He smiled, thinking that if she had only been the one to encounter the woman swimming almost nude in Lake Michigan this afternoon, she would hardly find the city staid. "Milwaukee has its charms," he said.

"But Chicago . . . I'll bet you're out every night and you could probably be out every night for years without doing the same thing twice."

Ryan laughed. "I'm not sure about years . . . months maybe," he teased.

Edward grinned down at the perky blond love of his life. "Lulu sometimes gets a bit restless . . . The Bergemans have given their daughters a great deal of freedom and opportunity. They both have this dangerous idea that the world is theirs to explore, not to mention challenge." This last he delivered with an affectionate tweak of Lu's cheek.

"I find Lu's enthusiasm refreshing," Ryan commented. He had been surprised, when he first started to make money and was subsequently invited into some of the finest homes in Chicago, to find that he had a natural gift for this kind of polite banter. Gift of the blarney, his father would have called it. "However, I will warn you, Lu, that many people think life is more stimulating anywhere other than where they live."

"Or you could perhaps take on a bit of Katrina's philosophy," Edward teased her and, at Ryan's questioning glance, added, "Katrina is Lu's sister."

Ryan nodded. "And what philosophy might that be?" he asked.

Lu grinned and shook her head in wonder. "It's hard to put into words . . ."

Edward cut in. "Suffice it to say if Katrina found Chicago as tantalizing as Lu obviously does, she would simply go there. Katrina tends to live life on her own terms."

Lu glanced at the stairway and frowned. "Speaking of my darling sister, I wonder what's keeping her? Will you gentlemen excuse me?"

At their nods she moved to her mother's elbow and whispered to her as they both looked worriedly toward the top of the stairs.

"I understand your expertise is in the grain market, Mr. Sullivan," Edward said as he helped himself to a second glass of beer from a passing tray.

"I thought Lu wanted us on first-name terms," Ryan reminded him.

Edward grinned. "Sorry, Ryan. It's just that in business one learns not to take liberties or stray too far from protocol."

Ryan could imagine that Edward Mueller had trouble being taken seriously in the marketplace. In spite of the mustache and sideburns, obviously grown to affect maturity, he had the wide-eyed gaze of an innocent and a boyishness that would plague him all his life. Still, the man had little to worry about. Clearly August Bergeman treated him as a son, and his match with Lu was unquestionably a good one.

"One never has expertise in the grain market or any other form of speculation," Ryan said with a smile. "I have been extraordinarily fortunate."

Edward's admiration was almost embarrassing. "I envy you," he said. "It takes courage to take risks like that. I know I could never—"

Ryan was uncomfortable in the face of praise on any account and particularly when he felt it undeserved. So with a chuckle he interrupted, nodding toward Lu, "I would say you are the courageous one, my friend. Miss Bergeman would be a test of any man's mettle."

Edward grinned and then added in a conspiratorial whisper, "I'll let you in on a secret, since it's my understanding from Lu that Cousin Eloise hopes to commence a possible match for Katrina and one of your friends by asking you here tonight."

Ryan smiled. He, too, had suspected some ulterior motive when Eloise Hauptman had insisted he come to supper. She certainly had little stake in any business he might be interested in promoting with her cousin August. And he knew Carlotta would have made it clear to her mother that Ryan was spoken for, even though that particular assumption was one-sided. "What's the secret?" he asked.

"Lu is an amateur in independence compared to Katrina. The woman is stubborn as a mule—just try to give her a hand with something . . ."

His voice trailed off as all eyes turned to the woman descending the staircase. "Mother, Father, I am so sorry to be late," she said softly, and then went straight to Eloise Hauptman. "Cousin, how lovely to have you here for a visit."

Ryan Sullivan had been about to ask Edward what on earth he was talking about when she appeared. The hair was unmistakable, and Ryan noted the way the gown molded her breasts and the wide sash accented her slender waist as her long legs moved against the fabric of the graceful skirt. Before him was not the fully clothed daughter of August Bergeman, but his lady of the lake, lying back in the cool water, naked but for a thin veil of cotton.

Lazily he had thought of the girl off and on through the afternoon, wondering that he had not taken the opportunity she had offered. He had been certain she was a shopgirl or perhaps a maid in just such a house as this, who had stolen an afternoon for herself. He had wondered if she had a boyfriend, or in lieu of that was her employer's mistress . . . something not all that uncommon in the homes of the rich and powerful, he had discovered.

At the hotel he had indulged in the fantasy of her lying on his bed in the same state of undress he had found her in that afternoon. That had been harmless reverie. Now, with her true identity clearly labeling her unattainable, she became an obsession.

It was his low, deep laughter Katrina had first recognized as she paused at the top of the stairs to make certain the streamers on her gown were straight. Her breath had caught in her throat when her fear was confirmed as she heard him conversing easily with Lu and Edward.

It could not be. Quickly she dropped to her knees and lay on the floor to peer through the banisters, as she and Lulu had done a thousand times when they were children and wanted to see the guests at the parties their parents frequently gave.

There he stood—all six feet and more of him, his broad shoulders now filling a handsome gray cutaway suit. His midnight hair glinted with the shafts of light from the stained glass window at the landing above where he stood. If he had glanced up, he would have seen her. If he had glanced up, she would have seen those eyes that reminded her so of the lake . . . one minute deep blue and calm, the next gray and brooding. But he did not glance up, and what she saw was the thickness of his lashes, the way his clean-shaven face reflected every nuance of his conversation with her sister—now exposing a dimple, now serious in concentration, now crinkling with laughter.

Lord, he had seen her practically naked, and she was supposed to walk downstairs as if nothing had happened? She considered feigning illness, rushing back to her room and ringing for Ernestine to deliver her regrets. It wouldn't be entirely a lie; she certainly felt decidedly ill.

But then she heard the grating voice of Cousin Eloise and knew that she had no choice. This man was the one Eloise had written Mama about, the one with so many eligible friends. The one Carlotta had claimed as her own. And since Eloise was here for the week, undoubtedly she had determined to throw this man and Katrina together at some point. She would not consider her mission complete until she found a suitable escort for Katrina at Carlotta's ball.

No, better to take her chances tonight, with lots of guests, than to risk having their first meeting take place in some cozier situation. She stood up and straightened her clothing—so much for this dress giving her confidence. Honestly, between Edward betraying her at the brewery meeting earlier and Eloise arriving, between the heat, and her encounter this afternoon . . . Now this . . .

"Miss Katrina?"

Ernestine stood just at the top of the back staircase, watching her.

"I'm going," Katrina muttered defiantly and started down the stairs like a prisoner on her way to the guillotine.

"Honestly, my dear, don't you think you could find something of this decade to put on when your family is entertaining?" Eloise took possession of Katrina's arm and steered her across the foyer, all the while lecturing her under her breath. "There's someone I want you to meet. I suggest you be on your best behavior. Mr. Sullivan is very high society in Chicago . . . *very* well connected. I'm sure he knows any number of eligible bachelors he could introduce you to."

Indeed, Katrina thought as she was brought to a halt a bare two feet from the provocative stranger. He was pretending an interest in a conversation with Lu and Edward, but she knew he was aware of her presence, just as she was uncomfortably aware of his.

"Ryan, dear," Eloise boomed, "I want you to meet August's elder daughter. Katrina, allow me to introduce Ryan Sullivan of Chicago."

"Mr. Sullivan," Katrina said, her eyes on his polished boots, her voice a croak above a whisper.

"Oh, we've already agreed to use first names, Katrina," Lulu announced. "From the sound of it, Ryan is going to be in Milwaukee on business often, and he's made us promise to introduce him to the city."

"Well, isn't that just lovely?" Eloise murmured, but she frowned at Lulu. "I'm so sorry Carlotta couldn't come with us this time. She always enjoys her visits so much." It was a territorial reminder, about Mr. Ryan Sullivan and Carlotta's claim on him, that neither Lulu nor Katrina could mistake.

"Yes, Carlotta finds Milwaukee so quaint," Katrina noted with barely concealed sarcasm. Carlotta Hauptman used any excuse to avoid visiting, and when she was forced to, she often took to her room, claiming the sheer boredom of such a provincial area gave her a sick headache.

"Well," Eloise tittered, "I'll admit Milwaukee is not one of Carlotta's favorite places, but I'm sure she would discover new wonders, seeing the city through Ryan's eyes." Eloise beamed coquettishly up at the dark Irishman.

The dark Irishman, Katrina noted when she dared to glance up, was grinning widely, exposing the maddening dimple and flirting shamelessly with his blue eyes. "Carlotta does know how to amuse herself," Ryan offered.

Now what the devil did that mean? Katrina was momentarily surprised to understand that a feeling of jealousy had come over her. She risked another glance at Ryan and found him looking at her, the devilish grin firmly in place.

"But we digress, and I have not yet greeted the charming Katrina," he said, and before she quite knew what was happening, he had taken one of her hands and lifted it to his lips. "May I call you Katrina, Miss Bergeman?"

"Well, of course, you can," Lulu interjected. "You'll find we don't stand on much ceremony in this family, Ryan."

"I warn you, I may be tempted to shorten it to Kate or perhaps Katie," he said softly, still looking directly at her, still holding her hand. "Kate is a favorite name for beautiful women in Ireland." His expression had gone serious, and the grin had softened to a smile, winsome and questioning.

Lulu and Edward exchanged knowing looks, Eloise huffed and tittered in absolute shock, and Ryan and Katrina stood there, staring at each other, neither willing to be the first to break the eye contact.

Finally Katrina realized they were making a spectacle of themselves and withdrew her hand from his. "You're from Ireland then, Mr. . . . Ryan?"

"My ancestors were Irish . . . My grandfather was born here in the United States, in New York."

"Then your family is in New York?"

Unmistakably, she had hit a nerve. His eyes clouded, and he frowned as a look of extreme sadness crossed his face for the barest moment. "No." He turned immediately to Edward. "What kind of annual yield is the brewery producing?"

Subject closed, Katrina thought. She was in a muddle. So far he had been gentlemanly enough not to reveal their earlier encounter, and just when she was prepared to give him points for that and ease into the natural sort of polite conversation that was expected of her at these gatherings, he acted as if she had asked the most impertinent question.

"Dinner is served," the butler announced, sliding back the pocket doors to reveal the dining room with its elaborate damask-covered table and high-backed chairs, its gleaming silver and crystal, and the gas-lighted brass-and-etched-glass chandelier that presided over the whole scene.

August offered his arm to Eloise and led the way while Sophie Bergeman asked Ryan to escort her.

"With delight," he said, and the charming smile that must have broken at least a dozen hearts was firmly back in place.

When the seating was done, Katrina found herself directly across from Ryan Sullivan. Not only that, but he was openly watching her, paying minute attention to the unfolding of her napkin, the sipping of her water. Her hand shook slightly as she replaced the crystal goblet by her plate. She had trouble knowing where to look. She was very relieved when her father struck up a conversation with him, occupying his full attention. "How did you come to be so involved in the grain market, Mr. Sullivan?"

"I made a small investment at the right time."

"You must have been quite young," August noted as he helped himself to three slices of the sauerbraten from the large china platter the hired girl offered.

"It was just after the war, sir." Ryan accepted the bowl of spiced applesauce Sophia passed to him.

"You were in the war, then. What division?"

"I had the honor of serving under Colonel Elmer E. Ellsworth. And you, sir?"

Katrina was well aware that nothing could flatter her father like the opportunity to discuss his military service. "The Sixth Wisconsin," he said with a proud smile. "I was a latecomer to the cause but reached the rank of colonel myself. Still, Ellsworth . . . he was renowned."

"Aye, that he was," Ryan agreed with a fond smile. "Mrs. Bergeman, this is delicious. How very kind of you to include me in your evening."

Katrina moved her food around her plate, unable to work up any appetite even though everything being served was her favorite. Normally Mama chastised her for eating too much and too fast. She saw Mama giving her a concerned look now and forced down a bit of the spicy hot potato salad their cook was famous for.

Ryan Sullivan did not seem to be having any problem with his meal. He took seconds and even thirds and all the while charmed the table with small talk that somehow included everyone . . . everyone except Katrina.

He seemed to talk around her—now addressing a question about the dry goods business to another guest, Mr. Chapman, on her right, then sharing a laugh with Lulu on his left, now complimenting her father on the fine workmanship in his home, then turning to Mama and seeking advice on finding good help. He even joined with Eloise in entertaining the entire company with tales of their train ride from Chicago. To Katrina he said nothing.

When the conversation turned to the brewery and Ryan asked how August had been able to keep the place going so successfully *and* serve his country, Papa beamed at Katrina.

"My daughter," he said and raised his glass in her direction. "And, of course, Edward," he added, turning to include his future son-in-law in the toast.

But Ryan's eyes remained on Katrina. "Really? Katrina has a head for business then," he asked, looking at her, but still addressing her father.

Katrina toyed with a piece of potato as their neighbor, Doc Clybourn, took up the story. "The women in this family are well educated and well read, Mr. Sullivan. Their mother sees to that."

Bergeman nodded. "One day the business will belong to them . . . and their husbands, of course, but Mrs. Bergeman and I have always agreed that the girls' future is best served if they are both beautiful and independent."

Eloise huffed on that note. "Honestly, August, sometimes, you'll forgive me, you and Sophie put a bit too much emphasis on the subject of independence, especially where young ladies are concerned. Willfulness isn't attractive, you know."

"Oh, I don't know," Doc said. "I find a smart woman far more interesting than one who's just a pretty face but dumber than a rock. How about you, Ryan?"

"When you put it that way, sir, there's little room for argument," Ryan agreed with a laugh.

Somehow the conversation moved from there to the way Mama had begun the local chamber music society and a woman's reading group, and with the focus once again off herself, Katrina relaxed. She even smiled at the hired girl when she came to clear the table and returned with the schaum torte.

"What a marvelous treat, Sophie," Clare Clybourn enthused as the confection of baked meringue, strawberries, and vanilla ice cream was served.

"I can take no credit where the strawberries are concerned," Sophie announced with pride. "Katrina has nursed them along until they are already ripe a full week before anyone else's. I think she reads to them or something."

While everyone else's attention turned to a discussion of gardens, once again Katrina felt Ryan's penetrating gaze. She looked up to meet it and was stunned when instead of holding her look, he allowed himself a lazy perusal of her—his eyes lingering first on her hair, then moving to her lips, and then lower to the prim row of tiny pearl buttons that suddenly seemed far too fragile to conceal what had been fully exposed to him earlier in the afternoon.

"Yes, they are unusually dark," he said quietly, "and equally sweet, I'll wager." Then he popped a berry into his mouth, biting it so that just a trickle of juice wet his lips and his tongue darted out to catch it.

Katrina wondered that the others did not react to his shameless display, his insulting insinuations, his . . .

Furious and with cheeks aflame, she glanced around the table. Surely Papa . . . But Papa was engaged in a lively conversation with Mrs. Chapman, and Mama and Lulu were caught up in the details of the ball Eloise was planning for Carlotta in October. Edward was talking to the other guests. Not one person had even noticed, had even heard . . .

She risked a look back at Ryan Sullivan and found him licking cream from his upper lip and watching her like a cat who has just cornered his mouse and is prepared to toy with it before the kill.

The butler brought the ornately engraved silver coffee service to Sophie. She poured while Heinrich delivered a cup to each guest and offered cream and sugar. Finally the meal was over. If only Papa had been one of those conventional people who invited the men into the library for cigars and brandy. But no, long ago Mama had told her husband she had no intention of missing all the interesting political and business gossip the men would exchange. "In the last century, the French were quite fond of their salons," she had announced. "They were a gathering place for all the most interesting people. I want our home to be a salon."

"Somewhere back in your mother's ancient history," Papa had told his daughters with a wink, "there's most certainly a Frenchman, or woman, most likely Joan of Arc."

But the truth was that he delighted in his wife's unortho-dox entertainments, and he shared her interest in creating gatherings that were lively and fun and even slightly con-troversial. No, the men would not retire to the library while the ladies gathered in the parlor. The evening would draw out with all of them in the same room. Well, at least Katrina could keep herself well away from him.

"Why don't you young people go for a walk in the gardens?" Sophie suggested as she stood to indicate that supper had ended. "It's such a lovely summer's night."

Lulu beamed. "Thank you, Mama," she said and moved around the table to give each parent an exuberant kiss on the cheek. "Wonderful supper," she called and then took Edward's arm. "I'll just get a wrap," she said.

"Bring one for your sister, too." Edward squeezed Lulu's hand and watched her lovingly as she ran up the stairs. Then he turned to intercept Katrina.

"I need to talk to you," he said quietly, walking with her toward the front door, "about this afternoon at the brewery . . ."

4

RYAN FOUND THAT he did not like seeing Katrina's face so close to another's man's, even if it was Mueller's, even if he was her future brother-in-law. He had gone to pull out Eloise Hauptman's chair and escort her from the dining room when he turned to see that the two of them had moved onto the veranda and were deep in what appeared to be a most serious conversation.

Throughout dinner he had tried to put the image of Katrina lying in the water out of his mind. Surely knowing who she was, whose daughter she was . . . Bergeman was a man Ryan hoped to do business with. There was that parcel of timberland up near Green Bay the older man was rumored to be willing to sell. But it was also well known that Bergeman took an almost parental pride in the natural resources of his state. It was no secret that more than once the German had refused a deal simply because the buyer was not someone with whom he wished to do business. Ryan wanted that land or at least some land in the area. He had visited there on the advice of his good friend former Chicago mayor William Ogden, and had been enchanted by the serenity of the region as well as its obvious business advantages.

But it was rumored that August Bergeman could be

stubborn. Ryan had noted the reserve with which the
brewer had treated him, a reserve Ryan recognized as
the sort of ethnic prejudice that was subtle but not at
all uncommon among powerful men. Each group stuck
together—the Germans, the Italians, the New England
Yankees who tended to view all others as "foreigners."
He knew full well the stereotypes that were held about
each group, about his own Irish heritage. He had sensed
that those stereotypes ran through Bergeman's mind during
their first meeting. He had also known the litany came as
naturally to Katrina's father as Ryan's own appraisal of
most Germans as conservative and ploddish came to him.

Such knowledge only heightened the charms of the
daughter. The very fact that he would not be considered
a suitable match provoked a need to prove himself. But
there was more. At the lake there had been little time or
opportunity to study her, to engage her in conversation.
Now he had learned things about her that intrigued him.
What had her father meant when he had given her the credit
for preserving the brewery during the war? She had been a
mere girl then. Still, Ryan had not missed how the credit
had gone first to Katrina and then to Edward.

He tried to pay attention to the chatterings of the corpulent
Mrs. Hauptman as he escorted her from the dining room
to the parlor. She clung heavily to his arm and seemed to
be raving on about something Carlotta had said. But his
thoughts were on Katrina. He had been shameless in that
comment about the schaum torte, even insulting. It had been
a lapse, one he was grateful no one else had heard. Still, he
had not mistaken the way her breath had quickened or the
way her cheeks had flamed. Carlotta would have taken such
a comment in all its crudity as a compliment. Katrina had
found it improper. No, she was not Carlotta, for all that
she had a penchant for bathing in her underwear in public
places.

"Are you going with the others, Mr. Sullivan?" Sophie
Bergeman had appeared at his side and was relieving him

of the chattering Mrs. Hauptman.

"Oh, my dear," Eloise said to Sophie, "I can't imagine that would be appropriate."

"Nonsense, Eloise. What could be more appropriate than Mr. Sullivan and Katrina chaperoning Edward and Lulu? After all, Mr. Sullivan is certainly of age." She smiled up at Ryan. "As is Katrina," she added.

When Eloise gave a frustrated gurgle, Sophie laughed aloud. "Oh, honestly, Cousin, we are discussing a simple walk on the lawn on a hot summer night, not a tryst in the back of some carriage."

There was no doubt about it. Sophia Bergeman was an incredibly modern woman. Ryan smiled down at her and in that moment realized how much Katrina resembled her, realized that this lovely woman was what Katrina would be like in years to come—intelligent, independent, with an understanding that times change.

"You won't take advantage of my daughter, will you, Mr. Sullivan?" Sophia gave him a stern look and wagged one finger.

"Absolutely not," he promised.

Eloise was speechless. "Well . . . that is to say . . . Perhaps . . ."

"Ah, here's Edward and Katrina. Now if someone can just locate Lulu." Sophie glanced at Katrina and nodded toward the stairway.

"Isn't Lu down yet?" Edward asked, but it was clear he was used to having to wait for her to appear.

Katrina laughed. "I'll see what's keeping her. We should know better than to let Lu get the wraps. She's probably redoing her hair, for heaven's sake." She turned and gave Edward's hand a sudden affectionate squeeze.

Ryan was a little taken aback that such intimacies with Edward could set him off. The man was clearly like a brother to her and obviously devoted to her sister. What was his problem? He frowned just as she turned and glanced up at him.

Again Katrina sensed that he was angry with her. She had felt it this afternoon at the lake and again when she had asked about his family in New York. Not anger, exactly, but a very definite shift in mood. The man was intractable enough to be Irish, she thought as she waited for him to step aside so she could pass, then chastised herself for indulging in a stereotype.

"I'll be right down," she said lightly and determined to move past him as quickly as possible, even though his position in the doorway seemed designed to block her way. There was no avoiding the brush of her shoulder against his arm, no evading the touch of his hand at her back as he turned to allow her more leeway, no escaping the fact that his palm and fingers easily spanned the width of her corseted waist.

Once through the door, she wanted to dash for the stairway but forced herself to move serenely through the foyer, stopping briefly to say something to her father and the other guests who were congregating in the parlor.

Lu was in her room, and as Katrina had guessed, she was busy rearranging her hair and applying fresh rose water. "Lu, Edward is waiting," Katrina said from the doorway.

"Ah, but it's who he's waiting with that's the topic of interest as far as I'm concerned," Lulu teased. "Is not Ryan Sullivan the most incredibly handsome, charming, fascinating man you've ever met?"

"Does Edward know you're so smitten?" Katrina teased and took a moment to glance at her own hair and the heightened color of her cheeks—a color she knew full well had been put there by the subject of their discussion.

"Ryan is the smitten one," Lulu declared.

"With Carlotta?" She sighed. "I'd like to give him more credit—"

"Not Carlotta, you *Dummkopf. You!*" Lulu's eyes sparkled with excitement. "I mean, it's as if he's known you before . . . the way he looks at you . . . the way his eyes followed you when you first came down the stairs tonight.

I'll give you that you are a knockout in that dress, even if it is a hundred years old."

"Will you and Eloise get it through your heads that I am not interested in being a fashion plate?" Katrina seized on any opportunity to change the subject. "Now, get your wrap," she added, picking out one for herself from the several in Lu's wardrobe.

"Not that one," Lu moaned, snatching the serviceable gray wool from her sister's hands. She paused for just a second before making her selection. "This one," she said, handing Katrina a dolman of turquoise silk. "It does wonderful things for your eyes."

Katrina looked doubtfully at the beautiful garment and then folded it over her arm. "Are you coming?" she asked when Lu stopped once more to study her perfect features in the mirror.

"Coming. Now, listen," she said as they moved down the hall together, "Edward and I want a moment . . . well, actually several moments . . . you understand. He's been working such long hours, and we hardly ever are alone now with the days so long and Papa sending him on his way practically before it gets dark . . ."

"Lu," Katrina said warningly.

"Please. Please. Please."

For most of their lives Katrina had been unable to deny her sister much. She envied Lu her natural gift for charm. Everyone loved Lulu. Everyone indulged her as well.

"I'll try," Katrina said with a sigh and was rewarded with a quick hug. "It won't be easy," she warned as they hurried down the stairs. "There's Ryan Sullivan, you know."

"Yes, sister dear, I'm well aware there's Ryan Sullivan, and that should make giving Edward and me a bit of time alone ever so much easier."

It was an incredibly beautiful night—starry and clear with a slight breeze coming from the lake that chased away the humidity of the day. The fireflies were out in force, and Katrina was surprised and delighted when Ryan suggested they see who might catch one first. It had been a favorite childhood game on summer evenings, but Katrina would have thought Ryan too worldly for such nonsense. She couldn't have been more wrong.

When they had all agreed to the rules, he pursued his quarry with zeal and did everything he could to sabotage the efforts of everyone else. There was much giggling and teasing as the four of them lunged drunkenly for the bugs, who seemed to dart out of reach just as a hand came after them, and then light up in triumph as they flew away.

"I have one," Ryan called out jubilantly.

"You do not," Katrina challenged, certain that his closed fist was simply a ploy to divert the attention of the others.

"You wound me, Miss Bergeman," he said with mock grief. "Have I ever lied to you before?" He had started back across the lawn toward her, his silhouette accented by the light streaming from the windows of the house.

"Let me see," she said, and again it was a challenge. She noticed that Edward and Lulu seemed occupied in the shadows of the giant weeping willow that spread its curtain of branches around them.

"If I open my hand, he'll fly away."

"How do you know it's a male firefly?" Katrina teased.

"Well, if it's a female, it will fly away for sure." He was next to her now, looking down at her with a grin, presenting his closed fist.

"That's a fairly judgmental comment, Mr. Sullivan. Why would a female have any more inclination to be free than a male?"

"I don't know. Perhaps you could tell me." His voice had gone soft and serious, and she sensed that his grin was no longer in place. She felt a sudden apprehension at the nearness of him—an apprehension that came not from any danger he might present, but seemed born of her own feelings whenever he was near. She took refuge in the minute study of his closed fist.

When she said nothing, he continued in a lighter tone. "It's just that I sense that you as a female feel, shall we say, certain constraints?"

The moment passed, and Katrina smiled. "It is a man's world, Mr. Sullivan, in case you hadn't noticed. Though why should you notice? As a man you are free to do and think and act as you please without question." There was no bitterness in her tone, though there was a twinge of envy.

"It's hardly so simple, Katie."

The nickname was an endearment the way he said it. Katrina thought she should probably take offense, but how could she when it came as it did . . . softly and accompanied by the tenderest brush of his fingers against the hair that blew across her brow.

"Do you want to see this bug or not?" He was back to being jovial. He loosened his fist just enough for her to see the glimmer of yellow through his fingers.

"You did catch one," she exclaimed.

He gave an exasperated sigh. "Katie, Katie, you're going to have to learn to trust me," he teased, then opened his palm and waited for the firefly to take off.

"Wait," Katrina said. "Let me call Edward and Lulu."

Ryan waved his hand slightly, sending the insect on its way, and took her elbow, leading her away from the willow tree. "I suspect Edward and Lulu couldn't care less about the game," he said. "I think they have other things on their minds, and we would do well to give them the few moments they want alone."

Katrina glanced back toward the willow in time to see the shadows of her sister and friend come together in an embrace. Her dilemma was not with them, but rather with the fact that she was now alone with Ryan Sullivan.

They walked in silence for a few minutes, his hand still at her elbow as if to courteously guide her over the uneven terrain of the lawn. When they reached the path that wound its way through the grape arbor back to the vegetable garden, he released her and walked beside her with both hands clasped behind his back.

As they entered the arbor, Katrina became increasingly uncomfortable. Not that he wasn't the complete gentleman. He even moved just slightly away from her, keeping a respectable distance as they walked along the graveled path. But there was something about the darkness that was both exhilarating and intimidating. Without being able to see him really, her other senses were heightened. More than ever she was aware of the scent of his cologne, the sound of his boot against the gravel, and the closeness of him. She thought about the afternoon and how strong and tan his bare chest had been and the musculature of his back when he had given her his shirt and turned away while she dressed.

There was a stirring she seemed to feel whenever he was near . . . and even when he wasn't. She recalled how she had been daydreaming about him in her room even before she had known he was to be the special dinner guest. How she had fantasized about touching his skin, being in his arms, having his lips touch hers . . .

"Is this where you grow your strawberries?" he asked.

It was an innocent and wholly conversational question, Katrina reminded herself. Then why on earth did her cheeks flame red and her breath quicken?

"The garden is just there," she replied, pointing stiffly as they came to the end of the arbor path.

They strolled the perimeter of the plot in uncomfortable silence. "We'd better go back," she said and reentered the arbor to return to the front lawn.

"I'm sorry," he said quietly. When she glanced at him, he added, "The comment at supper was rude. Sometimes, Katie, I forget myself and revert to . . . old ways."

"I'm sure I don't know what comment you mean," she said primly, thankful for the darkness that just a moment ago had given her cause for alarm.

He laughed then, and had it not been at her expense, it

would have been a wonderful sound . . . full and rich and completely unfettered.

She sputtered like Cousin Eloise and moved even a step farther away from him, catching her heel as she did and stumbling. Immediately his hand reached out to her. All he did was grasp her arm to steady her, but his fingers warmed her skin through the silk of her wrap, and the heat spread beyond where he touched her to fuel a deeper, more intimate, and completely unfamiliar sense of desire.

"I'm all right," she managed, praying that he would release her before she did something foolish like touch him back, and at the same time hoping against hope that he would give her just a few more seconds to savor the feel of his hand on her.

Instead of releasing her, he put his other hand at her waist, turning her until she was facing him. "Don't pretend nothing happened this afternoon, Katie," he whispered, his mouth close enough so she could feel the warmth of his breath. "Not when we're alone. I'll keep your secret with the others." He chuckled softly then. "I suspect, even though he clearly dotes on you, that your father would be less than pleased at your little adventure."

She could not stifle the smile that idea brought, and with the smile she relaxed slightly. "Thank you for not saying anything, Ryan."

"I have no desire to embarrass you, Katie." He trailed the backs of his fingers over her cheek while he kept one hand at her waist. "I do have . . . and have had all afternoon . . . an incredible desire to kiss you."

She stiffened and started to move away, but his hand tightened at her waist. She glared up at him then, her hands at her sides, her posture rigid and defensive. "You must not mistake what happened this afternoon, Mr. Sullivan. The fact that you . . . happened upon me in that moment does not make me a . . . loose woman. I—"

His fingers were against her lips. "Sh-h-h," he whispered. "This has nothing to do with this afternoon . . . Well, it does, of course. But I assure you, Katie, my desire to kiss you would be just as powerful had I met you this evening."

There was something about the way he called her Katie that mesmerized her. Perhaps it was the hint of an Irish accent. Perhaps it had to do with the fact that she had always been called by her proper name, unlike Lulu, who had hardly ever been Lucinda. Perhaps it was because she understood that to this man she was someone no one else knew. Because he had seen her this afternoon and decided to share her secret, she was free to be whomever she pleased with him. With Ryan Sullivan, there would be no rules.

She was looking up at him, her eyes at first wide with alarm and then something quite the opposite. There was just enough light to make out her features, especially the wide, expressive eyes, the lips parted slightly and incredibly innocent in their sensual invitation. Ryan flattened his palm against her back, and she swayed toward him, her breasts just a breath away from touching his chest. God help him, he wanted her in the most primal way. For a moment he regretted his chivalry of the afternoon. There by the lake they had been two strangers—a man and a woman with all things possible. Their formal introduction tonight had changed that.

With identity came decision and propriety. No longer were they simply a man and a woman. She had become part of a scenario, one that included business, one that carried with it societal guidelines one could not breach.

"You play a dangerous game, Katie," he said softly, allowing his fingers to caress the smooth skin of her cheeks, his thumb to trail across the fullness of her lower lip.

Katrina closed her eyes and swallowed. She was having trouble breathing, and had his hand not spanned the width of her back, she was quite certain her knees would not be supporting her. *Kiss me,* she wished with all her soul.

As if she had spoken aloud, he answered, "Not tonight, Katie. The first time will be when we can see each other clearly and understand there will be no going back, no pretending it never happened."

With his hand still around her waist, he started walking back toward the front of the house with her. "And Katie," he added as they stepped out of the arbor and moved across the wide lawn toward the willow tree, "it will be soon."

"I like him," August Bergeman argued, then added, "at least what I know of him."

"Well?"

Sophie's logic could be exasperating to say the least. To her way of thinking, there were far too many regulations for the way people were supposed to deal with one another. She liked the simple direct approach, especially when it came to relationships.

August helped his wife unfasten her gown. She was still beautiful, her figure as lithe and firm as it had been on their wedding night. Every time he saw her, he still felt the urge to take her in his arms. He finished opening the row of buttons down the back of her gown and then put his arms around her, pulling her against him. For all the servants in the house, he and Sophie had always reserved this private time for each other alone.

"Don't try to distract me," she teased. "You do that when you know I'm right and don't want to admit it."

August sighed and released her, reaching up to remove his stiff collar and unfasten his shirt. "Sophie, you'll just have to trust me on this one. Ryan Sullivan is a charming man, no doubt, and I have no problem with his being friends with the children . . ."

Sophie laughed. "Oh, Augie, the *children* are nineteen and twenty-four . . . One of them is practically married. We are not discussing playmates, for heaven's sake."

August frowned. This was more serious than he had thought. How did women take one evening's entertainment and turn it into a romance? Ever since they had retired to their bedroom, Sophie had been chattering away excitedly about

the obvious attraction between Katrina and Ryan Sullivan.
In some ways his wife was as bad as Eloise. Eloise he could
forgive; the woman was a fool. But Sophie . . .

"I want a better match for Katrina," he said quietly.

Sophie sensed the sobering of his mood and remained
quiet for several moments. She finished undressing, putting
on her gown and wrapper and moving to her dressing table,
where she took the pins from her golden hair and began to
brush it to a high shine.

"I do not understand your objections," she said after
a long silence. She was always unwilling to go to bed
with unfinished business between them. "Katrina has been
alone far too long. I am happy to see her interested in
someone."

"Sophia, he is Irish, and regardless of your willingness
to believe all men are created equal, there are differences.
Differences born of heritage and background, of the way a
man is raised, of ethnic history. Differences that may not
matter now, that rarely matter in the throes of courtship,
but that will come to matter a great deal later."

"Are you saying the only suitable match for our daughters
are men of German heritage?" Her brush paused in mid-
stroke, and she watched him in her mirror.

He sighed and sat on the edge of the bed to remove his
shoes and stockings. "Not necessarily. I am saying there
needs to be a commonality in values, in upbringing . . .
What do we know about this man?"

"Well, we know he's Irish, and that seems to be plenty
for you to judge him." The brush flashed as she stroked
furiously.

"Sophie, think. Do you know any Irish families who
came at the same time our families did and have made
anything of themselves?"

"But we already had—"

"The Clybourns didn't have anything . . . Edward's family started from nothing," he argued. "And think of the
problems I've had with the Irish at the brewery . . . late

for work or not showing up at all, and when they do, they're always pushing for change, not to mention drinking, fighting . . ."

"August Bergeman, do you hear yourself?" This time she turned around to face him directly. "Is this the same man who returned from that dreadful war torn apart because men were not allowed even the basic consideration simply because their skin was dark? Is this the man who has always stood for fairness and has taught his children as well as his employees to judge a man by what he is rather than where he comes from?"

"Sophie, the man speculates in grain futures. Today he has money. By morning he could be a pauper. Do you honestly want to promote a romance between Katrina and a gambler?"

It was unusual to hear her parents raise their voices, and that rarity was what had caused Katrina to pause outside their door as she returned to her room from her late-night chat with Lulu. It wasn't that they were shouting, but the murmur of voices held an uncommon tension, and Katrina had heard Papa mention her name.

She caught only her father's last statement before she was interrupted by the sound of Ernestine and Pauline moving up the back stairway to their rooms on the third floor. She did not want to be seen listening outside her parents' door, so she hurried on to her own room.

Still, the disapproval in Papa's voice stayed with her. At an early age she had learned the importance of financial security. Papa had made certain she understood that people's dreams were achieved through careful planning. From the time she was small, Papa had shown all of them how planning and saving and managing wisely could make all things possible. Only recently had Katrina understood the extent of the family's fortune. Throughout her childhood, her parents had placed financial responsibility on each child. There had been expectations of hard work and savings for the future carefully squirreled away, often at the expense of some present gratification. The fact that there were great sums of money available did not play a part when it came to teaching the children the value of financial security.

But the rewards had always been worth it. The pride she had felt when she finally had the money to purchase her own leather-bound set of Shakespeare's complete works; the delight Lulu had known when the silk for a gown she had craved for months was finally affordable; the pride Papa had shown when Katrina asked him to help her with the selection of a riding horse after two years of saving her earnings from working at the brewery.

She knew nothing of Ryan's business, only what she heard from talk at the brewery or in the after-dinner conversations in the parlor about the fluctuations of the grain market. She knew well the meaning of speculations and risks. She had heard her parents speak in hushed tones of friends who had lost money in the marketplace and had to make sometimes sudden and catastrophic changes in their lifestyle to compensate for those losses. She had known friends who had withdrawn from college and social clubs because they could no longer afford the fees. And she had known employees of her father's who had stopped by the office to beg for advances on their wages to pay pressing bills they had incurred without planning, money they had gambled away or used to pay for drinks instead of groceries.

On many occasions she had gone with her mother to tend the sick wives and children of employees who had good wages but never put aside the money for emergencies such as medical care. Using her own store of savings, more than once she had purchased shoes or winter coats for the children of employees who had had to be laid off in hard times.

She thought of the fashionable cut of Ryan's clothing, the silky softness of the shirt he had handed her that afternoon, expensive fabric hand-tailored with double-stitched French finishing of seams that fit only him. She thought of the townhouse Eloise had described in Chicago—a mansion really, where he lived alone with a cluster of servants. She thought of Eloise's answer when Papa had questioned her about Ryan's sudden rise on the Chicago social scene, as the family sat together after the other guests had left.

"Yes, Cousin, I'll admit his fortunes have been quite spectacular and quite instantaneous, and there were doubts about him. But then, many people made money after the war. Actually he is rather a mystery . . . No one knows his background . . . something about New York. But he is a war hero, and his manners are so impeccable there is little doubt he comes from breeding and money. And everyone seems to respect his business acumen . . . Why, I've heard he takes incredible risks and doubles, even triples, his money when more conservative investors are happy to simply garner a small profit."

As Eloise prattled on, Katrina had felt her heart swell with pride at the glowing report of Ryan's business savvy and personal reputation for civility. True, the way Papa had sat quietly, smoking his cigar, had not gone unobserved, but he must see what an unusually fine man Ryan was. Katrina had taken his silence for approval. Besides, Papa had given Ryan his blessing to look at some timberland the family owned up near Mama's family home place in Peshtigo. Ryan planned to leave the next morning.

"I'll be back by the end of the week," he had added, his eyes moving to include Katrina in this last statement.

Papa and Ryan then shook hands. "Perhaps we can discuss an offer for the timber when you return, Mr. Sullivan."

"Don't worry, Mr. Bergeman. I look forward to doing business with you in many matters." Again, his eyes had strayed to Katrina for the briefest second. She had felt a blush rise to her cheeks and had suddenly found the design of the carpet in the foyer extremely interesting. Most of the men she had known had been either so solicitous that their attentions were cloying, or so arrogant that a girl had to remind them she was even in the room.

Even though Papa might not have received the full thrust of Ryan's message, Katrina had, and it was for Katrina that the message was intended. Ryan had made her a promise in the arbor, and she knew that he was reminding her of his intention to keep that promise. It was this curious mix of upper-crust manners and nothing-to-lose directness that attracted her to him.

That night, unable to sleep, she climbed to the cupola that capped the house. From there she had a panoramic view of the city and Lake Michigan. This was her favorite spot in the house, a place she had come to all her life to sort through her feelings. Below her the grape leaves rustled against the structure of the arbor. In the distance the moon cast its reflection on the dark waters of the lake. Today both places had been inextricably tied to Ryan. She looked down at the place where the arbor ended near the willow tree and remembered his promise.

"Soon," he had whispered.

She thought about kissing Ryan Sullivan and knew that it would be an experience that had nothing to do with the hard mashing of lips she had shared with Abner, or even with the wet-tongued probings of some of her suitors more recently. Kissing Ryan would be different, she knew instinctively. Because Ryan was different. He was not like others who had gambled away family fortunes. He knew what he was doing; she was certain of it. Papa would see. After all, Papa and Mama were hardly the norm when it came to social standards, and Bergeman Beer was the success it was because, in his own way, Papa had taken risks.

All her life Katrina had held up the example of her parents' love for each other as the model she wanted for herself. Until now, she had had to content herself with romantic fantasies garnered from novels and stories. With the appearance of Ryan Sullivan had come the possibility of romance to rival any fiction. Hugging her wrapper to her, Katrina smiled. All in all, this had been a remarkable day.

5

"COME ON, KATRINA. I need your help."

Edward stood at her desk on Friday morning and waved the figures he had gathered for the commemorative stein. "You know you're much better at these things than I am, and it was your idea."

"Really," she said loftily and then grinned. "All right. Let me see what you've got."

After supper on the night of the dinner party, Edward had taken her aside to explain his motives in bringing the idea up at the meeting. "It's a good idea," he had argued, "and I knew you would never bring it up."

"I might have," she had told him, her arms crossed, her stance defiant.

"No, you wouldn't. You wouldn't risk your father's rejection in front of the others," he had said quietly.

"Papa does not 'reject' me."

"No, he doesn't. He loves you. But for all his New World ideas, he's pretty old-fashioned in many ways, and one of them is when it comes to taking advice from a woman, especially in business . . . even if she is his daughter."

"He takes Mama's advice on plenty of issues," she noted tersely.

"Yes, but I'll wager it takes some careful planning on your mother's part . . . choosing the right moment, the right words . . ."

He was right, of course. Katrina had witnessed it a hundred times, not only with Mama and Papa but between other men and women. No wonder women were relegated to be little more than children; they were constantly required to play some sort of stupid game to make any headway at all.

She sighed, taking the papers Edward held and spreading them on her desk. "Edward, do you play these stupid games with Lu? I mean, place her in a position where the only way she can make use of her brain is to carefully work her way around your fragile male ego?"

Edward laughed. "Well, at least you understand the male ego is fragile," he said. "And, no, I try hard to be as direct as possible with your sister and encourage her to be the same with me. However, I'm afraid such feminine wiles come rather naturally to Lulu . . . it's part of her charm."

"Well, it's not part of mine," Katrina muttered and turned her attention once again to the papers he had handed her. "Have you thought of other suppliers, Edward? Pilsop and Hunt make a fine stein, but they are the most expensive in the business."

Together they worked through the numbers until the proposal was ready for the scrutiny of the others, and more importantly for the close inspection of August Bergeman.

"There," Katrina said, handing Edward the final figures. "I think he'll accept this."

"I intend to tell him the idea was yours, Katrina. I always did. I just wanted him to accept it first."

Edward had been Frederick Bergeman's best friend. When he died, Katrina and Edward had comforted each other, and their friendship had grown. There had never been anything romantic about it. In so many ways he had slowly taken his place as her brother long before he and Lulu had begun their courtship. She smiled at him now. "No. You've done the work, Edward. It's easy to have the idea, much harder to actually make it happen."

Instead of going back to his own desk, he pulled over a stool and sat by hers. "You've got a good head for business, Katrina."

"Thank you." She waited. Clearly Edward had something on his mind. "And?" she prompted.

He smiled. "And I'm thinking of making a small investment in the grain market—nothing huge," he hastened to assure her, "but I'd like to start to get a little ahead . . . before I officially ask your father for Lulu's hand."

"Edward, I'm hardly qualified—"

"Well, actually I thought perhaps you might speak to Mr. Sullivan, to Ryan. I would value his advice."

"What makes you think I would have the opportunity to seek business advice from Mr. Sullivan?"

This time Edward laughed. "Now, Katrina, weren't we just speaking about how you hated feminine games? Don't be coy about Ryan Sullivan. The man is clearly taken with you, and perhaps your father missed the unspoken messages flashing around that house the other night, but I assure you Lulu and I did not. He's coming back this way for a great deal more than buying some trees from your father."

Katrina pretended an interest in finding a particular file but not before Edward had seen the smile that lit her face.

"Aha," he exclaimed. "I'm right. And it's about time. Lu and I have been wracking our brains to come up with someone willful enough and secure enough to make a good match for you. I guess we should have been looking in Chicago."

"You two are as bad as Cousin Eloise," Katrina said.

"Speaking of whom, if she gets wind of this, she and Carlotta are going to have a duck."

Katrina laughed. "She did make it very clear that Ryan was spoken for, didn't she?"

"Yes. Do you have other information?"

"Well, Carlotta's name did not exactly come up in our conversations."

"And what did the two of you talk about during those long minutes you spent in the grape arbor?"

She playfully punched his arm. "You have a lot of nerve. I was practically under orders from Lu to give the two of you some kissing time, and trust me, the willow does not hide everything. From what I observed, you'd better make your proposal to my father soon."

The return to that subject sobered Edward. "So, you'll speak to Ryan?"

Katrina frowned. "I don't know, Edward. Ryan seems to have unlimited funds, and you know how Papa feels about speculating on the market." She recalled her father's words, overheard in the hallway. *Gambler,* he had called Ryan.

"It costs nothing to ask," Edward said.

"I'll see if it comes up," Katrina agreed with a sigh.

"Oh, you'll have your chance. The circus is coming for the Fourth of July and I thought perhaps the four of us could go. We could take a picnic for the afternoon and then go to the late matinee . . . perhaps stop at the beer garden afterwards . . ."

"You seem to have this all planned out," Katrina said.

"It'll be a wonderful day, Katrina. What do you say?"

"I don't think you and Lulu really want a third wheel, and I'm not certain that Ryan—"

"Oh, I spoke to Ryan the other night. He gave me a ride home on his way back to the hotel. He's all for it."

"Really?" Katrina was a bit miffed that Ryan was taking it for granted that she would be at his beck and call, especially on a holiday. How did he know she didn't have a dozen invitations already? "Even in what everyone seems to perceive to be my desperate state of spinsterhood, I would still appreciate being asked," Katrina huffed.

"Then I'm asking" came a familiar bass voice behind her.

She whirled around to find Ryan Sullivan standing just inside the office door, his hat in his hand, his blue eyes sparkling. To her shock, he dropped to his knees and held our his folded hands in supplication.

"Please, Miss Bergeman, do me the honor of allowing me to be your escort on the Fourth of July. I am offering a picnic . . . the circus . . . perhaps a bit of dancing . . ." With each item, his dark eyebrows lifted as if asking what it would take to have her agreement. And then quietly and with the slightest twinkle, he added, "Oh, yes, and plenty of fireworks."

It rained on the eve of the Fourth, keeping Katrina awake most of the night. If it rained into the morning, the parade would be canceled, or at least her part in it. Independence Day was one of Katrina's favorite holidays. Papa, resplendent in his Union blues, would lead a regiment of the Sixth Wisconsin, while she, Mama, and Lulu would ride in a fine open carriage, the gentle breeze ruffling their summer dresses and leghorn straw hats. She loved the hoopla—the bands, the guns fired in celebration, and the flags snapping in the summer breeze.

This year Ryan Sullivan had given her even more reason to look forward to the day. It had been a week since he had extended his invitation on bended knee in Papa's office, a long week during which Katrina had spent an inordinate amount of time studying the clothes in her closet. She had finally given it up as a hopeless search and asked Lulu to go shopping with her. Lulu, of course, had been thrilled and had even held her teasing remarks about Ryan Sullivan to a minimum.

Katrina had looked forward to a good night's sleep after carefully laying out her finery for the following day, but the rains kept coming throughout the night, and she lay awake, willing them to stop as she wondered at the fact that only a few weeks ago she had been quite content with her life. Now here she was thinking of Ryan Sullivan constantly.

She had never experienced such feelings before . . . not even when she thought she was in love with Abner.

It was all so new . . . the way Ryan's presence intruded on her most mundane tasks, on her most routine activities. And there was the way she had begun to think of herself, to study herself really, spending long moments in front of the mirror playing with her hair, watching her expression with every thought focused on how she might be seen by Ryan. When Lulu indulged in such foolishness, Katrina had always tried to be tolerant, but in truth she had found such pastimes wasteful and downright foolish. Now suddenly she found herself moving into the realm of more erotic imaginings—his arms around her, his lips on hers, his body pressed against the thin cotton of her chemise.

She had spent more time than usual working in Mama's garden these past few days, hoping such industry would take her mind off Ryan; but she found herself recalling every detail of his face and voice, the pull of his shoulders against the fabric of his coat, the way his hair lay against his collar. When she retired to the porch or library after supper for her usual evening of reading, more often than not the book or magazine lay forgotten on a table or unseen in her hands as she replayed the brief history of their relationship.

Oh, she was captivated, no question about it. The only question was how he felt. Of course, there was Carlotta, but he had never so much as mentioned Katrina's cousin. On the other hand, what did she know of him? Perhaps he was one of those men who liked to collect hearts like so many trophies. She recalled how devilishly handsome and charming he had been that afternoon in Papa's office, how mortified she'd been when Papa came walking into the office while Ryan was still on his knees before her, pleading with her to allow him to escort her on the Fourth. Katrina had turned nearly purple with embarrassment when Papa came striding through the office door, just as Ryan made that comment about fireworks. But Ryan had hardly missed a beat.

"Excuse me," Papa had said politely, but the frown of disapproval was unmistakable as he glanced from the young man on his knees to Katrina.

Ryan had gotten gracefully to his feet and turned to greet the brewer. "Herr Bergeman, I have just asked your daughter to join me for the day when we celebrate our independence. I hope that my invitation meets with your approval."

Papa's bushy eyebrows had knitted with consternation. Katrina could practically hear him thinking, she knew him so well, and she remembered the bits of the conversation she had overheard between him and Mama. She held her breath waiting for his refusal to give his permission, and wondered what she would do. More to the point, what would Ryan do? Give up? Persist?

"Lu and I asked Ryan and Katrina to join us for the day, sir," Edward added nervously.

Then Papa gave an abrupt nod and headed for his office. "What did you think of the timber, Sullivan?" This last was thrown out over his shoulder, a clear indication that he expected Ryan to follow him into his private office and conduct the business at hand.

And that had been the end of it. Katrina had been busy in another part of the brewery when Ryan left, but she took some solace in the fact that Papa had announced to Sophie at dinner that the young Irishman would be buying a piece of timberland. "The Peshtigo tract. I asked what he planned to do with it," August said. "He told me he hadn't decided." Papa shook his head at that. "Said he just liked where it was, affording the view of the harbor."

"He's an unusual young man," Mama said noncommittally as she offered potatoes to Lu and Katrina.

"The four of us are spending the Fourth together," Lu told Mama, then turned immediately to see Papa's reaction.

Papa acknowledged this with a grunt.

But later that evening he had found Katrina in the library and pulled a chair close to hers. After some superficial inquiries into the book she was reading, he cleared his throat, signaling the commencement of a serious talk.

"Katrina, about young Sullivan . . ."

"Papa . . ."

He had held up his hand to forestall any interruption. "Hear me out, *Liebchen.* The man was born a charmer, not only of the fairer sex but on the business front as well. I don't think I've ever known a man with such a gift for saying exactly the right thing at the right moment." Papa shook his head and studied the polished planked floor before going on.

"He's very nice," Katrina said softly, as much to remind her father of her presence as anything.

He looked at her then, his reddish-gray sideburns working as he clenched and unclenched the muscles in his face. "Ah, *Liebchen,* you know I want nothing but your happiness, and since you've no other plans for the Fourth, he's a fine man to show you a lovely day. But you must keep perspective here. Ryan Sullivan's roots are . . . different. He comes at life from a variant direction than the one you were brought up with. In the conversations we've had, it puzzles me that the man seems to have no real plan . . . no real direction. Imagine, buying land with no plan in mind." For a moment, Papa seemed lost in thought, but then he returned his full attention to his daughter. "And yet, I cannot deny his success. Katrina, success is momentary . . . It is what follows, how a man builds on those moments, that counts. Ryan Sullivan, no doubt, has achieved some remarkable prosperity, especially for one so young. That can be exciting when you're first getting to know someone, but believe me, over the long run differences in backgrounds . . . in philosophies . . . can have their effect. They can be very devastating, very . . . confusing."

Katrina and her father had had serious talks before— about her education, about business, about the war, even about other boys and young men. Papa always got so solemn on these occasions, as if life itself hung in the balance.

The pattern between them was for Katrina to listen intently, and then when Papa seemed at the depths of earnestness, she would say something to lighten the mood, at the same time indicating she had heard every word.

"Papa," she said softly that night in the library, "we're going on a picnic and to the circus. This is not 'till death us do part.'" Papa smiled and patted her hand and sighed with relief.

"That's my girl," he said heartily. "Such a good head on those pretty shoulders." He hugged her and left her to her reading. During the following days he even teased her about her coming date, and she retorted with banter of her own.

But the truth was there was something very exciting, almost disturbing, about her anticipation of seeing Ryan Sullivan again, of spending an entire day with him. In a way, it was as if she stood at the brink of something momentous, something that might give her great joy or horrendous pain, but either way would change her. And either way, she knew she would not be satisfied with one day. The very fact that he was so different from anyone she'd ever known before only added to the intense attraction she felt for him.

For the first time in her life, she questioned the validity of Papa's counsel.

Independence Day dawned clear and perfect, the air purified, the atmosphere newly cleansed as if in anticipation of the celebration to come. The Bergeman household, like all other households in the city, awakened to the booming of the guns of the Light Artillery, calling the citizenry of Milwaukee to gather by the thousands for the day's festivities.

The house was alive with activity as Ernestine hurried between the dressing rooms of her mistress and the two girls, stringing corsets, hooking petticoats, lifting gowns over freshly coiffed hair, fastening rows of tiny buttons, tying sashes, finding misplaced slippers, fans, and gloves.

In the kitchen, Pauline had prepared a veritable feast of eggs, sausages, potatoes, fresh fruit, freshly baked rolls, and coffee. Heinrich served from the dumbwaiter as the family gathered in the dining room. Ignoring the girls' protests that their corseted waistlines could never withstand such a repast, Pauline tied large cloth napkins bib-style around their necks. "Eat," she ordered brusquely. "I won't have you fainting during the parade from lack of proper sustenance."

Then Rudy, the driver, appeared at the portico with the carriage; Papa strapped on his saber and gave one last bit of polish to the brass buttons that marched two by two down the front of his uniform coat; Mama adjusted the slant of Lulu's hat; and the group was off. The matched Belgian horses pranced along, their large hooves almost daintily tapping out a cadence on the brick street, as if they understood the importance of the occasion. The girls practiced various styles of waving as Papa rode alongside the carriage on his sorrel stallion.

Every shop they passed was decked out with bunting and evergreens for the celebration. Many houses and businesses flew the red, white, and black of Imperial Germany as well as the tricolors of the United States. People of all backgrounds had gotten into the spirit of the day by choosing the colors of the Union to wear. Katrina's dress was a deep blue lawn, embroidered with tiny white stars and featuring a sailor-styled lace collar piped in red. Lulu had helped her arrange her hair into a high twist with one curled lock on her shoulder to offset the jaunty angle of her flower-decked straw hat. A white parasol completed her costume, and she felt festive and pretty.

Crowds thronged the parade route along Broadway, Mason, and Wisconsin streets, sometimes standing four and five deep to see the passing spectacle. Many of them waved small replicas of the American flag as the parade passed, and from her family's carriage Katrina smiled and waved back. Now and then she spotted someone she knew— a family friend or a worker from the brewery—and for that person she had a special smile, even calling out a greeting. All in all, this was starting out to be a glorious day.

Ryan took in the extravaganza of Independence Day in Milwaukee, Wisconsin, with a wry smile. There was something so ingenuous about the atmosphere surrounding the event. In Chicago and New York, gatherings such as this were rarely the innocent fun they were made to appear. Almost certainly political agendas were at work along with factional competitions and financial considerations.

But here all that seemed secondary to the pure joy of the day's events. Ryan had chosen to wait at the Courthouse Square, where he had been advised the parade would conclude. A great many people filled the square and waited in excited anticipation for the commencement of the speeches and music that would make up the program for the day.

Ryan moved among them, listening with half an ear to their comments, tipping his hat to the ladies, pausing to shake hands when he met someone he knew from his dealings in the grain exchange. But in truth, he was moving purposefully toward a destination, looking for someone, scanning the crowd for some sign of her . . . knowing that her hair would be unmistakable.

It was insanity, of course, his wanting this woman. Certainly he could have his pick of any number of beauties, women whose fathers would not be nearly so concerned about the difference in background, the course of his future, the trail of his heritage.

August Bergeman was not likely to embrace the idea of his daughter becoming involved with an Irishman. Ryan had not missed the frown that day at the brewery when he asked to escort Katrina to the festivities today. Nor had he mistaken the direct, albeit subtly polite, questions designed to take his measure that first evening when he came for supper. No, August Bergeman would be consumed with Ryan's intentions: on the one hand, fearful that they might be too serious; on the other, troubled that they might be too trifling.

He knew that he had Bergeman's grudging admiration when it came to business. He also had the man's respect as a fellow veteran of the war. But when it came to his daughter, August Bergeman would draw the line. Knowing all of this, Ryan had spent the better part of his trip to Peshtigo reflecting on the foolishness of his infatuation with the girl. She was, after all, hardly more than that, regardless of her chronological age. As sheltered a life as she had led, she could hardly be considered experienced on any level. For all the Bergemans' free thinking on matters of education and women's rights, their daughters thought as they had been taught to think, following the example of their parents.

But then he had walked into Bergeman's office and seen her . . . the graceful slant of her neck as she bent over some papers with Edward, the slender hips, and the memory of endless legs he could not get out of his mind from that day at the lake. He had stood there watching her for a long moment before making his presence known, relishing the deep throatiness of her voice and knowing that nothing he had daydreamed about on his trip north compared with the urges and desires he felt in her presence.

Yes, it would be easier to go after another woman, but the combination of obvious innocence and suppressed sensuality that emanated from Katrina Bergeman like fine French perfume would not be denied. He only wondered that there wasn't a line of men ahead of him. He had told himself a dozen times this past week that the very fact there were no other obvious suitors should in itself serve as fair warning.

Then he saw her, sitting across from her mother and Lulu in a carriage that had been polished to the sheen of marble and upholstered in red velvet. The perfectly matched team of Belgians high-stepped their way through the crowd toward the expansive platform where the dignitaries were gathering in front of the scaffolding of the new courthouse. August Bergeman waited there and extended his hand to assist his wife and daughters from the carriage and up the steps to their place on the dais.

Sophie Bergeman and Lulu moved with a distinct feminine grace, the kind born of long moments spent in front of mirrors and in the study of ladylike deportment. Katrina's rhythm was very different, at once boyishly athletic and enticingly provocative. Ryan considered the difference and realized that both Sophie and Lulu wore the bustles that fashion dictated de rigueur for the times. Although Katrina's skirts were gathered and swagged high on her hips and derriere, there was no sign of that nonsensical pillow of padding bouncing perkily along as she moved.

The band played as the Bergeman family greeted other community leaders, were introduced to the speakers, and settled into their places. Ryan saw Katrina scan the crowd and wondered if she were looking for him. Then Alexander Mitchell began to introduce the chaplain for the occasion, and the crowd quieted as the invocation was offered. At its close Ryan noted the calm, thoughtful way Katrina crossed herself, not as a hurried afterthought as with so many others in the crowd, but as an act of deliberateness he realized was a reflection of the importance she placed on her faith.

But it was during the oration delivered by the honorable C. G. Williams that Ryan became hopelessly captivated by Katrina Bergeman. While other young women lifted polite faces toward the speaker and applauded whenever the crowd at large signaled their approval of the speaker's words, Katrina Bergeman's face reflected every nuance of the ringing emotional address. Ryan heard the words but filtered them through Katrina's reactions, how she watched the speaker intently, now nodding in agreement, now frowning slightly as the painful history of the war was recalled, now applauding heartily his sentiments of life, liberty, and the pursuit of happiness as every American's right.

Ryan was drawn to her, his eyes riveted on her rapturous face, as he took up a position under a tree at the foot of the platform stairs. There his view of her was unobstructed, and he studied the way she sat forward as if by doing so she might hear better, her face alight with the clear-eyed intelligence of one who loves learning and appreciates the opportunity for shared knowledge. In that moment, she made every woman Ryan had ever known seem dull and one-dimensional.

" . . . Who are the men today that in church, in state, and in nation hold the destiny of this country as in the hollow of their hands," Williams boomed, pausing dramatically to allow the audience a moment to consider his rhetorical question. "Trace back their lineage, and in nine cases out of ten, you will track them to the shop, the forge, the mechanic's bench, or back onto the paternal acre."

Katrina nodded involuntarily as she listened to the orator express the teachings her father had drilled into her since childhood.

"I walk the streets of this rich and beautiful city. I enter the mansions and decorated houses, and am greeted with true hospitality, culture, and refinement," Williams continued.

Katrina smiled as she recalled the speaker's visit to her parents' home the afternoon before. He had marveled over Mama's music room and Papa's vast collection of books.

But then Williams's voice grew quieter, sadder. "I look thence out upon the surging masses. I see mediocrity struggling to gratify a weak ambition—awkwardness, uncouthness, failure everywhere"—again the voice boomed—"and I say there is a difference between this and that. But no sooner has this conviction taken possession of me than I sit down to converse with the proprietor of this bank, that store, or yonder mansion, when he straightway informs me that he sprang from the humblest walks of life."

Williams paused as he was interrupted once again by thunderous applause. Katrina surveyed the sea of faces before her. In her festive mood she had seen every face as part of the whole; everyone had seemed beautifully dressed, amply fed, filled with the holiday spirit. But as she now studied the individuals, she saw what Williams had seen—faces that were weary yet hopeful, worn yet unde-feated. Women and men in clothing that had come to them through charity, holding small children on their shoulders or in their arms, their faces upturned to the speaker who fed them with the promise of America as surely as Pauline might fill the table with any feast or buffet. They deserved more, Katrina decided. They were Americans.

Katrina heard the words Williams spoke to conclude his oration, but they were webbed with her own racing thoughts. Her parents had taught her a love of country that was as firm as her Catholic faith. She was not German, as her grandparents had been, or German-American, as her parents were. She was American, the first generation of the newly reunited United States. Her heart swelled with the enormity of the possibilities, and goals that had flitted through her mind with little focus or pattern became sharply defined. Williams spoke of the promise of the future in a nation healing and ready to move forward. Katrina's eyes brimmed with the passion the occasion had aroused in her, and as she turned to find the handkerchief she had tucked in her purse, she saw Ryan standing there watching her.

If this had been a dream, she might have moved in slowed motion, unnoticed by everyone else, down the plat-form stairs and into his arms. The way he was looking at her seemed to mirror the passion that only in the last moment had been for the possibilities of the young nation and now suddenly, dreamlike, had turned its focus to the possibilities of an equally powerful connection between this man and this woman.

You know nothing of him, her brain argued as it had dozens of times during the last several days. *It doesn't matter,* her heart responded as it pounded in cadence with the thunderous applause that greeted the orator's conclud-ing remarks.

6

IT TOOK A moment for Katrina to realize that the oration had ended and that everyone was standing and applauding the speaker. A gentle nudge from her mother brought Katrina back to the moment. Dutifully she stood and applauded, and some of the patriotic fervor she had felt while listening returned. After the speech there were more speeches, shorter ones, and musical numbers from the band, but Katrina barely noticed. She was aware of only one person—Ryan. She wondered what he had thought of the speaker and whether or not he might find her enthusiasm childish and silly. The war had done that to some men— made them cynical in matters of patriotism and politics.

Then the program was over. She moved forward with her parents and Lulu to congratulate C. G. Williams, but she was aware of Ryan's eyes on her, and she was inordinately conscious of the tilt of her head, the sweep of her gown, the expression on her face as she visited politely with other guests on the platform. He stood just barely in the line of her peripheral vision. She knew he had not moved, that he stood as he had when the speech ended, one foot nonchalantly crossed over the other as he leaned against the large elm, his hat at a rakish angle that shaded his face.

Once the formal proceedings had concluded, an air of

informal chaos took hold of the crowd. The sounds surrounded Katrina—shouts of recognition, the laughter of
shared conversation, an occasional firecracker exploding
just as a crowd of boys ran from behind the platform. The
crowd was dispersing, gathering their belongings to move
on to the next activity of the busy day. Everyone would
have plans today—family picnics and reunions, a trip to the
circus, a day at the beach, all topped off by the fireworks
promised at eight that evening in Seventh Ward Park.

Edward had joined them on the platform, and he and
Lulu were clearly anxious to get started with their own
plans for the day.

"Katrina, Edward and I will get his carriage. You find
Ryan and meet us over by the cathedral steps," Lulu called
as she and Edward started down the steps of the platform.
"We'll go by the house and pick up blankets and the picnic
basket."

Katrina nodded and waved. She turned to the spot where
she had seen Ryan, and he was still there, observing the
passing parade of humanity with interest and a wry smile.
Every now and then he would nod in greeting to someone
or exchange some comment that changed the smile into
laughter. When the dignitaries began exiting the platform,
he straightened and moved forward to greet the men he
knew with a firm handshake. Katrina waited her turn.

"Ah, Miss Bergeman," he said as he climbed the first
two steps to offer his hand to assist her from the stage,
"you are looking particularly enchanting this morning."

"And you, sir, are looking especially handsome," she
replied. Lord, she was flirting. How long had it been since
she'd done so? Oh, she was known for her quick wit and
often quicker tongue, but to blatantly flirt—and enjoy it.
They stood there grinning at each other, he at the foot of
the steps, she just above him.

Sophie Bergeman cleared her throat. "Mr. Sullivan," she
said by way of acknowledgment, "how lovely to see you
again."

Ryan quickly helped Katrina down the remaining two steps and then turned to offer her mother his hand. "And, Mrs. Bergeman, may I say that the daughters clearly inherited their comeliness from their mother?"

"And may *I* say, Mr. Sullivan, that you have a gift of blarney that would do your ancestors proud," Sophie responded with a smile.

That made Ryan laugh, an action that showed his straight white teeth and made his eyes crinkle under the thick black ridge of his brows. "Ah, Mrs. Bergeman, no wonder you are so respected in this community—you are that rarest of creatures: a candid woman."

"I'm glad you admire that. You see, my daughter here not only inherited that particular quality of mine—she excels at it." Then she bent to kiss Katrina's cheek. "Have a lovely afternoon, you two. Mr. Sullivan, I hope you will join Edward in coming back to our house for the fireworks?"

"Thank you, ma'am. It would be my pleasure."

Sophie nodded and moved on to rescue her husband from a heated political discussion that had developed on the courthouse steps. So, Milwaukeeans had their agenda at these events as well, Ryan thought ruefully.

"Edward is bringing his carriage around to the front of the cathedral," Katrina said, indicating the large church just across the square. "Shall we meet them?"

Ryan offered her his arm. "We shall indeed," he said with a smile, and when she placed her hand gingerly on his sleeve, he anchored it firmly in the crook of his elbow. "I'm looking forward to this, Katie. How about you?"

His attitude of pure optimism and pleasure was so engaging that all she could do was nod. There was little opportunity for conversation as they made their way through the remaining crowd to where Edward and Lulu waited. Lu, as usual, was never at a loss for conversation. She kept up a steady commentary all the way to the house and had them all laughing by the time they reached the kitchen entrance.

"Why don't you and Ryan collect the basket and other things from Pauline, Edward?" Lulu directed. "Katrina and I need a moment to change our shoes."

"I should tell you Lulu loves getting everyone organized," Edward commented to Ryan, "just in case you haven't been forewarned."

Lulu gave her fiancé a playful punch on the arm as she exited the carriage and waited for her sister. "We won't be a moment," she called gaily as the two girls disappeared into the cool shadows of the house.

"Not likely," Edward said with a grin. "Let's see if the cook has some lemonade." He led the way into the large kitchen and introduced Ryan to the servant. Ryan could not help but note how completely at home Edward was in this house . . . almost like a son.

"Go on with the two of you now," Pauline ordered when she had served them large slices of thick-crusted bread dripping in butter and preserves. "Take your lemonade and sit out in the garden and wait. I've got tortes to make for tonight's party and I can't be having two overgrown boys underfoot."

"Aye, aye, Captain." Edward gave the older woman a smart salute.

"Thanks for the bread," Ryan added.

"Harrumpph," Pauline muttered, "you fellas are going to need something to tide you over. By the time that Miss Lulu gets herself together, it could be past time for lunch."

"Oh, she's not *that* bad," Edward defended.

Pauline grinned. "Tell me that after you've been married to her for as long as I've known her, young man."

They all laughed as Edward led the way to two old chairs made from willow branches, near the arbor. Ryan was reminded of his walk with Katrina through that arbor, how tempted he'd been to kiss her that night. He was glad now he hadn't. By the time he kissed her tonight, they would know a great deal more about each other. He already felt as if he knew her in many ways. Yes, tonight their kiss would take on a special meaning.

"I like this house," Edward commented as he polished off the last of his bread and licked butter from his fingers.

"You certainly seem at home in it," Ryan noted.

"Oh, that, too, but what I mean is I like the household, the interactions of the people who live and work here. The Bergemans are special people."

"I've noticed. You've known them a long time, then?"

Edward chuckled. "I probably have spent more of my life here than with my own family. Our parents were friends, and then my folks moved to Iowa. Father is a farmer. He tried city life, but farming is what he loves. So when I was sixteen, we moved."

"But you came back."

This time Edward laughed aloud. "My father is a farmer, I'm not. I thought I would die of loneliness."

"What happened?"

"Herr Bergeman offered an apprenticeship. I took it, or rather my father allowed me to take it." He shrugged. "I've been here ever since." Then he reflected for a moment and added quietly, "In some ways, August Bergeman is more like my real father than the man in Iowa."

Ryan studied Edward. On the surface, the man was affable and pleasant; in the world of business, he appeared to be something of a lightweight. But something in his tone, in the way he talked of this family and his part in it told Ryan that Edward had a depth of caring that would make him loyal and the kind of friend any man would want to have.

"I'm sure you've given as much as you've received. It occurred to me that evening when I was here for supper that Herr Bergeman looks on you as the son he never had."

"Oh, but there was a son." Edward leaned forward, clearly eager to share the story. "He died . . . of cholera just when everyone thought the threat had passed. It had been several years since there had been more than a couple of isolated cases. Frederick got it, and then he was gone. The family was devastated . . . as you can imagine." He looked off into the distance for a moment and added, "Frederick was very special."

"He was your friend," Ryan noted quietly, and it was not a question but a statement of understanding.

Edward nodded, then smiled. "We were the Three Musketeers—Frederick, Katrina, and I—we did everything together."

"How did Katrina take it . . . his death?"

"Hard . . . very hard. She wouldn't talk much about it . . . still doesn't. But his death plus the war made Katrina grow up in a hurry. Her parents were inconsolable for months . . . Sophie up in her room, going nowhere . . . August working but really just going through the routine day in and day out." Again he paused as if lost in that other time. "In those days this house was very quiet . . . very desolate."

"And Lulu?"

Edward smiled. "Lu was still so young . . . the concept of death escaped her. Oh, she mourned, but then as a child will, she went on. In the end she and Katrina saved the day."

Ryan raised his eyebrows in question.

"Katrina took on incredible responsibility . . . She was determined to make up for Frederick's death, I think . . . not replace him but show her parents, especially her father, that all was not lost. She was the one who spoke for her mother, directing the running of the house. Then she began going into the brewery on the pretext of helping out in the office but really because she was so concerned about her father. She's very smart, and before long she was doing quite a bit of the work."

Ryan realized this was the second time someone had mentioned Katrina's role in the family business. Clearly the woman was quick to learn and a good manager. He knew enough of business to know she would not have been tolerated for long if her role had simply been one of ornamentation.

"And Lu," Edward continued, "well, Lu was as impatient then as she is today. She was used to laughter and people coming and going and family outings, and she didn't like it when one by one those things disappeared from her life."

Ryan thought of the effervescent Miss Bergeman and smiled. "I can imagine," he said.

Edward chuckled. "One day we were all at supper . . . The Bergemans had given me rooms on the third floor during my apprenticeship. Meals had become as quiet and somber as every other activity in the house. Anyway, I could see these looks passing between Katrina and Lu— Katrina warning Lu not to start something. But she just piped up and announced: 'Aren't we ever going to be happy again?' "

Ryan could see her doing it.

"Well, the family was stunned, of course. I thought Heinrich was going to drop the platter of sausages he was serving. All eyes were riveted on first Sophie and then August. But Lu wasn't finished. She went on: 'Because if we aren't ever going to be happy here again, then I'm leaving. I don't think Frederick would like this place the way it is now. I know Katrina doesn't, and I don't either.' And with that she threw down her napkin and stood, preparatory to leaving the room."

"What happened?"

"Katrina and I kept exchanging looks, and then neither of us could keep a straight face a moment longer. I mean, if you could have seen this little girl with her bouncing curls and her hands firmly on her hips, stamping her foot . . ."

Both men laughed.

"And that was it . . . Before long, Sophie started to grin, and then August was trying hard to smother a smile, and within weeks things were on their way to being back to normal. In fact, Sophie loved to announce to callers how Lulu had gotten them all back on track."

"The Bergemans are certainly a remarkable family," Ryan said.

Edward lounged back in the chair, stretching his legs out in front of him. "What about your family, Ryan?"

"Nothing like this one," Ryan said with a shrug and then stood up. "Ah, here come the ladies."

They picnicked along the lake, north of the city. Ryan recognized its proximity to the spot where he had first discovered Katrina. She had tried her best to steer Edward and Lulu to another site, but they had been adamant.

"I don't know what you suddenly have against this spot, Katrina," Lu admonished. "We always come here."

"I just thought it might be nice to try something new," Katrina replied, but she knew it was but a weak attempt to cover her discomfort . . . and so did Ryan.

"Is there a way down to the shore?" he asked as he stood on the bluff looking out at the passing parade of ships, yachts, and steamers.

"Sure," Edward said. "We used to spend a lot of time here as kids, didn't we, Katrina?"

"These two and our brother were inseparable," Lu told Ryan as she helped Katrina spread the blanket and set out the food.

"So I understand," Ryan answered, but now he was watching Katrina. He noticed how she gave a quick look of surprise at his comment. "You must miss your brother a great deal," he continued. "I'm very sorry for your loss."

"Thank you," Katrina said quietly and then turned away on the pretense of looking for something in the large hamper. It was disconcerting to have him know things about her when she knew so little of him.

"Let's eat," Lu called, using a glass and spoon as an impromptu dinner bell.

"Well, finally," Edward said in mock exasperation as he plopped down next to Lulu. "Come and get it, you two, or I promise there'll be nothing left." To prove his point,

Edward took a large bite out of the liverwurst sandwich Lu had handed him.

Their talk over lunch was light and inconsequential, the sort of polite chatter people make when someone new joins a group. Lu and Edward carried the conversation, keeping Ryan amused with stories of their friends, their parents' friends, and other people in the town.

"Oh, yes," Lulu said as she reclined against a tree after finishing the last of her chocolate cake, "we do know some interesting people, and several of them are our relatives." She grinned slyly before adding, "Of course, there's also our cousin Carlotta." She made a study of her nails, all the time watching for Ryan's reaction to the name.

His reaction was to laugh. "Ah, Lulu, you are nothing if not subtle. Should I take it that you are concerned about my intentions where your cousin is concerned?"

Lulu smiled prettily. "You should take it that I am concerned about your intentions where my *sister* is concerned, Mr. Sullivan."

Katrina felt the color rise to her cheeks. Honestly, sometimes she wanted to strangle Lulu. Her impertinence could be charming unless you were the subject.

"I have no designs on Cousin Carlotta," Ryan said noncommittally.

Lulu grinned and gave Katrina a mischievous wink. "Then you do have—"

"Ryan, would you care to take a walk?" Katrina interrupted before Lulu could finish. "If I don't move about, I'm afraid all I'll be good for the rest of the afternoon is a nap."

Immediately Ryan was on his feet. "That's a wonderful idea. You can show me the path down to the shore." He turned his attention to Edward and Lulu. "You two will be all right here alone, won't you?"

"I think we can manage," Edward replied.

Katrina felt as if she were caught in the web of a conspiracy. All this flirtatious banter that seemed to come so easily to the other three was making her distinctly uncomfortable. She'd never been at such a loss for repartee before.

Ryan took hold of her elbow and helped her to her feet. "I must say I don't see how anyone, let alone a lady, could possibly make it down these bluffs." He reached down to retrieve one last cookie and then reclaimed her arm as he led the way toward the cliff. "Edward tells me you used to swim here as a child . . . Do you swim here anymore, Kate?"

"Have fun, you two," Lulu called out gaily.

"And don't hurry back," Edward added, moving to a position where he could rest his head on Lulu's lap.

Edward and Ryan had taken off their coats, ties, and collars earlier. Lulu and Katrina had changed into less formal clothing as well, and Katrina had taken down the elaborate hairstyle Lu had arranged for her that morning and tied her hair at the nape of her neck with a ribbon. She wore an old straw hat she often wore when gardening, to keep the sun off her fair skin.

"I like your hair that way," Ryan said as soon as they were out of earshot of the others.

"Thank you." Katrina relaxed slightly, although the light pressure of his fingers on her elbow was unnerving.

"Did we upset you back there?"

She glanced at him quizzically.

"When we spoke of Frederick?"

"No, it was all right. I was just surprised that Edward had talked to you about him. He's usually so reticent on the subject . . . They were best friends, you know."

"Funny, he says the same of you . . . that you don't like to speak of it."

She shrugged. "I miss him . . . I always will."

"I know," Ryan answered softly, and something in his tone told her he spoke from personal experience.

"Here's the path," she said, easing her way past some shrubbery and standing on the precipice.

Ryan laughed. "You call this a path, lady?"

She grinned at that and challenged him: "Are you scared, Mr. Sullivan?"

"Hardly. Last one down has to pay the price," he called as he gained a healthy head start.

"You cheated," she cried and raced after him: following the unmarked path of tree roots and boulders she had known since childhood.

Still he won the race and stood waiting on the shore to catch her as she sped pell-mell toward him. "You cheated," she said again, but this time her breath was shortened by the combination of exertion and the sensation of being in his arms as he caught her.

"I know," he said huskily and continued to hold her. His face was close to hers, and she was more aware of the press of his body than of anything that might surround them. For all she knew, they could be on a crowded street corner or under the scrutiny of a passing excursion boat and hundreds of people.

As was her wont in circumstances where she felt out of control, she took the direct approach. "Are you going to kiss me?" she asked huskily.

"Do you want me to?" He trailed the backs of his fingers over her lips.

"I think I do," she said, which made him smile.

The etiquette of kissing traditionally seemed to include closing one's eyes, but Katrina was so fascinated with the features of Ryan's face that she forgot all about rules of etiquette. *He has the longest, thickest, blackest lashes I've ever seen,* she thought in the second before his mouth brushed hers.

Then she did close her eyes as she savored the taste of him. There was the slightest hint of chocolate from the cookie he'd grabbed as they left the picnic. His lips were smooth and soft, and their touch on hers was tender. She sighed and relaxed against the strength of his arms, content to have this moment go on forever.

She frowned when she felt the slight lifting of his mouth from hers, and she heard him chuckle. That's when she opened her eyes and saw that he was watching her, the handsome grin that seemed to be his trademark lighting his face.

"What?" she asked. Was he laughing at her? Could he tell how inexperienced she really was? After all, a man like him . . .

"How old are you, Katie?" He was still holding her lightly with one hand as he stroked her cheek with the other.

"Twenty-four," she answered with slight irritation. "Why?"

He ignored her question and pulled her against his chest, resting his chin lightly on the top of her head as he continued to hold her. "Ah, Katie, did you ever have the feeling that for our generation life stopped during the war years, and what should have been the carefree times for us never got lived at all?"

This was a side of him she had not expected to know, and yet he put into words some thoughts she had had many times. She nodded. "Sometimes it seems as if one day I was playing dolls under the willow tree, and the next I was trying to keep a family business going while my father went off to war."

"Tell me about that."

She shrugged. "After Freddie died Papa was disconsolate. None of us knew what to do. Mama was lost in her own grief . . . Lu was so young . . ."

"So responsibility for everyone fell to you."

"I had to do something, so I started going down to the office on the pretext of helping out but really because I was so worried about Papa. Gradually I learned the business without really meaning to, and then when the war came and Papa longed to be a part of it, I had learned enough to keep things going while he went away. Of course, Edward was well schooled in the business. Papa does not give him nearly enough credit for his contribution during those times."

"I'm surprised Edward wasn't called to serve."

"Oh, he wanted to go desperately, but Father wanted him here . . . I think he couldn't bear the idea that having lost Freddie, he might lose Edward as well. He used his influence to keep Edward here."

They were quiet for a time, standing on the shore, holding each other and watching the traffic on Lake Michigan. Then, as suddenly as he'd become so serious, Ryan turned flirtatious once again.

"Excuse me, miss, but I do believe we had a wager." He held her at arm's length and grinned down at her.

She was puzzled for a moment and then remembered. "Are you speaking of that challenge at the top of the bluff, Mr. Sullivan? The one you *cheated* to win?"

He feigned hurt feelings. "I did not cheat."

"Ha! Well, name your price. I'll show you that we Milwaukeeans keep our word even when you bounders from Chicago use unscrupulous means to win."

"If you're thinking to shame me out of claiming my prize, Katie, you'd best think again." He indicated that they could sit together on one of the rocks.

She sat down and waited for him to join her. To her surprise, he began removing his shoes and stockings.

"So, name your prize," she repeated, her eyes riveted on his partially exposed calf.

"A swim," he said quietly and looked directly at her, the dare evident in the merry twinkle of his eyes and the way the dimple in his cheek twitched.

"I couldn't," she whispered.

"You did the other day," he reminded her.

"But . . . but that was . . ." She was absolutely at a loss for words. Surely he did not expect her to willingly remove her clothes in his presence or, for that matter, allow him to remove his. She looked away.

"Oh, all right then," he said in that same gentle teasing tone he had taken since bringing up the idea in the first place. "I suppose I'll settle for another kiss . . . a real kiss."

The impertinence of the man brought Katrina's attention fully back to him. He sat cross-legged and bare-footed inches from her, grinning and waiting.

"Mr. Sullivan, I may have given you the wrong impression before," she began and hated the way she suddenly sounded like an old-maid schoolteacher.

He shrugged. "Hey, Katie, the offer's on the table: a swim or a kiss. Take your pick."

"And if I refuse both?"

He laughed. "Come, come, Katie, you are your father's daughter. You have a better sense of business than that— you don't have an option. Pick one."

"All right," she said and leaned quickly forward to plant a chaste, tight-lipped kiss on his mouth, but before she could escape, he had captured her and pulled her closer, holding her there between his now outstretched legs so that she was half-lying against him.

"Kiss me, Katie," he whispered, his breath warm against her face as his eyes burned a message of desire. "Kiss me with the kind of passion I saw light your face during the oration this morning. Kiss me to recapture all those lost moments of our youth."

"Ryan . . ." She meant that one word to be a warning, but he took the opportunity to capture her partially open mouth under his.

7

KATRINA KNEW SHE should resist . . . that any proper lady would. She was giving him all the wrong ideas, and he would probably take what he wanted and then return to some young thing in Chicago. Perhaps Carlotta. But heaven help her, she wanted this. Not just being held and kissed, but being in the arms of this particular man. Ever since that first afternoon when they had stood together on these very rocks, he had been in her heart. Then he had been a stranger, a romantic hero straight out of fiction. Now he was very real, someone her family knew.

"Katie," he mumbled softly, lifting his head for only a second to gauge her reaction before kissing her again. She was incredibly vulnerable, and he was a cad to take advantage of her like this, but he could not help himself. Oh, he had planned to kiss her today—one sound good-night kiss before he had to return to Chicago and then go on to New York for several weeks. He had had no intention of leaving without tasting those full, ripe lips just once.

But he had lost his head, taking her in the way he would have the girls he'd known in the old neighborhood, before the war. Those girls understood the rules, Katie would not. She would expect more out of this. Still, he seemed unable to stop, and when her lips parted as he stroked them with his tongue, he was lost.

Katrina was not so inexperienced that no man had ever tried open-mouthed kissing with her before. But before she had always merely endured it, a passive participant who allowed a man to take his moment's pleasure. Such kisses had seemed too rough and crude to serve as a prelude for an act she had always fantasized as graceful and even reverent . . . or at least that's what she had gained from her conversations with girlfriends who had married.

But Ryan's approach was different. His tongue became an instrument of tenderness rather than brutality, his teeth nipped playfully at her lower lip, and his touch was light, always ready to pull back at the first sign from her. Kissing Ryan was . . . fun. He made it seem so acceptable, so right. There was none of the desperation she had felt from other men, none of the impatience to rush on to more intimate activities. No, Ryan seemed perfectly satisfied with kissing her. Instead of resisting, she found herself seeking more, moving her face under his to try and bind them together in a full kiss rather than these playful nips and pecks.

She balled her hands into fists of frustration as she clutched the fabric of his shirt. He allowed his tongue to settle at the center of her lips and began a slow probing and withdrawal that caused the strange sensation of a tightening in her lower body, a tightening that caused her hips to rise slightly as if to find release.

Then she placed her own tongue against his and heard a moan of pure pleasure. That moan gave her pleasure as well, empowering her with feelings about being a woman she had heretofore never understood. She relaxed the fists that clutched his shirt and moved one hand into the dense fullness of his hair. At the same time she felt his hands moving along her sides from her waist to her armpits, circling ever closer to her breasts, which felt unusually full and sensitive.

Touch me, her heart cried, and her hand pressed against the back of his head as she opened her mouth to receive him more fully.

Her desire and passion were unexpected and therefore all the more irresistible. When her mouth opened in surrender to his, his resolve to keep this light was lost. He turned her until his upper body covered hers and his hand cupped her breast. He felt the heat of the rocks seeping through his clothes and the beating of the hot sun on his back while inches away the cool water lapped gently against the shore.

Now their tongues and teeth collided again and again as they sated the hunger of their passion. There was nothing crude about this, Katrina thought. It was wild and exciting and certainly outrageously unbridled, but she knew she was incapable of calling a halt to it.

Reality intruded in the form of the loud braying of a steamer's horn sounding a warning to some smaller vessel. Suddenly the chatter of passengers on passing ships echoed across the deep waters, reminding them of the possibility of discovery. Ryan felt Katrina stiffen, and he understood that the moment was lost. She tried to struggle to a more proper sitting position the moment he lifted his lips from hers.

"No," he said huskily, "it's all right. We'll stop. No one has seen us, Katie. Just stay for a minute."

She relaxed slightly and watched him. Seconds before, he had cupped and massaged her breast to the point where she had thought it must surely explode. Now he gently moved his thumb across its point, soothing the exquisite pain he'd created there. Then he lightly traced his index finger up the line of tiny buttons on her shirtwaist until he reached her lips.

He watched her with a lazy smile, his weight now on one elbow as he tenderly traced the outline of her mouth with one finger. Katrina was suddenly aware that her lips felt swollen and bruised and her face was flushed and warm. As if reading her mind, Ryan leaned down and wet his fingers in the cool lake water, then gently bathed her face.

What now, she thought, and said the first thing that came to mind. "We hardly know each other, Ryan."

He smiled. "That's true. I'd like to remedy that."

He was going to try to make amends. Well, she didn't want that. She didn't want anything to take away from this. Somehow she knew the memory of this afternoon would be with her for the rest of her life. What had happened here was the kind of grand passion one usually found in books; they were like Cathy and Heathcliff.

He caught her face between his large hands and compelled her to meet his gaze. "I mean that, Katie. I want to see you again . . . after today." When her reply was to glance at her hands, he continued. "I won't lie to you. What happened here was spontaneous in the sense that it happened now, but I planned not to let the day pass without kissing you once."

Her eyes met his in panic. How should she take that? That she was simply another conquest, that he wasn't in the habit of letting women escape without at least some—

"Am I upsetting you? That comes from our knowing so little of each other. You're right about that. But, Katie, one thing I'll tell you, I do not take what happened here lightly. If it had been casual, I would have settled for one thorough kiss to pay the wager and let you go." He waited and then relaxed the tense grip he still had on her. "Will you please say something before I make a complete fool of myself?"

He had a knack for making her smile; she would give him that. Oh, who was she kidding? He had a knack for making her feel supremely feminine and alive. She smiled.

"That's a good sign," he said softly. "Am I to take it that I have not completely lost my chance to spend the rest of the afternoon with you?"

"That would be a safe assumption," she replied.

"Good. Now let's talk." He turned, so that he could dangle his bare feet in the water below, and looked back toward her. "Come on. Your stockings will dry in no time in this heat. Just take off your shoes and come sit here with me while we tell each other our worst traits."

He had an endearing quality that captivated her, so she did as he suggested. "I seem to have lost my hat," she noted as she took off her shoes and lowered her stockinged feet into the cold, comforting water below.

"Here," he said, reclaiming the straw bonnet from where it had fallen and placing it next to them. "Let me help you."

She had reached to loosen and retie the ribbon that held her hair at the nape of her neck, the ribbon that barely clung to a few strands of her hair now. She lowered her hands and allowed him to remove the ribbon. Then as he combed his fingers through the tangles of her hair, he talked.

"My worst trait is impatience," he began. "I have absolutely no patience, in business or pleasure, as was probably adequately demonstrated here this afternoon. Since the war, I find myself living almost completely for the moment. No one can say what might come with the morrow." This last was said in a more serious tone, but immediately he smiled and continued. "Nevertheless, one of my good traits is what has been called a strength of will that when necessary allows me to triumph over my weaknesses."

"Papa says I'm impatient," she offered. "Sometimes he gets so exasperated with me."

"Tell me about Frederick," Ryan said, again changing mood and subject so radically that Katrina felt thrown off balance.

"I thought Edward told you the story."

"He told me the facts . . . It's not the same thing." He was behind her now, continuing to work through the tangles of her hair.

She pulled away and brought the mass of her hair over one shoulder to finish the work herself. At the same time she turned to face him. "You already know a great deal about me, Ryan. It's time you told me something of yourself."

He frowned slightly and glanced out toward the horizon. "All right. What would you like to know?"

Faced with the direct question, she was momentarily at a loss. There was so much she wanted to know. Given his sudden change in mood, she sensed it might be safer to keep the conversation more general.

"Well, for example, how did you feel during the events this morning . . . I mean what did you think about during the oration and when you saw the parade and all?"

He smiled and relaxed. She was going to make it easy for him. "Well, there was little doubt of your feelings," he teased. "If President Grant could only take the patriotic fire that lit your eyes and bottle it . . ."

"We aren't discussing me," she reminded him.

"You're right." He rested his weight on his elbows and looked once again toward the seemingly endless horizon. "Before the war, I used to love the hoopla, the pandemonium, of patriotic events. I was always the kid setting off the illegal firecrackers under some dignitary's carriage or putting a stolen flag in the hand of the statue of the local hero. And there was a time when I dreamed of going into politics, of running for office, making a better country . . ."

His voice trailed off. Katrina understood the power of such childhood dreams. "What happened?"

"The war happened." He sat up, pulling his knees against his chest and holding them there with his tightly crossed arms. "I saw things, Katie . . ."

"Will you tell me, Ryan?" she asked softly after a minute. "I'm sure your father must have shared stories."

She shook her head. "He never wants to talk about it."

Ryan nodded as if he understood that all too well. Then he sighed and began. "When I first went in, I was lucky enough to hook up with Colonel Ellsworth's unit. That meant once I'd gone through the training, I was sent to train others. In those early days, the cause seemed so . . . noble . . . so basic. It was exciting to see the fire of righteousness that burned in the eyes of those recruits."

"And later?"

He shrugged. "Later reality set in. Wars are fought for political and economic power, Katie. Don't let anyone tell you any different. Oh, we wrap it all up in patriotic ribbon, but that's not what it's about."

"But it was right in this case," Katrina urged.

"Yes, maybe it was. But, oh, Katie, the terrible tragedy of it." He had turned to her now and clasped her hands in his. His eyes burned with the pain of memory. "The waste of human life . . . the lost youth . . . innocence. Toward the end, those were children out there, Katie, somebody's son, brother . . . lover . . . friend . . ."

"But war is like that, Ryan." She gave him the benefit of everything she'd been taught by her parents. "Innocent people die . . . good people die . . . but the greater good in this case has been served in the preservation of the Union and in the ending of slavery once and for all."

Ryan gave a sardonic laugh. "Oh, Katie, there are all sorts of slavery. The South hardly has a monopoly on slavery in this country."

"What does that mean?" She felt suddenly defensive, as if he were about to tell her something she already knew but did not want to acknowledge.

"Look around. We have not exactly embraced the runaways and other freed slaves with open arms in this part of the country, have we?"

"The underground railroad ran right through my friend's farm," she protested.

But he barely heard her. She had touched a nerve, opening a subject he had thought about long and hard. "And how many white children are working fourteen-hour days when they should be in school? How many men are really getting a fair wage for their day's work? How many fine Northern houses are run by servants who are paid with room and board and very little in the way of real cash? What chance have they of ever achieving the kind of financial wherewithal to have a house of their own?"

He was every bit as passionate as the orator had been this morning . . . the orator who had affirmed Katie's ambition to make a difference by changing life for the better.

"At least those people have choices . . . the slaves . . ."

"What choices?" Now that he had begun, he seemed unable to stem the tide of his emotions when it came to this subject. He had held his thoughts in check through too many political discussions, in the name of deference and good business. He could be still no longer. "Do these people have a choice of jobs? Do they have a say in their duties, their hours, their safety? No. Does anyone care that a large segment of the children in this country are growing up uneducated because they are working in factories to help their families live? No. Does anyone pay attention to the fact that those children are the future of this country?"

It was disconcerting to have him toss out these fully developed concepts that she had only begun to wrestle with. It made her uncomfortable. It made her angry.

"So I suppose you're saying my father . . . a much-decorated war hero, not to mention one of the most respected businessmen in this entire area, *including* Chicago, is guilty of *enslaving* people?"

"Your father is a businessman, Katrina. In the world we live in today, that means he holds all the cards. He decides what will be and what won't be, and if the men and children who work for him don't accept that, they can move on . . . Only they can't, because there is a giant recession coming, and jobs that are scarce now are going to be nonexistent in another year or so."

"What makes you so all-fired certain you have all the answers?"

"I don't have answers," he raged at her and then realized she was hardly to blame for the state of the world. He paused and added softly, "I just have a lot of guesses, doubts, and questions."

Katrina reached for her shoes and shoved them vehemently onto her feet, hooking the buttons with some difficulty, skipping those that seemed more trouble than they were worth. "Well, my advice, Mr. Sullivan, is that you not accuse innocent people of things you only surmise could be true." She stood up and shook out her skirts, then reached for her hat and anchored it none too gently onto her freshly tied hair. "My father is one of the kindest men you will ever have the privilege to meet. I doubt anyone who works for him feels enslaved."

He caught her just as she had taken the first step back up the trail that led to the top of the bluff. She turned so that she stood just above him, looking down at his apologetic face.

"I'm sorry to have spoiled the day, Katie. The war is too much with me yet . . . I'm sure you've seen that with your father. We all saw . . . things that were upsetting in ways we hadn't imagined possible. When we came home, we began looking at our lives with different eyes."

She did understand. How many times had she seen Papa get that faraway look when talk of the war came up or when he thought no one was looking and such an incredible expression of sadness would cross his face? She understood because she had friends who had been young brides when their husbands were called to serve . . . friends who had become young widows. She understood because she saw things in the world that bothered her—unfairness, prejudice that seemed out of place in light of what the country had suffered through in the last ten years.

"Your talk is upsetting for me, Ryan. We all saw things during the war, even those who stayed at home," she said seriously. "You talk of things I think about." She saw the slightest lift of his eyebrows. "Does that surprise you? That a woman would have thoughts of her own?"

He smiled and touched her cheek. "Katie Bergeman, I stopped being surprised by anything about you an hour ago."

She realized he was referring to their passionate kisses and blushed, which made him laugh, which broke the moment. "Come on," she fussed, "we'll never make the circus at this rate."

The New York Circus offered two hours of pure escape and fantasy. Katrina and Lulu emitted so many oohs and aahs that Ryan and Edward began to rank them.

"Oh, now that was the best yet," Edward exclaimed at Lulu's reaction to the Great Melville's steeple bareback ride with his son standing on his shoulders.

"Hush," Lulu fussed, but she was grinning. "Katrina and I used to do that kind of stuff all the time," she boasted.

"Right," Edward guffawed, "and I'm the President of the United States."

"We did ride bareback," Katrina argued. "We both learned that way of riding."

Edward laughed. "You learned to ride on the work horses down at the brewery. Of course, you learned bareback."

Lu gave a slight shrug and then pointed to where the Levantine Brothers were beginning their gymnast routine. "Sh-h-h," she ordered.

"Did you and Lu also try those little maneuvers?" Ryan asked Katrina. The Levantine Brothers were flipping around the ring as if they were boneless.

"Didn't you and your siblings ever play circus when you were kids?" Kate looked over at Ryan, expecting a smile of pleasant memories. Instead he was suddenly sad and seemed as if he were miles away from the merry setting of the circus. "Ryan?"

"No . . . no, we didn't play circus," he said softly.

"But you have brothers and sisters?" Suddenly all her attention was focused on him. The music and appreciative applause of the crowd were mere background.

He shrugged. "Doesn't everybody?" he said with a grin and offered a freshly shelled peanut before turning his attention back to the show.

And it was a splendid show. Before long Kate lost herself once again in the beautiful spectacle of it. She had always loved the circus, loved the way it appealed to all ages, the way people shared in the laughter and the wonder of it all. She especially enjoyed watching the children and noticed that Ryan was also getting a kick out of the small boy next to him, who, Ryan confided to her, had probably slipped in under the tent without paying.

"Something you seem especially familiar with," she teased.

At one point he took the boy on his lap to give him a better view of Joe Pentland, who was billed as the Great American Clown. The child screamed with laughter at the clown's antics, pounding Ryan's shoulder and accepting the steady stream of peanuts he offered. Kate noticed how both Ryan's eyes and the kid's were shining, but Ryan was watching the boy, not the clown. In that moment she came very close to telling herself she loved this man.

The finale was a parade of the performers, taking their bows as they were announced once again by the dramatic ringmaster. Everyone in the audience applauded in cadence as the long line of performers circled the tent for their final bows. When the show was over, Ryan handed the boy the rest of the bag of peanuts and sent him on his way.

"Thanks, mister," the kid yelled as he slid between the benches and hustled out the exit.

Ryan waved and grinned, then looked down to find Kate staring up at him, her face flushed with admiration. "What?" he said, suddenly embarrassed at the adoration he saw there.

"Nothing," she said happily and placed her hand in his as they made their way toward the exit behind Edward and Lu.

8

THE FOURSOME WENT from the circus to a nearby beer garden. As they sipped beer and lemonade, they observed the hordes of other young people who had gathered there. These were contemporaries from another world, Kate realized. They were men and women of their age, but whose roots and lifestyle differed vastly from the one she and Lu took for granted. She realized she was observing them through Ryan's eyes.

"Is he coming to the house for the party?" Lu whispered with a mischievous grin while Ryan and Edward were engaged in conversation about grain futures.

Kate nodded, her attention focused on a young man who stood on a barrel and was about to address the crowd. "I wonder what that's about," she mused.

Lu glanced toward the people gathering around the would-be speaker. "I don't know. This place makes me nervous," she said fretfully.

Of course, it would. They had chosen the place at random. Its location in a working-class neighborhood precluded its patronage by anyone but laborers and their families. A couple of men had recognized Edward and Katrina and nervously tipped their hats. Kate and Edward saw these people every day, but to Lu they were as foreign as the refugees and immigrants fresh off the train or the boats.

The orator had started to speak, and his friends were distributing pamphlets among the crowd. Several of his remarks brought applause and an occasional angry comment from the growing crowd.

"I think we ought to leave," Edward said, his conversation with Ryan overshadowed by the developing scene across the way. He dropped a coin on the table and held out his hand to Lu. Ryan stood also.

"I'd like to stay," Kate replied quietly and remained sitting. She was aware that all three of her companions raised their eyebrows, stunned by her declaration.

"Katrina . . . ," Edward began.

"Oh, honestly, sister, do you always have to be so obstinate?" Lu had a petulant streak when things did not go her way.

Kate looked at each of them in turn. "Please, do not feel compelled to stay if you'd rather not. I'd like to hear more."

Edward looked at Ryan, clearly expecting the man to take Katrina in hand. Instead Ryan took his seat next to her. "It's all right. I'll see that Kate gets home."

"Papa isn't going to like this," Lu said.

"I know," Kate replied and deliberately turned to face the speaker, so that her back was to Edward and Lu.

"Well . . ." Lu huffed and then left with Edward.

"We'll be less conspicuous if we move closer and become part of the gathering," Ryan said.

Kate nodded as he extended his hand to escort her.

The men who worked at the brewery noted Kate's presence with surprise and curiosity.

" . . . new day and a new world," the speaker promised, and the crowd roared its approval. "But nothing comes without a price," he continued, his voice hoarse from exertion. "Ask the bosses about that."

The crowd chuckled.

Kate looked at the faces now close to hers. Pressed as she was into the thick of the gathering, she became aware of the clean but patched clothing, the weary faces of men and women of her own age who looked a decade or more older. She was glad there had not been time to change again from picnic clothes to a dressier outfit for the circus. At least she wasn't as markedly different as she might have been.

A woman next to her rocked a colicky baby, her hand constantly massaging the child's back, her whispered "Sh-h-h-h" a constant lullaby. A man in front of her bellowed his approval when the speaker began to berate factory owners and businessmen for their indifference to the growing chasm between the classes. Several workers accented the speaker's calls for action with fists clenched and raised or pumped into the still afternoon air.

Ryan felt the hair bristle at the base of his neck. He had not heard such brazen challenges and criticism before in such a public forum. The young man was taking a huge risk in speaking out so openly, and it wouldn't take much to turn his audience into an angry mob. Ryan moved a step closer to Kate, his eyes constantly roaming the group for the first sign of trouble.

As the speaker continued, the crowd pressed forward. At times Kate was certain she would have been crushed had Ryan not been there, his body a barrier to any harm that might come her way. He was constantly alert to the mood swings of the mob, prepared to get Kate out of there at the first hint of violence.

But the speaker was merely a preview to a larger rally to be staged later that week. This was a call for participation. He distributed the leaflets and urged the crowd to see that they were distributed and posted. "And if they are torn down," he cried, "post them again. We will not be stopped. We will be heard," he cried, and raising his clenched fist dramatically in the air, he shouted, "Solidarity!"

And the crowd took up the cry, chanting it until their voices reached a fever pitch and smiles creased their lined and exhausted faces.

Kate joined them, her eyes burning with the passion of the moment, her heart knowing this was what her father feared most, her mind telling her that it was a fear born of being uninformed. If Papa could only talk with them, know that their demands were not unreasonable, that they did not seek to displace anyone, only to take their fair place in a society they were largely responsible for maintaining through their toil and sweat.

"Let's go," Ryan shouted above the fervent chant, and his hand at her waist left no room for argument. Firmly he steered her away from the increasingly charged atmosphere of the throng. He found a side exit from the beer garden and hurried her through it, then hailed a passing hansom cab and gave the driver Kate's home address.

"Oh, Ryan, did you see them? It was as if he offered them great wealth. And he's right. I mean, by what title do you and I hold our positions? By how much money we have . . . by the cut of our clothes? It's not fair . . . It really isn't. Here we fight an entire war on the premise that all men are created equal, but it's not true." She turned to him and clutched his hands between hers. "Oh, Ryan, I know there are two sides to all this, and certainly my father and his associates have their point as well, but you were right—slavery is not solely the disgrace of the South."

Ryan's mind raced with the sensations she ignited in him. Her father was going to be furious. Ryan knew it, and so did she, for Lu was sure to report her whereabouts. Even if she didn't, Ryan could see that Kate would not let this rest. She would go to the brewery, and her eyes would be wide open to abuses and offenses she had never given a thought before. Her zeal for change would be fueled by the events of today, and from the fact that her awakening had come on such a momentous occasion as Independence Day.

"So what are you going to do?" he asked.

"I have to talk to Papa, make him see . . ."

"Don't sell your father short," Ryan warned. "He knows both sides. I'm sure he's agonized over the disparities that alarm you."

"But . . ."

"Go slowly, Kate," Ryan cautioned. "You'll do no one any good if your actions only serve to close the door more tightly."

She was surprised that he was taking her father's side in all this. Was it because of his own position? What had he heard today? "I thought you would be on the workers' side."

"I am. But I've been both places, Kate. I know what they're up against, and you won't be thanked for getting in their way by setting up projects that are doomed to failure."

"Well, I've got to do something." She settled dejectedly against the cushioned seat and stared out the small window of the closed coach.

Ryan allowed the ride to continue in silence, using the time to gather his own jumbled thoughts. She was trouble . . . He knew that. Anything he might start with her would only end in disaster. Her bond with her father was a zealous one. August Bergeman was equally passionate about his daughters. He would brook no less than the best possible match for each of them, and he would not consider an Irishman, even if he was wealthy, a suitable match at all. If Ryan pursued this, somewhere Kate would be forced to choose between him and her father, and either way she could be badly hurt.

As the cab approached the Bergeman house, Kate turned to him, her face calmer, her demeanor more serene than when they had first started the ride. "Ryan, thank you for today," she said. "It . . . I mean . . ." She looked down at her hands, her lashes suddenly dampened with tears.

Ryan was alarmed by her emotion. "What is it, Katie?" Resolve or no resolve, he could not stand her tears. He pulled her into his arms and stroked her cheek.

"I'm being silly," she mumbled and swiped at the one escaped tear with the back of her hand.

"Just say what you're thinking," he said.

She lifted her face to his, and her eyes brimmed not only with tears, but with a fire that made his heart race. "I'm thinking that you have come along at a time when I was lost, figuratively speaking. My life had become so . . . unsatisfying . . . and I felt such a need to . . . do something . . . to take some new direction . . . Oh, this is not at all proper. I'm making a complete fool of myself," she moaned and turned away.

He caught her chin and turned her face back to his. "You are no fool, Kate Bergeman. You are perhaps the most exciting woman I have ever known. It is you who have stirred me from my apathy. Seeing you today has changed me . . . knowing you has changed me . . ."

God help me, Ryan thought, *I want her.*

His kisses were filled with all the drama of the day they had shared. He rained them over her face and neck, his experienced fingers releasing the buttons on her jacket and high-collared blouse to give him greater access to her throat. "Tonight," he whispered huskily, as the driver tapped on the sliding window, noting their arrival.

Kate nodded as she rebuttoned her clothing and tried to bring her breathing under control.

Ryan tapped to let the driver know they had heard, then turned back to Kate. "My God, you are lovely," he said and kissed her once again before opening the coach door and handing her out to the driver. "Tonight," he said once again by way of farewell.

Sophie Bergeman's annual Independence Day party was the highlight of the summer season. An invitation to it was considered a major honor. And invitations went to everyone from the brewery workers and their families, to the elegant and wealthy members of the many charities the Bergemans supported, to neighbors and family and friends.

Sometimes it seemed as if half of Milwaukee had gathered on the Bergeman lawn by sunset on the Fourth of July.

When the weather was good, as it was on this night, Sophie and the servants turned the lawn and gardens into a fairy-tale wonderland, using torches to light the way to the side yard. There was always music, usually from the members of the German Music Society, which Sophie had helped to found. Tonight it was a quartet as skilled at playing folk dances and beer-hall songs as it was at waltzes and classical pieces. The musicians sat in the gazebo surrounded by the party-goers at white-clothed tables set with fine china, glimmering silver, and centerpieces of candles and flowers.

Sophie and August personally greeted all their guests as they arrived by carriage or foot. Some of the working families invariably came with home-baked breads and sweets to add to the festivities, gifts that Sophie graciously received and made a great fuss over when they were added to the buffet.

The girls were expected to direct guests to their tables; Sophie used place cards and delighted in seating the lowliest laborer with the president of the bank. Everyone understood that on this evening, if at no other time, there was no place for putting on airs or designating class and ethnic differences. To her friends who had dared bring the topic up or who had attempted in a more subtle way to rearrange seating, Sophie had instructed, "This is an *American* party." She would let the phrase hang there and then smile and change the subject.

Edward arrived early and helped the girls direct the social activities. Once a goodly number of guests had arrived, there were games and contests, which Edward was a wizard at organizing. Even the most reluctant guest was soon part of the activity, participating in a relay or guessing game. The men removed their jackets and rolled back their sleeves as more strenuous games such as tug-of-war ensued.

Katrina had hoped Ryan would come with Edward and could not quell the sense of disappointment she felt when

Edward arrived with his parents, who were visiting from Iowa. She had dressed carefully for the evening in a gown of white taffeta trimmed with wide navy velvet ribbon. A blue cashmere shawl covered her shoulders where the open neckline revealed the long curve of her neck to perfection.

She had refused Lu's offer to pin up her hair in some fancy fashion of the day, choosing instead to bind it loosely with two long combs high at either side, which allowed the bulk of it to trail down her neck. And all the while she had been imagining the possibility of Ryan's removing those combs, touching her hair, her neck, her lips . . .

"Katrina, darling!"

Katrina turned for the halfhearted hug of her cousin Carlotta. "How nice to see you," she said, wanting to add that she had thought Carlotta was simply too swamped with plans for the October ball to allow for a visit with her country cousins.

"I've just arrived," Carlotta stated airily as she scanned the guests. "*Tante* Sophie insisted that Mama drag me here if necessary."

She pronounced Mama in the French way, while using the colloquial German for "auntie." The distinction was not lost on Katrina. "We're honored," she said wryly. Carlotta's gown was far too formal for the evening's picnic and games but somehow perfectly right for Carlotta, showing a good deal of cleavage while making a pretense at youth and innocence in its yards of pale blue tulle, lace, and ruffles.

It was unnecessary to be sincere with Carlotta since her attention was anywhere but on her cousin and hostess. She smiled and turned the full dazzle of that smile on Katrina.

"Would you excuse me, darling? They're playing a waltz, and I do so love the waltz." With a wave of her lace-gloved hand she was off. It did not surprise Katrina one bit that the smoky-eyed beauty headed directly for the group of bachelors standing off to one side and observing the dance. Without hesitation she playfully pulled on the arm of Lars Olsen, by far the handsomest and most eligible of the group. Kate watched his reaction with interest, noting the lazy smile, the way he took her by both hands and sort of swung her around to get the full effect of the gown, then threw his head back in laughter at whatever comment she had made. She substituted Ryan and herself in the scene and felt a twinge of envy.

"Definitely a romantic fool," Katrina muttered to herself and turned her full attention to the organization of the sweet table.

"Ah, *Liebchen,* you are here." Papa beamed down at his elder daughter with pride. "And such a picture you are tonight. Would you do an old man the honor of dancing the waltz?" He held out his arms and cocked one bushy eyebrow quizzically.

Katrina could not help but smile. "Of course, Papa. I've been hoping you would ask."

He led her to the dance area, where several couples were already spinning over the lawn to the music. They joined the dancers in perfect rhythm, and soon she was laughing and smiling at her father's running commentary on the guests.

"Don't laugh," he would order sternly under his breath, at the same time winking broadly and squeezing her hand, knowing full well she would burst into giggles any moment.

How she adored this man, who had given her not only life itself but a world filled with happiness and pleasures and education and opportunities. He had come through so many hardships . . . he and Mama both. Not only had they suffered through the war and Frederick's death, but also hard times getting started in this new world; hard times when after Lu was born, the doctor said no more babies; hard times when family members in Germany died. "You are my family," Papa had said in those times when Mama tried to console him. "You and the girls . . . and one day the fine men they will marry and the grandchildren. You are the center of my life."

Such sentiments had struck a cord with Katrina. It seemed unfair to her that two such giving and loving people as her parents should ever have to suffer any grief at all, let alone the huge burdens they had carried. It made her protective of them, determined that the rest of their lives would be as carefree and happy as she could make them. She was certain that if the workers at the brewery could only know what Papa had suffered, they would know that he could be nothing less than fair.

"I love you, Papa," she said suddenly.

August Bergeman looked momentarily startled. Outward demonstrations and declarations of love were not usual in his house. In fact, it was one area where he was downright conservative, preferring the privacy of their rooms for his embraces of his wife.

"Thank you, *Liebchen*," he said softly, then with a hearty laugh he changed the subject. "However, it is high time you focused your affections on some eligible young man. Who is it to be? Young Willem over there? Or perhaps Herr Schmidt—he's had his eye on you for some time, but I think he lacks courage."

"Well, we can't have that—a suitor who lacks courage in this house?"

Papa laughed. "I see what you mean." They danced, and the unmistakable sound of Carlotta's laughter floated across the lawn. "Your cousin Carlotta seems to have snagged our Mr. Olsen with her city ways," he noted. "I thought she was seeing Mr. Sullivan." It seemed an innocent comment, but Katrina knew Papa was watching her reaction closely.

She shrugged. "I think they've been seeing each other in Chicago."

"But this afternoon he spent with you."

"It was perfectly innocent, Papa. Haven't you always encouraged your girls to have men as well as women as friends?"

"H-m-m," Papa mused as the dance came to an end.

"I'll see if Mama needs help," Katrina said and ran toward the house before Papa could ask any more questions. She did not like lying to him, but for now she instinctively understood she could not confide her true feelings.

The guests sat down to supper with the fireworks in the background, and still Ryan had not come. Katrina sat with the rest of the family at the central table. It was the one thing Papa insisted on. Katrina knew that extra places had been set for Eloise and Carlotta, but though Eloise was present, Carlotta and her place setting seemed to have disappeared. It did not surprise Katrina in the least to see her sitting very close to Lars Olsen at a table of young people toward the shadows of the willow tree.

The fireworks were disappointing compared to other years. Everyone said so. So it was hardly personal disappointment on her part, Katrina thought. Still, a pall of sadness settled over her following supper and the last burst of rockets across the sky. And while the dancing and games continued in earnest, she slipped away to the arbor to consider the day.

In truth she would have rather gone down to the lake. It was her favorite place, and she knew any number of secret spots for reading and ruminating and just being alone with the multitude of thoughts and ideas that seemed to plague her. Tonight the arbor would have to do. Normally it was a perfectly good place to go, but now that she had been there with Ryan, his presence was everywhere along the shadowed path.

She walked the length of the arbor slowly, playing with the ribbons that trimmed the front of her gown, allowing her shawl to droop to her forearms in the sultry night. At the end of the path she spent a few moments attending to some of the plants in the garden, pinching back dead leaves, straightening a stalk, snapping off dead blossoms.

Still, she could not stay away forever. Mama would notice and ask questions, and Mama was very good at ferreting out secret passions. Katrina straightened her shoulders with determination and turned to rejoin the festivities.

"I've been looking everywhere for you," Edward said in an almost identical greeting to the one her father had offered earlier. "I have a message for you from Ryan." He handed her an envelope from the Plankinton House Hotel.

Kate clutched the note but did not open it. She did not know what it might hold, and she was afraid to betray her true feelings to Edward.

"He's gone to New York," Edward said and then added, "For several weeks." At her accusatory look that he had opened her letter, he added, "He sent a note of thanks and regrets to your parents."

"I see." Kate started to move back toward the party.

"Katrina?" Edward's voice was filled with pleading and concern. "Would you take some advice from an old friend?"

Kate turned and waited for him to continue.

"I like Ryan . . . very much."

"But?"

"But I don't think he's right for you and I think you are becoming too involved with him too quickly."

"I thought you and Lu approved."

Edward nodded. "We did, but this afternoon . . ." He shook his head slowly. "When he allowed you to stay there . . ."

"Allowed? No one allowed me to do anything, Edward. I chose to stay. Ryan stayed with me. I thought he was very gallant in that."

"It was no place for you to be or to be seen," Edward protested.

"Oh, now we come to it. You're upset that my presence there might cause talk. Well, I don't care what talk it might cause. It's high time these two opposing sides started to listen to one another instead of always listening to just themselves."

Edward seemed momentarily at a loss for words. "All of a sudden I don't know you, Katrina," he said huskily.

"I'm changing. There's nothing wrong with that. People move on in life, Edward."

They stood in uneasy silence for a couple of minutes as the polka music played a ridiculous accompaniment to their conversation.

"May I suggest that you are headed in a direction that can only cause you hurt in the long run?"

"I don't think so."

Edward took a step toward her, his hands coming down on her shoulders as if to shake some sense into her. "Katrina, face it. Your father may be a most progressive sort, but he will draw the line at Ryan Sullivan."

"I thought we were discussing my changing attitudes toward the problems of the working class and the privileged," Kate said defiantly.

"We are discussing Ryan Sullivan, and we both know it. He will hurt you, Katrina, mark my words."

She took a deep breath. Earlier she had had words with Lu about staying at the rally. Now Edward. What was worse was that they were both right, at least about Papa. It did not help matters one bit that she knew their concern was well placed. A relationship with Ryan was risky. Still, she had never wanted anything more, and nothing had ever felt more right.

"Edward, I know you mean well, but I'm a grown woman. There comes a time when I have to leave the nest and make decisions based on what feels right here." She covered her heart with her hand.

"No matter if those decisions will cause you pain?"

She smiled and touched his cheek tenderly. "Hey, what's the point of life if you never take a risk?"

Edward relaxed his grip on her shoulders and shook his head. "Lu and I will be there," he promised.

"To pick up the pieces?" she teased.

He nodded solemnly.

She laughed. "Oh, Edward, don't be so somber. We're talking about romance here, not life and death. Now how about a dance with your future sister-in-law?"

9

THE NOTE EXPLAINED that Ryan had been called back to Chicago on business, and from there he was leaving for several weeks on the east coast. It concluded with "Write!" and an address, and was signed "Ryan." Kate was beside herself with delight as she prepared for bed that evening, and Carlotta's chatter could not break her mood.

"Oh, darling, he is wonderful," Carlotta moaned to Lulu as she studied her face in Katrina's mirror and tried on various smiles and poses. "Every eligible woman in Chicago has her eye on him. Not only is he deliciously handsome, not to mention incredibly virile, but he has all this money and a townhouse on Terrace Row. *And* he's so wonderfully mysterious. No one knows a thing about his past, which of course drives Father absolutely mad."

"How did you meet?" Lu asked with a guileless smile, her intent clearly to ferret out as much information as possible for Katrina.

Carlotta sighed dramatically. "It was straight out of the pages of a novel."

Katrina's ears pricked at that. *Her* meeting was the stuff of fiction, not Carlotta's.

"Really," Lu said encouragingly, rolling her eyes at her sister as she settled onto the high sleigh-shaped bed to hear the details.

"Oh, yes. Mummy and I were having the most awful fight about where to dine, and suddenly he and Father appeared. Just like that he suggested the most perfect place. He just took charge, even Mama was captivated." She sighed and studied her reflection more closely.

Kate understood the power of Ryan when he decided to "take charge," but such mannerisms were hardly the stuff of great romance fiction, she thought. She was tempted to top Carlotta's story with her own first encounter with Ryan.

"And has he kissed you?" Lu pressed.

Kate was certain she did not want to hear the answer to this one.

Carlotta giggled and twisted one long blond curl around her finger, tilting her head modestly as she did. She was playing to an audience of one, however, uncaring of the effect her posturing had on her cousins. "Ryan has to be so very careful. Chicago society . . . while it's far more open than what passes for society in . . . other places . . . still has its standards."

Kate bristled. "Meaning?"

"Well, darling, the man *is* Irish, after all."

"Meaning?" Kate repeated emphatically enough that Carlotta gave her cousin her full attention.

"Meaning," she said as she turned on the dressing chair to face Kate and Lu, "that ordinarily he would not be welcome in polite society."

"But he is," Lu added.

"Well, of course. This is America, after all, and, as Father noted, there will always be the odd man who rises above his station to great success. For heaven's sake, Abraham Lincoln was President!"

That did it. Abraham Lincoln had been Kate's hero since childhood. "Carlotta," she said sweetly, "I wonder if you'd mind retiring to your own room. I'm afraid I'm very tired and I do have to work tomorrow."

Carlotta frowned. "I don't understand why you continue to spend your time at that . . . factory . . ."

"Brewery," Kate corrected automatically, her fists clenching and unclenching as she collected Carlotta's robe and handed it to her. "I continue to spend my time there because it's important . . . to me and to my father." *And so help me, if you dare say one word about Papa after already casting aspersions on the martyred President and Ryan, I may strike you.*

"Come along," Lu urged Carlotta, "we can talk in my room. I want to hear about Lars." She gave her sister a sympathetic glance as she ushered Carlotta to the door.

"Your sister is so . . . old-fashioned," Kate heard Carlotta stage-whisper as the two girls made their way down the hall. "If she doesn't watch out, she's going to turn into a hardened spinster and no man will give her a second glance. Lars says . . ."

Ha! Kate didn't care for a second what Lars Olsen had to say about her. He had pursued her and been so wounded when she found his company monumentally boring, that he salved himself by spreading malicious gossip about how uptight and prudish Kate was. She closed the door firmly and hurried to find paper for her first letter to Ryan.

Two weeks later she had her response.

Ah, Katie, do you have any idea what it meant to have your letter waiting when I arrived back in New York from a brief business meeting in Washington yesterday? You ask about my business—difficult to explain. I don't mean to condescend. It is simply the nature of the business. I buy pieces of paper, actually, papers that represent silos of grain or lots of lumber. I trade in futures, betting that prices will go up or down on any given day. It's complicated and risky to be sure. I have been fortunate, and when an investment pays off, I frequently invest in real estate, as I am doing on this trip, as I did with your Father when I bought the timberland in Peshtigo.

I have only recently begun to take an interest in lumber. Your father's property is my first ownership of actual acreage. Oh, I own real estate in other forms, but can you understand that to an Irishman the land is everything? The property your father sold me is in many ways a dream realized—to hold my own land with trees and fields. Katie, I have never told anyone this—I've never even said it aloud—but I've dreamed of a home, a real home, not like the museum I have in Chicago. The moment I saw the property in Peshtigo, I knew I had found the setting for my dream. Don't tell your father, but I would have paid twice the price he asked, just to be able to call those acres of woods my own.

Do you know the spot? If so, then you will know where I envision the house—on that knoll near the river with the view of the bay.

You ask about my family. It is a story I will tell you when I return. It is not for a letter. Rest assured that I do come from real people and did not just suddenly appear as Carlotta would have you believe. In fact, I am far less mysterious than her childish imaginings would have me be.

And speaking of Carlotta—you do ask a lot of questions, dear Katie—her parents have been very good to me. Her father has served as a sort of mentor, guiding me in the years when I first returned from the war, sponsoring my efforts to improve my station. Carlotta's brother served under me. Your cousin Emil claims I saved his life. Such is the fodder of war stories. At any rate, Carlotta's family has been very supportive, and I cannot deny that they have opened doors that would certainly have been closed to me regardless of my fortune. However, do not listen to her prattle. Carlotta is a girl caught up in the fantasy of her own beauty. While I find her amusing, I have no serious interest in her, and both she and her father are quite aware of that.

And now it is my turn to ask a question. What is this mysterious "project" you allude to? What are you up to now? And I want you to tell me all about your day— what you are reading, where you go, what you wear. I

*miss you, and the days here are long. I fear it will be
well into August before I return.*

*Yours,
Ryan*

Kate savored the closing most of all. *Yours.* He could
have chosen another word or no closing at all. He had
chosen a possessive, a promise.

"Katrina!" It was obviously not the first time Edward had
said her name.

"I'm sorry. I was . . ."

" . . . mooning over that letter for the hundredth time,"
he noted. "You apparently have an appointment?"

Kate straightened in her desk chair and glanced toward
the outer office.

"Millie Kopfmeier? From the settlement house?" Edward
wondered how many clues he would have to offer before it
all registered, and before she told him what on earth Millie
Kopfmeier was doing at the brewery.

"Oh, of course." Kate rose to go and greet her guest, but
Edward stopped her short of the door.

"What's this all about, Katrina?"

"Don't worry," Kate assured him. "It has nothing to do
with the union." She knew how concerned he had been
about meetings and organizational rallies that had sprung
up since the Fourth. There were already a number of strong
unions in force. So far Bergeman Brewery had not been
targeted for organization, but Millie Kopfmeier and her
settlement house were dangerous precedents. Millie had
her own ideas about what was necessary for the workers and their families, and those ideas grew more stri-
dent every day. Not only that, but the settlement house
was a known haven for union organizers and their rallies.

"Come in, Millie," Katrina called as she welcomed the
woman, who was only slightly older than she but seemed

far more schooled in the harsh realities of life.

Millie moved with confidence to the chair Katrina indicated and glanced warily at Edward. "I received your note," she said to Katrina, pulling the paper from a purse that had seen years of use.

Kate nodded and took her place at her desk. "Well, Edward, if you're going to stay, at least sit down," she said as she gathered papers and notes. "You'll make Millie nervous hovering like that."

Edward sat.

"You see, Millie . . . May I call you Millie?"

"Of course, Katrina." The ground rules were set—there would be no "yes, ma'am" here. They were to be equals regardless of the differences in their stations in life.

Katrina smiled at the woman and leaned forward with her notes. "We have at this time eleven boys under the age of sixteen in our employ. They each work a full week and sometimes overtime. My question is: What about their education?"

"What about their what?!" Edward exclaimed.

"Their education . . . their future," Kate said quietly but firmly, looking directly at him before returning her full attention to Millie. "Are any of these boys enrolled in your evening program at the settlement house?"

Millie scanned the list. "Not a one. I know these boys. When they aren't working, they're sleeping or loitering."

"I thought as much." Kate reclined in her swivel chair, tapping a pen against her desk as she appeared lost in thought. "I was wondering whether we might start some classes here," she mused as if the idea had just occurred to her.

"Classes?" Millie and Edward spoke simultaneously and with the same inflection of disbelief.

"Yes. Nothing staggering. Just perhaps during the mid-morning lull and perhaps again in the afternoon . . . perhaps during lunch break . . . half an hour here . . . there." She continued to muse.

"Katrina, it's summer. We're brewing nine to ten times a day—there are no lulls. Have you spoken to Herr Bergeman about this?" Edward was always very formal when strangers were part of the meeting, refusing to use the more logical "Have you asked your father?"

Kate glanced at him. "Not yet. I'd thought to get Millie's reaction first and perhaps some ideas about implementation I could take to the board." She looked expectantly at Millie, who clearly had been prepared for almost anything but this.

"Are you suggesting a school, Miss Bergeman?" In her shock, ingrained propriety won out.

"It's Katrina, remember—or better still, Kate. What do you think, Edward? Could you start to call me Kate?" Once again she focused on Millie without waiting for a response. "I would assume you are Millicent?" The woman nodded dumbly. "But you use Millie . . . It's so . . . approachable, don't you think?"

Edward shook his head. The woman had clearly gone off her rocker. "Katrina . . ."

Kate held up her hand. "Let's hear Millie out," she said as if the other woman had actually started to speak and been interrupted.

"Well, I . . . that is to say . . . your idea is a bit unorthodox, though not entirely unheard of. May I ask who would teach?"

"I would."

At this Edward rose from the chair and sputtered something that sounded like "Arghh," as he moved past Katrina to the window.

"I have a college education, Millie," Kate assured her. "I was trained as a teacher . . . I just haven't gotten around to using that training." She shrugged and smiled charmingly.

"I see." Millie pondered the idea for a long moment. "I suppose there is a possibility but, Miss . . . Kate, these boys are a bit on the rowdy side. Education is not exactly a priority."

Kate eagerly leaned forward. "I've thought of that and, see, I've developed a plan of rewards and promotions. They would not lose pay while they were in class as long as they work the full day . . ."

Edward spun around. "You intend to pay them to go to school during work hours?"

"Exactly." Kate beamed as if he had just grasped a very difficult concept.

"Where do I come in?" Millie appeared to be warming to the idea.

"You help me in the beginning . . . We would pay for your time, of course. I'll need help choosing the appropriate materials. The boys are clearly unschooled, but at their age I don't really think I can teach them with nursery rhymes."

Millie actually laughed. "I have some books that may work," she offered. "I'll bring them by later. When were you planning to begin?"

"As soon as possible."

Edward could see that for the two women he had ceased to exist as a presence in this room, so he reclined against the windowsill and waited until Kate had ushered Millie out.

"Are you out of your mind? Your father will not stand for this . . . You are talking about taking men off the job and paying them to boot."

"In the first place, we are discussing boys, not men. And in the second . . . you'll see," Kate said airily as she donned her hat and collected her papers. "Tell Papa I'll see him at home."

Dear Ryan,

    You are not going to believe my news. Do you remember the discussion we had about slavery when you said not being educated was a form of slavery? Well, I gave that a great deal of consideration, and when I realized we employed several young boys who work full-time and have never attended school, I came up with the idea of teaching them at the brewery during the morning and afternoon slow times as well as at lunch. It's not as good as regular schooling, of course, but it's a beginning. And of course, right now it will be difficult to find time—it is the peak brewing season. But by winter production slows to almost half, and there would be plenty of time then.

Edward thought I was out of my mind, but I had Mama and Millie Kopfmeier from the settlement house on my side. We were a formidable trio. Papa was a founder of the settlement house, so how could he deny the very principle of equal opportunity on which it was founded?

Then I showed him how the schooling would actually be an incentive for better performance and attendance. And, of course, there was Mama—he can deny her nothing.

So, he has agreed to let me try—one month. I am so nervous, yet at the same time I feel so alive. Ever since Papa returned from the war and Edward began to take on a more important role at the brewery, I've begun to feel less and less a part of things. But this— Oh, Ryan, can you tell how truly satisfying this is? I can make a difference. What a wonderful feeling!

You seemed so surprised that both Lu and I have been to college. Mama insisted that we needed "something to fall back on" in case the men in our lives could not provide. To finally use that education is very satisfying! I love being at the brewery and making a contribution. It has not escaped your notice that we are a close family, devoted to each other.

When Frederick died, I vowed to do whatever I could to fill the huge void he left, especially in Papa's life. I know I can't replace him, but I think Papa has begun to take a certain pride in me. I've even heard him bragging about his "smart" daughter to the other businessmen. It delights me to see Papa so happy and pleased.

Oh, when I first mentioned the idea of the school, he blustered and fumed, but before a week had passed, he was offering his own ideas. Do you understand that this is

going to work and it's all because of YOU? Hurry home.
I want you to see what you have created.

> Yours,
> Katie

The morning of the first class, Kate arrived half an hour early at the brewery. She did not miss the shielded looks the men gave her as she moved through the courtyard and into the stables. Classes would be held for the time being in the tack room, a relatively clean area that was usually quiet once the horses were dressed and out for delivery and work. Kate had confiscated one small cabinet in the corner of the room for her supplies. She felt a sense of exhilaration as she carefully stored the books, slates, paper, pens, and inkwells Millie had managed to loan her. She closed the cabinet and placed a single stool next to it. The boys would have to make do with sitting on the wide-planked floor. She glanced at the watch she wore on a chain like a locket. After lunch break they would begin. She smiled and headed for her office.

But when she returned to the tack room, the men were strangely silent as she made her way past them. She felt their eyes on her. Well, it was something new and for people like this, new was not always better. She would show them. She smiled as she opened the door to what for the next half hour would be her classroom. Immediately the smile turned to a grimace.

The tack room was a disaster—ink was spattered across the floor and walls; the cabinet stood open and empty. Every paper and page of the books had been shredded into confetti and strewn across the room. The slates she had cajoled her father into purchasing had been smashed, the chalk ground to dust under the heel of a worker's boot.

"I'll get your father," Edward said quietly.

She had been unaware of his presence, but something in the demeanor of the men had told him to follow her.

"No," she said firmly, then thrust a list into his hand without turning to look at him. "Get me these workers . . . now."

Edward glanced at the paper. It was her roll for the week, set up in all its optimism for taking attendance. "Katrina . . ."

"Now," she said barely above a whisper and moved to reset the stool and salvage one unbroken slate. Behind her she heard the shuffle of feet and the murmur of voices as the men stood by to see what she would do. "When the boys have gathered," she said over her shoulder, "they will have to clean this room. *Then* there will be class. You men will have to cover the work for them. Nothing will be slowed or postponed—not one order, not one brewing. I don't care how shorthanded you are, you will manage. If this happens again, you will have to cover again—for as long as it takes."

For a moment there was complete silence, and she was certain they had all left, never hearing her order. But then she heard the muffled clearing of throats and a couple of muted "Yes, ma'am's" as they slowly filed back to their posts.

Oh, Ryan, it's horrible. They are so sullen and disinterested. They look at me with barely contained resentment, and when my back is turned, they snicker and make rude noises. Once I felt a wet pellet-sized wad of paper strike my neck, but when I turned around, they were suddenly angels, all bent to their tasks.

I thought they would want this. Why don't they want it, Ryan? Oh, I couldn't stand it if Papa were proven right. When he first heard of the vandalism, he told me not to continue, that I would be hurt. I am not hurt. I am angry and confused.

You ask what I am reading. It is all tripe. My brain is too muddled to absorb anything of consequence. I am as dull as these dullards I pretend to teach. It has been weeks now and nothing—they only pretend to learn. I know some of them are truly capable, why don't they see what reading and knowing how to figure could mean for them? For their families? I am nearly defeated, but then I recall how the men were when Papa left for the war and I was left in charge. It was much the same, and I won them over. In time I won them over.

Still so long until you will be home to Chicago? And then what? Forgive me, my mood is that of a skeptic and defeatist. Already there are signs of the coming autumn. I have always dreaded the autumn. I will send my next letter to your Chicago address.

Katie

"Miss Bergeman?"

Kate looked up from the slates the boys had worked on during lunch. It had been a month, and still there had been no progress. It was hopeless trying to teach them; they deliberately thwarted her at every turn.

"What is it, Mr. Connors?" she said wearily. Mike Connors was one of her father's oldest and most valued workers. He was by far the strongest man in the brewery, even though he was several years older than most of the others. Through the years he had often been sent to the house to help with heavy work there. Kate had known him all her life.

During the time her father was at war, Mike Connors had served her well. His loyalty to her father was unquestionable, and he had cast himself in the role of her enforcer whenever some worker tried to get fresh or challenge her authority.

He practically filled the doorway to the tack room with his height and girth, but his eyes were downcast, and he nervously rolled the brim of his derby in his dirty fingers. "Some of the men and me was talking, miss . . . about this schooling . . ."

Kate sighed. So he had been sent by the others to talk her out of it. She was just about in the mood to let him do it. Why not? None of the boys cared for the gift she was giving them, for the opportunity to open doors they could never dream of walking through without an education of some sort.

" . . . and . . . well, that is to say . . ."

"I know, Mr. Connors. The school isn't working, but . . ."

His eyes focused directly on her for the first time, and he actually took a step into the room. "No, miss, that's the point. The boys are learning and bragging about how they can read when their pops can't, and, well, some of us was wondering if you might have a place or two . . . that is to say . . ." He looked forlornly at her. "I never learned reading neither, Miss Bergeman."

She had been so wrapped up in the misery of her failure that she needed a moment to comprehend what he had just said. "You're asking me to teach you?"

He nodded. "Junkerman and Osgood, too. We'd get our work done, make no mistake, and with the three of us in the class, there'd be no place for horseplay from the youngsters . . . and in time the boys might even . . ."

Kate smiled. He had thought it all through, built his case. Little did he know he needn't have bothered. "I'd be honored to have you and the others in my class, Mr. Connors."

The man beamed. "I'll tell the others." He started to leave, then turned back. "Actually, ma'am, 'twas the Irishman from Chicago who does business with your father who made the suggestion. That is, we old men never thought . . . although we wished . . ." He stuttered to a stop and looked once again to the floor as he turned to leave. "Tomorrow, then," he said with a shy grin.

"Tomorrow," she agreed absently, for her mind was racing with the news he had brought. He had spoken of Ryan, and if Ryan had suggested the idea, it could only mean one thing. *Ryan was back.*

10

HE WAS SITTING with some of the workers and a man Kate did not know. Their concentration on their conversation gave her time to savor this first sight of him. She wondered why she once again felt shy, as she had on Independence Day. She had barely known him then, but as they had corresponded for several weeks, she felt she had grown closer to him. Now, hearing he was back, she had felt herself on the way to greet someone who had become very dear to her. But as she watched him, she was once again taken aback.

He was, if possible, more handsome than she remembered. And as always, when he laughed as he was doing now, she was even more drawn to him. He had this abandon when he laughed, the act involving his whole being. He would throw back his head and slap one thigh with pure delight. Kate noticed how the sun had deepened the tone of his skin, making his teeth gleam ever whiter and his eyes sparkle in contrast.

When he saw her, he came immediately to his feet, snatching his hat off his head, his face suddenly serious as he moved toward her. When they were almost face-to-face, he reached out as if to touch her, then dropped his hand to his side.

"Hello," he said softly but with a smile.

"Hello," she replied and smiled as well.

They were both aware of the interest of the men. Kate caught some good-natured nudges and smiles among the workers, and the stranger watched them intently.

"Who's that?" she asked, nodding toward the man who had been laughing with Ryan and the others. He was slightly better dressed than the workers, but certainly not on a par with Ryan.

Ryan glanced over his shoulder. "Theodore Kerry. He represents the Chicago local of the union."

"You know him?" Her voice was still quiet, but there was an edge of apprehension.

"He's my cousin," Ryan said. "Is that a problem?"

"No. Just wondering."

He seemed little interested in pursuing that line of conversation. "I haven't much time, Katie." He took her hand and walked with her out to the sidewalk. "I got in last night and had to come here for some business with the exchange. I have to go back tonight. I haven't even been to my office yet." He started to walk with her toward the yard, noisy now as casks of beer were loaded onto drays for delivery. "Is there somewhere we can go?" he shouted.

She indicated the huge limestone arch that marked the entrance to the brewery and led to the street beyond. At the corner she pushed open a grillwork gate and followed a cobblestone path to the garden of the brewery's tavern. It was just after lunch, and they were alone except for the gaily painted statue of King Gambrinus, the patron saint of beer. The barkeeper brought them each a lager.

During the exchange of the order and the service, Ryan took the opportunity to study her. He had often wondered throughout these last weeks at his unusual absorption with this woman. It was completely out of character. His determination to remain unattached was legendary among his friends in Chicago. And yet here was this woman—totally unlike the women he usually spent time with. Oh, they were all pretty and had at least some degree of intelligence, but Katie . . .

"You look wonderful," he said after he had taken a long swallow of the brew. "Teaching agrees with you." He grinned at her and placed his hand over hers.

Kate groaned. "I don't know why I ever thought the idea of a school in a brewery would work. I do think having Connors and the other older men in the class will help. Thank you."

Ryan feigned ignorance. "What did I do?"

"You know perfectly well what you did. You suggested that perhaps the men might like to take advantage of the opportunity to learn, too. I'm ashamed I didn't think of it before. Of course, they are the logical students. The boys think they can conquer the world, but the men know better. So, thank you."

"Connors has a big mouth," Ryan muttered as he took another swallow. As usual he was embarrassed to receive gratitude or compliments, as if he did not deserve any recognition. As a boy, he'd heard often enough how his kind would never amount to anything. The message had stayed with him in spite of his success. He had never learned how to take a compliment at face value, without questioning its sincerity, its purpose. He wondered if Kate could ever understand that. She had grown up surrounded by love and money and praise for her smallest accomplishment. He touched her hair, smoothing back a tendril the wind played with. "I've missed you . . . all the more since receiving your letters."

"I know . . . me, too." She was tempted to turn her lips to his palm, to feel the warmth of it.

"I can't stay," he said again.

"Just for supper?"

He shook his head. "I have to get the four o'clock train. Come to Chicago." He knew it was preposterous, but . . .

"I couldn't," she said breathlessly, but in her heart the idea was tempting.

"Why not?" Now he leaned forward, his face close to hers across the small table, his fingers stroking her cheek. *Come with me, Katie,* his heart pleaded. *Seize this moment with me . . . a moment that may never come again.* Ryan had learned in hard and somber ways the dangers of postponing happiness.

"You know it wouldn't be . . ."

"Proper?" He teased her with a grin. "Then spend the afternoon with me and come with me to the station to see me off." He cut off her protest with a motion of his hand. "I've hired a carriage and driver, he'll see you safely home." She hesitated. "Please?"

Everything told her she should refuse. For all its city ways, Milwaukee was provincial. People seeing her with him in the middle of the day would talk. Papa wouldn't like it at all. Mama would worry even though she would understand . . .

"All right," she whispered, her eyes closed as she savored the nearness of him.

Without a word he pulled her to her feet. "Let's go now," he said exuberantly, as if she had just presented him with a gift.

"I have to get my hat . . . my things . . . ," she stammered.

Ryan nodded and changed directions so that they headed back toward the brewery's office rather than toward the carriage and driver waiting in the street. "Hurry," he said as he gave her a slight push toward the stairs to the office. "I want every possible minute."

Kate fairly flew up the stairs, and she was humming as she burst through the office door and moved quickly to the hall tree.

"How was school?" Edward asked without looking up from his ledgers.

"Wonderful." Kate sighed as she pinned her hat in place.

Her sudden change of mood brought her Edward's undivided attention. "Really?"

She beamed at him. "Really. Everything is going to be wonderful now . . . Ryan's back." With that she planted a kiss on the top of her future brother-in-law's head and raced back down the stairs.

"Was that Katrina?" August Bergeman emerged from his office, some papers in hand, a puzzled frown on his face.

Edward nodded. "I think she's left for the day," he noted.

August moved to the window as if to call to his daughter, but stopped. "Is that young Sullivan?"

"I'd guess it is," Edward agreed, turning his attention back to his work.

"Then could someone tell me what business he has that involves not only my daughter, but Theodore Kerry as well?"

At the mention of the union organizer's name, Edward hurried to the window. He was in time to see Sullivan, Kerry, and Katrina walking together toward a waiting carriage.

"I appreciate your agreeing to give me a lift, miss," Theodore Kerry remarked as the carriage moved slowly along the avenue.

"It's Mr. Sullivan's carriage," Kate replied. Then sensing this was less than courteous, she added, "But I'm pleased to have this opportunity to speak with you, Mr. Kerry."

"My friends call me Teddy, ma'am."

"And is that what we're to be, Teddy? Friends?"

Both men looked at her in surprise. Then Teddy laughed. "The men all told me you were the smart one, Miss Bergeman."

"I think on this occasion Katrina would be all right. After all, we're friends, isn't that right?"

She glanced at Ryan, who rolled his eyes as he reclined to a more comfortable position and prepared to serve as spectator to the sport unfolding before him.

"However," she continued, feigning a sudden interest in the way her glove fit, "if you cause trouble for my family,

Teddy, you can bet whatever you own that you will never meet a more tenacious enemy." She looked directly at him. "The Bergeman family has a long tradition of being fair and open-minded. We do what we can, but we are also in business. You understand that, don't you, Teddy?"

Teddy leaned forward, eager to engage in the debate. But Kate was not in the mood for debate. She was in the mood for taking this opportunity to make it clear that the Bergeman Brewery had no intention of tolerating the usual disruptive techniques that came with getting workers to unionize.

"Yes, I'm sure you understand about business, Teddy," she said as if she had in fact given him an opportunity to speak. "Because, after all, your union is a business, is it not?" He bristled at that. "Oh, let's be completely honest here, Teddy. The union uses at least some of its dues to pay the salaries of people like you and officers and others who would be entirely expendable if there were no union."

She shrugged and smiled benevolently at him.

"So, you'll understand that if there are the usual work slowdowns or perhaps a bit of midnight vandalism or even a strike, my family will have no choice but to put our money toward . . . addressing such problems. Our attention would be totally distracted from dealing with the real issues of our employees." She smiled radiantly at Kerry.

"Kate has started a school at the brewery," Ryan interjected when he saw the poor man had been struck dumb. "Tell Teddy about your school, Kate," he urged.

"That's all right, ma'am. I see we're about at my hotel." Teddy motioned to the driver to pull to the raised sidewalk, where he got out and then offered his hand to Kate. "It's been a pleasure, Katrina," he said.

"Next time you're in town, Teddy, I hope you'll take the time to meet with my father as well as the men. I'm sure it would be best if you knew the story from both sides. Good day."

The carriage moved off and turned at the next corner. It was then that Ryan released the bellow of a laugh he'd been holding in since before Teddy had made his hasty departure.

Kate gave him a startled look at first, then joined in his laughter. "Do you think I was too hard on him?"

"Heaven help me if I ever get on your bad side," Ryan said with a chuckle. "I had no idea, Miss Bergeman. No wonder your father felt he could leave his business in your hands during the war."

"He trained me well," Kate agreed with a satisfied smile. "Papa taught me that in spite of all our best efforts, there are fundamental differences in people, that's simply the reality of life. Mr. Kerry no doubt has some ideas about my family that are based on very few facts and a great deal of conjecture."

Kate was still enjoying her sparring session with Ted Kerry and did not notice the shift in Ryan's mood or the prolonged silence that stretched between them.

After several blocks Ryan gave the driver directions that Katrina recognized would take them to the area of the city where many immigrants settled when they first arrived, the neighborhood that housed the poorest dwellings and some of the most abominable conditions in the city. She also noted that when he turned from giving the driver instructions, Ryan was very quiet and very serious.

"Where are we going?" she asked after a long moment.

"It's time you saw my world, Katie," he said softly and looked directly at her for the first time since telling the driver where to go. "No more mystery." His usually robust smile was weak. He wondered what the next hour would bring. Why was he taking the risk of losing her just when it seemed they might have a chance?

But it was her devotion to her father that had decided him. August Bergeman had left no doubt of his feelings about any serious match between Kate and Ryan. She would have to defy her father if they were to be together. He could not ask her to do that unless she knew wherein lay her father's reservations.

As they neared the neighborhood, he ordered the cab halted and asked the driver to wait. He pressed some bills into the man's hand, then helped Kate down and began walking with her.

The first thing she noticed was the smell—rotting food mingled with cooking odors. As they passed an alley, there was the stench of raw sewage as the contents of slop buckets were dumped unceremoniously into the gutters. She glanced up and saw a network of clotheslines heavy with freshly washed but still-gray clothes. A stray dog stood on hind legs to scavenge in a barrel of food scraps behind a rundown and disreputable-looking saloon.

The second thing she noticed was the noise. Children raced through the streets dressed like ragamuffins in too large or too small clothing they had evidently inherited from other family members. Shopkeepers and street vendors, vying for the attention of passersby, practically knocked each other down to catch the eye of this well-dressed gentleman and his lady who had miraculously appeared in their midst. Housewives haggled over a penny's difference in the price of a piece of fish or a few potatoes, their faces creased with sweat and dust and constant worry.

At the second corner they were practically run over by a fire wagon that careened around the corner, its bell clanging, its generator throwing hot cinders in its wake. Kate glanced at the buildings—wood shanties and cottages with broken windows and doors akimbo. Every one of them was filled to bursting with the sounds of people talking, laughing, shouting, babies crying. Where did they go when one of these firetraps ignited, as one might with increasing frequency, given the hot dry summer? What happened when everything they owned went up in flames? How did they start over?

"You're very quiet," Ryan commented. He had deliberately allowed her time to take it all in and realized he had been right in his guess that she had been protected from places like this.

"Are you trying to say you were raised here?"

He shrugged. "Not in Milwaukee, but one slum is about the same as another. Mine was in Chicago . . ."

"But I thought your family was in New York."

"The family I have now is in New York," he said. "Distant cousins mostly." He pulled her to the side as a fresh group of immigrants came toward them from the Reed Street station. They carried all their belongings in heavy bundles on their backs, and their eyes were wide with wonder and confusion.

"Where is your famous Milwaukee *Gemutichkeit* here, Katie?" He used the German word that meant the good life and hospitality for which the city was renowned, and he could not temper the bitter edge that tinged his voice. It was one of the dichotomies of his recent life that at the same time he dwelt among the rich and powerful, he still deeply resented their ignorance of and disdain for the people who made that life possible.

"I don't understand." She looked up at him and remained standing in the doorway where they had waited for the refugees to pass.

He shrugged and placed his hands in his pockets as he started walking again. He was deliberately making this tough on her, more so now that he had brought her here. He figured he might as well play it out to a finish. Leaving her no choice but to follow, he strode along, expounding on the passing mass of humanity as she tried to keep up with his pace. "Look at them . . . For that matter look at the people who work for your father, Katie. I mean, have you ever really looked at them?" He strode on, his anger, long suppressed, seething to the surface.

"Ryan . . ."

"This is where people like this live, Katie. This is what the men who show up at your fine establishment every morning come home to at night. This is my ancestry, Miss

Bergeman. A bit of luck one way and I'm back here in a minute, and my fine society friends would offer handouts before they would offer a hand." The words were ripped from deep within him. He was bitter and scornful of himself that he also had avoided taking this walk very often since escaping the old neighborhood. *It's not Katie or her father who are guilty of forgetting those they left behind,* Ryan thought. *It's me.*

She was near tears. She could not imagine what it all meant . . . why he had brought her here. Why, after being away for so long, had he deliberately chosen to do this . . . to blame her for all this? She stopped and began to rail at him, her shouting barely noticeable in the noisy street where people had little enough time for their own troubles, much less the ravings of some well-dressed lunatic. "I don't know why you want to hurt me, Ryan, but you are doing a magnificent job of it! And if you don't stop blaming my family for everything evil in this world, I swear I may resort to violence myself." He paused and half-turned to her, but he wouldn't look at her.

"Why is it that when you walk here all you can see is misery and pain? There's a child laughing and having a wonderful time. Yes, he's poor, but does he know it? Yes, he's got little enough, but he may make something from the little he has."

When Ryan still looked everywhere but at her, she planted herself in front of him, her face as close to his as it could be, given the difference in their height.

"Is that it? Was your own childhood so miserable that you simply can't see anything beyond wretchedness and desolation? If you're so concerned, so outraged by what's happening here, then what are you doing about it?" She barely allowed a beat to pass while she searched his face for an answer. "I'm leaving," she announced quietly and turned on her heel to head back toward the cab.

He had no choice but to smile. She was extraordinary. What had he expected from her? This was a woman who, faced with a problem, took action. He remembered how stunned he had been reading her letters about starting the school, how there had simply been no problem as far as she was concerned. How she had met every hurdle with an attitude of unequivocal self-confidence. Immediately he caught up to her. "Katie, forgive me. It's this place plus being with Ted Kerry today and the men . . . the hopelessness of it. You're right, you know. I put my own guilt on you."

She refused to look at him but slowed her pace a bit. "I don't understand what this has to do with us."

"It has everything to do with us, Katie. This is what I come from, not the kind of society your family deals with on any regular basis."

"My family . . . ," she began.

" . . . is more open than most," he finished. "But Katie, they want more for you . . . better. They want you to have what they have."

"Why are you so angry, Ryan?"

"Because sitting there this afternoon with Kerry and the other workers, I knew that in spite of the tailored clothes and the fancy house, I am no different. Those men speak my language. We understand each other. In your father's eyes, I can never measure up to what he wants for you." He forestalled her protest with a finger on her lips. "You know it's true, Katie. If we are to have any future, it will mean sacrifice. I'm not sure it's fair to ask that of you."

Her heart soared at the word *future,* and she smiled. "Are you afraid I won't be able to measure up?"

He touched her cheek, his eyes tender and sober. "I'm afraid I'll ask too much of you," he said softly. "Come on. Let's go somewhere quieter." He led the way down a side street toward Lake Michigan.

"What happened to your family, Ryan?"

They were near an area of the docks not in use. No one was around, and the silence stood in sharp contrast to the chaotic scene they had just left. A gull screeched and landed on a piling near where they walked. A steamer's whistle blasted a warning to some smaller craft. A sidewheeler excursion boat bound for Chicago passed in the distance.

"Do you recall the *Lady Elgin?*" Ryan said softly, his eyes on the excursion boat until it was out of sight.

Everyone knew of the tragedy of the *Lady Elgin,* an excursion ship, just like the one passing, that had collided with a freighter and sunk on its way from Chicago in 1860, killing almost everyone on board.

Kate tried to recall what she remembered of the famous calamity . . . something about a large contingent of Irish . . . "Ryan, your family?"

He nodded, his eyes still on the horizon, his mouth set. The only betrayal of his emotion was the way his throat worked around a swallow.

"Oh, Ryan, I'm so terribly sorry. Everyone?"

Again the nod, then a deep sigh before he began to talk about it. "We were all so excited. My family had gotten on in Chicago. Cousins from Milwaukee who were on board had insisted we make the return trip with them. It was such a dark night, but the ship was alight with merrymaking. You've never heard such music . . . seen such jigs . . ." He smiled at the memory. "Ma sang . . ."

"You must have been very young."

"Sixteen."

"Brothers? Sisters?" Kate prompted him softly, unwilling to disturb his revery.

"Eight boys . . . one girl . . . Molly . . ." His voice trailed off and then added with a slight break, " . . . one on the way."

Kate was stunned. "And everyone . . . ?" She didn't even begin to know how to phrase such a horror, so she left her question unfinished.

He nodded. "Except me." He leaned forward against a piling, his head down, his face shadowed by his hat. "I tried to help, Katie," he said, and even now, a decade later, his voice caught. "But . . ." He shrugged and gave a slight shudder. "Twenty minutes," he whispered, "that's all it took, I was told later. It seemed an eternity . . . twenty minutes of chaos and screaming and the sounds of three hundred feet of water sucking down that huge steamer . . . and then nothing but the occasional moan of someone who had managed to hang onto a piece of wood or a door from the wreckage . . . a shout . . . a cry for help."

"How did you make it?"

"Two of my brothers and I got a fairly good sized piece of debris and used it for a raft for a while . . . took turns paddling to shore. But it started to break up, and they . . . couldn't hold on . . ."

She remembered the scar she had seen on his back that first day at the lake. In the following weeks, she had assumed it was a war wound, but now . . . "Ryan?" She touched his back, and her fingers traced the place she knew the scar to be. He flinched and then relaxed.

"Somebody tried to take away my piece of the raft," he said. "After the boys were all gone, this guy comes along, clinging to a piece of wood . . . I had seen him on board . . . a fat, loudmouthed businessman who'd made it very clear how he felt having to share the passage with a bunch of rowdy Irish. Well, I offered to help him, to share what was left of the raft, so he let go of his wood and grabbed onto mine. 'Paddle,' I told him, but he whined and moaned about how we were never going to make it."

"What happened?"

"We got within fifty yards of shore . . . I could see people waiting to help us, sending out rowboats, cheering us on. Just then the raft started to break apart again . . . probably from the weight of this overstuffed pig. 'We're sinking,' he screamed. 'Get off!' And then he was pushing me, and before I knew what hit me, he'd grabbed some daggerlike piece of splintered wood and was stabbing me in the shoulder. 'Off,' he screamed . . ."

Kate could barely imagine the horror of it. What if she had just lost Papa and Mama and Lu? It had been horrible enough losing Frederick, but this . . . this must have been unbearable.

Ryan finished the story in a flat tone. "I fell away, but somehow I managed to stay afloat, and finally one of the rescue boats reached me. They took me to the hospital. After a few days the bodies began to wash up on shore . . . Ma's among them. I saw her buried. Aside from the shoulder wound, I was treated for exposure and exhaustion. The doctors kept me in the hospital for months, afraid I'd do something rash, I think. Those were long days and nights with nothing to do but remember. In April I joined the army, trying to forget. It haunts me that I survived . . . of all of them . . ." His voice trailed off, and he studied the horizon.

Kate could think of nothing to say, so she moved behind him and circled his waist with her arms, leaning against him, her cheek on his back. After a moment he turned, and she saw that he had been crying.

"I'm sorry," she whispered and thought there had never been two more inadequate words in the English language.

They kissed then, a kiss of healing and solace, a kiss of understanding and compassion, a kiss of shared knowledge.

"Katie Bergeman?" He held her loosely and studied her upturned face. "I think it's quite possible that I am falling in love with you and I haven't the slightest idea what to do about it."

Her heart pounded at his words. It was impossible, and yet, she, too, had felt the stirrings of something deeper than mere attraction. She had tried to tell herself it was his mystery, his aura of fictional heroism, but now, knowing his roots, knowing his tragedy, had only drawn her more passionately toward him.

He watched the play of emotions that crossed her face and grinned. "It's your turn to say something," he teased.

"We're going on holiday tomorrow," she blurted.

"What about your school? You've just gotten started."

"I know, but Papa insists. He says my first priority should be family tradition, and going to Lake Geneva is traditional." She was doubly miserable now because not only was she having to leave the project she had just managed to get off the ground, but also she was leaving Ryan. "Sometimes I think my work counts for nothing with Papa."

"Lake Geneva, you say?"

"We have a summer cottage there as do our cousins . . . Eloise . . . Carlotta . . ." With each detail her heart sank. "The whole household moves out there for a month . . . Papa and Edward and Cousin Emil and Christian come out on the weekends."

"Really?" He smiled and kissed her. "I just happen to have friends who have a summer place on Lake Geneva, and frequently I spend time there on the weekends. Now, isn't that a coincidence?"

11

AT THE STATION, Ryan dismissed the driver when Kate insisted she would rather take the streetcar home. They walked to the train that chugged and hissed near the station platform.

"Come with me," he said, pulling her up the narrow steps to a car of private compartments.

"I can't," she said, her voice tinged with regret.

"Then come on board for a few minutes . . . We have a few minutes . . ." He led the way past other people who were aboard to see family and friends off.

"Here," he said, checking his ticket against the compartment number. He opened the door and, as soon as she was in, closed it firmly. "Come here," he whispered and pulled her into his arms for a long, fervid kiss.

Aware of the daylight and the passing throngs of townspeople and strangers just outside the windows and in the corridor of the car itself, Kate resisted. Lord knew she didn't want to, for it was heavenly being in his arms again, having his mouth on hers, not having to live on memories and fantasies.

"Ryan," she said with a breathless warning.

He stopped kissing her but held her, looking down at her with longing and confusion. "What?"

"It's . . ." She indicated the windows, where Mrs. Schwartz of the Women's Guild was scanning the train. Obviously she had come to see someone off. Certainly if she happened to recognize Katrina, she would have quite a tale to tell at the coming meeting.

Ryan started to laugh. "Is this the same independent lady who just leveled one of the country's leading union organizers? Not to mention how she just gave one of the toughest rascals I've ever met—namely me—fair warning to leave her family and its business alone?"

She felt the color rise to her cheeks. How could he possibly endure her lack of sophistication? Carlotta would have simply enjoyed the kiss, not worried what the townspeople might think. Ryan had hinted he might be falling in love with her, and all she could do was worry about her reputation—or more to the point, about what Papa would say if anyone told him. She had never felt more like an immature schoolgirl in her life.

Ryan reached around her and pulled the shades, then waited for her to decide to come back into his arms. He frowned as he once again reminded himself that Katrina was different. For all her society upbringing, she was basically unsophisticated, especially in matters of the heart.

A tear slid from the corner of one eye down the side of her nose. She wasn't usually given to such emotion, but here was a man she had dreamed of, waited most of her life for, and she was ruining the whole thing.

"Ah, don't cry, Katie darling. I didn't mean to upset you . . . it's just . . ." He sighed and collapsed against the upholstery of the train seat. "Ah, Katie, I tell you of these things in my life because I want you to know me. I still have a lot of rough edges for all my success. Then there's the war . . . the loss of my family . . . events that left me determined not to allow anything in my life again that I might lose, that might cause me ever again to experience that kind of raw, chilling pain. It's like an open wound I carry, Katie," he said softly, his hand reaching for hers.

"What right have I to ask anyone to share that with me?" He sat forward and grasped both her hands in his. "But you, Katie Bergeman, are good . . . good for me. It scares me to think of letting go of what we have. Does that make any sense?"

It was only what Kate herself had been thinking for weeks. What if she lost him? What if he found someone else? In New York and Washington there had to be dozens of beautiful women, sophisticated and willing. What if those kisses by the lake and in the carriage were all she would ever have of him? She had thought she could live with that, but it wasn't so. She wanted him and felt as if she would never have enough of him.

"All-l-l 'board!" The conductor's cry rang out repeatedly up and down the corridor.

Ryan stood up. He looked as miserable as she felt. "Kiss me . . . I promise to be a gentleman." He grinned and gently embraced her.

She went willingly into his arms. Their kiss quickly escalated to something far more involved, far more intense, far more reckless than anything they had shared before. Both of them knew that through the weeks of writing and thinking of each other, and now this afternoon, their relationship had risen to a new plateau.

The kisses they had shared before today had been exploratory, questioning. With this kiss they entered the realm of commitment. Ryan's hands, so tentative as she came into his arms, had now become possessive, roaming over her back and around to embrace the fullness of her breasts.

" . . . 'board," the conductor cried.

"You have to go," Ryan rasped while reaching for yet another taste of her.

"Yes," she whispered, then kissed him again.

"On the weekend," he said, "I'll come to Lake Geneva."

"Yes." Then immediately, "Not till then?"

He smiled. "A few days only," he promised, kissing

her fingers, her eyelids, her hair as he eased her toward the door.

The train lurched. " . . . *'board!*"

Kate shrieked. "Oh lord, it's moving. I have to . . ."

He stopped the words with one last passionate kiss, then hurried with her down the narrow corridor to the exit. The train moved ponderously forward as with one arm around her waist he swung her to the platform, where she stood watching until he was out of sight.

" . . . sitting there in my courtyard with my workers and that scalawag Kerry . . ."

Papa's voice could be heard booming across the lawn as Kate stepped off the streetcar and walked along the ironwork fence that encircled the property.

"What do you mean, what's the harm? He knows the man. What does that say of him? No, Sophie, I do not trust this Irishman."

Kate could not hear her mother's replies as she walked up the drive, but it was easy to fathom the conversation.

"I know Katrina likes him—so much the worse. I don't want you encouraging this, Sophia . . ." Papa meant business whenever he referred to his wife by her true name.

"Guten Abend, Pater," Katrina said as she started up the steps to the veranda. She had found that using German words soothed her father when he was upset.

He glowered at her. "I'll see you in the library, young *fräulein,* as soon as you've made yourself presentable."

Kate could only hope he referred to the dust and sweat on her clothes and not to any telltale sign of her encounter with Ryan. Nervously she licked her kiss-swollen lips and glanced at Mama.

Mama studied her for the barest second before indicating with a nod of her head that the wisest course would be to retire to her room and change.

"Ja, Papa," she said softly and entered the house.

"You're in trouble," Lulu said as she eased into Kate's

room, closing the door quietly behind her.

"So it seems," Kate replied as she resisted the urge to study the full aftereffects of Ryan's raid on every fiber of her being. She changed into a gown she knew her father favored and tied her hair into a girlish braid.

All the while Lu chattered on. Edward had told her of Kate's leaving with Ryan and the union organizer. "My stars, sister, didn't it occur to you that Papa would positively explode seeing you with Theodore Kerry?"

"Actually, no," Kate replied absently. Nothing had occurred to her except that she had only a few hours to be with Ryan before he had to return to Chicago.

"Well, Edward told me that Papa . . ."

Kate barely heard the account of Papa observing the threesome leave the brewery, of his reaction, of his arrival home *before six,* which always meant trouble.

"The signs are all in place," Kate observed as she finished the last button on her shoes. "I suppose I'd better go and meet my punishment."

Lu studied her sister. "My lord, you went somewhere with him? You had a . . . an assignation?"

Kate looked at her sister for the first time since Lu had entered the room. "Lulu, please don't say anything, but . . . yes . . . that is . . . Oh, Lu, I can't seem to help myself when he's around," she moaned. "I . . . I think I'm in love with him."

To her surprise Lulu gave a shout of exuberance. "Well, glory be. After all this time, you've finally found someone you're willing to take a chance with."

Kate bristled. "I thought you and Edward disapproved."

"Katrina!" Papa's voice boomed up the stairwell.

"Papa and Edward disapprove. *I* think it's fantastic. I mean it's so-o-o incredibly romantic."

"I . . ."

"Katrina—*now!*"

Kate opened the door. "Coming, Papa." She glanced back at her smiling sister and stuck out her tongue, which caused

Lulu to change her grin to bald-faced laughter.

"Yes, Father," Kate said demurely as she entered her father's book-lined study and stood by the door.

He sat behind his desk, which was also not a good sign.

"I'm waiting, young lady, and none of your sister's coy tricks, please. They work well for her, but you fail miserably at any semblance of charade."

"What is it you want to know?"

"Young Sullivan was at the brewery today."

"Yes."

"He did not make his presence known to me."

"He did not come to see you."

Papa's eyebrows narrowed at that. "Don't be impertinent."

Katrina remained silent, standing behind the high-backed, tufted velvet chair directly across from her father.

"I'm waiting," he said, refusing to make eye contact as he lit his pipe.

"May I sit down?"

He nodded in the general direction of the chair as he sucked hard on his pipe against the flame of the match.

Katrina took her place in the chair and arranged her skirts to buy time. "Ryan . . . Mr. Sullivan has been away for several weeks . . ."

"And you have corresponded with him," Papa noted, taking some small pleasure in her surprise that he knew this.

"Yes, we corresponded. We have become friends," she said with a hint of defiance.

Papa drew on his pipe for several minutes as he pondered the intricate plasterwork of the ceiling. "Friends," he said once.

"Yes. Today was his first visit back to Milwaukee since returning from New York. He came to say hello and to see how the school was proceeding."

"And in all this proper concern between two friends, exactly where does Mr. Theodore Kerry figure?" Papa's voice was quiet but forceful.

"I . . . Mr. Kerry was . . . there . . . with the men . . ."

Papa held up one finger. "With the men *and* Mr. Sullivan," he corrected.

"Well, yes, but . . ."

"Are you aware that Mr. Kerry and Mr. Sullivan grew up together? That they both started out as the rowdy sons of immigrant Irishmen? That they are cousins?"

This last gave Katrina pause. "How do you know?"

Papa turned his full attention on her for the first time since she had entered the study. "Because, *Liebchen,* when one of my daughters becomes *friends* with a man who has at best a mysterious past, I make it my business to find out what I can. Your Mr. Sullivan and his cousin were raised in the bowels of Chicago. It was through the war that the young man made the invaluable contacts that eventually led to his success . . . stupendous success, I will grant you."

Kate was dumbfounded. Her father knew as much about Ryan as she did. It placed her at a disadvantage. It made her uncomfortable. "I thought you admired his war record," she challenged.

"I do. I admire a great many things about him, but . . ." Here he paused for effect and leaned across the desk toward her. "But, *Liebchen,* he is not for you . . . Do you understand? It is the nature of the Irish to be somewhat . . . casual about their relationships with the fairer sex. I would not wish to see you hurt."

"We are friends," she protested, and noticed how easily the lie came when it seemed as if the truth might deny her the opportunity of ever seeing Ryan again.

"And that's fine. Edward certainly admires him, as does your mother. I have no problem with the young man calling to see the family whenever he is in town." His emphasis on *the family* was unmistakable.

He took his time tapping out the ashes of his pipe. Kate knew he was pausing to allow the full effect of his words to register. Her mind raced. How could she see Ryan and not disobey Papa?

"Now, let us speak of happier matters," her father said heartily. "Are you all packed for our trip tomorrow?"

"Papa? I've been meaning to speak to you about that." How easily the lies tumbled from her lips now that she was desperate to come up with a plan that would allow her and Ryan to be together.

Papa frowned. "Yes?"

"Well, the school has really just gotten started, and it seems . . . Oh, Papa, couldn't I stay in town during the week and go to the lake on weekends like you and Edward?"

"I thought you liked the country."

"I do, but, Papa, I've begun something with the school . . . I don't want to risk losing ground." She tried to phrase her pleas in arguments he would identify with, business arguments.

Papa grinned. "I am already ahead of you, *Liebchen*. I have made arrangements for Miss Kopfmeier to teach the sessions while you are away. She can also help in the office. I believe she is quite grateful for the extra work and funds."

Kate's spirits plummeted. In town she could have sent word to Ryan, and they could have had any number of opportunities to be together while her father and Edward were occupied at the brewery. Now she had no choice but to go with the others to the summer cottage, where her every move would be subject to scrutiny.

Papa stood, indicating the end of their meeting. "So you see I have thought of your school. I will admit to you that I thought it a terrible idea in the beginning, but it has merit, and I have considered that in agreeing to bring in Miss Kopfmeier." He was obviously pleased with himself, viewing his action as some reward for his daughter's creativity and perseverance. "Now let's go and see what your mother has for our supper on this eve of our holiday."

Without another word, Katrina walked ahead of her father into the dining room, where Lu, Edward, and Mama waited expectantly. Katrina sensed the general sigh of relief when

Papa placed his arm around her shoulders and escorted her to her usual place. But she barely heard any of the table conversation. Her thoughts were on Ryan Sullivan. As the evening wore on, she replayed her conversation with her father, searching for any hint that he might change his mind about a union between Ryan and his daughter in the future. The more she thought of his words, the more she resented Papa's insinuation that all Irishmen were flirts and cads.

Her situation was worse than Kate had predicted. Because the summer was so terribly hot, Papa decided the family should stay at the cottage through most of September, so the visit was to be six weeks instead of four.

The days crept by. She was too restless to read and it was too hot to ride, so she spent hours pacing the shore of Lake Geneva. In all of those long six weeks, Kate and Ryan were able to see each other only three times.

There was the barrier of his only being able to come up for the weekends, and sometimes not even then if he had to attend to business. But more importantly, there was Papa. Every weekend when he and Edward arrived to join the family, Papa brought along Willem Frear, whose family was also in the brewing business, also lived in Milwaukee, and, most importantly for Papa, also was German. Clearly Papa hoped to promote a match between Willem and Katrina.

Willem wasn't any more interested in such a match than she was. He came because it was politic to do so. The Bergeman Brewery was larger and more powerful than his family's, and clearly his father hoped for the merger of the two young people in order to boost his own business. Willem, however, was far more taken with Carlotta than he was with Katrina. He obviously found Kate's forthrightness and involvement in the family business annoying.

Still, she had little choice but to entertain him. On weekends she and Willem would join Edward and Lu for swims, picnics, concerts in the park, and other traditional summer holiday gaiety. Kate suffered through all the activities with barely concealed restlessness, her mind racing with plans for seeing Ryan.

But on the two occasions when Ryan accepted the family's invitations, Carlotta was in residence, and Eloise made certain that Ryan was her designated escort for every event. Kate wondered that Papa had no words of disapproval for the obvious promotion of a match between Ryan and his cousin's daughter, but she kept her thoughts to herself.

When they were together for social occasions, the six young people made a comical portrait—Willem pining for Carlotta, Carlotta clinging to Ryan and flirting shamelessly with Willem, Ryan casting long, miserable looks at Kate, Kate seething in silence, while poor Edward and Lu tried desperately to hold the whole affair together.

Late at night Lu would comfort Kate in the privacy of their shared room as she bemoaned Papa's obvious plan to keep her from Ryan. It seemed as if Papa knew which weekends Ryan might appear even before Ryan himself did, and Carlotta was always visiting.

"And she loves it," Kate wailed one night as she and Lu sat by the window in the dark, talking. "If I hear one more word about that stupid ball and how Ryan wants to dance every waltz with her . . ."

"But he doesn't," Lu reminded her. "He barely tolerates her silliness . . . I'm sure the only reason he comes here at all is to see you."

"Perhaps. But in the last three weeks he hasn't come. Oh, it's hopeless. Why must Papa be this way? He barely knows Ryan."

"Maybe you should talk to Mama," Lu suggested. Just then, Kate had little patience for new ideas. Nothing would work, and that was that. She and Ryan were doomed. She stared forlornly out the window, at the moon over the lake. "I can't talk to Mama. In matters such as this, she stands by Papa, and you know it."

They sat in uneasy silence for a while. Lu wanted so

desperately to help, but nothing she offered seemed to be right. Kate was so miserable that she had begun taking out her frustration on the one person who was clearly on her side. "I'm sorry, Lu," she said softly.

"Sh-h-h," Lu whispered urgently and leaned out the window, staring at the shore. "Someone's out there." Lu pointed to a cluster of trees just past the dock.

Kate recognized the tall, graceful figure immediately. It was Ryan. Her spirits soared at the sight of him. "Ryan," she whispered, then looked at her sister pleadingly.

Lu understood. "Go," she urged.

In moments Kate was dressed and out the window, using the tree she and Lu and Frederick had used as children when they wanted to leave the house for a midnight swim or some childhood adventure without their parents' knowledge. Kate fairly flew across the expanse of the yard to where Ryan waited in the shadows of a stand of pine trees. She could see the shape of the dinghy he had used to paddle silently along the shore from his friends' cottage.

When she was near enough, he stepped out of the shadows and caught her in his arms. Without a word his mouth was on hers, their hunger and longing obvious in the way their tongues tasted and savored each other. The night was still and muggy, and there was not even a breeze to stir the lake. Around them the cicadas chattered, and occasionally a fish or a frog broke water, but they heard none of it.

Ryan drew her farther into the darkness of the evergreen trees, kissing her all the while. He wore trousers and an open shirt, and she could feel his heart beating against hers.

Without a word he untied the ribbon that held back her hair, then buried his hands in the voluminous masses while he kissed her temple, her ears, her neck.

"I had to come," he whispered. "I didn't know if . . . That is, I had no plan but to see you . . . alone." He continued to kiss her, his words coming in a breathless rush. "Oh, Katie, I want you."

She pressed her hands to his bare chest, exulting in the sensation of touching him without the barrier of clothing. During these weeks of abstinence, her fantasies had run wild. Many a night she had lain awake imagining what it would be like to lie with him, to feel his skin against hers, to have him make love to her. If this was all they could have—clandestine meetings in the shadows—it would have to do. She did not like defying Papa, but he left her no choice.

"Yes," she whispered.

Ryan took a step away, and his fingers shook slightly as he began to unfasten the long row of buttons that closed the front of her gown. Kate barely breathed as she watched him. When the last button was open, he looked at her and eased the gown off her shoulders and down her arms until the bodice hung loose at her waist. She felt the press of her nipples against the thin cotton of her camisole, the only garment that separated her chest from his.

"I've thought of you . . . of us . . . like this," he said, and opened the bow that held the lacing of her camisole. "My beautiful Katie," he whispered as his fingers worked their way down, spreading the fabric to expose her skin.

She traced the hollow that ran between his chest muscles and then let her hands drift down to the tight waistband of his trousers. He shuddered, and she reveled in the ability to give him the same heightened pleasure he was creating in her. Lightly she circled her fingers over and around and down again until he pulled her hard against his hips, wanting her to understand the sensations she created. "You're playing with fire, Katie," he warned.

In the embrace her camisole came fully open, and they experienced the first heady, forbidden contact. Ryan groaned and moved to kiss her throat, her bare shoulder, and finally, when she thought she might faint from want and need, the full ripeness of her nipple. The explosion of the embrace carried them first to their knees and then to the soft ground, where Ryan's mouth and hands seemed to surround her, making up her entire world.

For long moments their passion transported them. She pushed off his shirt. He moved over her, bathing her from her lips to her waist with kisses. Instinctively she discovered the movements that would give him the greatest access, the greatest pleasure. Her hands moved over his back and down to his waist, then up again. Once, she gave a soft whimper as the buckle of his belt pressed against her waist. He opened the belt and the top two buttons of his trousers as well.

"Touch me," he implored, taking her hand, guiding her. Her palm cupped him, then her fingers closed on the straining fabric. The sound he uttered was unadulterated gratification. He seemed to move into another realm, moving against her hand, his face contorted with a kind of sweet agony that startled and terrified her. Immediately she stopped and withdrew her hand.

He froze and looked at her, searching her face in the shadowy moonlight for some explanation. "I don't know how . . . what . . ." She felt very near tears, wanting him so and yet intimidated by her innocence.

He rolled away but pulled her with him, holding her so that his arm was around her shoulder and her head against his chest. "It's all right, darling," he whispered soothingly. "I didn't mean to scare you." He cursed himself for rushing her, for treating her as if she would have the knowledge of other women he had known. It pleased him to be her first, to be her tutor. This was enough for one night's lesson, he decided.

She gave a shuddering sigh of relief that he wasn't angry or upset. "Sh-h-h," he whispered, and then again, like a lullaby, "sh-h-h."

They lay together until their breathing steadied and hers became deep and regular. He let her sleep, pulling his shirt over her bare shoulders, stroking her hair, and thinking how it might be possible to make her his without destroying the happiness she had always known.

12

RYAN WOKE KATE just before dawn. The servants would be stirring soon, and her chances for discovery would be great. He watched from the shore as she ran up the slope to the apple tree she had used to climb down from her bedroom. When she was safely inside, she leaned out the window and blew him a kiss.

There had to be a way for them, he thought as he paddled along the shoreline. His friends were not in residence this weekend, and he had the huge estate to himself. He wandered the grounds in the predawn stillness, imagining a home of his own with Kate as its mistress. It was only a short step from that fantasy to one where children, their children, played on the lawn, rolling down the slope in wild abandon as their parents looked on with delight. Or perhaps he and Kate would be right there with them, rolling down the hill themselves, their shrieks of laughter mingling with those of their offspring.

The transition from resistance to any sort of serious relationship to planning for a complete commitment seemed perfectly legitimate. When he had watched as his entire family slipped into the vast depths of the lake after the collision of the *Lady Elgin,* he had thought he would never again allow himself to feel such pain.

But his experiences during the war had mellowed him. There he had witnessed the immense pain of so many and watched as their indominitable spirits, as well as the uniquely human will to live life to the fullest, triumphed over tragedy. After the war he toyed with the idea that one day he, too, would want more than power and success and position in order to be fulfilled.

Now he knew that what he had waited for was Kate. She was so absolutely right for him, combining intelligence with wit, beauty with a genuinely selfless caring for others. He had been completely captivated by her letter telling him of the plan for the school at the brewery. It was a preposterous idea, born out of the most casual conversation between the two of them, and yet she had acted on her convictions. Yes, with this woman the dreams he had for his childhood friends and neighbors could be realized. With this woman his money and position would be used to its best advantage. Together they could build toward a world where there was indeed more opportunity for everyone.

He thought of the land he had bought from Bergeman in Peshtigo and wondered how Kate would react to moving away from the city. Of course, she had family in Peshtigo. Sophie's relatives were very active in town politics and business there, so it wouldn't be a complete break. A sister and brother-in-law of Sophie's had welcomed Ryan into their home when he first went to look at the land. They had talked of Katie, regaling him with accounts of her childhood escapades on her grandparents' farm nearby.

Ryan chuckled to himself. How Ted Kerry was going to laugh when he heard that his cousin, the confirmed bachelor, had been completely captivated by Katrina Bergeman. He laughed out loud. Then he gave out with a whoop of unadulterated joy that brought a startled glance from the caretaker and his wife, who were setting up his breakfast on the terrace that overlooked the lake. Ryan waved and moved quickly to the house to pack.

He was actually planning a life with her. He, who had once sworn he would never again allow himself to become so close to anyone, to risk losing someone. And here this extraordinary woman had, in a matter of a few weeks, brought him to the point of actually considering the idea, not only of commitment, but of marriage and a family and a real home.

Still, marrying him would mean a serious break with her father, and Ryan understood how devoted Kate was to August Bergeman. How could he ask her to choose? Could they ever really be happy if there was tension between the two men she loved most?

But even as he considered the uncertainties of a match between them, he could not entirely abandon the idea of their finding a way. There had to be a solution, and having arrived at that decision, he was characteristically impatient to act on it. He was anxious to get back to Chicago. There was much to arrange between now and the week of the Hauptman ball.

Kate lay on the bed and watched the sunrise. She had slipped in without waking Lu and changed into her nightclothes. But she had not slept. Her mind raced with thoughts of what had almost happened last night. No man had ever seen her naked body or touched it. Yet she had found herself wanting to be rid of all clothing, all barriers to the magic of Ryan's lovemaking. She wondered what might have happened had she not stopped him, and relived every moment of his hands and mouth on her, touching herself everywhere his lips had been.

Who was this woman? Certainly not the prim and proper girl who had always agonized over the propriety of every touch, every kiss, with other beaus. Unlike Lu, she rarely confided such thoughts with her sister, but they were there nonetheless . . . what a touch might mean or how allowing that small liberty might seem. She was constantly aware of her role as the daughter of one of the most respected families in Milwaukee. It would never do for her to cause even the hint of scandal.

With Ryan there were no reservations. She was his to do with as he pleased, fully understanding that while he had suggested he might fall in love with her, he really had never indicated he would consider their relationship more than a summer romance. Even last night his words had been of wanting her . . . not loving her.

She didn't care. Whatever she could have, she would accept. Besides, there was just something about the way he looked at her, the way he was so tender and gentle, that gave her hope that he shared her feelings . . . feelings that far exceeded a simple flirtation. Surely, if all he felt was a longing for her physically, he would not have pulled back last night.

She glanced over at the sleeping Lulu, and thought, *By this time next year, we might both be married.* It was an idea that pleased her. For some time she had known that it was a good thing Abner had left before they could be married. She shuddered to think of the life she would have had, the opportunities she would have missed. Abner would no more have condoned her working in the brewery than Willem Frear did. And what would their conversations have been about? Lord, whenever she dared express a political opinion, Willem looked as if he might actually faint from the impropriety of such a thing.

But Ryan sought her opinions, encouraged the expression of her ideas and thoughts, applauded her efforts to change things. No man except Papa had ever made her feel her ideas were worthy of consideration, and even Papa had constraints on when such expressions were appropriate. Ryan, on the other hand . . .

She smiled and hugged the pillow to her face to smother a giggle of delight. Everything came back to Ryan. *Ryan says . . . Ryan believes . . . Ryan . . . Ryan . . .* Even Papa paled in his presence.

Kate stopped smiling and watched how the curtains stirred in the already hot breeze. Papa would never stand for a match between her and Ryan. It was one thing to have him as a guest in his house, or as a friend or business associate. It was quite something else to have him as a suitor for his daughter, especially his elder daughter. Kate put the pillow aside with a heavy sigh and sat on the edge of the bed, considering what she could possibly do to make Papa see what a fine husband Ryan would be.

She heard Mama outside talking to the servants. In two days the family would return to Milwaukee, and today the packing would begin. Perhaps Lu was right. Mama was really her last hope. Kate dressed quickly and hurried downstairs. She wanted some time with her mother before the others claimed her attention.

"Good morning, darling," Mama said as Kate came across the yard and began helping to gather the flowers Sophie chose every morning to place in bouquets throughout the house. "Did you sleep well?"

"Yes." Kate searched for words. How to begin? Mama could help. "Mama, I love Ryan Sullivan," she blurted suddenly, "and I'm sure he loves me."

Mama paused only a moment and then continued cutting blossoms with the kitchen knife. "I see," she said softly.

Kate waited for something more, but Mama just moved on through the rows of flowers, choosing this one, leaving that for another day.

"I know Papa doesn't like him, but—"

"On the contrary, your father seems to admire Mr. Sullivan very much. I think he's a bit envious of one so young being so successful."

"But he'll never—"

"Never is a long time, darling," Mama said, turning to glance at her daughter for the first time since the conversation had begun. "Forever is also a long time. I wonder if you've considered the magnitude of that," she mused, as if to herself. "I wonder if you've considered the possible complications of that," Mama said, looking directly at Katrina.

"I don't know what you mean," Kate said with more than a little petulance. The conversation was hardly going the way she'd hoped. She had counted on her mother's support.

Sophie took a seat on an old fallen tree that the caretaker had fashioned into a rustic bench. She patted the spot beside her, inviting Kate to join her, and brushed the back of her hand across her brow to catch the sweat. "So hot already. Such an unusual autumn," she reflected, squinting up into the sultry September sun.

Kate sat, her posture one of dejection. "I don't know what to do, Mama," she said.

Mama put down her basket of flowers and rubbed Kate's back. "I think," she said with a smile, "that this is the first time I have ever really seen you in love. Oh, I know there was Abner, but I always had my doubts about the two of you. For some time now, I've been aware of a change in you . . . a change that speaks of a new maturity, a new womanliness that hasn't been there before."

Kate contemplated the baked and cracked earth, allowing her mother's words to nourish and soothe her. "What am I going to do?"

"I think you must give it time, Katrina."

Kate groaned in protest.

"I know," Mama assured her, "but try not to think of time as the enemy. Think of it as your ally. If Mr. Sullivan is patient enough and persistent enough, he can perhaps win your father over. When your father knows Ryan better, is more sure of him . . ."

"But Mama—"

Mama held up her finger to forestall any interruption. "You have led a sheltered life, my darling, for all our efforts to educate you. You have been surrounded with all the love and kindness we could offer. I am not at all sure I have done a good job of preparing you to face the world at large. It's a place that can be unkind, even brutal. There is much prejudice out there. If you and Ryan persist, such brutality is bound to touch you. I share your father's reservations. Do you understand what such a match could mean, not only for you but for your children? People can be most unfeeling, Katrina, and matches that cross ethnic lines are not especially . . . well tolerated."

"Ryan is the most honorable, tender, remarkable, gentle man," Kate protested.

"I'm sure he's all of that," Mama said as she stood up and resumed her gathering. "But the fact remains that he is also Irish, and you are German, in a community where such backgrounds matter a great deal. Even if you lived in Chicago, there would be times . . . comments. Oh, my darling Katrina, don't you understand that your father and I don't want that for you? We want your life to be one of pure joy and happiness insofar as it is within our power to give that to you."

"Mama, no one can guarantee happiness or freedom from pain. I assume I will have my share of both, as you have had. After all, wasn't it you who taught us when Frederick died that there can be no pain if there never was joy? That our grief was evidence of the love and happiness we all shared with him?"

Mama frowned slightly. "I know what you are saying, darling, but you speak of unpredictable pain and suffering. If you and Ryan attempt a life together, we are speaking of an avoidable hurt. Besides, you have given me no evidence at all that Mr. Sullivan's intentions are anywhere near as serious as your feelings for him obviously are."

Katrina could be as determined as her mother. In fact, at such times they resembled each other most. "He has asked to escort me to Carlotta's ball, and I have accepted."

"I see. Then I would remind you, Katrina, that not more than two months ago it was Carlotta he planned to escort."

Kate frowned. "So Carlotta and Eloise said," she retorted. "But Ryan says he never asked her. You saw how he was with her these past weeks, Mama. I know you saw."

Mama nodded. She could not deny that Ryan had been obviously and thoroughly miserable.

Hope sprang to Kate's eyes. "Then you'll help me . . . with Papa."

"For the ball," Mama replied, wagging one finger. "After that . . ."

Kate did not allow her to finish, but grabbed her mother in a hug and whirled her around. "Oh, thank you, Mama. Thank you."

"Absolutely not," August Bergeman roared when his wife told him of the plans for the Hauptman ball.

"Augie, dearest Augie, if you deny her this, you are setting the stage for disaster," Sophie warned.

August frowned. "How so?"

"She is in a state of defiance. This man has her completely captivated. She will do almost anything to be with him. If you forbid her, it will only increase her resolve. Yes, Augie, right now . . . for this man . . . she will defy even you."

"I don't like this."

"I know, but I honestly think it will run its course. Once she is in Chicago, in his surroundings, she may see the gap between them for herself. Katrina is very wise, darling. She's acting out of character for the moment, but I believe she will come to her senses as long as we don't force her hand."

"Sophie, it is not just meanness that keeps me from approving this . . . romance. There are things . . . This labor union movement is becoming a major issue throughout the land. Here in Milwaukee, as often as not, we of the German community find ourselves on opposite sides from the working class Irish and Italians. This air of prejudice that now is only manifested in subtle ways will flourish in an atmosphere of dispute."

"But Ryan is not of the working class," Sophie reminded him.

"No, but his heart is." August paused as if lost in thought. Then he turned to his wife with fresh evidence to prove his case. "And there is the economy. There are difficult days coming, and again different groups will find themselves on opposite sides. If Ryan and Katrina are together, how will having to choose between us and his friends affect them?"

"She isn't thinking of that, Augie. She's thinking of today, of next week. You cannot convince her with talk of next year. She is in love for probably the first time in her life. There is enormous power in that," Sophie warned.

August stroked his chin and nodded. "I know," he agreed.

Except for his wife, August Bergeman loved his daughters more than anything in the world. Katrina's obvious infatuation weighed heavily on him. "Perhaps if we allow her to attend the ball with him, she will come to her senses," August repeated as if it were his idea.

"You may be right."

"Still . . ."

Sophie put her arms around her husband. "Augie, we cannot protect them forever. Katrina is a grown woman, and she is in love with him."

"She *thinks* she's in love with him," August corrected.

"No, darling, she's in love . . . That's what makes it all so painful. Besides, we'll be there."

But that night two events concurred to change all their plans and to put in motion events that would change Kate's life forever. As the family sat down to supper, Mike Connors pounded on the front door with the news that the cooperage at the brewery had caught fire. No sooner had Papa and Edward dashed off to take care of that than a messenger appeared with a telegram for Mama. Sophie's brother-in-law sent word from Peshtigo that her youngest sister, Fanny, might lose the baby she was expecting and die in the process. Could Sophie come?

"Mama, I'll go with you," Katrina argued as she helped her mother pack, all thoughts of balls and courtships put aside. Fanny was her favorite aunt. This was her first child after years of trying unsuccessfully to produce.

"No. Chicago means a great deal to you and your sister, and I won't have you miss the ball. Edward can stay here and help your father and then take the train down on Saturday in time for the ball. You go along with Lu. Eloise has made arrangements for the two of you to stay with their neighbors, the Drakes. Take Ernestine, and we'll leave Pauline and Heinrich here to see that your father eats and gets some rest."

As always, Mama had everything under control within a matter of hours.

"But Papa . . . ," Katrina protested.

"Your father has Edward, and the staff will see that he gets food and sleep. There is little you can do. He needs to be at the brewery himself. He's been afraid of a fire all summer, and I know him well enough to know he won't rest as long as there is any danger. No, there's nothing you can do for your father. Please, darling, go. Everything will be all right."

The house seemed suddenly quiet and empty without Mama's omnipresence. Every curio, every vase of flowers, showed her touch. Mama made all things possible. Kate thought of the baby trying to be born in Peshtigo and prayed that her aunt would pull through.

Two days later, Lu chattered excitedly as the train carried them across the plains, past the parched farms and into Chicago. Inside the station they were surrounded by people going and coming and shouting greetings and instructions. Outside, where they found a hansom cab to take them to the home of the Jason Drake family, where they would be guests for the weekend, the lineup of drays and cabs and carriages was impressive.

"One hundred passenger trains every day," the driver told them proudly. "And more being added all the time." On their way down the avenue, he kept up a running monologue. " . . . dusty as the dickens . . . no rain for the last three weeks . . . but still the most exciting city you ladies will ever see in this part of the country . . ." He pointed out the sights, showing them the skyline, behind which could be seen the tracery of rigging he identified as ships and yachts on the Chicago River. "Yessir . . . boom town, boom times," he bragged.

Lu and Katrina strained to see every building, read every sign, peer in every shop window, and in general follow the constant commentary of their self-appointed guide. Even Ernestine's neck craned to take in the hustle and bustle of a city that seemed worlds away from Milwaukee.

"Ooh, I love it," Lu squealed with delight, squeezing Katrina's hand as she turned to catch a display in a shop they had just passed. "Let's go shopping first thing," she begged.

Katrina laughed. Why not? Shopping was Lu's very favorite pastime. "Driver?" Katrina gave the driver instructions to take Ernestine and their luggage to the Drake home, requesting that he let Lu and her out at the entrance to Field and Leiter's Department Store on State Street.

"Field and Leiter's," Lu breathed reverently as they entered the store. "They have everything, simply everything."

They moved through the store at a frantic pace, Lu's eyes constantly moving from one display and counter of wares to the next. On the third floor she spied a beautiful lace evening gown on exhibition. "It's from Paris," she whispered in awe.

"How do you know, and why are we whispering?" Katrina teased.

Lulu giggled and resumed her normal tone. "I saw a sketch of it in last month's issue of *Peterson's*. Isn't it simply magnificent?"

Katrina could not deny that it was indeed the most beautiful garment she had ever seen.

"Oh, Kate, try it on," Lulu urged.

"I couldn't," she said as a saleswoman approached. "Besides, I have a perfectly nice gown."

"You can wear that one to the opera on Monday. This one is so much prettier and perfect for the ball."

"May I be of assistance?"

Before Katrina could refuse, Lulu spoke up. "Yes, please. My sister would like to try on this gown, and please call for a seamstress for alterations."

"Lucinda," Katrina protested, but she was outnumbered. The saleswoman as well as a seamstress urged her into a fitting room and, under the watchful eye of Lulu, helped her to try on the gown.

"You see, it's too small," Katrina noted as she indicated the display of her bosom against the low neckline.

"Oh, no, my dear, quite the contrary. The cut is the latest thing in necklines from Paris," the seamstress assured her. "Our customers have been clamoring for the new design, and since we've frequently run out of stock, I've altered many a gown."

The saleswoman rushed in with gloves, ecru satin pumps, and ornaments for Katrina's hair.

"We'll take it," Lu announced.

"Lu . . ."

Her sister ignored her, leaving with the saleswoman to handle the details while Katrina dressed. " . . . delivered to the home of Mr. Jason Drake this afternoon. I believe my father has an account here?"

"It's ridiculous," Katrina continued to protest when they were back on the street and waiting for a hansom cab to take them to the Drake home. "Papa will be furious. You know his account is only for special occasions."

Lu dismissed all protests with a wave of her hand. "This is special. Besides, I was never satisfied with the gown you settled on in Milwaukee. Neither was Mama. Honestly, you show about as much interest in choosing a dress for a momentous occasion like this as you would picking one to wear for work. Ryan Sullivan's heart is absolutely going to stop when he sees you tonight."

13

Lu UNDERSTATED RYAN'S reaction. He had looked forward to the ball, to spending the evening as Kate's escort, dancing with her, having her at his side as they moved together through the gala event. But the moment he saw her, he was filled with desire for her and suddenly wanted her all to himself with no interruptions, no need for the polite amenities demanded in this social setting.

She entered the hotel ballroom on the arm of her host, Jason Drake. When they arrived, Ryan was standing across the large room, near the high, arched windows that led out to the balcony. The evening was unusually warm for October, and the doors were open to catch whatever breeze might stir.

Kate was a vision in a gown of melon-colored lace over rust taffeta. The color complemented the fiery highlights of her hair. She wore her hair loosely arranged in a cascade of curls that were lifted and caught here and there with combs trimmed in the lace of the gown. The wide neckline barely skimmed her shoulders, and in the candlelight of the room her features were accented by the play of shadow and light. In that moment she was every inch the woman she had been raised to be—wealthy, socially important, secure in the knowledge that her future was assured, as it had been from the day she was born.

Not for the first time since Kate had come into his life, Ryan felt the stirrings of his own baser roots. His position had been gained through luck and hard work, and at any given moment it was hardly assured. Only this evening he had had to endure Hauptman's displeasure when he realized that Ryan would be someone other than Carlotta's escort. "There are some elements of breeding, young man, that come as a birthright. They cannot be learned, only copied. Given your manners in this matter, I must say I am vastly disappointed, but somewhat relieved. I have told Carlotta for months that she can do better than you, sir, and perhaps now she will take my advice."

Ryan had taken the man's insults with barely a change in his expression. Even though he had never asked to escort Carlotta to the ball, he had accepted that she and her mother might simply assume his attendance on her. Weeks ago, he had gone out of his way to speak with Carlotta about his intention to spend the evening with Kate, ending his public visits to the Bergeman place in Lake Geneva in the process.

But though Carlotta had assured him she had her choice of many escorts and would hardly miss his attentions, she had clearly gone crying to her father. Carlotta had a vengeful streak and must have known that to make an issue of this would embarrass not only Ryan, but Kate as well. Ryan waited politely for Hauptman to finish, then commented, "I hope your daughter will find the happiness she deserves, sir. Would you prefer that I leave?"

At that Hauptman had been aghast. "Of course not. People would talk if you were not here. We are in business together, and no doubt several people here know of your attentions to Carlotta in the past. No, you would do her greater harm by leaving. Do you honestly think I would embarrass Mrs. Hauptman and Carlotta by throwing you out? This is a celebration, sir. Please mind your manners and stay away from my daughter, and everything will be fine."

A few moments later Ryan had overheard his host admonishing the hotel manager to "keep an eye on the Irishman. I want no trouble tonight."

Now here was Kate, clearly at home in her surroundings, at ease with the ostentatious finery of the place, comfortable with the chitchat of these people, who even though they were strangers, had everything in common with her and her family. She moved through the room on the arm of Jason Drake, gracefully nodding her head as introductions were made, extending her lace-gloved hand for a kiss from male guests, smiling politely at small talk.

Then she saw him, and in her expression Ryan saw that for her as for him the room had suddenly emptied. With barely a word to the Drakes, she started toward him, and he moved to meet her, take her in his arms and onto the dance floor as the string ensemble played a waltz.

Kate barely heard the names of the people Mr. and Mrs. Drake introduced as they moved with her into the large and crowded ballroom. Her eyes scanned the room for one person . . . Ryan. The use of only candles gave the room the effect of night shadows, which of course was the idea, as Lu had informed her. "She's actually going to have live swans swimming on little lakes!"

And swans and lakes there were, along with huge potted trees and fountains, bridges to span the distance from the tables to the dance floor, and the twinkling of a thousand candles to light the way. Lu and Edward were already on the dance floor. The Drakes had been some of the last guests to arrive, due to a business problem that had detained Mr. Drake. Kate had never been so nervous waiting to attend a social function. Usually she took such spectacles in stride, understanding their necessity but barely tolerating the anxiety and excitement others attached to the occasion.

Tonight she was to be with Ryan, and that made all the difference. Someone kissed her hand, and she heard a name. She nodded and smiled and looked past the gentleman's shoulder to where Ryan stepped out from the shadows and waited.

Had he ever looked more handsome? Had the features of any man ever set off the elegant black garb of evening so splendidly? In an instant Kate started toward him, drawn there by the expression that told her more clearly than any compliment how lovely she looked to him. Almost as an afterthought, she murmured apologies to the Drakes and then locked her gaze with Ryan's, speaking not one word until she was in his arms and moving with him in rhythm to the waltz.

"I thought you'd changed your mind," he said, flashing the wry smile that made her heart somersault.

"You look wonderful," she replied and then felt the color rise to her cheeks. What more stupid remark could she possibly have come up with? Damn her penchant for saying exactly what was on her mind. In the next breath she'd be announcing her love for him, for surely she did love this man. He filled her dreams. He was the beginning and end of every thought. Every plan she made was colored by what Ryan might think, want, or do.

Throughout the evening, they danced and exchanged gossip and dances with Edward and Lu. Ryan introduced Kate to several of his associates and their wives, and she could not help fantasizing that perhaps one day these women and their husbands would be her friends, coming for dinner, sharing information about the best place to go for meat and the availability of reliable help.

Around ten o'clock, the orchestra played a fanfare, and Carlotta was led by her father to the center of the room. Everyone gathered around for the inevitable toasts and speeches.

"Let's escape," Ryan whispered, his hand at Kate's waist, his breath warm on her ear.

She glanced at him over her shoulder. They were standing near a set of French doors that led out to the balcony.

"No one's going to notice," he observed, indicating everyone's rapt attention to the festivities before them.

"Shouldn't you make a toast?"

At that he laughed out loud. "I doubt that would be very welcome. Come on."

As he had predicted, no one noticed their exit, and the air was ever so much cooler on the balcony. The only light came from the ballroom behind them and the city before them.

"Why aren't you making a toast?" she persisted.

He told her of his conversation with Carlotta's father.

"But that's horrible. You told her . . . She told Lu . . ." Kate faltered for a moment as she remembered Carlotta's flippant remark that Ryan was beneath her social standards anyway.

"She told Lu what?"

"Never mind."

He was quiet for a moment. "Katie, are you going to be able to live with this?" He did not look at her but stared out toward the skyline.

"I don't understand. Live with what?"

"The comments, the prejudice. After all . . ."

Her mind was a jumble. What was he asking? Her heart raced with anticipation and fear. "Ryan?"

He sighed and turned to her, taking her hands in his and pulling her close. "I love you, Katie Bergeman. I've no right to love you. I've told myself a thousand times there will be nothing but heartache for us if I love you . . . that you deserve more. Certainly your father knows that. Still . . ."

Kate could not keep the smile off her face. "Say it again," she whispered, having digested nothing more than his declaration.

He grinned down at her and caressed her cheek. "I love you . . . from the impertinent flash of those gorgeous eyes to the tips of your satin shoes. I have tried to tell myself it is nothing more than raw desire for something I cannot have, but it goes deeper. You move me, Katie, in ways I thought were long dead. You arouse not only my passion, but also my zeal for living. You make me want to do things, accomplish things, build a future. I see a future when I think of you . . . and that is new for me, Katie. For a very long time now, I have seen only today, never tomorrow."

Kate had never been so happy, and yet the tears welled. No one had ever spoken words that moved her so. With Ryan all things were possible . . . all dreams were possible. They would have such joy, such bliss.

"But, Katie—"

Immediately her fingers were against his lips to silence him. "No," she whispered, not wanting to hear even one doubt. Not now. Now she wanted only to savor the moment.

He seemed to understand, for he nodded slightly as he pulled her into his arms and kissed her with an ardor that left no doubt of his feelings. For the second time that night, there were only the two of them, alone on a balcony, high above the city that stretched on to the lake. There in the shadows she reveled in the taste of him, the sensation of his mouth on the exposed skin of her throat and shoulders, his hands possessing her breasts, his hips pressed hard against hers.

"I want you, Katie," he said as his mouth moved over the decolletage of her gown, his fingers pressing the fabric lower to give him access. By instinct her fingers locked in his thick hair, encouraging his most intimate contact.

Knowing he could not have her here or even tonight, Ryan understood the need for restraint. Still, even as he reluctantly came to his senses, he could not resist trailing kisses up the slim column of her throat. "I have something for you," he said as they stood close together and allowed the passion that had flamed through each of them to ebb.

He reached into the pocket of his white waistcoat and removed a thin silver ring, engraved to resemble entwined vines. "It was my mother's wedding ring," he said softly. "Her body washed up on shore two days after the wreck. Before I buried her, I decided to keep this." He placed it on the ring finger of her right hand. "It's not the kind of jewelry you deserve, but for me it represents something very beautiful between a very special man and woman. Will you wear it as a pledge of my love until we can shop for something more fitting?"

"I will wear it always," Kate said, and then reaching to kiss him, she added, "I love you so much."

The solitude they had enjoyed was suddenly interrupted by the arrival of several of the male guests on the balcony. Ignoring the lovers in the shadows, they seemed intent on straining to get a view of the orange glow that lit the sky to the west.

"Fire," one of them declared, and others took up the cry. "Fire!" The clanging of the courthouse bell accented their calls.

Ryan moved to join them, his arm still protectively around Kate. A fire engine careened around the corner on the street below, its horses driven at full gallop, its wood-burning boiler sending clouds of steam and smoke from its stacks. In a moment it was gone, leaving only a wake of glowing cinders to mark its path.

The men were abuzz with commentary. Dozens of fires had broken out across the city just in the past week. While Chicago enjoyed the services of a professional fire department, the men were exhausted, and the equipment was badly in need of repair and maintenance. The men on the balcony began to speak of volunteering.

"We could at least help with crowd control," one man said, and others agreed.

"As dry as it's been, the whole city is nothing but tinder. I have warehouses in that area, packed with merchandise . . ."

"Aye," Ryan agreed, drawn into the conversation as the courthouse bell sounded the second alarm. "It could spread."

"Listen," one man said, holding up his hand for silence as they concentrated on the tolling of the courthouse bell.

"What is it?" Kate whispered.

"A telegraphic network carries the alarms from the alarm boxes to a central office in the courthouse. From there the signals are relayed to the closest fire station and tolled on the bell." He listened for a moment. "This is a new signal," he said tensely. "The fire has already spread."

In moments a plan was made. The younger men would leave immediately to offer their services to the fire department. The ladies would be seen safely home by the older men. Carlotta could be heard wailing her dismay at how this turn of events was spoiling her party.

"I'm afraid for you," Kate whispered as Ryan led her back inside to the Drake table.

He stopped in the shadow of a large potted palm and kissed her hard. "I have to go. I know people with property in that area; there are families nearby that cannot afford to lose the little they have. I have to go," he repeated, his eyes beseeching her to understand.

She knew he spoke of working people, people he had known as a boy, people he knew now because he did not divorce himself from his roots ever. Of course he had to go. "I understand," she said and kissed him again.

On the ride home the conversation was of the fire, the unseasonably warm weather, and the foolhardiness of young men who dash off to assist people they don't know and who probably will not appreciate their daring. Kate turned her attention to Lu, who was trembling with fright because Edward had elected to follow Ryan.

"Ryan will see that he doesn't get hurt," Kate promised.

When they arrived at the stately Drake mansion, Kate noticed that the courthouse bell was silent. She hoped that was a good sign.

No one could think of going to bed. They all gathered in the parlor to await some news. Mr. Drake had several callers, men he did business with, who came to report the progress of the fire.

"It seems to be fairly well confined to one area," he told

the women, but his expression of anxiety did nothing to reassure them.

A few hours later, Edward arrived, reporting that the fire had been devastating, laying waste four city blocks of warehouses, mills, and factories. "I never saw anything like it," he muttered again and again as the Drakes plied him with brandy to control the shaking of his hands, and Lu hovered next to him, her face lined with worry.

"It was the most incredible thing," he continued after a while, going on as if he had never stopped speaking. "People everywhere . . . on rooftops, clogging the streets and alleys with their carriages and carts . . . all come to watch . . . as if it were a damned circus . . ."

He was so distraught he did not apologize for or even seem to notice his language, and no one seemed to expect it of him.

"You're exhausted," Mrs. Drake said. "Let me have Evans draw a bath for you."

"Ja." Edward nodded, lapsing into German. *"Ja,"* he repeated quietly, but his eyes were riveted on the crystal glass he held. Then after a moment he looked at Lu with tears in his eyes. "Some people probably lost everything," he whispered. "Can you imagine having to start again . . . with nothing?"

"Oh, Edward, it's all right. You did what you could," Lu soothed, cradling his head against her shoulder and rocking him.

All the while Kate longed to ask of Ryan. Edward had arrived alone, and so far he had said nothing of his friend. Kate tried to quell the horrible thoughts that passed through her mind. Ryan could be hurt . . . Ryan could have been burned . . . Ryan might be pinned under some smoldering piece of debris . . .

"Edward," she ventured, and the fear in her question was plain on her face. Instinctively she played with the silver ring Ryan had placed on her finger.

"He's fine, Kate. Exhausted . . . seems this is not exactly

his first time out this week. The professionals all seemed to know and respect him. I'd say he's been there before. He went home to get some rest."

"A good idea for all of us," Jason Drake said and rose from his chair as an indication that the evening was at an end. "Mueller, so glad to have you back in one piece. Mrs. Drake will send Evans to attend you. Ladies . . ." He nodded toward the door and the stairway, indicating they should precede him and go to their rooms.

Kate led the way and, reluctantly, Lu followed. The butler, Evans, passed them in the hall on his way to minister to Edward's needs. They heard Mrs. Drake giving directions and then the house was quiet.

On Sunday Kate, Lu, and Edward attended morning mass with their cousins. Kate watched for Ryan, but he did not appear. The only thing she saw was Cousin Eloise's disapproving frowns.

After church Eloise, Kate, Lu, and Carlotta shared the family carriage while the men rode home on horseback. Eloise seized the moment to make her displeasure known.

"Katrina, my dear, I hope you understand that in the absence of your mother I feel duty-bound to watch out for your best interests. I can tell you frankly that I do not believe Mr. Ryan Sullivan a suitable escort for your stay here."

"Really, Cousin? And yet not a few months ago he was perfectly suitable for Carlotta."

"Don't be impertinent, missy. It cannot have escaped your notice how he cast poor Carlotta aside on the very eve of the ball. I wonder that you have the nerve to give the man the time of day. After all, his lack of breeding goes without saying, but—"

The look Kate gave Eloise stopped her in mid-sentence. "Cousin Eloise, I do not doubt that you feel a responsibility for my honor, as you seem to have felt a responsibility for saving me from the eternal damnation of spinsterhood."

The shocked gasps of Carlotta and Eloise did not deter Kate from delivering the message she had held back for years. "Allow me to set your mind at ease and free you to pursue your good deeds on behalf of some other poor soul. You see, not only am I of age and therefore perfectly capable of choosing whom to spend time with, but Mr. Ryan Sullivan has solved all your worst fears by asking me to be his wife."

At this she flashed the silver band which she had quietly moved to her left hand during the making of her speech. She only prayed that Ryan would not be too upset with her small lie once she explained it was for the best of causes. He had called the ring a pledge of his love. That was hardly the same as a proposal of marriage.

Lu squealed with delight. "You stinker! Why on earth did you keep this to yourself?"

Kate grinned. "It was a busy and frightening evening. I thought this could wait for a more appropriate time." She turned her attention back to Carlotta and Eloise. "Well, cousins, don't I get your best wishes as well?"

"You . . . you . . . can't be serious," Eloise tittered, then collapsed against the upholstered carriage seat as if she were about to faint. "What on earth will your father say?"

"He'll probably say I'm making a mistake," Kate said. "I'll have to disagree with him, of course."

"It's hardly much of a ring," Carlotta smirked. "Or has Ryan had another financial setback?"

"It is a ring that has more value than any diamond or emerald you could find," Kate said quietly. "It is a ring that was forged from love and trust and respect between a very special man and woman. I hope you are fortunate enough to wear such a ring someday, Carlotta."

There was no more conversation as the carriage pulled up to the Hauptmans' portico. Carlotta sulked, Eloise moaned, and Lu just kept shaking her head and giggling with delight.

"Sweetheart, guess what?" Edward and Lu said simultaneously as Edward assisted Lu from the carriage.

"You first." Lu giggled again, barely able to contain her news.

"Ryan is here. He's proposed a tour of the city for the four of us. We're invited to lunch at his home." He nodded toward the curb, where Ryan waited with his driver and carriage, his eyes on Kate.

"Then let's go," Kate said, and without a word to Eloise or Carlotta, she led the way down the walk to where Ryan waited. Behind her she could hear Lu excitedly whispering the news to Edward.

"What?" Edward exclaimed. Then he added a puzzled "But, Herr Bergeman . . . ," which Lu dismissed as she admonished him to be happy for her sister and not spoil anything by expressing his doubts, at least for today.

Kate hastened her step, determined to get to Ryan before Lu and Edward. When she reached him, he took both her hands in his and kissed them.

"I have to speak with you privately for a moment," she said, glancing uneasily over her shoulder to gauge the arrival of Lu and Edward.

"And I have to speak to you . . . darling Katie, do you know how much I love you?" he said softly. "Do you know how much I would like to run away and leave your sister and Edward, as much as I adore both of them, to spend the afternoon with just you . . . kissing you . . . holding you . . ."

"Congratulations, Ryan," Edward called as he and Lu reached the carriage. "I couldn't be happier for both of you."

Kate took in Ryan's confused expression and then the dawning of realization as Lu added, "Of course, Cousin Eloise practically had a cow, but that was half the fun. I mean, Kate was magnificent—just flashed that ring and announced it."

Kate's grip on Ryan's fingers tightened, hoping to send some silent signal that he should not give her away, especially since she could see Eloise and Carlotta watching from the portico. Instead, he turned on her and frowned.

"You told them we are to be married?"

She nodded miserably. If only she had had a chance to explain, if only he had heard Eloise, if only . . .

"Ah, Katie, darling, I was hoping we could tell them together." His disappointment was tempered by the smile he gave her.

"What?"

"I had hoped we could make the announcement together, and of course your parents should really be the first . . ."

Lu interrupted, ever eager to smooth over any situation. "Yes, but if you could have heard Eloise, and she's been tormenting Kate forever, and it was just so delicious the way Kate was able to just spring it on them."

Ryan laughed at the image, then glanced toward the portico and tipped his hat with a low bow to Carlotta and Eloise. "Thank you for your good wishes, ladies," he called. "With you on our side, we're off to a good start."

The reaction of the Hauptmans was to scurry into the house. Ryan's reaction was to laugh with delight and then give Kate a resounding kiss on her beautiful, puzzled mouth. "You will marry me, won't you?" he whispered.

All she could do was nod.

14

WAS IT THE extraordinary events of the day that made it seem as if the air stood still and the entire city of Chicago functioned in an atmosphere of almost eerie calm? As if in a dream, Kate moved through the rest of that Sunday afternoon.

Lulu insisted on following the throngs of carriages to the scene of the previous night's fire. The mood of the sightseers was almost festive, as if the devastation were some show for them to view and admire. But faced with the ravaged ruins of businesses that had been completely leveled by the fire, Lu fell silent, and she was moved to tears when she spotted the charred remains of a child's stuffed toy. Kate could almost see the child dropping the toy as his family ran for their very lives.

"Let's go," Lu whispered. "It's horrible."

Edward put his arm around her, and Ryan gave his driver instructions.

"It was dreadful," Edward said after a moment. "By the time Ryan and I and the others arrived from the ball, there was little we could do."

"Indeed, we probably contributed to the mayhem already present," Ryan added. "People are so strange. They had actually left their homes and climbed on top of roofs and fence posts for a better view. Their carts and wagons made passage impossible for the fire equipment, jamming the streets and sidewalks." He shook his head at the memory of the catastrophe.

"It seems to have spread so far and so quickly," Kate noted.

Ryan nodded. "Four city blocks . . . gone." He snapped his fingers for emphasis. "Not to mention that several pieces of needed equipment were rendered useless, and with this drought continuing . . ."

"And where will the people go? How will they manage?" Kate looked around and saw that there was little chance of salvaging anything.

No one answered her. Edward simply shrugged. Lu closed her eyes, and Ryan stared into the distance, his thoughts clearly elsewhere. It was little comfort that few families had been affected. Even one person left homeless with winter on the way was one too many.

By contrast to the scene of devastation they had just left, Ryan's home was magnificent. Kate was struck by the simple elegance of the furnishings. Nothing was over-done. Every piece of art and furniture seemed to have been chosen carefully for the way it would fit with every other piece.

In the library, where Ryan left them while he went to confer with his cook, the walls were lined with volumes of oft-read books on many subjects. Kate could not help noticing the amount of shelf space given over to literature and poetry, a discovery that made her feel even closer to Ryan.

Lunch was served in the sunny dining room and consisted of baked chicken with vegetables, freshly baked lemon bread, and wine. For dessert the butler offered bowls of fresh raspberries on shortbread biscuits, with mounds of whipped cream to top them.

"Did you grow these berries yourself?" Kate teased, reminding him of the comment he had made about the strawberries at her parents' house.

Ryan looked uncomfortable enough that she knew he was remembering as well, and he sent a warning glance toward Edward and Lu.

"Really, Katrina, where on earth would Ryan raise berries in the city?" Lu protested.

Kate just raised her eyebrows and smiled as she bit into a berry. "Well, they certainly are dark and surprisingly sweet," she said softly.

Ryan actually blushed. "Coffee, anyone?" He stood and went himself to the sideboard for the coffee service.

One thing Kate had noticed since they arrived at Ryan's home: he was very uncomfortable with servants. In fact, the butler had had to rush to perform his normal duties of opening the door or taking the men's hats and the ladies' wraps, lest Ryan beat him to it. Lunch had been served as unobtrusively as possible, with a minimum of ceremony. Having always seen Ryan in other settings, where he seemed self-assured and firmly in charge, Kate found it endearing to see him at home, where he clearly was uncomfortable with the details of entertaining.

"This is such a lovely townhouse," Edward commented as Ryan ushered them back to the parlor after lunch. "What kind of staff do you employ to manage it?"

"Oh, just Emma and Thomas."

"Really?" Lu was aghast that two people could handle such a large place. Kate found it charming.

"Well, if they need help, they know they can bring anyone in. Of course there's also Kevin, the driver . . . He's Emma and Thomas's son. Speaking of which, are we going to spend this whole afternoon indoors? I thought you folks wanted to see the city."

The rest of the afternoon was spent walking around Ryan's neighborhood, enjoying the changing colors of the season and the warmth of the October day. Kevin drove them to the Tremont Hotel, near Ryan's office, where they shared afternoon tea. Then they drove along Lake Park to the elegant estates and homes of the Hauptmans and their neighbors.

"Will you come to church with me?" Kate asked Ryan as he helped her from the carriage. "The family is expected at evening services, and I think we've upset Cousin Eloise quite enough for one day," she added with a smile.

"Would you forgive me if I said no? You see, I've been thinking about those friends who were burned out last night. I have an idea for setting up some sort of relief. I thought if I could reach some business associates and friends, we might be able to have something in place by tomorrow."

"Ryan, what a wonderful idea. I want to help."

He smiled and gave her a hug. "Tomorrow. This part is all talk—calling on the contacts, getting them to make some commitment. You go on to services with your cousins. Tomorrow you can help me . . . I'll call for you early, and we'll have the day together before the opera tomorrow evening." The finale of the weekend's festivities was to be the gala reopening of the renovated Crosby Opera House.

Kate was reluctant to leave him. So much had happened in just the past twenty-four hours. Had he really asked her to marry him? Had she really accepted? Or was this all just a fantasy?

"I love you, Katie." He said it out loud in the full bright glow of the late afternoon sun. She was not dreaming.

"I love you too," she answered and could not suppress the smile of joy that thought brought with it.

They both laughed in delight and then reached for each other, kissing in full view of anyone who might happen to pass or to peer out from the draped windows of the mansions that lined the street.

"Tomorrow," Ryan said, then kissed her again. "I'll arrange my schedule and return with you to Milwaukee on Tuesday so that I may speak with your parents as soon as possible."

"Yes," she answered and kissed him back.

"Katrina . . . ," Lu whispered, and her tone was one of warning.

Kate glanced over her shoulder and saw Cousin Eloise standing at the open door, but she took her time leaving Ryan's arms.

"I don't care," she fussed as Lu and Edward chastised her, when the carriage had pulled away and they were moving up the walk to where Eloise waited.

"You should care," Edward warned. "This is all going to get back to your father—with embellishments only Eloise can provide. You are already in a great deal of trouble, I fear."

Kate shrugged and looked back in time to see Ryan's carriage turn the corner with Ryan hanging out the back, waving and blowing her kisses. The ridiculousness of that sight made her smile.

"*Guten Abend,* cousin," she said serenely as she moved calmly past Eloise and into the house, where Carlotta sulked at the opening to the music room. "Oh, dear Carlotta," Kate said, "thank you so much for including Lucinda and I in your festivities. It has been the happiest time I've ever known." Without further ado, she planted a kiss on her cousin's cheek.

When Christian Hauptman started to lecture her on deportment, Kate gave him her most radiant smile. "Oh, Cousin, I know my behavior has been . . . questionable, but do you understand that I am in love . . . that I have become engaged? Surely I cannot be held completely responsible for all my lapses at such a moment. Come along, Lu, we really must get changed for dinner and church."

She led the way up the stairs to the room where their things had been moved from the Drakes' home. Now that the ball was over, family members who had stayed with Cousin Eloise had left for home, and Lu and Kate were to spend the rest of their visit in the Hauptman home.

Dinner was a strained affair with conversation that stopped and started again, surrounded by uneasy silence and the clink of silver on china. By the time the meal was finally at an end, Evans had appeared to announce the readiness of the family carriage to convey them all to evening services.

Kate did not hear a word of the priest's sermon, nor did she really absorb much of her surroundings, but rather used the time and the solitude to reflect on the incredible day.

Ryan loved her. More than that, he wanted to marry her. How like him to dispense with the normal propriety of a long courtship following the declaration of his intentions. No, being Ryan, he would take action. They had talked before about the shared feeling that they had been robbed of many good times because of the war. No, Ryan would not tolerate any custom that prevented their being together. He was going home with her to speak to Papa, for heaven's sake!

She could not suppress her smile as she knelt with the others for the benediction. It was then that she became aware of the tolling of the bell.

At first she thought it was the carillon of the cathedral, but once outside, she realized it was coming from the courthouse. It was nearly ten o'clock.

"Another fire," Edward said and looked worriedly toward the south.

"You aren't going," Lu protested.

"No. I'd be little help."

Kate scanned the sky for signs of smoke or flame. The wind had picked up, blowing warm and gusty now out of the southwest. "Edward, you have to find Ryan," she said, clutching her friend's arm. "He'll go there and he's already exhausted. He could be hurt."

Edward began to shake his head.

"Please," Kate pleaded.

"I'll go to his house. It's the best I can do. If he's not there . . ."

"His office . . . do you remember where his office is?"

"I remember, but—"

"Go there. He was going to organize some relief. He's probably working there now. Please, Edward."

"He'll be all right, Kate," Edward said soothingly, but she was near tears.

"I'm so afraid he'll try to go and help, and what we saw today . . . it was so awful."

"All right, Kate. But I'm sure you're making too much of this."

Kate agreed. She didn't know what had come over her. She had complete confidence in Ryan's ability to slay dragons, much less survive a simple fire. But throughout the day she had felt this undercurrent of something powerful, something that now seemed ominous. The idea of losing Ryan after having just found him had popped unbidden into her thoughts. Her sense of panic was unfamiliar. She felt on the brink of something whose outcome she couldn't predict.

"Thank you," she whispered, and hugged Edward.

The Hauptmans seemed unconcerned with the prospect of another fire. It was clearly miles away, on the other side of the Chicago River which bisected the city on its way to Lake Michigan. They had had an exhausting weekend and wanted nothing more than to get all their guests settled for the night and go to bed themselves.

"There's no cause for us to lose sleep tonight," Christian Hauptman announced. "Tomorrow will be soon enough to survey the damage."

"But, Christian," Eloise protested tearfully when the courthouse bell continued to toll long after they had reached the house.

"There, there, my dear. The fire is on the other side of the river. The flames can hardly move across water." Then he chuckled and gave his wife a comforting hug.

Lu and Kate shared a room that faced south. In silence they changed into their nightgowns. When Ernestine had hung their clothes and turned back the covers on their beds, she bid them both good night and retired to the servants' quarters on the fourth floor. Uncustomarily, Lu did not chatter on about the day or Edward or even the remarkable news of Kate's impending engagement.

"Good night," she said softly and settled into the covers.

Kate remained where she had been for the past several minutes, near the window, gazing out at the ever brighter sky. Edward had returned just before midnight to report that the financial district was in flames. Kate had noticed that Christian Hauptman's reaction to this news was something less than the hearty and secure outlook he had offered just an hour earlier.

"And Ryan?"

Edward had looked at Kate for a long moment. "I couldn't get through. The streets are jammed with traffic, and the police are trying to prevent spectators from gathering. I'm sorry."

She now stood at the window in the dark room, wondering where he could be and trying desperately to quell the overwhelming feeling that he needed her, that he was in danger.

The courthouse bell reverberated somberly in the distance.

Because the alarm boxes were locked to prevent false alarms and keys were given only to citizens considered trustworthy, the first alarm had not been registered until the fire had already been blazing for half an hour. Fed by a strong wind, the fire spread in what seemed no time at all from the O'Leary barn, where it had started, to the very heart of the city.

Ryan first became aware of the sounds of panic before he actually heard the alarm. He was working in his office. Having had some success in contacting his associates, he was engrossed in establishing a relief plan for those who had been burned out in Saturday night's fire. He had thought himself alone in the large building, but soon became aware of the sound of shouting and running and doors opening and closing.

He moved into the hall, where he was met by a chaotic scene of panicked men dragging papers and trunks and whole file cabinets from their offices, bumping them along behind them as they hurried down the stairs and out to the street.

Following them, Ryan encountered even greater pandemonium once he reached the street. Fire engines tore down the street, pulled by teams of horses frothing at the mouth and rearing in excitement. The sky to the south and west was bright as day, and everywhere people were running, shouting, arguing, yelling, screaming. Men he recognized as business associates rushed to and from office buildings, piling reams of files and documents and possessions onto carts and wagons, waving sums of cash at any passing conveyance that might carry them and their belongings to safety.

He returned to his office and quickly unlocked the safe, removed the cash he had there, and paused to retrieve a few bonds and certificates before racing back down the stairs, along the way dodging men crazed with panic and fear.

Outside he moved toward what was obviously the center of the catastrophe. He fought his way against the flood of people who moved rapidly toward him. Finally spotting a policeman, Ryan asked about the fire, but the man just kept walking in the other direction, his eyes glassy, his features without expression.

The wind was hot with the heat of the flames and came in gusts that sounded like waves breaking off Lake Michigan onto the shore. At Adams Street he encountered a group of men wandering around, looking frightened, as if unsure of where to go, what to do. Ryan had seen those expressions before . . . that night on the *Lady Elgin* . . . that same terror, the horror of being completely at the mercy of something uncontrollable.

He turned onto Clark and kept moving. Now he was running, his thoughts focused only on getting there, helping in any way he could, not letting disaster take over again. By the time he reached the next block, he was racing through showers of cinders that fell all around him. With every step the sky grew lighter.

Everywhere there were people, standing in the street or leaning out from their windows. They were quiet, as if waiting for something or someone to tell them what to do. He passed a tavern and saw the proprietor rolling barrels of beer into the street, pouring drinks for everyone, hoping to prevent the looting and vandalism that could accompany such a disaster.

Ryan started to run toward Van Buren Street, the southern boundary of Saturday's fire, dodging the places where the raised wooden sidewalks had been ignited by the flying cinders, carried on the wind from the heart of the fire, still blocks away. When he reached Polk Street, the crossroads was solidly packed with people and carts and carriages. A man stood on the roof of a four-story brick building and shouted to the crowd, his hands wildly gesticulating to emphasize his point. But whatever he was shouting was lost in the roar of the wind.

Suddenly a murmur raced through the crowd. " . . . river . . . both sides . . . leapt the river? . . . both sides . . ." and all of Ryan's focus turned to Kate. If the fire had crossed the river, it could reach the Hauptmans—it could reach Kate.

Ryan turned and pushed his way back through the crowd. He had to get to the nearest bridge. He had to get across the river. He had to get to Kate.

The pounding on the Hauptmans' door started around one in the morning. Kate was awake, keeping her vigil by the window, watching as the sky lightened, as the window became warm to her touch, as the trees swayed as if in a January blizzard. She heard the excited voices of Christian Hauptman, her cousin Emil, and the servants.

"Lu, wake up," she urged, drawing on her wrapper and instinctively putting on her shoes.

"What," Lu fussed, but one look at the orange sky outside the window and her eyes were wide open and filled with alarm. "Oh, Katrina," she wailed.

"Get dressed," Kate urged.

Just then the door flew open, and a very agitated Ernestine burst into the room. "Oh, it's terrible," she cried as she raced through the room throwing anything she could find into valises and trunks. "The mistress says we're to pack as much as possible and bring it out to the street. The mister is getting a wagon for hauling. The Drakes' carriage house is on fire. The butler is burying some money in the backyard. Oh, Lord help us all."

There was mayhem throughout the house. The laments of Eloise carried up the wide staircase from the front foyer, where she was admonishing the servants to gather the silver, the china, everything of value.

Kate assisted Ernestine while Lu dressed. For herself she grabbed a shawl to pull over her gown and wrapper as she raced with Lu and the others down the front stairway and out to the street.

Had there not been genuine reason for panic, the scene that greeted them there would have been quite comical. Up and down the street people had heaped their worldly goods into teetering piles in the middle of the street. Furniture, baskets loaded with silver and art objects, even a grand piano, had been dragged out into the road. Some of the finest homes in the city of Chicago stood open-doored and gaslighted but empty, as the residents fled.

Christian Hauptman was bidding with his neighbor for the use of a passing wagon already loaded with goods. "Here," Hauptman screamed, pressing bills and coins into the hands of the driver. Then with Emil's help he began to hoist trunks and cartons onto the already overloaded conveyance.

"Christian," Eloise wailed. She was encumbered by several gowns and three cloaks she had donned, one on top of the other, in an effort to save them. In her hand she clutched a satchel of jewelry.

"Mama!" Carlotta shrieked as she was pushed and shoved by the passing parade of terrorized citizens running, galloping on horseback, and whipping their teams into ever greater action, as their wagons and carriages crashed through fences and along sidewalks toward safety. People ran about as if insane, shouting and crying and knocking into one another.

Emil lifted his sister and deposited her on top of a trunk on the back of the wagon, then climbed on with her. Christian assisted Eloise into the family carriage, which was also brimming with possessions, and shouted an address at Edward. "Bring the girls and come to . . ." The rest was lost on the wind.

Edward said something to Kate and Lu, but even though he shouted, his words were only a pantomime against the competition of the screaming masses and the incessant wind. Realizing the pointlessness of words, he grabbed Lu's hand and gestured for Kate to follow as they started off in the general direction the Hauptman family had headed.

As they ran, Kate became aware of the choking smoke and stifling heat and the shower of cinders, carried by the wind and descending on them like a snowfall. She watched in horrible fascination as flakes of smoldering ash settled on her sister's gown and cloak and on Edward's back. She reached to brush them away, only to have them replaced by a dozen more.

It seemed as if the entire populace of the world were running down that street, their faces blackened with dust and soot, their mouths open and twisted by their shouts and moans of desperation. Twice Kate was nearly knocked down as some citizen rushed past, pulling a trunk or some other valuable behind. When Lu fell after being bumped by a horse, the tidal wave of humanity paused only to step around or over her and keep going. It was only through the quick action of Edward and Kate that she was saved from being trampled and was pulled to the relative safety of an abandoned heap of household goods.

"I can't," she wailed, and Kate saw that she was quite terrified, trembling and wild-eyed. And with every moment they delayed, the smoke was getting thicker, making it almost impossible to see and breathe.

Among the cluster of rummage around her, Kate spotted a wheelbarrow filled with cartons of books and motioned to Edward. "Take that," she shouted. "Lu can ride . . . You can push . . . Go on . . ."

Edward unceremoniously dumped the books into the street and presented the wheelbarrow to Lu with a flourish. "Your chariot awaits, my lady."

Kate could see that he was trying hard to stem his own rising panic. Alone they could make it, but he did not have the time or the strength to worry about Kate keeping up. "Go on," she urged. "Try to head for the station."

Edward and Lu were already being swept along by the throngs. "No," Edward shouted. "The Hauptmans said to come to the Sholes' house on Fullerton Avenue."

So he had heard Christian Hauptman after all. Kate felt a sense of relief at having some destination. "I'll come," she shouted.

"Come on," Edward cried, and she saw that Lu was straining to keep her in sight.

But the running and the smoke and the fear had made Kate short of breath, and the never-ending stream of men, women, and children widened the gulf that separated them.

"I'll get there," Kate screamed, waving, forcing a reassuring smile to her smoke-blackened face. Helplessly she watched them go, wondering if she were seeing them for the last time, knowing now what Ryan had experienced that ghastly night when the *Lady Elgin* went down, taking his family with it.

She sank down onto a damask-covered sofa in the middle of the street and watched as a spark caught and followed the trail of ivy up the pillar of the house across the street. She looked up at darkened windows, lighted now by the glare of the approaching fire. She closed her eyes and fought against the wave of fear, nausea, and sobbing that threatened to overpower her. She struggled to breathe deeply but could not because the air was thick with choking smoke and soot. She could hear explosions as combustible items caught fire. This must be what it's like to go into battle, she thought.

Ryan loves you, she heard from somewhere deep in her soul, and then it became a chant. Something inborn gave her the will to get up and move on. He would find a way to get to her, and she had to be there. She could not give up. Ryan knew how to survive; now she must learn as well. She beat out an ash that had ignited at the hem of her robe and tore away the smoldering fabric. Wrapping the shawl tightly around her face and hair, she dove into the mass of people once again and allowed herself to be carried along toward what she prayed was safety.

15

BY THE TIME Ryan reached the courthouse square, it was after two in the morning, and yet the flames made every street bright enough to read by. The wind acted as a giant bellows, fanning the fire and giving it a constant energy to seek out new fuel. Firefighters had long since abandoned the effort, having seen that even as they tried to contain the blaze at one point, fireballs were literally leaping over their heads and igniting the buildings behind them.

The sound was dreadful—buildings crashing to the street, explosions from storehouses of oil and kerosene, the crackle of wood up and down every alley, where in every yard residents had laid in their store of fuel for the coming winter, and always the ceaseless roar of the wind. Against this tumultuous background, the wails of the people were like open-mouthed but silent screams of agony. It was a city brought to its knees, a city that had once seemed invincible now being systematically destroyed block by block by the raging fire.

At the courthouse people were gathered as if lost. Abandoned animals wandered around, skittish to every sound, every touch. Men shouted directions and instructions while their women wept and their children stared wide-eyed at the inferno that surrounded them seemingly on every side.

Along the river and on the lake the hoots of tugs could be heard occasionally above the chaos as they tried to steer larger vessels to safe harbor. The streets had become nearly impassable with carts, wagons, and discarded possessions.

Ryan watched with the others in silent awe as the courthouse belfry caught, burned, and finally crashed to the ground with a shock that shook the earth where they stood. That bell had tolled a thousand events, Ryan thought, remembering how he had stood in this very spot on the night it tolled for slain President Lincoln lying in state.

As if the fall of the bell tower were some signal, the masses began to move north. Along the way Ryan witnessed every possible spectacle such a disaster could offer. Here were looters raiding the piles of forsaken possessions, uncaring of the cartons and trunks they discarded into the passing throng as they searched for treasure. There were citizens drunk and still drinking from the barrels and bottles tavernkeepers offered in the hopes of preventing their establishments from being looted and sacked. And as they moved north into the more affluent neighborhoods, Ryan observed the yawning desolation of the mansions where he had socialized and conducted business with many of the city's leaders, houses standing abandoned and deserted, their doors open to anyone who wished to enter.

Every step the masses took was dogged by the relentless fire. At one point the crowd was stopped cold as the narrow passage ahead suddenly flamed and closed, and people were literally surrounded on all sides by the conflagration. Then suddenly the wind shifted, and a way was clear; the mob poured through, running for their very lives, lest the passage close again.

When he reached the block where the Hauptmans lived, Ryan's heart pounded, and his eyes strained to see the house. It was still standing, open-doored and empty. In the street he saw the settee from the parlor and Carlotta's piano. Nearby lay the shattered remains of the family china. He raced up the walk and into the front hall.

"Kate," he shouted. "Kate!" He then returned to the yard and ran around to the back, where the barn had just ignited.

He saw a servant at the Drake house across the way, racing from the house with some treasure. "You there," he cried, hoping for some news, but the man, thinking himself caught in the act of stealing, ran faster and disappeared down the alley.

Where might the family have gone for safety? *Think,* he ordered himself and mentally ticked off the closest associates of the Hauptmans. Seizing a horse blanket from the stables, Ryan wrapped his face and head to ward off the escalating blizzard of cinder and ash. There was only one direction they could have gone. He started trudging north.

Once he saw a woman huddled against an abandoned wagon, her features blackened, her hair singed and burned. At first his heart stopped, for she could have been Kate. He hurried to her and touched her shoulder. The woman opened her eyes and stared blankly at him. It was not Kate, but he lifted her all the same and carried her through the streets until he found a driver who would take her.

He had to find Kate. *Please God, let her be all right.* He walked with his head down, his face averted from the heat and smoke. When he reached Ontario Street, he turned toward the lake. Perhaps if he could reach the shore, it would be easier to breathe, easier to move. He could make better time along that route. If he could get to Government Pier, he might be able to find a way to his yacht. He could sail along the shoreline, seeking information, looking for Kate and Lu and Edward. He doubled the rhythm of his steps with a renewed determination to find them.

By four in the morning Kate had wandered up and down strange streets, pulled along with the ebb and flow of the crowd, until she was thoroughly disoriented. She was surprised to turn a corner and find herself within sight of Lake Michigan. Of course. Why hadn't she thought of it before?

The fire would have to stop at the water—the lake would save her. It had always been a source of comfort and rescue; now it would be her very means of deliverance.

But the scene that greeted her there was less than glorious. Thousands of refugees huddled along the shore or wandered aimlessly through the growing crowd. Their constant movement reminded her of the perpetually shifting design of Mama's kaleidoscope, as shapes melded and separated in unceasing motion. Fights broke out, and everywhere men who were drunk or lecherous or both reached for her, grabbing at her arm, touching her skin, calling out their lewd suggestions for how she might find solace with them. Some of them wanted more than her body. One crazy-eyed man grabbed her from behind and held her with one arm while with the other hand he searched her for hidden pouches of jewelry or money. "I know you've got something, girlie," he breathed rancidly against her face. "Now give it up before I have to hurt you."

With a strength she would never have believed herself capable of, she kicked and twisted and screamed. Finally she landed one successful upthrust knee to the man's groin that caused him to release his grasp enough for her to run away.

But where to run? She could do little better than lose herself in the milling hordes. She was suddenly overwhelmingly aware of the danger she had placed herself in—she was completely alone and she was wearing no more than a nightgown and robe. Not that there weren't hundreds of other women in the same situation, but she felt vulnerable and totally defenseless. Pulling her shawl close to obscure her features and her relative state of undress, she sought a position where she might be safe and less noticeable.

She chose a spot near a large family, where several women sat together while their men stood a little apart and considered their dwindling options. One of the women breast-fed a baby while the others tried to soothe the other whining and exhausted children.

Relaxing slightly, Kate took in her surroundings. Besides the thousands of people, there were horses and dogs and even a few cows wandering about. The area itself seemed one she would never have ventured into in broad daylight, much less at night. There were buildings that looked like some sort of storage or warehouse structures, piles of debris and lumber, some of them smoldering, and smaller abandoned places that bore the signs of saloons and other enterprises of questionable repute.

Her eyes strained to see by what route she might make her next escape, for the fire now surrounded her, and the lake at her back had become less of a comfort and more of a potential foe with each passing hour. Some refugees had already moved out into the shallows, pressed there either by the growing throngs or their conviction that the fire would hunt them down wherever they went on land.

Kate's throat burned, and her lungs ached with each breath she drew. She was bone weary, and her clothes and skin were black with sweat and soot and ash. There were several holes in her gown and robe, and even her hair was singed. What was to become of her, she wondered . . . of all of them?

She watched as the women gathered around one of their sisters, a young girl lying on the ground, her cries barely audible against the din of the place. Still, she was clearly hysterical, wild with fear and exhaustion and panic. Kate understood her feelings. At least the woman had her family. Where were Lu and Edward? Had word yet reached Papa? If so, how worried he must be! Always foremost in her mind was the thought of where Ryan might be.

Before she was even aware that she was crying, tears dropped onto the backs of her hands, folded now listlessly in her lap. The fire surrounded her, its orange glow illuminating the scene like some eerie stage lighting, the stench of burned goods everywhere, the sounds of devastation and terror a clamor in her ears, and everywhere the heat and ceaseless roar of the inferno.

Unable to bear her total despair, she collapsed against a pile of rugs and allowed the sobs to come. She had to rest. She could not go on. Let the fire come. She was little match for its fury.

Someone shook her. "Lady, we're moving," a voice shouted hoarsely. It was still necessary to shout even after all these hours.

Kate blinked and focused on the face of the woman who stood over her.

"I'm needing my stuff," the woman noted, indicating the rolled-up rug and bundle of clothing where Kate had found her resting place.

Kate nodded and moved away. In a daze she noted that the fire line was closer. She must have slept. The throng was oozing north again. Tiredly she considered her options and decided to move toward the water.

Soon she was ankle-deep in the lake, the coolness of it like a soothing bath after the turmoil of the night past. There were the beginnings of a light in the east that she recognized as having nothing to do with the fire. Day was breaking. It gave her a new energy, a new hope.

In the distance she made out a long pier. At the end was a lighthouse. If she could make it to the pier, she might be able to get the lighthouse keeper to wire her father that they were safe. Perhaps she could get word to Lu and Edward. The lighthouse meant communication . . . She had to try.

She saw how several people were cautiously inching their way over a series of barges toward the pier that jutted far into the lake like a finger pointing the way. Clutching her now-soaked gown and wrapper high in one hand, she crawled onto the first barge. It swayed and tilted crazily from the weight of so many people. At times the churning water washed over it, and it was almost submerged.

A man fell into the water and was pulled to safety by his friends. Who would care if she fell? Who would reach out a hand? She looked at the faces surrounding her, all focused on only one thing: escape. Still, she had to try. There was no other choice available. Like the tightrope walkers they had watched that Fourth of July at the circus, she eased her way from one rocking and bobbing platform to the next. She was pushed and shoved from behind and almost lost her footing more than once. Her shoes were soaked, and the surface was slippery. Once when she slipped, her ankle twisted and she went down to her knees. The crowd threatened to engulf her, but she fought her way upright and, favoring the ankle, moved on.

The worst part was when one barge ended and she had to leap to the next. Sometimes the distances were negligible, a mere step away. But once the chasm seemed impossible, and many people gave up and turned back, unwilling to take a risk. Kate considered the gaping distance. If she made it, she would reach the pier by crossing that last barge. If she didn't . . .

"I wouldn't try it," a man warned as he studied the situation and turned back. Kate looked back at the scene behind her—a sea of humanity silhouetted against the stark devastation of what yesterday had been the city. Ahead was the pier, the lighthouse, and possible rescue. If she went back, what then? She considered the jump, and gathering her skirts high around her hips and waist, she took a running start. Closing her eyes, she took flight, fully expecting that in the next moment she would find herself in the water, weighted down by her soaked and heavy wrapper, with no one to care whether she lived or died.

She heard the gasps of several people and one woman's "Oh my sweet Jesus . . ." and then she fell—hard. She had made it—bruised, battered, but in one piece and on the last barge. She glanced back and saw that those who had watched her in stunned silence were waving, and several of the men had clearly decided that if she could make it, so could they. They were leaping the distance like so many ballet dancers.

The last barge rocked precariously as each new daredevil landed. In moments the end to which they had all leapt became dangerously overcrowded, and the barge threatened to dunk the lot of them into the water. Kate moved forward as quickly as possible. Crawling at first, as she favored her injured ankle and badly bruised hip, she watched as the pier came closer. She stumbled to her feet and hobbled as fast as she could. Finally, after what seemed an eternity, she placed her foot on solid ground.

Once there, she made her way to the very point, where it seemed at last as if she might breathe deeply of air that was unblemished by the smoke and ash. But although the smoky air was not as thick, it still hung heavy like fog, burning her eyes, throat, and lungs.

The lighthouse loomed above her, its beacon still lighting the way in the hazy dawn. Below, the lighthouse keeper and his wife tried desperately to organize the growing mob. "Water," people cried, and hands reached forward, grasping and straining. "My child has not eaten since yesterday," a woman begged and was met by a chorus of agreement.

"I have some supplies," the lighthouse keeper's wife said to her husband.

"Let me help you," Kate volunteered and stepped quickly to the woman's side.

The older woman nodded and led the way to the kitchen.

As the day broke, Kate moved to and from the lighthouse, doling out water. The mistress of the house offered to cook what she had and share it, a gesture that had a calming effect on the multitude, as if already they had received sustenance. The activity of dipping up water for the steady line of refugees refreshed Kate, and she momentarily forgot her own despair as she brought solace and relief to the dozens of souls who waited patiently and quietly now for their turn.

Ryan followed Ontario to "the Sands," a district of ill repute along the shoreline that only recently the city fathers had, ironically, ordered burned in preparation for rehabilitation. The clamor of the mob there was almost as deafening as the fire itself. Everywhere people milled about like lost souls, uncertain of where to go, what to do, in some cases exhausted to the point of madness by the long night of flight.

The fire was everywhere behind them. There was no source of escape save the lake itself, and that meant finding passage. Ryan moved determinedly through the crowd toward the water, where he saw that people had already started to use the several barges there as floating bridges to the Government Pier.

The pier stretched far out into the lake. A lighthouse anchored the point. If he could reach it, he might be able to get someone to take him to his own yacht, assuming it had not already been burned or stolen. He fingered the cash in his pocket and worked his way through the swarm of people. Nimbly he moved from one barge to the next, easily bypassing timid souls who paused to gauge the choice of perhaps missing a step and ending up in deep water or staying where they were and facing the encroaching fire.

At the lighthouse he encountered even more chaos. Those who had successfully navigated the treacherous trail of the barges were lined up now four and five deep as they waited for the tugboat *Magnolia* to carry them out to waiting boats. The lighthouse keeper and his wife were doing their best to soothe the masses by offering water and bits of food, but Ryan could see that such ministrations would not last long.

He had hardly noticed the dawning of the new day but now realized that with the hazy light came the opportunity to reach his goal. Amid the angry protests of several in the crowd, he struggled toward the lighthouse. It was not his intent to push ahead of the others, merely to get a message to the tugboat captain to look for his yacht. If it was still there, he would stay and wait his turn. If not, he would take other flight. Now that he had daylight, it would be easier to trace Kate and the others.

With apology but determination he moved forward. There was a girl handing out water and food, just ahead. If he could reach her and explain . . .

"Please, miss," he croaked hoarsely when he finally broke through the line to where she was dipping water. His throat was parched and burned, and his voice was barely audible. He reached out to touch her shoulder, and when she turned, he looked up into the one face he had prayed through the long night that he would see again.

16

THEY FELL INTO each other's arms, the dipper and water bucket forgotten as Kate stared incredulously at him. Ryan . . . here . . . safe . . . It was a miracle. His voice was a smoky rasp as he said her name again and again, but it was music to her soul. Uncaring of the onlookers, she kissed him, wrapping her arms tightly around him, holding on as if she would never again allow him out of her sight. She felt tears of joy bathing her face, and when she looked at him as if to assure herself she wasn't dreaming, he was crying, too.

They talked at the same time. "I never thought . . ." "I was so afraid . . ." "I prayed and hoped . . ." In between they hugged and kissed and held each other, their eyes shining out from blackened faces like the beacon on the lighthouse behind them.

"We'll be all right now," he said soothingly, and she nodded, her face pressed against his chest, her body savoring the comfort of his arms around her.

After a moment she introduced him to the lighthouse keeper's wife, and he explained his dilemma. A message was dispatched to the captain of the tugboat, and while they waited for word of his yacht, Kate and Ryan worked together with the keeper and his wife to minister to the others who had gathered along the length of the pier.

Inside the house, Kate and Ryan were offered coffee and hot bread, which they devoured hungrily and guiltily, knowing there wasn't such a repast for the hundreds who waited outside.

"Go on with you," the older woman said. "No one else cared a fig for anyone but themselves but your missus here. She stepped right up first thing and offered to help. And now you here . . ."

Kate and Ryan smiled at the woman's assumption that they were married. He reached across the table and clasped Kate's hand, fingering the ring he had given her. Once they had fortified themselves with the bread and hot coffee, they returned to tend to the others. For hours they moved along the pier, bathing faces, bandaging wounds, treating the burns as best they could.

Behind them the blackened ruins of the city smoldered, and the scorched and singed remains of buildings and homes reflected the ravaged dreams and lives of the masses huddled now quietly along the shores and the length of the pier. In contrast to the roar and chaotic din of the night before, an eerie quiet settled over the city with the coming of the new day.

Ryan's fortune here in Chicago had been represented by mere pieces of paper, paper that surely had burned along with everything else. Even the few certificates he had stuffed into his pockets as he left his office now crumbled into dust as he fingered them. The heat had been overpowering enough to simply disintegrate the paper. Fortunately his money had been rolled, and only the outer bills were destroyed. It would take time to reconstruct the paper trail that would prove his ownership.

His plight was ironic. Decades before, his father had arrived in America with little more than the clothes on his back and a small stake of cash in his pocket. From that he had built a life. Ryan glanced ruefully down at his own clothes, now burnt full of holes and grimy with the filth of the last sixteen hours. Building his fortune before had been easy enough. Could he do the same again? He thanked God for the foresight to invest in real estate outside of the city, especially the property in Peshtigo. Looking at Kate, he realized that land had brought him a good bit of luck already.

Kate sat holding a baby while its mother slept. She had wrapped the child in her tattered shawl and now cradled it against her breast and the bedraggled remains of her nightgown and wrapper. She was the most beautiful woman he had ever seen. Her courage awed him. Again he was struck by the thought that with Kate, he had no question that all his plans and dreams for a better future, for people he knew and cared about, could be realized. He thought of her rocking their own child and placed her in a setting of the serene pasture and woodland acreage he had purchased from her father in Peshtigo.

Yes, they could start again . . . There in that peaceful setting they could build their own life, their own family. Everything would turn out right. He moved to where she sat on the hard ground and gathered her and the child to his chest, rocking the two of them to the rhythm of some unsung lullaby.

By late afternoon the reports had begun to filter along the pier about the extent of the damage. The death toll numbered in the hundreds so far, but was not at all what might have been feared. The worst toll was in property loss and the resultant tens of thousands who were now without homes or shelter of any kind. Some rumors placed the damage to property in the hundreds of millions. Still, they were alive, Kate thought, and if they had made it, she had to believe Edward and Lu were all right as well.

An hour later a wonderful sight greeted them as they watched yet another tugboat of refugees being carried off the pier and on to safety. As the tug pulled away, Ryan spotted a second tug coming in to dock, towing his yacht behind. With hugs and promises to stay in touch, they bid their farewells to the lighthouse keeper and his wife. They took with them as many of the refugees as would safely fit.

As soon as they were on board, Ryan steered a course north along the shore. Kate had told him where Lu and Edward had headed. He knew the house. Soon they would all be reunited.

But two hours later, after leaving the others in a safe place near Lincoln Park, Kate and Ryan arrived at the address Kate had been given only to be told that Lu and Edward had headed by train for Milwaukee earlier in the afternoon. The Hauptmans had returned to their home and planned to stay with friends until the full damage could be assessed.

"Do you want me to get you on the next train?" Ryan asked Kate as they debated their options.

"No," she said with a small waver of panic in her voice. She had no intention of being separated from him even for a moment.

"If we sail through the night, we could work our way along the coast and be in Milwaukee tomorrow," he suggested.

"I just wish we could get word to my parents."

They tried to send a telegram, but the lines were jammed, and they were told it would be at least the following day before a message could get through. "We'll keep trying," the operator promised, but he didn't seem hopeful.

"Come on," Ryan said as they left the telegraph office. "Let's get you home." Kate was limping badly now, favoring her injured ankle and hip.

Back on the yacht Ryan set their course for Milwaukee and insisted that she get some rest. "When it's dark, you can bathe in the lake. You'll feel better."

"And what about you? You're as exhausted as I am." She felt close to tears and knew it was the result of finally being able to release all the pent-up stress and tension she had kept a tight rein on all through the last night and day.

He smiled wearily. "Hey, the one thing everybody agrees on with the Irish is that we are one tough breed." He flexed his arms in a tired parody of a weight lifter. "Now get some rest."

"Aye, aye, Captain."

In the small living quarters below deck, she found a tiny kitchen—galley, she mentally corrected herself—and a sort of all-purpose room that served as bedroom, reading room, and dining room. A table could be lowered from its place on the ceiling by means of a pulley system. The walls were lined with shallow shelves that held several volumes of poetry and novels along with the basic supplies of the vessel. She pulled aside a curtained partition to reveal a sleeping chamber built into the side of the hull.

With a heaviness born of total fatigue she lay down on top of the patchwork coverlet and was immediately asleep.

Ryan made good time, but by midnight he was so weary, he could hardly keep his eyes open. Anchoring in a cove near shore, he removed all his clothes and lowered himself into the cold, refreshing water. He swam and scrubbed himself as best he could, noting the soft stubble of nearly two days' growth of beard. The water revived him, and as he hoisted himself back on board, he wrapped a blanket around his waist and went below to find fresh clothing and check on Kate.

She was sleeping fitfully, tossing and turning in what he expected were the nightmares of her recent ordeal. He pulled on a pair of pants and then went to wake her.

"Darling," he whispered, pulling the tangled and soiled wrapper away and tossing it on a bench across the small room.

She jumped in a startled reaction, and her eyes flew open. Then, seeing him and sleepily taking in her surroundings, she breathed a sigh of relief and smiled. "I was dreaming."

"I know. How about a bath?" He offered her a piece of soap from the galley and then pulled several towels from a nearby cubbyhole. "Here, take these and go up on deck. The water is cold but warm enough if you're quick about it. I'll find something for you to put on." He laid the supplies on the bed beside her and began rummaging through a small trunk, his back to her. "Go on," he muttered, and she knew he was giving her the privacy to go without him watching her.

She hurriedly climbed the brass-railed ladder to the deck and saw that the yacht was anchored in a cove where the water was calm and inviting. Quickly she rid herself of the gown and, holding the soap in one hand, lowered herself into the water.

The feeling that came over her was heavenly. She released her matted and tangled hair and dunked her face and head in the water. Then she worked the soap into a lather and scrubbed herself from head to toe, spending a long time on her hair, wanting to rid herself of every residue of the stench and grime of the fire.

Even after she had bathed, she was reluctant to leave the water, knowing that she would be chilled once she returned to the deck. On the other hand, Ryan was on board, and he would keep her warm. She smiled and swam a little toward the shore, her hair trailing behind her. At the sound of a soft splash, she turned to watch Ryan swimming toward her.

Without a word they swam toward the shore until they could stand shoulder-deep in the sandy-bottomed water. Then his eyes locked with hers, he slid his hands slowly, sensuously over her shoulders . . . her back . . . her breasts . . . and down her hips.

"I love you," he whispered just before his mouth settled over hers. As his tongue began its erotic dance with hers, he flattened one palm against her hips and pressed her to his.

He was naked and fully aroused. Startled, she pulled slightly away, but immediately relaxed and relished the sensation of his naked body against hers.

With the contact, their hands and mouths were kindled with a fury of need. Grasping each other as if it would be impossible ever to be close enough, their mouths collided and melded and searched for release.

He lifted her, and instinctively she wrapped her legs around him, feeling the probe of that part of him that could bring her the closeness she craved. "Love me," she whispered, her tongue wet against his ear.

"It will hurt just at first, Katie, only at first." He hated the idea of ever causing her even the slightest pain.

"It's all right," she said. Then with a whimper of longing and desire, she whispered, "Please."

Slowly he lowered her onto himself, ready to withdraw at the first sign of pain. She was so slender and felt so fragile in his arms. He fought the urge to plunge into her, to take her with all the passion that raced through his body.

At the first contact Kate flinched only slightly and then settled herself more firmly onto him, feeling him slide inside her, filling her in a way she had never imagined could be possible. She obeyed every instinct, lifting and tightening and moving in ways that would pull him ever more deeply inside her. Yes, there had been one moment of pain, followed immediately by such a sweet ecstasy that the distress was immediately forgotten.

Ryan knew the moment he broke through, saw it in her face, but she did not pull back. Instead she moved restlessly against him, exploring every means of holding him tight inside her. Gently he held her at her waist, lifting and lowering her as he buried himself ever more deeply inside her. The water was cold, but he could not stop now.

Her soft moans of rapture echoed on the quiet night air, and when her nails dug into his shoulders, he was lost. With increasing fervor he plunged into her, urging her toward that rarest of pleasures. When she cried out his name and arched her torso in the exquisite agony of release, he poured himself into her, his own outcry of fulfillment joining hers.

Spent, they stood holding each other for one long moment. Slowly he withdrew himself and lowered her to her feet. "Are you cold?" he asked.

"Never with you," she replied.

He laughed at that. "Nevertheless, I think we'd both better get back on board."

They swam back to the yacht, and she had no thoughts of shame or shyness when they stood naked together on the deck. In the distance there was thunder, and a soft rain began to fall. Sadly it reminded them of all they had been through. If only the rains had come sooner and more often, they thought.

"Come on," he urged, leading her below. "I can't have you getting sick after all you've been through."

Tenderly he dried her and settled her in the berth. He wrapped himself in a towel and made tea, bringing her a steaming cup and settling himself in the narrow bed with her. "I love you, Katie," he said seriously.

"I know," she replied happily.

That made him laugh. "Pretty damned sure of yourself, aren't you, woman?"

She allowed the steam of the tea to warm her face, flirting with him over the rim of the mug. "Yeah, I am."

"Pretty cocky, too, for a woman who just began her first real love affair," he teased, taking the mug from her and setting it on the floor with his own as he stripped off the towel and joined her beneath the covers.

"How did I do?"

He raised an eyebrow. "Let me think . . . There are so many to compare . . ."

She gave his naked rump a hard slap.

"Ow," he bellowed. Then he pinned her with the length of his body. "You free-thinking women are all the same," he said. "A little too feisty for your own good. What's a man to do but show you who's boss early on?"

"You can try," she taunted.

"I can do better than that," he warned with a sly grin. He spent the next hour showing her that when it came to making love, he was indeed her master. On the other hand, he had to admit she was a quick learner, so he was going to have to work hard to stay one step ahead of her.

Ryan woke a couple of hours before dawn and went back on deck to lift anchor and set sail for Milwaukee. Normally the trip would take less time. But normally the yacht would be manned by a crew. Sailing alone, he needed to stay close to shore and take his time. He was anxious to get there now and knew Kate would be, too, when she woke. She wanted to reassure her worried family, but he had a different reason—he wanted to speak to her father and then move on to Peshtigo and hire builders for the home he would design for the two of them to live in once they were married.

Throughout the day, they felt as if they were already married. Kate found a few supplies and put together sandwiches, serving him as he steered them toward home. She read aloud to him to help combat the fatigue that threatened to overtake him by late afternoon. He taught her how to maintain a steady course long enough for him to grab an occasional nap. And in between they touched and talked and planned their future.

She had found an old nightshirt of his to put on. It came to her ankles, and she had belted it with a piece of rope. He found a pair of casual pants and a shirt. As evening came on and the air turned cooler, Kate wrapped herself in a blanket and brought Ryan the oilskin slicker he kept on board. When it rained, as it did off and on, they covered themselves with a tarmac, huddling close to each other, his hand searching beneath the fabric of the nightshirt to touch her soft bare skin, hers massaging his chest and stomach, taking great delight in her ability to arouse him by such a simple device as raking her fingernails lightly across his inner thigh.

And they talked . . . of the fire and their harrowing escapes . . . of the things they had witnessed . . . and of their future.

"When we are married, how would you feel about living in Peshtigo?" he asked.

"You mean permanently?"

"Oh, we would have the house in Chicago as well, but . . . would you mind so awfully much if our real home . . ."

She smiled. "I've always loved Peshtigo."

"You wouldn't miss the city?"

"You'll be traveling there often enough on business, I expect."

He nodded.

"Well, then, I'll be there as often. I have no intention of letting you out of my sight once we are married."

That made him laugh. After a few moments he asked, "What about your school? I hate to see you give that up."

"Millie Kopfmeier is a wonderful teacher, and in truth, she understands the boys better than I do." The acknowledgment seemed to make her sad.

"Katie, do you understand that in starting that school you did something quite wonderful? It was unique and completely original. What other young woman in your position would have cared?"

"You give me too much credit." But his praise pleased her, and she snuggled against him, comforted by his closeness, by their growing understanding of each other. "Perhaps there will be a need for a school in Peshtigo . . . at Mr. Ogden's woodenware factory . . . or perhaps at the Ryan Sullivan Sawmill?"

He grinned. "Are you planning on taking an active role in my business when we're married, Katrina Bergeman?"

"It's *our* business, and the answer is most definitely, yes."

It was night when the lights of Milwaukee finally came into view. They stood together, their arms around each other, and rejoiced in the sheer mundanity of the unblemished cityscape. It seemed incredible to see a skyline where buildings stood whole and carts and cabs and vessels went about their business in the most routine ways.

As they passed the boardwalk, Kate moved as far forward as she dared, her fingers tensely gripping the ends of the blanket, her eyes straining for the first view of the family's dock. There! She spotted Lu and Edward racing down the wooden staircase toward the small pier, waving and yelling. Papa was there, too, pacing, his hands clenched behind his back, his posture a portrait of concern and worry. Kate looked for her mother, but there was no sign of her. Of course, she was probably still with Fanny in Peshtigo.

Kate was thankful they were all safe, and Mama had been spared the agonizing worry of not knowing their fate during the fire. Her eyes welled with tears, which she recognized as a sign of both her relief to be home and her exhaustion from the ordeal of the past two days.

Ryan hastened to dock the craft, afraid Kate might actually try to leap the distance between the deck and the pier before he could get her there. Lu waited with open arms and tears streaming down her face. Edward reached for the ropes to secure the yacht. Neither said a word as August Bergeman stood waiting just behind them.

The first moments were filled with a jumble of talk and exclamations between Lu and Kate. Edward simply hugged his future sister-in-law and then turned his embrace on Ryan. "Thank God," he muttered emotionally as he clapped Ryan on the back several times.

"Lucinda, take your sister up to the house and find her something decent to put on. Edward, accompany the girls."

These were the first words August Bergeman spoke. He did not embrace his daughter. On the contrary, he spared but a glance for her, his face a mask of barely controlled anger as it focused on Ryan.

"Papa . . . ," Kate began.

"Now!" Bergeman roared, and Ryan saw that his jowls trembled with rage as he gave his order.

"Come on, Katrina," Edward urged, and Lu put her hand on her sister's arm and led her away from the pier.

"Katrina," Lu said softly, "come now . . . please." Then with a sob, she added, "It's Mama."

Kate looked toward the house and then back at Ryan. Something had happened to Sophie? She started up the stairs, practically running as she went. "Mama," she called in a shaky voice. Lu and Edward hurried to follow her. By the time she was halfway up the stairs, Ryan could hear Lu and Edward trying to explain, their own voices shaking with emotion.

"What's happened?" he asked August Bergeman when they were alone.

Kate's father ignored the question. Quietly and with a dangerous edge, he began to speak. "You, sir, will leave my property. I am indebted to you for your safe return of my daughter, but judging by her state of undress and the means you chose to secure her return, I have no choice but to believe that you have already taken your reward."

Ryan's own fists clenched, and he took a step toward the older man. "I love—"

Wild-eyed, Bergeman flailed at the air between them. "Do *not* speak to me of love, Sullivan. You do not know the meaning . . ." His voice broke, and he stood there for a moment, his face a tortured blank.

"What has happened to Mrs. Bergeman?"

At the question Bergeman recovered his focus. "There has been another fire," he said. "We have just this afternoon received word, just after receiving the telegram telling of Katrina's safety. I am sad to report we do not have such good news about Mrs. Bergeman."

"Peshtigo? A fire there as well?" It was unbelievable. What cruel hoax of nature could have brought this about?

"I expect you will be wanting to survey the damage to your property," Bergeman said, his anger returning. "You have been most severely devastated, Mr. Sullivan, to the north and to the south of your somewhat fragile empire. What have you to offer Katrina now . . . as if I would allow . . ."

"Sir, your wife . . . is she . . ." Ryan could not find the words. Loving Katrina as he did, he could only surmise what the man must be going through, and understanding that, he forgave every barb the brewer hurled in his direction.

"Get out of here," August thundered. "Go away from here. I have told you that you are not welcome, that you have violated my daughter's honor, that I will not tolerate your presence in my house, do you understand?"

Ryan retreated to his yacht, afraid if he made no sign of departure the man would collapse. "I will leave," he said. "Please tell Kate—"

"I will tell Katrina nothing . . . *nothing,* do you understand? She is through with you." He stumbled along the pier, toward the stairway up the bluff. His voice breaking with tears and the long strain of worry and grief, he turned. "I have lost my wife, Mr. Sullivan . . . You have only lost a bit of property. I am sure you will recover from the events of the last few days."

An hour later, Ryan was still trying to digest what had happened. Sophie Bergeman was surely dead, killed in a fire miles from the conflagration he and Kate had just survived. His heart broke for Kate. She needed him now, and he could not go to her. Perhaps August Bergeman was right. What had he to offer her now? Most of his holdings had literally gone up in flames. And by taking her without seeking at least her father's blessing for their union, he had defiled her reputation, even if no one ever knew. He should have insisted on putting her on the train. He should have understood the ramifications of sailing with her alone for a day and a night. Bergeman was right. Regardless of the tailored clothes and the cash in his pocket, Ryan Sullivan was little more than he had always been, a slum kid who had had a bit of luck.

17

KATRINA WOULD NOT hear what Lu and Edward tried to tell her. Another fire . . . even more devastating . . . Mama surely among the scores of victims . . . few escaped . . . no word except of death . . .

She ran the distance from the top of the bluff to the house, calling for her mother. Pauline waited indoors, her face streaked with tears, her arms open. "There, there, child. Thank God, you are safe."

"But Mama?"

Pauline's tears started again, and all she could manage was to hug Katrina tighter and shake her head sadly.

Once Kate had accepted the news, she calmed herself enough to ask questions. Lu was near hysteria whenever the subject was brought up. She had not yet recovered from her terror in Chicago, and now this. Later that night, Kate spent several hours sitting with her, comforting her until she finally cried herself to sleep. "Sh-h-h," she soothed. "We don't know for sure yet."

"But . . . ," Lu had blubbered.

"You must have faith," Kate coached, hearing her mother's words in her own voice.

When Lu was finally asleep, Kate lay in her own bed, trying to put together the pieces of the last several days. At every turn, when she had thought nothing could be worse, something more had happened. When would the nightmare end? In between there had been the pure joy of Ryan and their love for each other. How cruel it seemed to have lived perhaps the most wonderful moment of her young life at the very moment her mother lay dead in some other disaster.

After hours of lying, wide-eyed, trying to make some sense of the maze of events, Katrina dressed and roamed the house, praying that it not be true, that by some miracle God had spared her mother. But God had been busy performing many miracles on that night. Was it possible He had not been able to save Mama?

She wandered into the darkened music room, where Mama's piano was positioned so that Sophie could look out onto her gardens as she played. Kate stood for a long time at the arched and leaded glass doors that led out to the veranda; she considered the outline of the gazebo in the distance. She remembered clearly the look of pure love her mother had given her father the day the structure, the perfect accent for her precious garden, had been completed. She remembered how her parents had sat together in the gazebo long past dusk, talking, laughing . . . perhaps holding and caressing each other there in the shadows.

I'm being punished, she thought, and felt the sobs she had thought spent welling up through her chest. In her growing hysteria, she began to imagine that somehow she was responsible for what had happened to her mother. She had gone against her parents' wishes for the first time in her life by insisting on being with Ryan. Now she had been with him in a way that even Mama in all her progressive ways could never condone. "Oh, God," she wailed as the tears fell freely and unchecked, "what have I done?"

She could not shake the thought that somehow her making love with Ryan had created this new horror. During those long hours of sleeplessness, it seemed her newfound love was more a curse than cause for celebration. And yet . . .

In all her life she had never felt like this. What she shared with Ryan made her feel strong and alive and free. With Ryan she felt as if she had been reborn to a life filled with purpose and meaning, to riches beyond material wealth. She felt that with him at her side there was nothing they could not accomplish. Surely there was good in that.

At the same time, she could not erase the one thought that had sustained her through the endless hours of her own ordeal: *I love him.* Surely that had to count for something . . . surely God's hand had been in that as well . . . God would never be so wrathful, so vengeful as to . . .

She reminded herself that Mama had always taught her daughters that God was loving and good. She swallowed back one last sob and forced herself to focus on the positive. In time, her natural optimism prevailed. There had been no official word, and without that there was still the possibility that Mama was alive. She recalled how she had made her way alone through the fire to safety and knew that all the instincts that had led her to survival were as present in her mother as in herself. She thought of how difficult it had been to get word out from Chicago; surely in rural Peshtigo, the hardship would become an impossibility.

As long as they had no official word, there was still a chance that Mama was alive . . . She had to hold to that. If it were so, then Kate certainly was not being punished for her love of Ryan. It would be a sign.

And if Mama were dead?

She shook off that thought. Moving through the house now with purpose, she took a shawl Sophie always kept by the kitchen door and let herself out into the predawn. Soon the servants would be up and about, as would Papa. He had banished her to her room, the expression on his face clearly indicating that he shared her idea that somehow her behavior was connected to this calamity.

"Papa," she had pleaded, reaching out to him, to comfort and be comforted, when he came through the front door after returning from the pier.

But he had brushed her aside on his way up the stairs. "I do not wish to deal with you right now, Katrina. Go to your room. Your behavior has . . ." He shook his head slowly from side to side, his face struggling for words to express all he felt. "You have dishonored your mother. You are no daughter of mine," he had said dully before continuing on his way.

That, too, had been a source of her distress. At a time when she needed him as at no other time in her life, he would not be there for her. His own pain was greater than his ability to see to the torment of his daughters. He had possibly lost the one person he loved above life itself, and he had nothing to give to anyone else.

Kate understood that. In those hours when she had struggled alone, not knowing whether she would ever see Ryan again, not knowing if she would live to see him again, she had thought only fleetingly of her parents or Lu. She had focused on Ryan, on how horrible it would be for him once again to lose the one person he held dearest. She had also had to face the fact that Ryan himself might be taken by the fire. Those had been the worst moments of all. How would she go on? What would her life be without him? Years stretched before her—lonely and solitary—when she considered a life without him. Oh, yes, she understood Papa's terrible grief, especially because he and Sophie had had such a good life together. She, Kate, hadn't known Ryan for long and already felt this way.

One day she would make her father see that just as Mama had been a lifelong companion for him, Ryan was that person for Kate. She would make Papa understand that her love for Ryan was no less powerful than what August had shared with Sophie and wanted for both his daughters.

As the sky lightened, Kate made her way down to the dock and released the small dinghy. Ryan had needed rest. He would not have been so foolhardy as to start for Peshtigo after the ordeal they had just lived through. She had to believe he would anchor along the shore and sleep. She rowed north to the spot where she had first met him.

Ryan was exhausted, but sleep would not come. His mind was a jumble of conflicting emotions and information. His love for Kate was the one constant he kept coming back to, yet in between he was haunted by questions. How could he possibly hope to win her family's approval now? He had little to offer. From her father's dock he had sailed first downtown and up the river, where he had listened to the gossip of the fires, Chicago, and the more recent news of Peshtigo. With each story the prospects that anything remained in either place grew worse.

Completely fatigued, he nevertheless felt the need to go to Peshtigo, assess the situation for himself, face the reality of what his future held. So he had set sail. And once out on the water, his panic had eased and his thinking had cleared some. As he once again passed the Bergeman dock and recalled the ravaged, grief-stricken expression on August Bergeman's face and the panicked cries of Kate calling out for her mother, he knew that whether or not his property had somehow survived the fire was immaterial. Nothing meant anything without Kate to share it.

He had considered any number of ways to contact her— a note delivered to the kitchen and spirited to her by the cook, Pauline; a message to Edward, who might help them arrange a meeting; or one to Lu, the eternal romantic, who could surely be counted on to help.

But what of Kate herself? He tried to imagine what she must be going through. She adored her mother and with good reason. Ryan himself felt an aching grief at the thought of never seeing Sophia Bergeman again. He also remembered his own grief following the wreck of the *Lady Elgin*—that pain he had carried for years, coming as it did in the midst of the most ordinary activity, reminding him that they were truly gone, never to be seen again. In the midst of the fire, he had felt the familiar panic, the helplessness that nothing he did would make any difference.

He heard a soft thud against the side of the yacht, and his senses were immediately on alert. On bare feet he moved cautiously toward the ladder that led to the deck. It was just beginning to be light. Someone was coming aboard. An intruder? He was far too weary to fight off some ruffian.

"Ryan?"

Her voice was a hushed whisper, and he thought perhaps his overtired mind was playing tricks. But then she was there—in his arms, holding him, kissing him, crying, and gripping him as if he were a lifeline.

He responded in kind, murmuring over and over between kisses how sorry he was.

"But maybe she's alive," Kate said as they finally broke apart. Her eyes flamed with her need to believe.

"But . . ."

"There's been no official word . . . only about the fire and the terrible toll in deaths, but no one has specifically brought word of Mama, don't you see?"

He understood that she wanted to cling to any hope, any possible thread. "I see," he whispered and pulled her once again into his arms, holding her lightly as he stroked her hair and her back.

"You're going there, aren't you?" she asked, her voice muffled against his chest.

"I have to," he began, expecting her to protest. Oh, how could he explain that until he knew the full extent of his losses, he had no right to his love for her?

"Good," she said and pulled away enough to look up at him. "Then you'll find her."

Surely grief had momentarily demented her. She could not possibly believe her mother had survived. No one would be so cruel as to bring such news if it weren't all but certain.

"Katie," he whispered soothingly and tried to pull her back to the comfort of his embrace.

"No, I mean it. We have to know. I mean, what if she is

alive and Papa is going through this . . . this hell? Mama is strong . . . a survivor, Ryan. If anyone could make it . . ."

"But what if she didn't make it?"

Her eyes met his without a trace of panic or hysteria. "Then we need to know that as well," she said evenly. "Either way, we need to bring her home."

"I'll do what I can," Ryan promised, knowing that in that moment he would have promised her the moon and stars were it in his power to do so.

They stood on the deck, holding each other as the sun rose over the straight, even line of the horizon.

"When you come back . . . ," she began after a while.

"Sh-h-h. We won't talk of that now." He had meant to soothe her, but his words had the opposite effect, for suddenly she pulled away and moved several steps from him.

"What do you mean?" She looked absolutely stricken.

"I . . . that is . . . Katie . . ." It was a supplication.

Restlessly she began to pace. "Is there any chance you won't be coming back, Ryan?" She asked the question without looking at him. In fact, she had turned entirely away from him, facing out toward the rising sun, her hands tightly gripped behind her back.

He went to her and put his arms around her from behind. "Katie, we have to take this one step at a time. Right now your father . . ."

"Father is grief-stricken. Whatever he may have said to you last night, he didn't mean it. You have to understand that."

"I understand that for the moment all his predictions about me have come true. I may have lost a great deal, Katie. Before I knew you, that news would have irritated me, even distressed me, but I would have known that having done it once, I could work my way back. After all, I had only myself to consider. Now . . ."

"What's different?" It was as if she held her breath.

"Now," he said, turning her to face him, "there is you. Now I must be less selfish . . . I must think of you. If I cannot give you the life you deserve . . . the life you've had . . . the life . . ."

Her eyes flashed with anger. "What about the life I want?" she demanded.

"And what is that?" He was close to smiling. She could be so damned charming when she got her dander up.

"Did this mean nothing to you?" She waved under his nose the ring he had given her in Chicago. "Did our . . . our lovemaking mean so little?" Her anger dissipated, replaced by doubt.

Now he felt the rise of his own ire. "How can you believe that? You mean everything to me. I have told you that, and as for our making love, it was far more than that simple act." He seized the hand where she wore his ring and held it between them. "When my mother wore this ring, she was married to my father. In my mind we were married the day I placed it on your hand, and our making love was the consummation of that marriage." His hold on her and his facial expression became more tender. "Ah, Katie, I should have waited, but after what we had both been through . . . knowing from the past how easily and quickly life can change . . . I had to have made love with you once. Do you understand?"

Oh, how she wanted to believe him, to give in to the feelings his words aroused. "And yet you speak of going away as if you might not return. What kind of marriage is that?"

"I can't promise you anything, Katie," he roared with frustration. "Don't you understand? I'm not leaving you, but I have to go and make a life for us and I have no right to expect you to be there when I do come back."

"But you will be back?" she argued.

Now he was bewildered. "Well, of course I'll be back." How could she think otherwise? Didn't she know how much he loved her? Needed her?

"All right, then," she said with a stern glower. "Then I'll be here. Though why on earth it hasn't occurred to

you we might actually build this new life together, I'll
never understand. Still, you men are all so stubborn, always
thinking you know the best way. Mama warned me . . ."

She was chattering on, which made him smile. Then he
started to chuckle, and that felt so good he laughed out
loud. "Oh, Katie Bergeman, do you know how much I
adore you?" He shouted it to the gulls that circled the
shore.

Then she was laughing with him, and for the first time
in days they were caught up in the pure joy that was life,
that moment of absolute bliss when two people know they
have found the singular love that stands above all others.
When their laughter subsided, they stood for long moments
enjoying the purity of the new day, secure in their love, if
not their future.

"Let me make you some breakfast," she said.

"You'd better head back."

"You have to eat." Her expression told him that they
were not speaking of breakfast, but of her determination to
live her own life, despite the boundaries her father would
continue to try to impose.

"You mean you cook?" he teased, and she responded by
punching him hard in the arm as she moved toward the
galley.

They shared the preparation of their meal in an atmosphere of comfortable domestic camaraderie, but as they sat
together on the deck to eat, their mood grew quiet and
pensive.

"You'd better go," he said again after he had carried
the dishes to the galley and come back to find her staring
north toward where her mother's fate remained a mystery.
The morning sky was hazy with smoke . . . smoke from
the north.

She turned and hugged him. "Hold me," she whispered,
and he knew the tears had begun.

"I'll find her," he promised and kissed the top of her
head.

"And you'll come back?" She turned her tear-streaked face to his, her eyes entreating him to agree with her.

He frowned. He wanted to provide for her in the same way her parents had provided all her life. She knew nothing really of how hard life could be. He wanted to protect her from that. "I'll come back," he said and kissed her before she could ask more. "Now go, so I can get started."

By the time Kate got home, everyone else was in the dining room, having a silent and somber breakfast. Papa concentrated on his food, but she knew that he had registered her presence and the fact that she had been out.

"Shall I set a place, miss?" Heinrich asked nervously.

"No, thank you, I've eaten." This brought raised eyebrows from Lu and Edward, who immediately returned their attention to their plates.

"Lucinda, I will be leaving this morning for Peshtigo. Heinrich and I will take the noon train to Green Bay and rent a carriage from there. If you need transportation, have Edward see to it. Edward, you can send a driver from the brewery or take time to see to whatever errands are needed for the household yourself."

"But, Papa, Katrina . . . ," Lu began, about to say that it was Katrina who always saw to the running of the business of the house in Mama's absence.

"Are you not to be a married woman soon?" Papa snapped at his younger daughter. "Then perhaps you might wish to gain some practice in the art of managing a proper household." With that he stood and threw his napkin on the table. He glanced around the table as if waiting for some argument and then stormed out of the room, brushing past Kate on his way, as if she were nothing more than a part of the room's decor.

When they heard the front door slam, Lu burst into tears, and Edward rushed to comfort her. Kate waited for the tears to subside and then said quietly, "Lu, we are all needed in this terrible time. I know you can manage the household staff as well as anyone, and actually it would be a great help to me if you would do so."

Lu looked up at her sister and nodded. "I just . . . Oh, Kate, he's being so horrible about you and Ryan . . . I've never seen him so angry . . ." All of which brought on a fresh jag of crying.

"Now listen, both of you. Papa is the person who counts most right now. If Mama is . . . gone . . ."

Edward caught the qualification. "What do you mean? Have you heard something?"

"I just mean we don't know for certain, and as long as there is any hope . . . and even if it turns out that . . . well, we need to conduct ourselves as Mama would have us. That means seeing to the care of Papa and the management of the house in as nearly a normal way as possible."

"And what are you going to do?" Lu asked.

"Kate, I don't know if it's a good idea, given your father's present state of mind, for you to be at the brewery," Edward added.

Kate smiled at his tactfulness. "I agree. And this morning I was thinking of what Mama might be doing today if she had come home to such horror stories as we have."

Lu smiled in spite of her worry and grief. "Mama would be beating the bushes for every possible donation of goods and funds for some sort of relief effort."

"Exactly." Kate turned to Heinrich. "Could you ask Ernestine to check the closets where Mama usually saves those items she intends to donate to charity, Heinrich? Oh, and on your way past the kitchen would you ask Pauline to make a list of supplies that might best make the journey to Peshtigo?"

Edward and Lu began making their own suggestions of how best to organize a relief effort, and soon the three of them were sitting around the large dining room table, making lists and dividing up tasks toward putting together blankets, clothing, and food for the victims of the fire.

Later in the day Edward sent word that several efforts were already under way, although most were concentrating on getting supplies to Chicago. That news made Kate double her efforts toward reaching as many of her family's friends and neighbors first, before they gave whatever they might have to the Chicago cause.

"Many citizens will help Chicago," she entreated. "Their calamity is news throughout the land, but Peshtigo . . ." She repeated her speech up and down the streets of the city's wealthiest neighborhoods as Mike Connors drove her door-to-door in the buckboard wagon, where he would load whatever goods she managed to scavenge.

Nearly everyone had heard the rumor that Sophia Bergeman had been a victim of that very tragedy. Seeing the dear woman's daughter on their doorstep begging for donations, no matter how small, they opened their hearts and their pocketbooks. By the end of the day she and Connors had made three trips to the railroad siding at the brewery, where a flatcar waited for the goods they collected.

Late into the night Kate sat at her father's desk in his study, counting up the cash donations and planning her purchases for the following morning. Shopkeepers had agreed to open their doors early for her and to give her a generous discount on her purchases of not only clothing and blankets, but also tools and other supplies.

As soon as she had made her purchases, the railroad car would leave. Kate had ordered two more flatcars loaded with wagons for delivering the goods overland, since railroad service to Peshtigo had been under construction at the time of the fire. At the last minute she urged Edward to send along teams of oxen and horses as well, recalling the animals she had seen wandering through the flames in Chicago. Even if work animals had survived the fire up north, the chances were good that they were badly burned and certainly skittish, making them difficult or even impossible to work with.

She leaned back in her father's high-backed leather desk chair and wondered if he would be surprised to see railroad cars and wagons bearing the Bergeman name in and around Peshtigo. Would he understand that such an effort had come from her? That she was doing what he would have wanted her to do had he not been so angry? Would it soften his heart?

18

WHEN RYAN SULLIVAN had first traveled north to consider the purchase of August Bergeman's plot of timberland, he had marveled at the untouched wilderness surrounding him. He'd viewed acre upon acre of wild and majestic woodlands as far as the eye could see, to the north or west of Green Bay. At that time he could have taken the narrow-gauge railroad the seven miles from the harbor to Peshtigo, but he had opted for renting a horse and been glad of the decision, stopping now and again to explore a newly opened road or freshly cleared land where a farm would be established.

On that wonderful summer day he had exulted in the beauty of rolling hills leading to valleys filled with tract after tract of hardwoods—maple, oak, ash, beech, elm, and the soaring white pillars of birch. The hills themselves were overgrown with sweet-smelling cedars and spruce and tamarack. He recalled how he had taken the unceasing plaudits of his friend, William Ogden, with a grain of salt, until he had viewed the area for himself.

Ogden had raved about not only the beauty of the countryside, but also the opportunity for investment. Ogden himself had added to his already considerable enterprises in Chicago and surrounding areas by establishing a woodenware factory along the river in Peshtigo, a factory that had grown to be the country's largest provider of pails, tubs, broom handles, clothespins, and all manner of necessary items for every household.

"There's room for another good sawmill there, my boy," he had urged. "Everything's in place . . . plenty of raw materials, good cheap labor, proximity to the harbor, and with the railroad coming . . ."

He had not had to explain further. The coming of the railroad would move Peshtigo from its present status as a sleepy rural village to that of a thriving town, maybe even a significant city. Ryan had taken the first opportunity to seek land in the area, knowing that a purchase early on would give him a stake in the community. That first opportunity had come through August Bergeman, a mere three months earlier.

Now once again he sat astride a rented horse and surveyed the scene before him. In any other October, there would have been a riot of color—vivid reds splashed against the splendor of yellows, rusts, burgundies, and all of it accented by the emerald opulence of the evergreens. He thought now of the irony of how often the colors of autumn were compared to flame and fire.

For what he saw was complete and absolute devastation—the charred and blackened remains of centuries-old forests. Trees whose trunks had spanned the width of three men lay uprooted, twisted, scorched. A constant film of gray ash sifted over the scene from the piles of refuse that surrounded him on all sides. As his horse walked along the dirt road, his hooves kicked up clouds of ash and soot. The noon sky was as gray as a winter evening in January.

Ryan rode slowly on, his heart growing heavier with every step. As he topped one rise, he searched the horizon for evidence of the small but bustling town that had so captivated him before. He thought at first he must have taken a wrong turn, for where there had been the miniature skyline of the woodenware factory, church spires, storefronts, houses, and outlying farms, there was nothing but the skeletal remains of the brick and stone walls of the factory and the melted and grotesquely sculptured rails of the narrow-gauge.

Making his way into the valley, he saw horrors that took him back to the days of the war. Never had a battlefield scene upset him more, for this was indeed the place of battle: defenseless man pitted unexpectedly against nature in all her fury. His mount picked a path through the charred carcasses of horses, cows, oxen. Here and there he saw a mound of something at first unidentifiable, then realized he was looking at the remains of human beings. Often the bodies were grouped together, families perhaps or neighbors who had tried in vain to reach the river. There were dozens of them, more with every step that took him closer to town.

Outside of town he came upon crews of men, freshly arrived from outlying areas, who had taken on the task of burying the countless victims. His eyes met those of the gravediggers. Stunned, hollow-eyed, they stared back at him, then they returned silently to their work. He rode on. What if Sophie's body or what remained of it were there? How would he know? How could he ever identify . . . He was thankful Katie was not here to witness this.

In town, where in June there had been a thriving community of shops and businesses and women gossiping over backyard fences, there was an air of stunned disbelief. People spoke in hushed murmurs. He passed the blackened columns of the store Sophie Bergeman's brother-in-law had owned, the store where he had first stopped for directions upon his arrival in town. That day Helmut Schmidt had greeted him heartily, and his pretty and very pregnant wife, Fanny, had insisted on providing him with a repast of freshly made strudel and cold beer.

They had sat together in the little courtyard to the side of the store, talking and laughing. Helmut had called passing citizens over to meet him, making Ryan feel at once respected and welcome. That afternoon had gone a long way toward making him consider the possibility of leaving

Chicago and settling here. His first view of the acreage Bergeman was offering for sale had cinched it. It stretched from three miles east of town to where the river and harbor met.

The moment he had seen the timberland all his plans had changed. Oh, yes, to be sure there was opportunity here, a sawmill was an excellent idea—but not with these trees, not with this land. This land called for something more permanent, something that would preserve and revere the splendid grace of it. He had never traveled to Ireland, but from his mother's stories he had a picture of the land, and this came as close to it as anything he had ever seen before. On that summer's day, for the first time in a very long time, Ryan Sullivan felt as if he had come home.

"Could I help you, sir?"

He was roused from his revery by a raspy voice. He looked down to see an old man standing next to his horse. He leaned against a shovel and swiped at his ash-and-sweat-stained face with the back of one hand.

"I came to look for . . . That is . . . Is there some . . . list?" It occurred to him that the man offering help had probably lost everything, and yet here he stood offering aid to a stranger.

The man shook his head sadly. "Give me a name, and maybe I can help."

Ryan doubted it would help to offer Sophie's name, so instead he said, "Helmut and Fanny Schmidt?"

The man looked down, rearranged the street dust with the toe of his boot, then looked up and shook his head. "I'm sorry," he croaked, and more than the damage of the fire caused his voice to crack. "Such good people," he said, more to himself than to Ryan. Then he blinked up at the gray sky, and Ryan saw tears brim. "Sorry," he said again and took his shovel and wandered away.

Ryan rode on. Near the river he had noticed a large tent. He assumed it was a makeshift relief shelter of sorts and headed there. His hope was slim that Sophie had survived, especially if neither Helmut nor Fanny had. Still, for Kate's sake he had to find out what he could.

Inside the tent he witnessed a scene that brought back all the chaos of the fire he and Kate had endured in Chicago. People sat or stood in huddled masses, wrapped in blankets and makeshift covers. The stench of burned flesh filled the air as volunteers rushed from one person to the next, offering clean bandages, a dipper of water, a tin mug of coffee, or a slice of bread.

Supplies had begun to trickle in. On the road up, Ryan had passed a few wagons loaded with a variety of items to help in the relief effort. Almost as soon as he set foot in the tent, he was enlisted to assist in the unloading of one such wagon.

"You got relatives here?" asked the man he was taking boxes from.

Ryan almost said yes, for Sophie was Kate's mother and one day would indeed be family to him as well. "I'm looking for someone who was visiting relatives in the area," he explained. "Sophie Bergeman? Family name was Haber?"

The other man shook his head. "There's some Habers around in these parts. Myself, I'm from up at Marinette . . . came down to do what I could. The captain's your best bet . . . He's been overseeing the relief effort and generally keeping order between here and Marinette."

"Where would I find him?"

"He left at dawn with a wagonload of survivors, taking them up to the emergency hospital. Up there in Marinette . . . They got hit, too, though the town's pretty much intact. I expect he'll be back in the morning sometime."

Ryan nodded, and the two men resumed unloading the supplies.

When that task was completed, there was no lack of things for Ryan to do. He helped unpack and dole out the blankets the boxes contained. With other men he carried those who were still too burned or too hysterical to walk or

those who had made it to the shelter only to die there. He
wrapped the dead in blankets and helped to place them on
carts and wagons that would carry them out to the cemetery.
One of the gravediggers had come in for coffee and some
rest and told them there was no choice—some would have
to be buried in a mass grave. With this news the volunteers
in the tent redoubled their efforts to identify as many of the
dead as they could before sending them out.

Through the long afternoon and into the night Ryan
worked. He observed the incredible condition of some of
the victims. In some cases they were completely unmarked,
not a scorch or burn on them, yet when he touched their
clothing, it would disintegrate in his fingers, and once when
he searched the pockets of a man for some identification, he
found only a handful of fused coins. The coins had melted while the man's person seemed completely untouched.
Ryan remembered what the heat had done to the papers in
his pockets. How much greater had the maelstrom been here
that coins could fuse?

Just after midnight he and a crew of men made a rough
camp near the river and huddled next to a small camp fire
for the night. There were no extra blankets. They would
have to make do with their coats and the fire. Ryan stared
at the flames and thought how something that had caused
such a total sacking of the land and its populace could now
be the one source of warmth and comfort for survivors.

In spite of his almost complete exhaustion, he slept in fits
and starts. His dreams were interrupted by the reality of his
surroundings, as others tried to comfort the orphaned and
homeless and those who had become completely deranged
by the experience through which they had lived. As the
endless night wore on, Ryan's hopes for Sophia Bergeman
darkened. How could anyone have survived this?

"Faster," August Bergeman ordered the hired driver as
the carriage started for Peshtigo from Green Bay at just
past dawn. First his train had been delayed, and then he

had had to spend the night in Green Bay, being warned that the roads to Peshtigo were no longer clear and often were obstructed by smoldering piles of debris, fallen trees, or worse. After the delay he wanted only to be there, to find Sophie, to get her home.

"Sir, if I drive the team any harder, we might lose one of them to a fall, and begging your pardon, sir, but that would take a great deal of time—turning back to Green Bay or going on with just half the team . . ."

"All right. Pay attention to your business," Bergeman ordered irritably. He chewed on his cigar and fumed. The world was conspiring to beset him with impudent young men who thought they could do as they pleased while he sat idly by. Like Sullivan . . .

The thought of Ryan Sullivan carried with it thoughts of Katrina. What had happened between them during that long night on his yacht? Neither had denied his accusation of scandal. He had to assume he was correct. And if he were . . .

He rubbed the drawn features of his face. *Ah, Sophie,* he thought miserably. The news had been so unbearable, so undeniably bleak. There was so little reason to hope, and yet hope he did. Surely she had found a way to survive. He thought of her single-minded determination, and the memory made him smile.

Katrina was like that—resolute once her course was set— and it appeared her course was set for Ryan Sullivan. August had warned his wife of the danger of allowing the relationship to continue for even one day, much less for something as head-turning as a gala ball in one of Chicago's finest hotels. But Sophie had prevailed, as she usually did, and in the past more often than not she had been right.

He frowned. But she had misjudged this. Fate had seen to that. Fate had conspired to throw the young fools into a setting of peril and rescue where Sullivan could not help but appear the hero. And now, if Sophie was . . . gone . . . how would he manage this? The children had always been her priority . . . even Frederick . . .

The thought of his only son brought fresh pain to the wounds he already suffered. How he missed the boy. How he had looked forward to taking him into the business, to making him a partner, to seeing him married and carrying on the dynasty through children and grandchildren.

His dreams for Frederick had had to be shifted to Edward and the girls, and over time he had grown to accept that. But to go on without Sophie? It was too much . . . far too much. He watched his hands tremble; his body seemed to have slumped overnight into the posture of an old man. He sighed and tried to swallow around the hard knot that had settled in his throat the moment he first heard the news of the fire and devastation in Peshtigo.

When he and Heinrich had arrived in Green Bay, the news had not been any better. There were survivors, but most were from outlying areas. No one, it seemed, was from town, and that's where Sophie had been—in the worst of it. He closed his eyes and thought of her lovely face, the sound of her singing as she walked through her garden clipping something here, pinching back something there. How he used to tease her, coming home and staggering up on the porch as if he'd just survived a terrible attack.

"What is it, dear?" she would always ask, her voice full of concern, but her eyes twinkling with merriment.

"It's your flowers, my love. I fear they may actually begin to take over the street soon, or have there already been reports of persons missing among the foliage?"

He smiled and opened his eyes . . . and the smile faded. They were driving through the path of the fire now. August Bergeman was no stranger to disasters. During the war he had seen more than enough for a lifetime, and he knew well the damage even a small fire could do. But this . . . how could anyone . . . even Sophie . . . survive this?

The following morning, after another stint of grave-digging duty, Ryan had to get away, if only for a brief moment. Striding toward the tent where he hoped to get a cup of coffee, he spotted August Bergeman. For a moment the two men stood there, their faces mirroring the horrors they had already seen and the foreboding they shared of what such a catastrophe meant for Sophia.

"Herr Bergeman," Ryan said and found that his voice failed him. He had spent the morning inhaling the omnipresent ash, and his throat was raw and parched.

Bergeman's eyes widened in fear, and Ryan realized he had mistaken Ryan's failed voice for delivery of a message of sympathy. "No," he hastened to add, grasping the older man by the shoulders. "I haven't heard yet . . . haven't found her."

Bergeman's face relaxed only slightly with relief. He nodded once and moved past Ryan into the tent. "Who's in charge?" he said to the first volunteer he saw.

"Captain Daniels," she replied, "but he's not here."

"He's due back soon from Marinette," Ryan provided as the volunteer hurried on to assist others in restraining a man who had just found out his wife and baby had perished. "Can I get you some water, sir?"

Bergeman turned on him then. "Why are you here, Sullivan? This is no affair of yours."

"Katrina asked me to come, sir. How is she?"

"How do you think she is? For the moment this . . . tragedy overshadows everything else, but once we find Mrs. Bergeman . . . once we get her home . . ." He stumbled for words, and Ryan saw that he was overcome not only with fear and worry and grief, but also exhaustion. He doubted the man had had much sleep in the past few days.

"Sir, please come and sit down. We can wait for the captain together."

At that moment Heinrich appeared at the brewer's side and offered his employer his arm. Ryan went to get both men some water. When he returned, the three of them sat just outside the tent, on the banks of the river, in an unyielding and uneasy silence. A chill wind blew, and

Ryan noticed how August Bergeman sat huddled under a blanket. He had grown old overnight, since hearing the news of his wife.

Finally Ryan spotted Daniels. The captain looked as if he had viewed the essence of Hell and lived to carry back reports. His eyes were swollen and bloodshot, his face and uniform smudged with soot, his hands wrapped in bandages, grayed by the constantly drifting ash.

"Captain Daniels," Ryan called and knew that Heinrich had helped August Bergeman to his feet; the two were close behind him.

Daniels squinted and paused.

"Captain, we are seeking news of—"

"My wife . . . My sister-in-law, Fanny Schmidt, was expecting a baby . . . My wife, Sophia . . ."

Captain Daniels's face softened, and he nodded. "Your wife and the child are at the emergency hospital in Marinette . . . I took them there myself yesterday."

With a cry of disbelief mingled with pure joy, August Bergeman grasped the soldier's tattered sleeve. "Are you certain?" His face had paled considerably, and his hand trembled uncontrollably.

Daniels nodded. "However, I'm afraid the others . . . Fanny and Helmut . . ." His eyes welled. It was a message he had had to deliver too many times to neighbors and family of his own. He seemed very near collapse himself. "It's easy to remember the survivors, sir," he said brokenly.

August put his arm around the captain's shoulders, comforting him as he savored the news the younger man had brought. "She's alive. Can we go there?"

"If you can wait till this afternoon while I take stock here, I'll take you myself."

Ryan, August, and Heinrich filled the hours while they waited for Captain Daniels with more volunteer efforts. Heinrich and Ryan worked with a team of gravediggers, while August assisted in identification. From time to time

Ryan looked on with concern as August Bergeman came face-to-face with the reality of the disaster. Still, the old man seemed to have found a rebirth of energy, and his natural instinct for leadership and management served everyone well in establishing a more efficient method for handling the casualties.

"Let's go," Captain Daniels said, indicating the loaded wagon at the far end of the tent.

"My valet and I will follow in our carriage," Bergeman told the captain, signaling to the hired driver to bring the vehicle.

"And you, sir?" Daniels turned to Ryan.

Ryan saw that August waited for his response as well. "I'll ride alongside," he replied without looking at Kate's father.

Along the way, they viewed more horror. The captain explained that several people had committed suicide rather than endure the flames. Passing the road to one farm, he told of finding the bodies of the seven members of the family in the well, where they had hoped to save themselves but had been suffocated when the flaming walls of the house fell on top of it. He told his stories in a grim monotone and seemed to have not the slightest shred of emotion left with which to color them.

With every step, with every horror story, Ryan's resolve to begin his life with Kate as soon as possible was strengthened.

In Marinette the captain gave instructions for unloading the survivors and refilling the wagon with supplies to be dispatched immediately back to Peshtigo. Then he indicated the entrance to the emergency hospital and led the way through wards filled to overflowing with victims of the fire. He stopped a nurse and held a brief conference with her. She consulted a listing and indicated a cot at the far end of the room.

Sophia Bergeman's hair had been burned off. Her body was swathed in bandages, and even in her sleep she grimaced with pain and twitched with nightmares of her ordeal. But she was alive, and miraculously her beautiful face was unscathed by the flames.

The moment he saw her, August gave a cry of relief mingled with shock and fell to his knees at her bedside, his face buried in the sheets, his body racked with sobs as again and again he mumbled her name.

Sophia opened her eyes and gave way to her own tears when she saw her husband. "Augie," she whispered in a hoarse rasp. "Augie, *Liebchen.*" She struggled to rise, but August prevented her by moving to sit on the side of the cot, stroking her face, looking at her as if she were some illusion that might disappear.

They spoke quietly and emotionally in German. Sophia's voice would sometimes strain as she obviously described the terrors of her agony.

"She is talking of the noise," Captain Daniels translated when Sophia repeated *Geräusch* over and over. "It was like the roar of a hundred freight trains bearing down at full speed . . . a roar that started in the south and grew louder and louder . . ."

August was attempting to console Sophia, but she clung to him, her eyes clouded with memory of all she had lived through without him. *"Das Rauch,"* she whispered and closed her eyes in pain.

Ryan recognized the word for "smoke" and recalled how thick and omnipresent it had been in Chicago.

"The smoke came first . . . throughout the day," the captain said. "By nine the streets were black with it, so when the fire did come, everyone had lost all sense of direction. And the fire came"—he paused and took a shuddering breath—"with such sweeping force . . . Suddenly it was . . . everywhere." He gazed out the window, lost in thought.

"How did she survive?" Ryan asked, nodding toward the now sobbing Sophie.

"My understanding is that her sister and brother-in-law

thought they could all make it to the river. The sister was weak from childbirth, so her husband was carrying her. Mrs. Bergeman had the baby. At some point she apparently realized they would not make it and found a ditch, where she lay down with the baby. My men found her there and brought her here."

Ryan noticed the crib standing near Sophie's cot. When he moved closer for a look, Sophie saw the movement and gave her husband a sad smile, indicating that he, too, should look at the crib. August moved to lift the small bundle from which emanated one tiny red fist and several fierce guttural cries. It was the baby Fanny had delivered and Sophie had saved. "Frederick," she whispered, nodding toward the child her husband held. "Frederick," she repeated as they both began to cry, and Ryan caught words of German that told him Fanny had named the child after her sister's dead son.

After a few minutes the captain excused himself, and Ryan was left standing at the foot of the cot, eavesdropping on the reunion of two people he hoped would be his in-laws. He observed the tenderness with which they gazed at each other, evidence of the love that years could not dim. He recalled the anguish August Bergeman had exhibited in Peshtigo as they waited for word. He understood, recalling his own fears and torment in Chicago when he thought he had lost Katie forever.

In that moment he understood also the rage with which August Bergeman had greeted him at the dock in Milwaukee. Here was a man who placed his family above all else; his wife and daughters were his life, his whole purpose in anything he did. Harm them, defile their reputations, in any way open them to potential injury or misuse, and you would have August Bergeman to face.

Ryan looked down at the couple smiling now as they cuddled the infant, and he felt a fresh respect for them and something more—genuine affection.

"Sophia, I've got to get word to Katrina and Lucinda,"

August said, settling the child at her side and moving to retrieve his hat and coat.

"Nein," she cried and gripped his arm tightly.

For the first time August looked up at Ryan, and in his face there was something akin to a request for help . . . not a plea certainly, but still a need.

"I'll take care of that, sir," he offered quickly. "Shall I say when you will be returning?"

"As soon as Sophie can travel," August said. "Heinrich can handle it." The valet had remained with the driver outside.

"I'd like to do it, sir," Ryan said, and his eyes met Bergeman's directly.

"All right. Tell Heinrich to get us a room for the night."

Ryan nodded and left the ward, his boots making hollow sounds along the tiles of the corridors, as once again he passed the rows of cots and beds filled with people who were homeless but alive, in some cases the sole survivors of their families.

Kate passed the few hours of spare time she had in her mother's garden. Her days were long between hours spent with Edward managing the brewery and hours spent organizing relief efforts for Peshtigo and Chicago. She felt closer to Sophia in the garden than anywhere else in the house and moved along the rows of shrubs and flowers long after the sun had set, clipping back plants and collecting seeds her mother would want for the next growing season.

She tried to keep her thoughts focused on positive things, but after two days without any word, she began to lose hope, to fear the worst. To have no word at all from Ryan or her father . . .

"Katrina!"

It was Edward. He ran up the gravel drive and across the lawn, waving a paper. "She's alive," he cried happily. "They're coming home." He caught her in a hug and swung her around. "Oh, Kate, it is a miracle!"

"Praise God," she whispered and clutched the telegram in trembling fingers while she read its contents.

Sophia in hospital. Stop. Sends love. Stop. Coming home soon as possible. Stop.

"Oh, Edward," Kate murmured, rereading the message as if she could not believe her eyes. Then she hugged her friend once more. "We must tell Lu and the staff," she said happily.

"I'll do that. This came for you." He handed her a second telegram and hurried off to find his fiancée.

Katie. Stop. Must return to Chicago. Stop. Will wire plans from there. Stop. Love. Stop. Ryan.

She saw that both wires had originated in Marinette. That meant Ryan and her parents were together, and surely that meant something good, didn't it?

19

DAYS WENT BY with no further word from Peshtigo. A week later, her parents came home. Sophie was weak and frail, her appearance both shocking and sobering to her daughters, who had always thought of their mother as invincible. She was deeply depressed as the reality of her loss of family sank in.

August had aged as well, and Kate's heart went out to him as she watched him going through the motions of managing the brewery when his mind and heart were constantly with his wife. Their mutual concern for Sophie, however, had done little to resolve the differences between them.

Kate had tried to broach the subject of Ryan and what had happened to bring him together with her parents in Peshtigo. But Papa had glared at her and snapped, "I think I have made my position clear on Ryan Sullivan, Katrina. We will talk of him no more."

Which, of course, added to her turmoil. Her parents needed her now as they never had before. Her mother's convalescence might take weeks or even months. Her father was so distracted that once again she and Edward were the ones the men came to for solving problems at work. Then there was the matter of the baby, Frederick.

He was certainly the one bright spot in their otherwise bleak days, but his presence added a whole new dimension to the household. For one thing, the child was a constant reminder to Sophie of the loss of her family. On top of that he reminded them all of their own Frederick, another loss. Yet his very innocence and vulnerability made him absolutely irresistible.

Kate's days continued to begin before dawn and last sometimes past midnight. Aside from her added work at the brewery, she insisted on continuing the school, only now and then allowing Millie to step in and teach in her place. She was still as active as possible in the efforts to get relief supplies and funds to both Chicago and Peshtigo, efforts that had even earned her a letter of admiration from Cousin Eloise. But her days began and ended with Frederick.

From the very day he entered the house, she had been drawn to him. After Mike Connors carried her mother upstairs and settled her in her own room, Kate had asked that he and Heinrich go to the attic and bring down the cradle and a trunk of baby clothes she knew Mama had saved there, even after she had found out she could have no more children.

"Where do you want it, miss?" Connors had asked as he and the butler maneuvered the cradle down the narrow stairway to the upstairs hall.

"In here," Kate directed, making the decision almost without thought or plan. She led the way to the small sitting room that connected her bedroom to the guest room. "Here," she said with more certainty than she had felt about anything for days. She indicated a place near the fireplace and a rocking chair that had once belonged to her grandmother.

"Kate, don't you think it makes more sense to have the baby nearer to my room or even up on the third floor with Pauline and Ernestine . . . at least for now?" Lu had taken her duties as household manager far more seriously once Mama came home, and had learned that she was indeed vital to the continued smooth operation of the household.

"No," Kate answered firmly, and there must have been something in her tone, for no one argued with her.

So, with the garden in dormancy, her focus turned to the baby, Frederick. In the mornings she spent an hour feeding him and playing with him before going on her way to face whatever conflicts and problems the day might bring. At night she retired to the sitting room after supper and her nightly visit with her mother. She would take Frederick with her as she sat with Sophie for an hour or so. She did not imagine the spark of interest that shone in her mother's eyes whenever she entered the room, carrying the child. As the days passed, Sophie began to offer small pieces of advice for caring for the baby.

"Keep his head covered when you move through the house with him. The hallways can be so drafty." Or, "Are you testing the heated milk? On the inside of your elbow is best."

Later Kate would sit by the fire and read or work on the lessons for the school or details of the relief effort, while Frederick slept. The Peshtigo project took on new meaning now: She was doing it for Frederick, for the memory of his parents. If he became restless, she picked him up and sang softly to him as she rocked him back to sleep. All the while she thought of Ryan . . . of their future . . . of their children . . .

Meals were somber affairs during those days. As often as not, August chose to take his meal in Sophie's room, hoping that by so doing he could encourage her to eat and to regain her strength. That left Lu and Edward alone with Kate at the large dining room table. What little conversation there was centered around the day's routine at the house and the brewery and the schedule for the coming days and weeks.

They were all depressed by the trials they had endured during the past weeks and exhausted by long days filled with responsibility for the present as well as uncertainty about the future. Usually the conversation dwindled away to silence as each of them sat and reflected on the events of the past month.

Every day Kate waited for some word from Ryan. A week went by with nothing. Then she received a brief telegram telling her he was settled in a room in Chicago and would let her know as soon as he had news of their future together. She thought of writing, but he had sent no address. Maybe there was no address. From what Papa had told them of the totally ravaged town of Peshtigo, it was possible that in Chicago there was little left as well. It was strange that life had gotten back to normal in Milwaukee while familiar routines were impossible to follow in Chicago. Housework, jobs—all had been disrupted.

When the letter had come from Eloise asking about Sophie, praising the girls for their work, and profusely thanking August for his generosity toward the relief efforts, Kate thought of writing back and asking her cousin to inquire about Ryan. But how would that look? Eloise might have mellowed toward Katrina, but she was hardly likely to be sympathetic where Ryan was concerned. Indeed, she would probably see his lack of contact as clear evidence that she had been right about him all the time.

Kate hated the doubts that crowded in on her as one day followed the next with no word. She told herself that it had only been a matter of days, that it only seemed an eternity. She told herself that he certainly was as preoccupied with mere survival and recovery as her own household was. After all, they were all right, their losses in terms of property and fortune had been small, while Ryan had possibly lost everything. She told herself to be patient.

And that made her smile. When had she become the impatient one? Ryan was the one who constantly admonished her to live in the moment, for who knew what tomorrow might bring? Her thoughts and actions had urged caution, even when she was most drawn to him. She had been raised to consider all sides of an issue or situation carefully, to look beyond momentary reward toward the long-term merits of an action.

Of course, having done all that and come to a conclusion, she could be headstrong and impetuous. When another week passed with no further word from Ryan, she was not about to sit idly by. She understood what he was doing. Because he had fallen on hard financial times, he thought himself unworthy to pursue her. He would not be satisfied until he could arrive on her father's doorstep with proof of his merit as a suitor for her hand. But Kate had no interest in his portfolio. She wanted only to be with him. He was her future. Yes, her family needed her as well, but they had each other. Ryan had no one but her.

"I'm going to Chicago," she announced to Edward the following day.

He looked up from the columns of figures he had been checking. "I see," he said quietly.

"I'll be going tomorrow with the next load of relief supplies." Her tone showed that she anticipated an argument.

He nodded again and turned his attention back to his ledgers.

"I think I should see the situation for myself. After all, we keep sending carloads of supplies and never really know what happens to them. For all we know—"

"You don't have to explain," Edward said. He was leaning back in his chair, studying her as she paced the office.

"I'm not explaining," she snapped, but she was. Worse, she was making excuses.

"You haven't heard from Ryan?"

She shook her head miserably.

"Then I think you should go."

Kate couldn't have been more surprised if he had suddenly announced he thought she should try swimming to Michigan. She found herself making all the arguments she had expected from him. "Of course, Papa will be furious."

"Yes, he will," Edward agreed.

"And this probably is the worst possible time what with Mama and the baby . . ."

"Lu and I can help with that."

"I wouldn't be gone too long."

"I think you should wait and see what the situation is before deciding how long to stay."

Kate stopped her pacing and stood in front of him, completely at a loss for words. "I thought . . ."

Edward smiled sadly. "You thought I would disapprove. Before, I would have. I would have given you the argument you expected. But everything has changed. I know what I felt as Lu and I were trying to get away from that fire. I see what your parents are going through. I saw your father's face when he first heard the news . . . I honestly thought he was going to die of a broken heart on the spot. Life's far too short, Katie, to take a chance on missing out on your own joy."

Her heart swelled with love and gratitude for this man's lifelong friendship. He had always been there—a sounding board for her rantings, a barometer for her multiple moods. "Thank you," she said softly.

Edward stood up and hugged her hard. "What are brothers for?"

That night, when she went to the sitting room after supper, she found her father sitting in the darkened room rocking the cradle and talking quietly in German to the baby. " . . . *ein schlafen, kleine Frederick* . . . sh-h-h . . . sh-h-h."

She stood at the door and watched him, realizing that once she had been the child he had spoken to so lovingly in that cradle. How dear this man was to her. How much she hated the estrangement between them. Surely, there had to be a way to regain their closeness.

"Papa?"

He turned, startled at her presence, his hand still on the cradle. "Ah, Katrina." He turned back to Frederick, reaching down to rearrange the covers over the sleeping baby. "He reminds me of you as a baby."

"Not our Frederick?" she asked, taking the opportunity to move into the room and stand next to him by the cradle.

"No. Our Frederick was always settled, even as an infant . . . not like this one. He fights sleep as if it would deprive him of something. You were always restless like that. Your mother was just speaking of it tonight."

"I did not mean to give you so much trouble," Kate teased, and for an instant there was in the room a remnant of what father and daughter had once shared, a sort of easy companionship that allowed them the freedom to talk of thoughts and ideas and worries. Kate smoothed a wrinkle in her father's waistcoat, a gesture that was merely an excuse to touch him in some loving way.

"He will be all right . . . your cousin," Papa said, turning his attention once again to the baby. "Your mother and I will see to that."

"Then he will be most blessed," Kate replied. She hesitated, unwilling to spoil the moment but knowing she had to tell him. "Papa, tomorrow when our train of relief supplies goes to Chicago, I'll be going along."

His grip on the side of the cradle tightened, but he said nothing. Instead he once again adjusted the covers over Frederick, then turned and started from the room.

"Papa, did you hear me?" She knew full well that he had.

"Does your mother know?" He kept his back to her, his hand on the brass doorknob.

"I will tell her tonight."

With that he turned and took the three steps necessary to place himself face-to-face with her. "No. I understand that I can no longer prevent you from making the fool of yourself that you are determined to be over this . . . this . . . gambler. But I can and I will prevent you from upsetting the lives of anyone in this family, especially your mother. Do you understand?"

The tears streamed silently down her face. So it had come to this. He almost seemed to hate her, his eyes were so filled with fury.

"Why do you hate him so?" she cried.

"I do not hate him. I hate what his presence has done to you and to our family. Before he came here, we were happy . . . you were happy . . . our life was—"

"Surely you cannot blame Ryan for—"

"Has he turned your head so completely, Katrina, that you don't even see how you are prepared to desert your own ailing mother?"

"But Mama is recovering . . . She actually came down-stairs today for a little while. She is better and she has you and Lu and the rest of the household. Ryan has only me."

August closed his eyes tightly for a moment in pure frustration. "How can I save you, *Liebchen?*" he said almost to himself. Then focusing on her once again, he added, "Katrina, I know that he is a good man. He will always be a good man. But why can I not make you see that for you he is the wrong man? Your life with him will be . . . difficult, no matter how much money he makes. There are hard times coming that will have their effect. How do I make you see that I do not want you hurt?" He spoke in a whisper, mindful of the baby, but his whisper was filled with the substance of his bafflement, his impotence to make her see a future he was sure she faced.

"Papa, I love him."

Those four words took the wind from his sails. "And therein lies the root of it," he said sadly, and this time he did not pause as he left the room.

Kate was stunned when she arrived in Chicago. She had expected to see a desolate city, one completely brought to its knees by the catastrophe of only a few weeks before. Instead she saw a city at work. Everywhere buildings were going up, debris was being cleared away, the streets were filled with carts and wagons carrying lumber and supplies, and the place was alive with the sounds of hammers, saws, and crews of men rushing about, shouting directions, and working feverishly to rebuild.

Mike Connors had been assigned the job of overseeing the relief effort from the first day. Now he accompanied Kate through the busy and congested streets of Chicago as she began her search for Ryan.

"Do you know where we might find Theodore Kerry, Mr. Connors?" she shouted above the din of a city under reconstruction. Ted Kerry was the only contact besides her cousins who might know how to reach Ryan.

"I'll ask around." The brawny foreman flagged down a hansom cab and ordered the driver to wait with the lady while he made some inquiries. Ten minutes later he returned and called out an address as he hauled his large body onto the seat beside the driver.

Kate opened the partition window. "Did you find Mr. Kerry?"

Mike leaned down so that his face was framed by the small opening. He was grinning. "I did better than that, ma'am. I found you Mr. Sullivan as well."

Ted Kerry and Ryan were attending an organizational meeting. Union members had gathered to chart plans for the most efficient use of labor in the task of rebuilding as much of the city as possible before winter set in. Many new men who had lost jobs in other fields due to the fire were anxious to join the ranks of the laborers and construction workers.

With Mike at her side, Kate eased her way into the packed room and stood listening to Theodore Kerry's oratory. There were far too many men standing in the aisles and around the perimeter of the room for her to get even a glimpse of the stage, but Kerry was magnificent. He made the young man she and Ryan had heard in the beer garden on Independence Day seem a hopeless amateur by comparison. With a voice that was filled with drama one minute and hushed with distress the next, Kerry had everyone in the hall completely under his spell. Kate felt a grudging respect for the man, even though he still could be trouble for her father and Edward.

Her father and Edward, she had thought, not her. When had she stopped thinking of the brewery as her business, as her future?

She felt herself being pressed forward as more men entered the room. Then the men were cheering and moving toward the front to shake hands with Kerry, who had left the stage and was making his way toward the exit. Kate observed how the sea of men seemed to part for him, the workers watching him with a mixture of envy and deference. He was coming toward her.

"Miss Bergeman," he called, his eyes wide with surprise at seeing her here. Then over his shoulder he shouted, "Ryan, over here. Get Sullivan . . . now," he ordered, and several men rushed to obey. "A pleasant surprise," he said loudly to be heard above the clamor of the masses as they began leaving the hall. "How is your family?" His concern was genuine, and in that moment Kate felt that this was a decent man, a man one could work with. She would tell Edward that when she got back to Milwaukee.

"They are recovering, thank you. And you, Mr. Kerry? How did you and your family fare?"

He smiled, and she saw that he was handsome in a rugged sort of way. "Now then, Katie, I thought we were to be on a first-name basis . . . being friends and all."

He had dodged her question. Ryan did that, too, never wanting to talk of personal things. She wondered if it might be an Irish trait. "It's good to see you, Ted," she said and smiled back at him, accepting the handshake he offered.

"Would you take your hand off my lady, Cousin?"

Ryan placed a brotherly arm around Ted's shoulders, but his eyes were on Katrina. Until that very moment he had had no idea of just how much he had been missing her. His days had been so packed with work and worry that at night he had fallen into an exhausted slumber, only to rise the following morning and start again. One day had pretty much melded into the next, and he had literally lost track of passing time. But the moment he saw her, he realized the full agony of the past several days.

"If you two will just come with me, I think there's an office over here you might find a bit of privacy in," Ted said with a grin. "Then me and Mike here will just go have ourselves a brew, catch up on the news, be back in say, what? An hour or so?"

"Fine," Kate murmured, having barely heard a word the man said. Ryan looked haggard, he probably hadn't been getting much sleep. She wondered where he had been spending his nights. His clothes were dust-covered and wrinkled. He had a two-day growth of beard and was badly in need of a haircut. Conditions must be even worse than she had imagined. Of course, he had obviously lost everything—oh, Lord, why hadn't she come sooner?

"Lead the way," Ryan said to his cousin in a distracted voice, his eyes fastened on Kate as if she might disappear if he looked away for even a second. "I can't believe you're here," he said softly as he put his arm around her waist and pulled her close.

"Me and Mike'll be going now," Kerry said from the door after ushering them into what appeared to be an unoccupied office, with only a table and two chairs.

"Anytime," Ryan answered and did not wait for the man to close the door before he grasped Kate's face between his palms and kissed her hard.

Between fervid kisses they tried to talk at the same time. "How did you find me . . . ?" "Never thought I would . . ." " . . . missed you more than . . ." " . . . love you . . ." " . . . love you . . ."

And then they stopped talking and gave in to the pure pleasure of kissing each other, holding each other, touching and rediscovering each other. He took off her bonnet and ran his hands over her hair, his eyes telling her more than words could possibly tell how much he had missed her.

She flattened her palms against his chest, feeling the rapid beat of his heart against her hands.

His fingers shook slightly as he began opening the top buttons of her high-collared blouse, pushing the fabric aside so that he could kiss her neck.

Then they were in each other's arms again, holding on as if each were the other's lifeline, their mouths open and hungry for the taste and touch of one another.

After long moments they laughingly agreed that the hard oak table might not be the most romantic spot to play out their reunion.

"Cousin Eloise would be further scandalized," Ryan teased.

"I don't care," Kate shot back, and then she grinned. The room was exposed to the street by windows that ran from floor to ceiling. A few yards away, Chicagoans were bustling about their business, but any one of them could have been witness to the explosion of need and passion that had just taken place between them. Just like that day at the train station in Milwaukee, when Kate had begged him to close the shades before anyone could see them. Today she really did not care who saw, who knew, who protested. Eloise herself could have come strolling by. Kate was with Ryan, and nothing else mattered.

"You're remembering the train," he said with a provocative grin. "How brazen you have become, my love."

She nodded and ducked her head shyly.

Ryan laughed out loud. The sound filled the room as well as her heart. How she had missed the sound of that laughter. Then he hugged her tight, swinging her off her feet and around the room. "Oh, Katie, Katie, Katie, have you any idea how much I love you?"

Suddenly they did not want to keep their joy to themselves. They wanted to be out among people, sharing their happiness, flaunting it.

Outside a wind that foretold colder weather caused people to wrap their cloaks more tightly around themselves.

But Ryan and Kate hardly noticed as they strolled hand in hand through the streets. They went in search of a place to have coffee and found Mike and Ted. For an hour the foursome sat discussing the astounding resurrection of Chicago. Then Ted offered to help Mike oversee the unloading of the supplies he and Kate had brought from Milwaukee.

"Will you be coming back on the train, Miss Bergeman?" Mike asked shyly as the two laborers prepared to leave the restaurant.

"What time do you have to leave, Mike?" Ryan asked before Kate could open her mouth.

"I'd say two hours, sir."

Ryan nodded. "I'll see that she's there."

Satisfied and more than a little relieved that she would indeed be on board, Mike left with Ted, and Ryan turned back to Kate. She was defiant.

"I'm not going back," she said adamantly.

"Oh, yes, you are. I'm in quite enough trouble with your father as it is." He noticed how Kate's mood darkened at the mention of her father, and not wanting to spoil the rest of their brief reunion, he continued, "Katie, we're going to have the rest of our lives together. Let's not take any chances that might further upset your parents now. And speaking of them, I want to hear all about them . . . about Lu and Edward and the baby. Tell me about the baby."

She filled him in on Sophie's slow convalescence and how Lu and Edward had seemed to mature as a result of the fire. "Lu runs the house almost as well as Mama ever did. But what of you? Did you . . . that is . . ."

"The house . . . everything in my offices . . . my offices . . . everything," he said quietly.

"And in Peshtigo?"

He nodded, then smiled ruefully. "The nice part of that is I still own the land, and trees do have a way of growing back."

She loved him more for the brave face he was trying to put on everything. He turned the conversation once again to her, remonstrating her for working too hard, for trying to do too much, be all things to all people. Then he laughed and relaxed for the first time in weeks as she regaled him with stories of the wonders of the baby, Frederick.

They sipped the last of their coffee, holding hands across the small table, their eyes memorizing every detail of each other's face.

Suddenly Ryan stood up and grinned. "Well, we can't waste this wonderful day sitting in this dingy place. Let's go shopping."

"Ryan, no . . . ," she protested.

"Yes," he insisted, caressing the slim silver band that represented their engagement. "This is not at all what I had in mind as an official engagement present."

"But I love it."

"Good. But, see? You have all these other fingers, not to mention these beautiful wrists or that delectable neck." He sighed. "We have to attend to them all, I think."

"But . . ."

He pulled out her chair, leaning down as he did so and whispering into her ear, "Did I mention these earlobes? I do love these earlobes." With that he gave her a gentle nip, which brought her to her feet at once. "Ah, good, you're ready," he teased. "Shall we?" He offered his arm.

"Ryan." It was a protest and a warning. How did she tell him she did not need baubles? How did she tell him what was really on her mind: that in his present circumstances he probably could ill afford anything beyond the necessities?

Along the street, Ryan nodded and smiled and tipped his hat to almost everyone they passed.

"Do you know everyone in the city?" Kate asked with more than a little awe.

"I know many people," he agreed. "However, I don't know a single one of these. But you make me feel like greeting everyone I see. It's all I can do to keep from stopping them and telling them how much I love you."

She smiled with pleasure. He made her feel so incredibly beautiful and special.

"Ah, the very place." He led the way into a shop that was doing a brisk business in the midst of recovering from the ravages of the fire.

"Good afternoon, sir. May I be of service?" The clerk was formal in his address and attire, deferential in his manner, and standing behind a display of some of the most stunning pieces of jewelry Kate had ever seen.

"You have a fine selection," Ryan noted.

"Ah, yes, sir. We have just received these items from our New York store. The fire, of course, made some . . . restocking . . . necessary."

Kate almost laughed out loud at the irony of that. The chances were the store's entire inventory had been reduced to one large melted mass in the aftermath of the fire. Still the sales clerk spoke as if no misfortune at all had occurred.

"Could we see that?"

The clerk scurried to pull the necklace Ryan indicated.

"And perhaps those," Ryan added, eyeing a matching pair of earrings. "And we'll want to see something in a betrothal ring . . . emerald, I think."

The clerk practically tripped himself in his zeal to do Ryan's bidding.

At first Kate was resistant. "Ryan," she protested.

"Oh, try it . . . There's no harm in trying something on," he urged.

His pleasure in seeing her model the jewels seemed to be so genuine that she soon became caught up in the venture as well. She preened and posed and played along with Ryan's praise or disappointment in the stones. They giggled like errant children when the salesman's back was turned. Kate had begun to enjoy the sport of it all when Ryan pointed to three pieces and said with all seriousness, "This brooch with those earrings . . . and, of course, the ring."

Kate watched in stunned silence as he prepared to pay in cash from a roll of bills he pulled from his inner coat pocket.

"Ryan, no," she whispered urgently and firmly. He smiled benevolently down at her and nodded to the clerk to continue the transaction. "Excuse us," Kate said and practically dragged him away from the counter. "I cannot let you do this," she insisted.

For the first time that afternoon he frowned. "I want to do it."

"What are you trying to prove?" she argued.

"Nothing." He seemed confused at the turn of events.

"Well, this has gone far enough. Now, please, may we leave?"

"No. Why can't I buy a present for the woman I plan to marry?"

"You don't have to buy me gifts."

Their voices strained to maintain a level of decorum in the suddenly silent shop.

"Does this have something to do with your father?" He was confused. Had the old man finally won her over? Had she really come to break it off with him?

Now she was exasperated, and she was embarrassed by the heads turning in their direction. "It has nothing to do with my father. It has to do with the fact that you can little afford . . ."

His eyes darkened with anger. "I'll be the judge of what I can and cannot afford," he retorted and turned back to the clerk. "Are my purchases ready yet?"

"Yes, sir." The clerk glanced nervously from Kate to Ryan and back again.

"I assume you will accept my cash," Ryan said as he peeled off the bills.

"Thank you, sir . . . miss. Good day to you both."

Ryan accepted the small stack of boxes the clerk presented to him and headed for the door. He opened it and waited silently for Kate to join him. Once they were on the sidewalk, he took her by the elbow and began striding down the street. "We'd best hurry or you'll miss your train" was the last thing he said before depositing her at the station with the waiting Mike Connors.

20

MAYBE HE DIDN'T know her after all. Maybe she was just like her father and all the rest of those people who made assumptions about a man simply because of his heritage. Maybe he'd been fooling himself all along. But, damn it, after all they'd been through, a man would think she would believe in him . . . trust him . . . know him.

Ryan wasn't certain of the exact moment it had dawned on him that Kate believed him financially incapable of affording the jewels he had selected for her. All he knew was that when he realized that she doubted him, that she actually for even one moment believed he would be so reckless, even for love . . .

"Ryan!"

Ted Kerry loped across the busy street to where his cousin studied the plans for his new town house. He recalled how Ryan had insisted on several design ideas that clearly showed his intention to occupy the house with a wife and more than a couple of children. Ted grinned as he slapped his cousin on the back.

"So when's the happy day?"

The only response he got was a low growl, followed by a muttered "Women!" as Ryan turned and shouted at a workman nearby. "Could you watch what you're doing there? That stuff costs money, you know."

"Would you care to discuss the problem?" Kerry perched himself on a pile of lumber and prepared to listen.

"The problem? The problem is that I will never understand women if I live to be a hundred and five," Ryan ranted.

"I see." Ted paused and then added, "Or could it be that you are having trouble understanding a very particular lady?"

Ryan's shoulders slumped with the weariness of several long days and the stress of the aborted reunion with Kate. "Doesn't she know that I am pushing myself to get everything in place for us? Doesn't she understand that I would never expect her to accept me until I could offer her a home to live in? Doesn't she know that this"—he gestured to the skeletal structure behind them—"not to mention everything else, is for her?"

"My guess is that she doesn't understand that at all. My guess is that true to form, you have kept all these thoughts to yourself and expected the lady to somehow know them instinctively."

Ryan wasn't listening. "It's not as if I was stupid enough to put all my eggs in this one basket. I mean, she knew I'd bought property in New York . . . we talked about that . . . or does she think that burned as well?"

"I think . . ."

"And did she never hear of insurance? Damn it, she's spent years in the world of business. Has she not learned a thing?"

"Aye, and I suppose you expect her to understand that much of your fortune is contained in so many pieces of paper that can be traced and remain quite valid, not to mention profitable. And, of course, what woman wouldn't simply assume one of the first orders of business would be to build her a mansion? Yes, my guess is . . . knowing you as I do . . . that you expected she would somehow simply divine these activities."

"I wanted the town house to be a wedding present. How could I show it to her? It would ruin the surprise. Have you no romance in your soul?" He was pacing now. He was a man used to working alone. It had never occurred to him to discuss it with her. Of course, he had assumed she would understand that he needed to put his house in order, so to speak, before they could be together.

That's exactly what he had been killing himself to do. There were so many details to attend to. Property out east to be sold, a portfolio to trace and reestablish, a life to rebuild both here and in Peshtigo. So many details. Why, the staff alone that would be necessary to manage the house he was building made him nervous. He understood it was necessary, but he had grown so used to managing on his own. The staff at the burned house had been a cook and a butler, neither of whom lived in.

Ryan was a man used to putting together deals and plans that worked smoothly. He had left Peshtigo with just such a plan for Kate and himself, and up until now he had been ahead of schedule.

Ted lay back on the lumber and considered the coming dusk. "Ah, romance. You think I do not understand the concept of romancing a young lady? I have too much romance in my soul, Ryan. Had I a bit less I might well be building a town house on one of the most exclusive streets in Chicago as you are." Ted shrugged and smiled. "Still, at the moment I would not trade places. When it comes to understanding the ladies, I am a millionaire to your pauper."

Ryan pretended to return his attention to the house plans, but Ted knew he was listening.

"A woman wants to be courted, Ryan . . . but she also wants to be *included,* do you understand me? Especially a woman like Katie Bergeman . . . A woman like that who's been used to being in charge and making plans of her own . . . you can't be ignoring that."

"Aye," Ryan agreed, knowing Ted was absolutely on the mark. He thought back to their conversation in the café. It had centered on major events—the fires, the relief efforts, the rebuilding. They had barely gotten around to speaking of more personal things, and when they had, the conversation had focused on Sophie and the baby and Lu and Edward. They hadn't even discussed her father; they'd tiptoed around that obstacle to their happiness.

When the conversation had turned to the somber subject of the terrible losses her family had suffered, Ryan had been seized by a need to do something fun, something spontaneous and frivolous. Thinking about it now, he realized he had assumed she would understand that his willingness to spend money on expensive gifts was his way of telling her everything was all right—he was all right. Due to careful planning he hadn't even realized was prophetic, he had escaped with a great deal of his fortune intact.

"I thought she would understand," he said softly as he reconsidered the details of the afternoon.

"Talk to her," Ted said as he jumped down from the lumber pile and pulled his jacket collar high around his ears. "It's coming on winter," he said as he looked up at the gray evening sky. "Well, I've got a meeting. See you, Cousin."

"Aye," Ryan called as an afterthought when Ted was already half a block away. A plan was forming, and he headed for the nearest telegraph office to set it in motion.

The train ride back was interminable. It was dark by the time Kate reached Milwaukee, and she stepped off the train into a chilly wind. *Good,* she thought morosely, *weather to suit my mood.*

She thanked Mike Connors and the other men for their help and sent them home. Then she spent an hour at her desk in the deserted brewery office. Her aim was to bury herself in work; this had certainly been effective before. But she found she could not concentrate. She kept seeing Ryan's face clouded with anger and disappointment . . . emotions she had obviously been responsible for, and yet she could not for the life of her understand how.

Surely he could not be upset that she was concerned for his financial status. After all, if they were to be married, his financial security became hers as well, not to mention the children he talked of having. Or was it that he had been trying to protect her from the full extent of his losses by pretending that all was well? How dumb did he think she was? Was he just like everyone else who assumed a mere woman could never have the brains to contemplate the economic aftereffects of the fires?

Irritably she took a stack of files and began putting them in order. She had thought he respected her mind, her intelligence. And if that were so, why didn't he grant her just a modicum of ability to understand this? She slammed the door of the file storage and heard it rattle in protest.

She might as well head home. There was as much to do there as here. In both places she felt needed. What was she to Ryan? Hadn't he told her often enough that the reason he loved her was her strength, her quick mind, her instincts for survival? If so, why the devil was he keeping her from taking an active role in planning their future?

As she trudged home, she barely noticed the way the dry leaves swirled around her skirt and caught on her hat and capelet. Nor did she pay much attention to the golden moon that rose over the lake.

The sight of the house cheered her some. Every floor was brightly lit, and there was music and the sound of laughter as she opened the etched glass front door and shut it quickly against the chill force of the wind.

Lu came into the hall from the music room. She was smiling with genuine delight for the first time in days. "Oh, Kate, you're home. Come, see. Mama has come down for dinner, and Papa has gotten her to play for us."

Kate moved to the open pocket doors that led to the music room, removing her hat and cape as she went. The scene that greeted her was one of pure domestic bliss. There was Mama with her burnt-off hair covered by an exotic arrangement of silk and ribbons. She was sitting at her piano, playing a folk song she had taught them all as children. Next to her sat Papa, who sang along in a deep bass tinged with unadulterated happiness. Edward was on the settee, holding the baby, rocking him in time to the tune. Lu joined her fiancé on the sofa and leaned over to tickle Frederick. How happy they all were.

Slowly but surely Mama had come back to them. And with each step of her progress, the house had emanated a sense of life renewed. It affected everyone from Papa to the household staff. This morning, as he was driving Kate to the brewery from the train, she had heard their driver whistling for the first time since the fires.

"Katrina, come sing with us," Mama urged when the folk song was finished. She glanced at Papa, and he quickly moved aside, offering his spot to Kate. It was clear that he was surprised and pleased to see her back from Chicago so soon.

"Do the lullaby," Papa urged. "Katrina does the lullaby so beautifully." He smiled at Kate and patted her shoulder, and she understood that with the emergence of Mama from her sickroom, all was possible . . . even forgiveness from her father.

Sophie began to play, and Kate sang along, her eyes locked on her mother's as they harmonized on the melody. Edward and Lu moved to the piano with the baby. Frederick indeed seemed calmed by the song. His agitated movements quieted, and he sighed contentedly as his eyes closed in sleep.

He was so very innocent, Kate thought as she and Mama sang the second verse of the song. He knew nothing yet of what the world had already done to him, robbing him of his parents, placing him here in this loving household. He knew nothing yet of how hard life could be, how cruel and disappointing.

This should have been one of the happiest nights of her life. Mama was going to be all right; her father was not going to sustain his anger. She was in love . . . She felt the tears well, and thought how frequently she had cried since the fire. It occurred to her that so much had changed since then, and once again her life seemed little more than a jumbled mess. Unable to stem the display of emotion, she broke off singing and excused herself as she rushed from the room and up the stairs.

"I think it is just a reaction to all the stress of these times," Sophie assured her husband as they prepared for bed.

August removed his collar and cuffs and stored them in the lacquered box on his dresser. He shook his head firmly. "Sullivan has abandoned her," he said with certainty. He did not add that in his view Katrina would not be back from Chicago so soon if all had gone well.

Sophie waited a beat, studying her husband from behind. "And if so? Is that not what you hoped for?"

August turned, his face a study in parental concern. "Of course not. I do not want her hurt."

Sophie smiled sadly. "She cannot lose Ryan and not be hurt," she said softly. "She is in love with him."

August sat on the side of the bed, his large hands hanging in limp dejection between his knees. "Ah, Sophie, she's such a good girl. Why does she have to be hurt again? With Lu it's always been so easy, but for Katrina . . ."

"Do you really have so little faith in Ryan Sullivan? Or in Katrina, for that matter?"

"What are you saying?"

Sophie shrugged. "Perhaps it does have to do with them, but, *Liebchen,* everything in our lives these past few weeks has been colored by tragedy and near tragedy. She almost lost him . . . she almost lost me . . . she had to escape a horrible ordeal alone and without help. In such moments even the smallest altercation can take on remarkable proportions. I think they have probably had a little spat, nothing more. You will not get rid of Mr. Sullivan so easily."

August grunted and rose to finish preparing for bed. "I was surprised at his actions in Peshtigo," he said after a while.

"How so?"

"He had lost everything . . . The land was a complete wasteland. There was nothing for him there . . . no ties. I would have thought him relieved that at least he hadn't started to build the sawmill or some other business."

"And yet he stayed on."

August nodded. "He did. When I arrived, the man was working as intensely as any local. He insisted on coming along to Marinette, to see for himself how you were. There was no call for that."

"He's a kind man," Sophie said softly.

August rubbed his face wearily. "That's part of the problem. I like the man. I like him a great deal."

"Better than Willem Frear?" Sophie teased, reminding him of the romance he had tried to foster over the summer.

"Harrumpph," August growled. "No wonder Katrina has little interest in such a man. Did you see how he behaved at the summer house? He was downright insulting the way he ignored our Katrina and spent all his time drooling over Carlotta. I had half a mind to—"

Sophie laughed. "I doubt Katrina minded. After all, she only had eyes for Mr. Sullivan . . . who, I might add, only had eyes for our daughter." She patted the place beside her on the bed. "I think we may have to give in on this one, Augie. From everything I can gather, it is very possible that they have already . . . that their devotion to one another has been sealed."

So she knew. August smiled at the foolhardiness of ever thinking he could keep anything from his wife. "When did you become so wise?"

Sophie reached to caress his cheek. "I have always been wise, my husband. Sometimes men do not notice. Perhaps that is Mr. Sullivan's problem as well . . . that he does not fully appreciate . . ."

"You would approve the match," August said without surprise.

"Augie, he is a good man, and time is so short . . . If she loves him and he makes her happy, who am I to stand in her way?"

He knew she was right. The same idea had occurred to him in a different way these past few days. When he had thought he had lost Sophie forever . . . when he had had no word about Katrina or Lu that terrible night as the news filtered in from Chicago . . .

"Sophie, I love you so," he said, drawing his wife into his arms as he felt rise in his chest the now familiar swell of gratitude that she had been spared.

"If what Katrina and Ryan feel for each other comes even close to the love you and I have been blessed with, Augie, how can we deny them the chance for such happiness?"

"But—"

Sophie shushed his protest with a kiss. "She's our daughter, Augie. She can succeed at anything . . . even this. Besides, times are changing . . . They will change them."

August sighed. "I'll speak to her tomorrow."

"Tonight would be better," Sophie urged.

"Tomorrow," August replied firmly. "I have more important matters to attend to tonight. My wife has come back to me."

With a girlish giggle, Sophie moved aside to make room for her husband under the covers.

"Papa wants to see you. Alone . . . in the dining room," Lu said with some awe the following morning when she went upstairs to see what was keeping Kate from breakfast. Meetings alone with Papa were rare things and portents of great trouble. Her sister was still in bed. "Are you ill?"

Kate pushed aside the quilt and pulled herself into a half-sitting position. "I'm not sick. I was simply thinking of staying home today."

Lu's eyes widened in surprise. "But you never miss a day of work."

"Well, perhaps it's time I did. What does Papa want?" She had spent a restless night going over and over her meeting with Ryan. Still not understanding what had transpired between them and having lost another night's sleep in the bargain, she was in no mood for lectures.

"I have no idea, but it must be very important. He sent word that he would be late coming in to the brewery. Mama has gone back to their room and asked Ernestine to bring baby Frederick there so she can give him his bath. *And* Papa asked me to find something to keep me occupied."

Kate sighed. "I suppose this will be the lecture about my going to Chicago yesterday."

"Something horrible happened, didn't it?" Suddenly Lu was full of sympathy, her eyes imploring her sister to share her obvious misery. "I mean, when you went running from the music room in tears, everyone . . . that is, I started to come up, but Mama said to leave you alone for a bit. What happened? Did you and Ryan quarrel?"

"I'd better dress. Papa is waiting, and there's no reason to add to his irritation."

"I understand," Lu said and crossed the room to the door. "When you're ready to talk about it, I'll be waiting."

Lu only thought she understood, Kate reflected as she dressed. Her sister was an incurable romantic, and in her world of romantic fantasy, she probably had already constructed a scenario in which Ryan and Kate were cast as the doomed lovers. Kate only wished she understood what had transpired between the two of them the day before.

"Guten Morgen, Papa," she said as she slid into her place at the dining room table and spread her linen napkin on her lap.

Papa nodded and waited until Heinrich had served Katrina her breakfast. When the servant had left the room, Papa seemed at a loss as to how he should begin. He stalled by refilling his coffee cup.

"Did you sleep well?"

Kate glanced up at him in surprise. A tone of solicitous concern was not what she had expected.

"I was restless," she said softly and pushed her fried potatoes and sausages around her plate as she waited for his next move.

"And things went well in Chicago?"

"They are very well organized," she replied noncommittally. "Relief has been pouring in from across the country, and people are rebuilding everywhere." She recalled her surprise at the level of activity she had witnessed in the city and remembered that her first thought had been how this would have pleased and interested her father. Before their feud over Ryan, she would have been anxious to share her observations with him. She had missed talking to her father about business and world affairs.

Papa nodded and waited.

"Block after block is under reconstruction. It really is quite astounding. I would have thought it would take months before anything of substance got started."

"That's good," Papa said and fell silent.

Kate took a bite of her biscuit and sipped her coffee. An uncomfortable silence stretched between them.

"And Mr. Sullivan?" Papa said a little too heartily just at the moment Kate had decided their conversation would end with no mention of the real purpose of her trip.

"Ryan was well."

Again Papa nodded. "I understand Sullivan came through the fire quite unscathed actually, except, of course, for his considerable losses in Peshtigo. But as far as Chicago goes, it would seem your Irishman indeed leads a charmed life."

Kate practically choked on her coffee. What was her father saying? What was going on here? How could he know what she did not? "Father, everything in Chicago is burned," she said gently. "There may not have been the toll in lives there was in Peshtigo, but in goods and property, it was . . . there could not possibly be . . ."

"Goods and property can be insured, *Liebchen,*" Papa explained gently. "Aside from that, Mr. Sullivan dealt in pieces of paper . . . certificates . . . such things can be traced and replaced. Then there is the matter of his penchant for investing in real estate in other locales. New York, for example . . ."

"How do you know all this?"

"Your cousin Emil was here yesterday. He says Carlotta is to be married, by the way."

"That's nice," Kate responded automatically. "What did Emil want?"

"Actually he wanted help. The Hauptman Brewery was destroyed during the fire. They have to start again. We spoke of a possible partnership or merger . . . They would use our facilities until they could rebuild."

"And you talked of Ryan?" Why on earth would any member of the Hauptman family even mention Ryan's name? Why on earth would Papa allow anyone to speak of Ryan Sullivan in his presence?

"Sullivan is to be their partner, albeit an inactive one."

"And you approve of that?"

Papa shrugged. "Not really. But I understand that the Hauptmans must do whatever they need to do in order to get their business back in operation as soon as possible. If that means lying down with . . ." He stopped and seemed embarrassed.

Kate smiled. "Lying down with the devil, Papa?"

Her father tried to look stern, but then he began to chuckle, and soon they were laughing together. After a long moment, he said, "Ah, *Liebchen,* many strange things happen when it comes to business."

Evidently Heinrich had taken their laughter as a sign that it would be safe to clear. He removed Kate's barely touched breakfast dishes and served fresh coffee before he left the room again.

"Strange things can also happen when young people think they are in love," Papa noted. He focused on stirring the three lumps of sugar he had added to his cup. "Did you quarrel?"

Kate concentrated on her own coffee. Her mind was racing with the information her father had given her. Ryan's fortune was secure. She had made assumptions based on appearances and what had seemed at the time to be reasonable observations. On the other hand, Ryan had not exactly told her—

"Katrina?"

"We had a misunderstanding," she answered.

"I see. Does this mean you will see him again?"

Katrina's eyes met her father's. "Yes." *If he will see me.*

Papa sighed and drained his cup in one long swallow. He stood up, saying, "So it will be." Then he left the room.

That was it—no lecture, no threats of disownment, no orders or demands. In his way, Papa was giving her his blessing. Oh, what wonders Mama wrought! But had her efforts come too late? And why hadn't Ryan told her of his good luck? Why did everything have to be so complicated? Should she return to Chicago this morning? No. That was no good at all. After all, he had had a hand in all this confusion. Was he willing to let what they had die because of a misunderstanding? Surely not. Of course not. So what to do? Make the first move? Let him come to her?

"Damn," she muttered.

Not knowing which direction to take, Kate returned to her room and dressed for work. She could concentrate there. She would come up with a plan. Surely Ryan knew her well enough to know she would not give up so easily.

21

"THERE'S A WIRE for you, Miss Bergeman," the secretary said as soon as Kate arrived at the office. "I put it on your desk."

"Thank you."

Wires came into the office daily now that Milwaukee had become a central shipping point for beer to the rest of the country. It amazed Kate how something as devastating as the fire in Chicago could actually be a boon to business for her family. Before the fire they had averaged twenty thousand barrels a year. In recent weeks the orders had poured in from around the country. If this kept up, they would double that yield.

Edward came in from the yard as she hung her cloak and hat. Kate noticed how he rubbed his hands briskly together to restore the circulation from being outside. "Are you all right?" he asked.

"Fine," she said. "I'm sorry about last night . . . over-wrought, I think. Don't you think gloves would be a good idea in this weather?" She took the telegram that stood propped against her inkstand and opened it.

Edward seemed relieved not to have to delve into her reasons for running from the music room in tears. He was swamped these days with the increase in business, and he hardly had time for Lu, much less her sister. "Another order?" He nodded toward the telegram Kate was reading.

"No. It's . . . I'll take care of it." She folded the paper, replaced it in its envelope, and turned her attention to the billing.

But the message on that thin sheet of paper was already committed to memory.

On my way. Stop. Meet me. Stop. Dock. Stop. Nine. Stop.

It was unsigned, but she had no question of the sender.

Throughout the seemingly endless day, she fingered the telegram she had slipped into her skirt pocket. She dreamed of seeing him. She pictured him with the moon over the lake placing him in silhouette. She imagined rushing down the wooden staircase to the dock and into his arms. He would lift her and swing her around, and his laughter would fill the air and echo across the water. Then he would kiss her, and once would not be enough. A thousand times would not be enough.

"Katrina?"

Edward stood just behind her, and his hand on her shoulder brought her upright in a startled realization of where she was.

"I must have been daydreaming," she said apologetically.

Edward looked skeptical. "I was saying how I need your help in trying to get Lu to keep things simple." When Kate looked confused, he added, "You do remember that this is the night the family is meeting to plan our engagement party?"

Oh, Lord, how could she have forgotten! Lu would want to savor every detail, which would mean agonizing over everything from buffet items to the exact color and size of each flower stem in the centerpieces. She'd been gathering ideas for this party for months. She had entire folders filled with ideas and sketches. By nine o'clock, Lu would just be getting started.

"I . . ."

Edward barely noticed her reserve, so excited was he about the plans. "I've never seen her like this . . . so eager about every little item. I told her we should just elope if this is how she was going to be over the engagement. My heavens, how will she ever make it through an entire wedding?" But clearly he was delighted with Lu's enthusiasm and charmed by her agitation. "Do you know that she asked me to write Mother for her strudel recipe? She says Mother makes the best she's ever tasted—I have to agree, but isn't that just like her?"

Kate could not help but smile. Her sister was a wise woman for all her outward flightiness. Already she was endearing herself to her in-laws . . . as if she needed to. "It's going to be a wonderful party," Kate assured Edward.

The clock on the mantel chimed eight-thirty.

Kate's spirits plummeted. On the one hand, she did not want to risk her father's renewed displeasure by secretly meeting Ryan on his yacht. On the other hand, she wanted only to see him, to explain how she had misunderstood, to be in his arms and vow never to allow such a misunderstanding to keep them apart again.

Of course, now that Papa had practically given his blessing . . . but Ryan didn't know that, and they did need to speak in private to work out their disagreement.

If she wasn't at the dock at nine, would he leave? Would he misunderstand again and think she did not want to come? There had to be a way to get word to him or to persuade Lu to speed things along.

But Papa had been late for supper, detained by the rush of business that made extra brewings necessary. The family had finally sat down to eat at seven-thirty. Pauline had just sent up the dessert on the dumbwaiter. Heinrich seemed to be serving more slowly than ever before.

"I have everything arranged in Father's study," Lu announced. "We'll start with invitations . . . then menus, music, decorations . . . oh, and Kate, gowns . . . Wait till you see the sketches I picked up from the seamstress today. And, of course, there's the guest list. Oh, Mama, how many can we have?"

"Heavens, do we have to decide everything in one night?" Mama teased.

"Mama, do you think the community will be scandalized by our plan to be married over the Christmas holiday? I mean, everyone expects a long engagement."

Papa laughed as he polished off the last of his custard pie. "No one will be the least bit surprised at anything that happens in this house, I'll wager. Your mother has seen to that. Besides, it's hardly going to come as a surprise that the two of you will wed."

Mama smiled at her husband, and Kate found herself enjoying the obvious affection and love her parents shared.

Then the clock struck the quarter hour.

She had dressed carefully for supper, in fact, she had changed three times, wanting to have exactly the right gown, the right hairstyle. Her cape lay on her bed ready to be grabbed as she made her carefully planned escape down the back stairway and out the servants' entrance.

Of course, she had counted on supper being long over and the servants being otherwise occupied, leaving the kitchen deserted. She had counted on getting a start on the party plans and then making some excuse about illness or exhaustion after a decent interval and retiring upstairs.

She had not counted on this.

"Well," she practically chirped, "we'd best get started if we're to get anything at all decided before midnight."

The others gave her a strange look, but then followed her lead and adjourned to her father's study.

At last, she thought and tried to decide how long it might take for something she had eaten to disagree with her. No, if she pleaded a stomachache, Mama would insist on attention. Exhaustion was her best bet.

She yawned broadly and then smiled. "Excuse me," she said demurely, "it's been so hectic at the brewery. I suppose I'm more tired than usual."

Mama frowned and touched the back of her hand to her eldest daughter's forehead. Papa looked concerned, and Lu looked about to burst into tears.

"It's nothing," Kate hastened to assure them. She crossed to where Lu stood and put her arm around her sister's waist. "Show me everything." Ryan would have to understand. She could not dampen her sister's spirits; it had taken so long for her to recover from the fire.

Immediately Lu brightened and launched into a detailed explanation of invitations, type styles, paper quality . . . and on and on . . .

The clock struck nine.

Kate wondered how long Ryan would wait before he decided she was not coming. Were they doomed to drown in a sea of stupid misunderstandings? She considered excusing herself and sending Ernestine to the dock with a note, but that would never do. They would all want to know what needed her attention. She would have to write the note . . . talk to Ernestine— No, that would not work at all.

" . . . could have yellow . . . Edward loves me in yellow . . . don't you, darling?"

The clock rang quarter past.

Kate could not take her mind off meeting Ryan. She saw herself flying into his arms . . . their passionate kisses, which would carry them below deck to the scene of their first lovemaking. The taste of him . . . the feel of his skin on hers . . .

" . . . but then it might be too much . . . What do you think, Kate?"

"I like yellow," Kate agreed.

They all looked at her blankly. She saw immediately that time had passed while she imagined her secret meeting with

Ryan. She hid her blush with a sudden interest in the fabric swatches on the table.

"Katrina, we're discussing the music. Are you sure you're feeling all right?" Again Mama touched her cheek. "You seem flushed."

"I'm fine, Mama. Music . . ." She forced herself to concentrate.

The clock chimed the half hour . . . then quarter to . . . then ten . . .

"Excuse me, ma'am."

The butler stood at the entrance to the study.

"Yes, Heinrich."

"It's Mr. Sullivan . . ."

Ryan strode past the servant and into the room, bringing the cold night air with him as he swept off his cloak and hat and handed them to Heinrich. "Forgive me for the lateness of the hour, sir, but I wonder if we might have a word." He walked to Katrina and took her by the elbow, preparatory to leading her from the room.

Papa stood as if to protest. He had been holding the baby and listening to all the fuss over party plans with a bemused smile. Mama stopped him by sweeping across the room and offering Ryan her hand. "How lovely to see you again. I'm afraid you've caught us rather off guard here, but please accept my deep though belated gratitude for everything you did in rescuing my daughter."

Ryan's resolve was momentarily shaken. He accepted Sophie Bergeman's hand and bent to kiss it. "I am thankful to see you in such good health, ma'am," he said softly. Then he focused his attention on Kate. "You did not tell them I was coming?"

"I . . . you . . . I . . . ," Kate sputtered. "Your telegram seemed to indicate . . ."

"Telegram?" August thundered, looking from his daughter to Sullivan.

"I sent a wire to the brewery asking Katrina to meet me tonight, so that we could speak to you together."

"Well, what a lovely surprise to have you here. You will stay the night?" Sophie settled naturally into her role of hostess. She kept a light restraining hand on her husband's arm and spoke quietly to Heinrich. She instructed the servant to bring refreshments and alert the staff to prepare a room for their guest. Meanwhile Lu and Edward gathered around to welcome Ryan. Lu chattered on about the planning of the engagement party. " . . . Had we known you were coming, perhaps we could have planned a *double* announcement?" To add to the carnival atmosphere of the moment, the baby started to cry, and all attention turned momentarily away from Ryan and Kate.

"I thought you wanted to talk privately," Kate whispered fiercely.

"I do," he hissed back.

"Well?"

"I just wanted a moment to straighten out yesterday's misunderstanding before I came on up here to speak formally to your parents."

"Well, I wish you had taken the time in Chicago to let me know that everything was . . . all right with you."

"I know," he agreed. "It was stupid of me. After I got home and saw the way I looked . . . I can imagine what you must have thought." He grinned.

She could not resist that smile. It went directly to her heart, spoke to her in ways no man's smile had ever done before. "You don't play fair," she said lightly.

"Miss Bergeman, that's the second time you've accused me of cheating," he chided her. Then he touched her cheek, and his eyes darkened with desire. "I don't like fighting with you," he said softly.

"Me neither," she agreed.

"So, all is forgiven? I can speak to your father?"

"You came to speak to Father about—" The light was dawning.

"Us," he finished. Then he was grinning at her and fingering the ring on her finger, and she was smiling back at him as they forgot the presence of anyone else in the room. August Bergeman loudly cleared his throat.

"I'm sure everyone will excuse Mr. Sullivan and me while we have a short talk." It was not a request, despite the tone of courtesy. It was a command.

Lu and Edward scooted from the room immediately. Sophie gently pushed Katrina through the doorway just as Ernestine appeared with a tray of coffee and cakes.

"We'll serve those in the parlor," Sophie instructed as she balanced the baby on one hip and pulled the sliding doors closed, leaving Augie and young Sullivan alone.

Bergeman moved past his desk to stand in front of the fire, his back to the young Irishman who had come to claim his daughter.

"Come warm yourself, Mr. Sullivan. I expect it's a chilly night to be out on the water." He moved to a sideboard and held up a bottle of brandy, offering his guest a drink.

Ryan had been prepared for anything but hospitality. Still, he should have guessed. Whatever reservations he might have, August Bergeman was first and foremost a gentleman. "Aye, that it was, sir. A might chilly." Ryan nodded his acceptance of the brandy and moved closer to the fire, holding his hands out to the flames.

The room was silent except for the snap of the dry wood as it burned and the clink of the crystal decanter on the snifter as Bergeman poured the brandy.

"Sit," Bergeman said, handing Ryan the glass and indicating one of a pair of leather wing-backed chairs, one to either side of the hearth.

"Thank you, sir."

Again the silence stretched as they sipped their drinks and concentrated on the flames before them.

"Do you know the word *Zeitgeist,* Mr. Sullivan?"

"I believe it has something to do with time, sir?"

Bergeman nodded. "Literally it means 'spirit of the times.' My daughter, as you've no doubt noticed, has an uncanny ability to see potential in what are impossible situations for the rest of us. *Der Zeitgeist* is a concept that has always held enormous appeal for our Katrina." He smiled at some memory and then chuckled. "During the war, there were many who were less than enamored of our Mr. Lincoln . . . I'm sure you know that."

Ryan nodded, unwilling to break the moment with a comment.

"Not Katrina. From the beginning she embraced the man's ideals and demeanor . . . Everything about him that gave the rest of us pause was to her clear evidence of his genius. She was not more than thirteen or fourteen, but she was on me constantly about voting for the man." He chuckled, sipped his brandy, then added, "Imagine a mere girl being that good a judge of character." He shook his head with wonder and smiled again.

"I know that the President is a hero of Kate's," Ryan noted as much because he felt he should say something as to add anything to the conversation.

Bergeman peered at him steadily for a long moment. His bushy eyebrows furrowed and his eyes narrowed as he considered the man before him. "It would appear that you also have become something of a hero to my daughter, sir."

Ryan leaned forward so that his elbows rested on his knees and his eyes met the older man's directly. "I love your daughter, Mr. Bergeman. It is my hope that we can be married with the blessing of you and Mrs. Bergeman."

August's eyes widened in surprise. "Are you issuing a challenge, young man?"

"I am stating a fact."

"And the fact you are not stating is that while you prefer our blessing, you will be married with or without it?"

Ryan did not flinch from the question. "We are both adults, sir. Kate is no longer a child who needs your permission." He saw the flash of anger that crossed Bergeman's face and added, "Though obviously our lives would be happier . . . not to mention easier . . . if we had that permission."

August relaxed in his chair and pondered the idea of Ryan Sullivan as a member of his family. He knew the man to be fair in his dealings, to be successful in business, to be a decent and concerned citizen. He also now had little doubt of the man's feelings for Katrina . . . or hers for him. Still they were so young . . . On the other hand, he and Sophie had been younger . . . barely twenty. And Sophie's father had not been completely thrilled with the young upstart Deutschman who would carry his favorite daughter off from the family farm in Peshtigo to live in the city.

August sipped his brandy and smiled. "So, this match between you is to be the new *Zeitgeist* for my Katrina?"

Ryan relaxed as well. "You must know, sir, that Katrina is very much like you."

"Ah, now we have the Irish charm?"

Ryan chuckled. "I am sincere, though I'll admit that I've chosen my time to share this observation with you. Much of what I love about your daughter she has inherited from you. I would hope that some of what she finds lovable in me is a reflection of my own parentage."

August sobered. "She has told me of the loss of your family. You have my deepest sympathies."

Ryan nodded, and the two men returned to their contemplation of their brandies and the fire.

"What can be taking so long?" Katrina moaned for the third time.

Sophie sat in her favorite chair, feeding the baby. Edward and Lu had settled on the settee to await the outcome of the meeting next door. Katrina paced. And she ate, nervously devouring another tea cookie every other time she passed the sideboard, where Ernestine had placed the refreshments.

"It hasn't been that long," Sophie noted.

"Oh, Kate, wouldn't it be wonderful if we could announce our engagement together? What a party that would be! And a double wedding at Christmas! Oooh!" Lu was beside herself with delight.

Edward placed his hand over his fiancée's. "Darling, Kate and Ryan may prefer to have their own party," he suggested.

Lu looked stricken. "Oh, of course. But, Kate, won't it be fun? Don't you think it will be fun, Mama?"

"Delightful," Sophie agreed pleasantly. "Katrina, little Frederick is starting to fuss. Could you perhaps pace with him as long as you're up? It might calm him."

Kate bent and took the baby. Gently bouncing him in her arms, she resumed her promenade from the window to the parlor door and on into the hall, very close to the doors of the study, where she held her breath, trying to hear anything, and back again.

"They aren't making a sound," she reported worriedly.

"Did you expect fisticuffs, darling?" her mother asked with an innocent smile.

"Mama, what do you think is happening? Papa has been acting so strangely . . . this morning at breakfast and now this. Is there a chance?" She barely dared say it out loud. Papa had indicated his willingness to approve the match, but that had been when he thought such a thing might be some time distant.

"There is always a chance, Katrina. You know that. Now stop stuffing yourself with those cookies or you'll never fit into another gown. Besides, you're getting crumbs all over the baby."

Tension stretched between the two men in the study. It had followed Ryan's calm statement that he had made arrangements for the marriage to take place the following morning.

"Now see here," August erupted, losing his genteel control for the first time since their meeting had begun. "I have said I will approve the match, but there are proprieties, young man." He rose from his chair and paced the length of the room. "Do not presume to push too far, Sullivan."

Ryan waited him out, allowing him to walk off his surprise and shock. When the brewer paused and looked directly at him, Ryan finally spoke. "I believe I can convince you that it is not only proper for Katrina and I to be married as soon as possible, it is absolutely necessary." Too late he realized the double meaning the man might take from his words.

"Are you telling me that my daughter . . . that you have . . . Is my daughter pregnant?" August Bergeman's jowls shook, his face flamed with indignation, and he raised one fist and pounded it onto the table between them.

"No, sir. Please allow me to explain." Ryan had risen as well, more to calm Bergeman than to confront him. "Please." Now he indicated the chairs and invited his host to be seated.

"This had better be some explanation," Bergeman muttered with a disgruntled growl.

Ryan chose his words carefully. "When you first heard that Mrs. Bergeman was alive . . . when you saw her lying there in that hospital . . . I saw your face. And I know exactly what you felt in that moment. For you see, sir, I had experienced just those same feelings when I climbed out onto that pier and found Kate alive after the city had burned down around her on all sides."

Bergeman softened only slightly, but Ryan pressed the advantage. "When my family was lost in the wreckage of the *Lady Elgin,* I wanted never again to allow anyone to mean so much to me that I could experience that sort of terrible pain . . . the feeling that your heart is being ripped from your body. I know that's what you experienced when you first heard the news of the fire in Peshtigo, sir."

August focused on the fire and nodded. The ache was still very real in spite of the outcome. He found he indeed understood what the boy was saying.

"But then Katie came into my life. Oh, sir, I wanted very much not to fall in love with your daughter. For many of the same reasons you wanted it not to happen.

But it did happen. She captured my heart . . . She has quite frankly become my reason to get up in the morning. When I look ahead to my life with her, I am more content and at peace than I have ever been before. Can you understand that, sir?"

August was lulled by Sullivan's eloquence. He nodded but still did not speak.

"The reason I have arranged for Katrina and I to be married as soon as possible is very simple, sir. I have seen my entire family swept overboard and into the black depths of the lake out there. I have walked and ridden across battlefields and seen boys dead and dying for a cause they only barely understood. I have struggled through hell's fury itself, praying that I would not lose Katrina to the disaster of the Chicago fire. You understand what I am saying, sir, I know you do. I am begging you not to let one more sun set before Katrina and I begin our life together . . . We have been robbed of too much time already."

There was only the sound of the clock striking eleven. Bergeman seemed to count each chime and allowed the room to echo with the count for a long moment after the clock was still. He stared at the fire and did not look at Ryan. *"Der Zeitgeist,"* he murmured and then stood up. "We will compromise," he said in his strong businessman's voice, which brooked no argument. "The wedding will be here in the parlor at sundown tomorrow."

Ryan nodded once and accepted the older man's handshake solemnly. Then he grinned broadly and clasped his future father-in-law in a bear hug.

"Welcome to the family," August said, clapping the boy on the back as he returned the hug. "Now, may I make a suggestion for surprising the others?"

"Sophia!"

August Bergeman's voice boomed through the hall as the study doors were opened with a bang and Katrina's father strode into the parlor.

"Yes, dear?"

"Mr. Sullivan has asked to marry our Katrina."

Sophie calmly continued working on her embroidery while Kate froze in mid-pace and hugged the baby to her bosom. Lu and Edward glanced quickly from August to Ryan to Sophie.

"That's nice, dear," Sophie said. "And what has she replied?"

August frowned at his eldest daughter. "I have no idea . . . What have you replied, daughter?"

"I . . . I . . . have said yes," she stammered. She understood that her mother was being deliberately coy, but then she sometimes did that to disarm Papa when he was upset beyond reason about something. It was a way of calming him. She risked one look at Ryan, who seemed completely miserable.

"I see," Papa growled and paced the room, stroking his chin as if deep in thought.

"What have you said, dear?" Sophie asked.

August stopped abruptly and threw up his hands in frustration. "What have I said? What do you think I've said?"

Sophie put her needlework aside and came to stand beside her husband. She stood on tiptoe and kissed his cheek. "I am fairly certain that you have given the match the blessing we agreed to give it."

Kate wondered if she had heard correctly. In the few quiet seconds following her mother's comment, she glanced around to see Ryan grinning broadly, her father smiling and nodding his head, her mother moving to embrace Ryan, and Lu and Edward dancing and hugging with delight. Even Frederick was gurgling and cooing.

Then Ryan crossed the room to stand with her. He removed a small box from his pocket. "I believe this will make it official," he said, removing the ring they had selected in Chicago and sliding it onto her finger. He kissed her lightly on the lips, and the room exploded with congratulations and cries of delight. Even the staff was called to share in the good news.

"All right," Papa announced loudly above the din that promised to continue for several more minutes. "Enough. There is much to be done. Sullivan, I want you out of here." He took Ryan by the elbow and steered him toward the door.

"But, Augie . . . ," Sophie protested.

"Don't argue. It's nearly midnight, and he has to be gone."

Now even Sophie was confused. "Why? We have a room all made up for him here."

August shook his head firmly. "Absolutely not. You know it's considered bad luck for the groom to see the bride before the wedding."

"But that's the day of, Papa," Lu protested.

August heaved a sigh and made a great show of taking out his pocket watch and showing its face to all assembled. "Exactly. It is nearly midnight . . . No doubt by the time these two say their good nights, it will chime the hour . . . It will be tomorrow and . . ." Suddenly he grinned devilishly. "Oh, did I fail to mention the wedding is tomorrow?"

Again everyone was talking at once. Seeing his opportunity, Ryan took Kate aside, handed the baby to Ernestine, and pulled her into the deserted study. "Is that all right?" He appeared worried. "I mean tomorrow? Teddy tells me I need to consult you . . . I know I should have asked, but, darling, I cannot wait another day . . . Still, if it's not what you want . . . if you need more time . . . I know the trappings are important to ladies, but honestly—"

Kate silenced his babbling by pointing to the clock. "It's almost tomorrow," she said, "and if you don't kiss me now, you're going to have to wait an entire day. Papa was not kidding about that."

Ryan grinned. "Have I told you that I love your father?" He kissed her. "And that I love your mother?" He kissed her again. "And Lu?" Kiss. "And Edward?" Kiss. "And baby Frederick?" Three quick kisses on her eyelids and nose. "I even love your Cousin Eloise," he proclaimed, which made her laugh.

"And me?"

His expression turned serious as he gazed down at her. "You, Katie Bergeman, are for me what your mother is to your father . . . quite simply the best thing that ever happened in either of our lives."

They kissed, and suddenly the doorway was filled with family. Glasses of Bergeman's finest wine were pressed into their hands. "To *der Zeitgeist,*" August Bergeman shouted, raising his glass to Ryan.

"Der Zeitgeist," Ryan called back, and then he and August Bergeman laughed like two men who have shared something momentous.

CHAPTER ONE

My Name Is Mallory

I STEPPED INTO the stone entranceway set a few feet back from the sidewalk and rang the bell. The house had a solid, midwestern look to it, like houses I'd seen in suburbs north of Chicago where there's a Frank Lloyd Wright on every corner. It was in a rich neighborhood in Brookline, Massachusetts, opposite a small park of oak trees where an unfriendly sign said ball-playing and dogs were not permitted. In the glass of the door a red decal warned visitors that the house was protected by Anderson Security Systems, but I knew what that was worth. Anderson is a former colleague of mine. He hates my guts because I went to Harvard and once played golf with Tip O'Neill. The door opened to a stony-faced woman who cocked her head and said, "Yes?" with the sharp British accent of the private secretary, Miss Phoebe Goodrich, who'd summoned me from the office.

A British servant in America is a rare and wonderful thing to see, and my heart lifted. My own grandmother was an upstairs maid imported by the Guggenheims, I'm told, after one of their shopping trips to London.

"I'm the investigator you rang up, Miss Goodrich. I'm James Maxfield Mallory."

She wanted to see identification, then said, "Come." Only one of four doors leading into the central hall was open, and I peeked in and saw a study furnished like a period room in the Museum of Fine Arts. Then we stepped onto a wide, formal terrace in back where Morgan Streeter was using the telephone at a table set for afternoon tea. Beyond the terrace, at the foot of the incline of a long, landscaped garden, a high board fence held back suburban woods lit up by the afternoon sun. Not a bad spread, considering we were just a forty-five-minute stroll from my not-so-posh office in downtown Boston's red-light district.

Mrs. Streeter finished talking and looked up. She was gray-haired and past fifty, blue eyes set in wrinkles. She wore a well-tailored blue dress and held a heavy white china cup with a picture on it commemorating the coronation of Elizabeth II. The wrinkles gave her a look of frowning annoyance. The souvenir cup was chipped and didn't match the rest of the tea service and struck me as an odd touch for a woman of her position—the *Social Register* said she'd been bred by one of the oldest and wealthiest families in Boston. But that could be eccentricity. I noticed an open book on the table, with my name spelled out in capital letters halfway down the right-hand page.

Phoebe introduced me, disconnected the phone, and took it back into the house. A servant in a black uniform and white apron came out with a tray and set pastries onto the table. I sat down and Mrs. Streeter started talking.

"This meeting is difficult for me, Mr. Mallory. I have never been involved with a person in your field before today, and I abhor the necessity for it. I see from information Phoebe has provided that you are an educated man—you graduated from Harvard some years ago, and even went to the law school for a year. How did you happen to become a private investigator? The money can't be as good."

"It isn't," I said. I always feel a little pompous explaining myself, but I went ahead. "I think of my work as the 'private justice' business, Mrs. Streeter. I went to law school to study justice, but they weren't teaching it. And I didn't want to be a cop."

The wrinkles deepened when she smiled—if it was a smile. "That's a good answer. I too have found, to my chagrin, that lawyers concern themselves very little with justice. I dislike them, especially these new young cutthroats. That has some bearing on my asking you here to talk about my father.

"I also understand that a woman's attention to her father's affairs is generally viewed with suspicion, due in large part to the pernicious influence of Mr. Freud and his followers. I ask for the benefit of the doubt when I tell you my present course of action is provoked by nothing more than a full sense of familial responsibility.

"You should know that, despite his position in society, Father has always been an exceptionally irresponsible man. He comes from an old family and squandered the lion's share of his fortune many years ago. When Mother died she vested control of her personal resources in me. The income from various trusts supports him in the style to which he is accustomed, but the principal cannot be touched without my authorization."

She said that last with smug satisfaction, then finished her tea and set the cup onto the marble table.

"Notwithstanding my attention to his affairs, he has become attached to a much younger woman, a woman of inappropriate social background. I am concerned."

"Because of her youth or her social background?"

"Both. She is twenty-five years younger than I. She is a blonde and quite attractive. I want you to determine her intentions before she becomes more deeply involved with Father."

"Young women fall in love with older men all the time."

"I want her investigated, Mr. Mallory. I'm not interested in platitudes. If love is her motivation I suppose I shall have to be satisfied, but I doubt if that will prove to be the case. Father has a propensity for getting into bad situations."

I reached across for the silver teapot and filled the thin

bone china heirloom set for me, then refilled Mrs. Streeter's cup. We were drinking English breakfast tea. I know that because I read the tag on the teabags. The pastries all looked too sweet to eat.

"Have you told him your concerns?"

"I have. He tells me they are without rational basis. As if he could comprehend rationality."

"Assuming he's wrong, Mrs. Streeter, what could the woman do, given that you control the trust funds? Do you think she's under the impression he's richer than he is?"

"Certainly not. The woman in question has particular knowledge of Father's financial circumstances. She is Susan Winston, formerly an associate in the law firm that handles our family's affairs. Which I might add makes her present actions quite inexplicable to me. They are a very old and reputable law firm. She has resigned her position in favor of living with my father."

What I knew of the lives of young associates in old and reputable law firms made her actions seem perfectly explicable to me, but I understood what Mrs. Streeter meant.

"You mean she's not a floozy, a dancer, or an actress?"

"Not a dancer or actress in any event."

"What's the name of the law firm?"

"Choate and Masterson."

"Have you consulted them?"

"Of course. They tell me not a penny of Mother's money could be shifted to this woman, even were she to marry Father. As long as I am alive, nothing can be done without my authorization. And I intend to live a very long time, Mr. Mallory."

I knocked on wood for her. As if on cue, a short-haired blonde in a white tennis outfit jogged onto the terrace. She stopped to make a face at me, kissed Mrs. Streeter on the cheek, took a cream-filled pastry, and dropped into a chair.

For the first time I saw Mrs. Streeter really smile. "My daughter Melissa," she said.

The sudden appearance of this modern creature made me realize just how old-fashioned my conversation with her mother had been up to that point. We had actually been talking about gold diggers, spendthrift widowers, and the pernicious influence of Mr. Freud, while drinking tea. But mother and daughter obviously belonged together. They both looked rich. Melissa stuck out a hand to shake. Her hand was sticky from the pastry, and she looked at it and made another face.

"I think this is crazy," she said. "I think you should let Grandfather have his fling."

"Melissa knows what I'm hiring you for, Mr. Mallory." She turned to her daughter. "There have been too many 'flings' by members of this family. It is important for people in our position to maintain a positive image."

Melissa crinkled her nose, as if to demonstrate the inaccuracy of her mother's statement, and started eating a second pastry. She was pretty and quite slim, and I wondered about that. Probably burned up lots of calories making faces. I put her at about twenty-five.

"What do you say?" Mrs. Streeter said. "Will you help me?"

I drank some tea and considered. Just as a snap judgment, Melissa looked like trouble, and the mother was an obvious candidate for a few years in analysis—why else would she feel hostility for Freud? But I probably wouldn't have to deal with them once I got started on the job, I wasn't working on anything else at the time, and maybe the old guy really was in trouble. I said, "Okay. I'll make some inquiries."

"Excellent," Mrs. Streeter said. "The place to begin is the Bombay Hunt Club in Hamilton. Father plays golf every morning. I can arrange an introduction to the Club."

"We could play tennis," Melissa said.

"An introduction won't be necessary," I said to the mother. "And probably wouldn't be advisable."

"Are you certain? Since our friends refuse to see the two of them socially, the only place Father appears with the woman is at the Club. Phoebe and I selected you for this job, Mr. Mallory, because we thought you would be able to mingle with Father and this woman on a social basis. Can you manage it without an entrée?"

"I'll manage. I have a few friends in high places."

"Then so much the better." She made a dismissive gesture that involved lifting her chin and half closing her eyes. "My daughter will show you to Phoebe's office now. Phoebe can provide whatever particulars you require, and also write a check for your retainer."

"One question first, Mrs. Streeter. I assume we've been talking about your stepfather, Caleb Johnson?"

"Of course. My natural father has been dead for many years. I take it you have researched the family?"

"How long has he been seeing Susan?"

"She moved into his home in Marblehead in April. There is one other point I suppose I should make. Five years ago I authorized a special disbursement of trust income for one of Father's young women. It was intended to make the woman disappear, and it was effective. If necessary I would be willing to make a similar arrangement with Miss Winston."

"If she's conning him, we'll stop it without your having to pay her. You can spend the money on me instead."

I stood up and Melissa got up beside me. "I'll try the Bombay tomorrow," I said. "If Phoebe has addresses and vital statistics, and a picture of Mr. Johnson, I won't need to take any more of your time."

Mrs. Streeter nodded once and reached across the table to shake my hand. Her hand was cold.

"Thank you, Mr. Mallory."

"Thank me when I have something," I said.

CHAPTER TWO

On the Road to
the Bombay

SO THE NEXT day I sat in my office with a Styrofoam cup of coffee and reviewed the carefully typed resumés Phoebe had provided from the neat files in her tidy office in the Streeter house. Along with the resumés, Phoebe gave me a check for $5,000, which she'd typed out on her IBM Selectric and signed using Mrs. Streeter's name. It was an enormous amount of money for what seemed like a simple job.

I had my copy of the *Social Register* out to check the relationships between the various actors. Morgan's real father died young. Caleb Johnson married Katherine Loring in 1949, when Morgan was nineteen. At the time Caleb was only twenty-nine. Ten years later Morgan married Peter Streeter, who was exactly Caleb's age and had graduated from the same prep school. There was nothing about a subsequent divorce, although I'd had the impression from my visit to the residence in Brookline that it was an exclusively female household. When I checked Melissa's date of birth I discovered she'd come along only six months after the wedding. She was twenty-six now.

I put the book aside and looked through the wire-mesh window down two levels to the indoor swimming pool of the Trojan Gym and Health Club. My office is on the third floor front of the old building that houses the Club, close to the intersection of Charles and Stuart streets, at the edge of the so-called Combat Zone.

People tell me I'm bright enough to do better, that after ten years in the business I should have a fancy office in a building downtown with a score of young operatives, secretaries, payrolls, workers' comp insurance payments, high rent, high blood pressure, lawyers and accountants, retirement plans, and annual Christmas parties. After I have all of those things, they tell me, the business would take care of itself while I was off having fun.

But it never works that way in practice. I prefer taking off to travel or hike or fish whenever I put a little cash aside, on the theory that money in the bank goes inevitably to minor catastrophes like valve jobs for the car, new hot water heaters for the house you inevitably buy, and, somewhere down the line, braces for the kids. When necessary I'm perfectly willing to share the expensive toys my friends have managed to acquire, but that's where I draw the line.

And I like my office in the health club with the telephone answering machine that answers with the voice of an actress I was close to five years ago and haven't seen for four years. When she made the recording she said she was pretending to be Della Street, and when I'm feeling whimsical I sometimes refer to the machine as Della.

I checked the clock on the wall and put in a call to Michael Garrison. He's one of my friends in high places, exactly thirty-five stories high—when he's not in West Palm Beach, or Saratoga, or playing polo in Argentina—in a corner office with a wide view of the ocean in a firm that was old and reputable when Boston businessmen were running Lincoln's blockade of the South. Getting into a corner office is very important to a lot of lawyers, and architects have responded to the need by designing most of the new glass monsters downtown with eight or nine corners. That's one of the dangling carrots I didn't respond to when people were trying to convince me to stay in law school. Michael, on the other hand, was born to have one, and I once rescued him from the consequences of an indiscretion that might have made having one impossible.

He's gotten so important now he can't be bothered to pick up a phone, and he answers all his calls by switching on conference speakers and talking into them. It's an effective ploy, since his voice comes out wrapped in a hollow echo, like the voice of doom, and it's only natural for people to want to get the voice of doom working for them.

"Hello, hello," he rumbled when his secretary had put me through.

"It's Jim Mallory," I said. "I'm gonna tap you for an afternoon at the Bombay." On the other end of the line I knew my own voice was being broadcast over the squawk box to every underling's office within fifty feet of Michael's suite. I considered launching into one of a dozen show tunes in my repertoire, but Michael spoke.

"When?"

"Today, if possible. In about an hour."

"I'll tell my secretary to call. You after anyone I know?"

"Not for anything devastating."

"Don't tell them I sent you." He laughed and switched off.

I looked at the clock again, went to the small wardrobe built into one corner of the room, and changed into my country club outfit, blue slacks and a white shirt with an alligator on it. I looked in the mirror and decided not to comb my hair—maybe the folks at the Club would think I'd been riding a polo pony. Going out I locked the door into the corridor, went down two flights and out to the small lot where I keep my '69 Rambler station wagon.

It's a huge, steady, comfortable old relic, easily recognizable in any parking lot, and its only problem is that it's conspicuous at places like the Bombay. There was nothing I could do about that, so I climbed in and drove down the alley and out to Stuart Street.

* * *

I enjoy the ride out of Boston to the North Shore, partly because of the view you get over Boston Harbor crossing the Mystic Tobin Bridge, and partly because I've travelled it so many times on the way to good restaurants and the small harbors north of the city. I don't even mind all the miles of schlock architecture and commerce that hem in the old road after you cross to Chelsea, then Revere, Saugus, and finally hit Route 128.

Route 128 runs northeasterly all the way to the Atlantic at Gloucester on the tip of Cape Ann, and about halfway there Route 1A branches off toward Hamilton. Shopping centers and suburban sprawl give way to progressively bigger houses with progressively bigger lawns, until you come to real farms with long, manicured horse pastures where stalwart young men and women rise each morning to drink coffee and read the business news in *The Wall Street Journal.* It's the country that inspired *Town and Country* magazine, and, if properly distributed, its resources could feed half of starving Africa.

In amongst the farms is the Bombay Hunt Club, its white-fenced pasture facing the highway and its golf course disappearing toward the sea. The Club is announced by a small red sign, similar to one at a roadside vegetable stand run by kids, except instead of advertising tomatoes it says simply "POLO."

The Club's name has nothing to do with safaris to India. It was founded at Harvard around the turn of the century when Rudyard Kipling was at the height of his popularity with young American men. It moved to Hamilton after its founders graduated, and now it's a golf, tennis, and polo club. One of its oldest possessions is the skin of a tiger slain by somebody's great-uncle, which hangs on a wall in the grand dining room. On the tennis court the all-white clothing rule applies, and there's a bar that doesn't allow women. It's the only bar at the Club. The women sit outside at the unheated pool watching the children.

I drove up the sunny entrance drive with a line of oak

trees and horse pasture on my right and an ancient oak forest on my left. I parked at the far end of a gravel lot, beside the stables, and walked to the clubhouse exactly at noon.

I'd been out there several times before to play golf with Michael. On one such occasion Tip O'Neill joined us and we got into the papers and I earned the distrust of Chuck Anderson of Anderson Security Systems, then a fellow operative at Cahill Inquiries. The men's entrance is through a comfortable porch furnished in wicker, old prints of horses hunting or racing across the walls, and backgammon sets open on small tables.

A short hallway connects the games room to a bar that's more primitive than you might expect—but not if you stop to think about the kind of place where heterosexual men prefer to drink without the company of women. The walls are dark, there are no chairs or tables, and the wooden floor is scarred by a century of stamping golf cleats. There is the smell of leather and horses. Across one wall is a dark mahogany bar, and as I came in and stood to let my eyes adjust, the first thing I focused on was an intelligent looking bartender serving St. Pauli Girls and gin and tonics to six aristocratic types wearing shorts and polo shirts. They all looked to be at least sixty. I got a few polite hellos.

I would know Caleb Johnson from an old photograph Phoebe had given me, and he wasn't in the group. I ordered a gin and tonic, signed the chit using Michael's name, nodded to the men, and took the drink back through the games room and outside to the shade of the veranda. As a rule I don't like to drink in bars that don't permit women, and since it was early I figured I had more chance of finding Caleb out in the fresh air.

I settled into a comfortable wicker couch and reflected on the advantages of being extremely wealthy. My drink was made with a healthy portion of Bombay gin, in a big glass filled with ice and cut lime, and the bartender had added bitters. It was hot in the shade but not uncomfortable, and a light breeze brought the smell of mown grass and flowers. An attendant came by to check me out. I told him I was Michael's guest and he went away.

I noticed a young woman taking practice shots on a nearby putting green. She was nice to watch, dressed in white shorts and blouse and framed against the bright green of the fairway. She had a long waist and a lot of loosely curled blond hair.

After disappearing the yellow practice balls for five minutes, she straightened to watch a party gathered a hundred yards away at the nearest green. Yet another gray-haired man got set for a chip shot from the nearside of the hole. His ball went up and straight at the flag, then rolled into the cup. It was an impressive shot. The woman shouted and the man looked over with eyes shielded against the sun and waved. A conspicuously young, dark-haired fellow had stopped on the veranda to watch the shot and I asked him who the old guy was. He said, "Caleb Johnson," with a smirk, and continued toward the parking lot.

I set the gin and tonic down and went out to meet Susan Winston.

"You're pretty good," I said, "but you'd have more accuracy if you choked up a few inches. Let me show you."

She frowned, which might have been because the sun was over my shoulder and caught her in the eyes. She watched the fellow I'd spoken to go down the steps to the parking lot, then turned abruptly toward the clubhouse and disappeared into the women's locker room. I walked back to my drink on the veranda.

I was puzzled. I had been pushy, but not so much so that a person of normal social instincts wouldn't have felt obliged to at least acknowledge my presence. I wasn't sure whether I'd been deliberately snubbed, but it looked like it. Had somebody clued her to my purpose—perhaps Melissa or Phoebe?

I decided not to worry about it, but to skip Susan

Winston for the moment and try a good-old-boy routine on Caleb Johnson when he came off the course. I'd buttonhole him in the bar and tell him I'd seen his fancy chip shot by the clubhouse. If he didn't want to talk about that he wasn't human, and I should be able to tell by his reaction whether he knew about me.

But it didn't work out that way. I watched him ride up in a golf cart with two of his cronies and go into the clubhouse. He was a big man, with iron-gray hair and steel-rimmed glasses, and looking at him I could believe Susan might be attracted to him for reasons other than his personal financial statement. I gave him about five minutes and got up to follow. When I got into the bar Caleb Johnson was collapsed on the floor beside a shattered highball glass. He was already dead.

CHAPTER THREE

Call Me
Max

ONE OF THE men from Johnson's party was bent over the body about to try mouth-to-mouth resuscitation. I pushed by a tall, bulky athlete who was younger than all the other patrons and was probably the Club's golf pro. I got down onto one knee beside Johnson's buddy and caught the smell of burnt almonds just as the guy turned and goggled at me.

The athlete took a step forward and said, "Is he okay, Doc?"

Somebody on the other side of the room said, "My God."

I got up and moved back into the group. The men in the room were all holding half-empty highball glasses. The doctor said, "He's dead," as if he didn't believe it, then turned abruptly to the bartender and said, "Call the police, Peter. Don't let anybody touch that bottle."

We all looked at the crystal decanter standing on the bar, full almost to the neck with amber liquid, a glass stopper sitting beside it. I knew what he was talking about—the smell of almonds is a characteristic of cyanide poisoning, and Caleb must have been drinking from the bottle. Somebody said, "Is Susan at the Club?"

I fixed the scene and faces in my memory. At the far exit the attendant who'd questioned me earlier had come in and stood dazed, a stray ice cube melting at his feet. The bartender took a black telephone from under the bar. I moved back into the small corridor and the games room where the horses in the prints on the walls were still fixed in their rush to the finish line or hot on the tails of the desperate red foxes. Johnson wasn't going to get any deader, and I wanted to see Susan Winston before the cops showed up.

Outside I questioned a woman coming from the locker-room, and she pointed across the parking lot to Susan climbing into a red Mercedes sports car. I saw the dark-haired guy with the smirk standing not far from the car. Susan backed from the space and went out fast past the stables.

I ran across the gravel lot. At the Rambler I looked back and saw the athlete from the bar coming after me, and as I opened the door he shouted, "Not so fast, buddy," and reached a long arm out to restrain me. From the look of him I would have thought he'd have known better, since I'm tall and don't look like a pushover—but he was probably used to dealing exclusively with the idle rich. I swung my elbow up and hit him hard under the point of the chin, and I was in the car before he hit the ground. The dark-haired guy smirked at me from across the lot as I drove out past the red-painted stables and back onto the long drive under oaks. The wide, empty pasture shimmered in the sun on my left. Susan didn't look back. Her wheels kicked up dust as she turned onto 1A.

I slowed to keep well behind her. I could have pulled her over then, but I wanted to see where she was going. I had the Rambler's windows wide open, and hot wind plugged my ears and shuffled papers in the back. She retraced my route out to 128 and went south.

Watching the sunlit trees at the verge of the freeway and the dance of blonde hair in the open car ahead, the memory of the scene in the bar didn't seem part of reality. It had happened too quickly, and I knew from experience that I was suppressing the horror evoked by Caleb Johnson's face, and his sour smell mixed with that of the cyanide—my subconscious wasn't going to let me get involved until it had all my reactions sorted out. I was aware of the fact that my elbow was sore, and I wondered what was happening back at the Club. I also wondered if the coincidence of Caleb's sudden death just as I started my investigation was really coincidence, or maybe cause and effect?

But for now I was following Susan Winston. She cut over at the last second and got off at the exit for Salem. The secondary road was crowded, and a red Rabbit and old Chevy van got between us, then she began to cut around cars that hesitated too long at the green lights and sped up to make the yellow ones ahead of me. I managed to keep her in sight until we came over the bridge past the junkyard by the estuary and the half-dozen billboards advertising witch museums just outside Salem. Then I lost her in the center of town.

I kept on, east along Route 114, through a hodgepodge of rich suburbs and working-class triple-deckers over pizza parlors, into the town of Marblehead. I went past Abbott Hall, a fine brick building that is named for the ancestor of a short, balding friend of mine. Phoebe had briefed me on how to get to Caleb Johnson's house. It was across the harbor from the town, on a rocky peninsula aimed at Europe, a yellow Victorian on the edge of the water with a wide porch on two sides. There was gingerbread work at the eaves, and a narrow widow's walk at the peak that, in the days when the maples behind the house were young, must have had a fine view out to the ocean. The red Mercedes was parked under the maples. Beyond the house the harbor was as calm as a vacation lake in summer.

I parked across the street and sat thinking. My first impulse when I'd left the bar had been to watch Susan Winston's reaction to the news of Caleb's death—on the theory that if she were guilty of murdering him she wouldn't be able to hide it. It was not implausible, but her rush from the Club had thrown me off and now I wasn't sure what to do with her. If she were a murderer, would she have run? If she were innocent, did she know he was dead? Should I barge in now to catch her doing cartwheels or weeping hysterically?

I got out of the Rambler, crossed the road, and went down a half-dozen steps to the porch. A slight wind carried the smell of saltwater and the steady creaking of what might have been an anchor chain in the harbor beyond. I wondered if there'd been a boat and if she was headed out to sea.

There was no doorbell, so I rapped on the wooden screen door. I could see into the shadowy interior where there were armchairs and a baby grand piano. Through one of the front windows I saw the profile of her blond head against the blue of the harbor. Her voice came from around the corner and I went that way and found her sitting on a cushioned metal couch swing, a glass of lemonade in one hand, a book in her lap.

"You?" she said.

"Yes."

"What do you want?" She put down the lemonade and reached for a telephone.

"I'm a private investigator. I want to talk about Caleb Johnson."

She kept one hand on the telephone and with the other put aside the book. It was the Durrell travel book on the Greek Islands.

"What about my husband?" she said, and then her eyes narrowed. "You're surprised by that. I thought Morgan would know we'd been married."

I didn't answer, but sat in a chair against the railing. I wondered briefly if Morgan had in fact known about the marriage, and what Freud would say about her forgetting to tell me. With knees up on the cushions Susan was twisted slightly to keep her hand on the telephone. She had nice legs. She wasn't wearing a bra under the loose green t-shirt, and that made her look younger than she had at the Club. I noticed for the first time that the blue of her right eye was marked by a tiny wedge of amber.

"What makes you think I'm working for Morgan Streeter?"

"Who else?"

"It doesn't matter. I'd like to ask just one or two questions. Then I'll leave."

"You'll leave now or I'll call the police."

"It might be easier to answer the questions." I took my i.d. out and tossed it onto the cushion beside her curled up bare feet. She took her hand from the telephone to get it.

"James Maxfield Mallory," she read from the photostat. She seemed to think the name was funny. She tossed it back.

"Why don't you go the hell back and tell Morgan Streeter it's too late to do anything about us. What does she want from me?"

"How long have you and Caleb been married?" I asked.

She picked up the glass of lemonade and took a long drink. Maybe it wasn't just lemonade. The breeze over the water had picked up a little, and not far out, in the sun, a twenty-foot sloop with a varnished wooden hull swept by under a carefully controlled mainsail, headed for the opening to the sea. The man at the helm waved.

Susan looked at the telephone, then decided I wasn't worth the bother. "Last weekend. In Reno. It's quite legal."

"I noticed when you left the Club you were talking with somebody by your car. Who was that?"

"A friend."

"You seemed to be having an argument." I wasn't sure of that, but thinking back I remembered something tense and hostile about the dark-haired fellow as he watched her getting into the Mercedes.

"No," she said.

"Isn't that why you left the Club in such a hurry?"

"I was on my way out when I ran into him. He's an old friend. I'm not going to give you his name. What does this matter?"

"You're going to Greece?" I said and pointed to the book. "I've always wanted to go to the Greek islands."

"Great. Listen, I know you're trying to do your job and I'm being rude. Can you understand why?"

"Sure."

She looked closely at me. "So okay, why don't I make you a glass of lemonade. Then you can go back to Morgan and tell her I'm really quite nice and civilized, maybe even nice enough to invite to dinner sometime."

That surprised me. It occurred to me she really might not know her husband was dead, and I should tell her. But I wanted to ask more questions. And, contrary to much popular wisdom, I believe that bad news is something that should be avoided for as long as possible.

So I said I would love some lemonade.

"Fine," she said, and stood up from the couch. It swung as her weight freed it. We walked toward the turn of the porch and the edge of her domain of warm breezes and the smell of the saltwater. Then she stopped, put her hands on her hips, and surprised me again. "This is crazy," she said, "but you seem like a nice guy. What did you say your name was?"

"James Maxfield Mallory."

She smiled. "That's a good name. I bet your friends call you Max."

"All my friends call me Max," I lied.

We rounded the corner of the porch. Two state cops were up on the hill behind the house. One of them was poking around the Rambler and the other was already halfway down the steps. He had his gun out.

CHAPTER FOUR

I'm Friends with the Cops

I HAD A copy of *The Autobiography of Alice B. Toklas*, which I'd stolen when it appeared mysteriously in the waiting room of the station after one of my visits to the john. I put it on the scarred wooden table of the interrogation room and sat down behind it. Across the table a bland-looking cop in a heavy wool business suit sat watching me. It was about 85 degrees in the room. He looked down at the picture pasted to the private investigator's license he held in a fat hand.

"Mallory," he said.

He tapped the i.d. on the table twice and threw it across to me.

"I am Simon Mangenello and this is Sergeant Tuckerman." A big state trooper in campaign hat and knee-length leather boots sat across the room with the back of his chair tilted against the stained wooden paneling. I nodded, but he didn't respond.

We were at the state police barracks in Lynn, one town over from Salem. My flight from the Bombay and pursuit of Susan Johnson across town lines had created suspicion and a jurisdictional problem, and Hamilton had called in the state cops.

"We checked you out with your sponsor at the Club," Mangenello continued. "He says you're a bum, but not homicidal. Tell me what you were doing out there."

"The widow must have told you."

"Mrs. Johnson? She said you were hired by Morgan Streeter to investigate her relationship with Johnson."

"Makes sense, doesn't it?"

The trooper dropped his chair to the floor.

"It does make sense," said Mangenello. "Mrs. Streeter thought the girl was a gold digger. Now she thinks the girl murdered Johnson. I spoke with her in Brookline before I came up here. I bet she would appreciate her employees cooperating with the police in this investigation."

"You first."

"Me first what? Is that a tough-guy routine? I don't know you from borscht, Mallory, and right now, at a minimum, I've got you for assaulting that guy at the Club."

I'd been sitting on a wooden bench for three hours reading *The Autobiography of Alice B. Toklas*, and I was tired. I said, "If it'll help, Jim Cromerty at Boston homicide knows me. He's chief of detectives."

"I know Cromerty." Mangenello turned to the big trooper and said, "Watch him," then got up and went out. There was dead silence for a few moments in which I tried to stare down my guardian. Then he opened his big mouth and grinned at me.

Mangenello came back and settled about two hundred pounds of flesh into the big wooden chair behind the table. "Based on what Cromerty tells me, I think we can talk about the details of this case. But first, questions. Accepted?"

I nodded.

"Why did you take off from the bar in such a hurry after Johnson died?"

"I wanted to talk with Susan Johnson."

"You didn't want to stick around? You were hired to protect the man. There he is, murdered right before your eyes, and you hightail it without even stopping to take a look at the evidence."

"I didn't think the killer was in the bar, and even if he

was I doubted he'd be making confessions. I would have stuck around, Lieutenant, if Susan Johnson hadn't taken off. I followed my imperatives."

"Like beating up the golf pro on your way out?"

I shrugged and congratulated myself on having correctly identified my victim as a golf pro. "I wasn't hired to protect Johnson, you know, I was hired to investigate Susan. And it didn't happen right before my eyes. Just for the record."

"Let's have it from the beginning." He started me through the afternoon and the day before. I told him everything. He wanted details and went over the same ground about five times, which is what he's supposed to do. He was particularly interested in my conversations with Susan Johnson.

"She tell you why she took off from the Club in such a hurry?"

"Saw an old boyfriend she didn't want to see. At least that's the way I figured it. Wouldn't give me his name."

"Stephen Littman. A guest of one of the members—and Johnson's lawyer, by the way. He wasn't in the bar at the time of the murder."

"He was talking with Susan out by the car. Tell me about the cyanide."

"It was in a bottle of scotch the victim brought to the bar himself. The bottle was mailed to the house in Marblehead and Johnson picked it up on his way to the Club. It was wrapped first in gold wedding paper, then wrapped again in brown commercial paper. He opened the package in the locker-room and we found the wrappings, no note or letter. Package was postmarked Tuesday, Boston. Plenty of prints, but no return address."

"You'd expected one?"

"It could have been a legitimate gift and someone poisoned it in the bar. Johnson'd left it with the bartender while he played his nine holes."

"I think it would have been difficult. Too many people."

"The bartender also claims the tax seal hadn't been

broken when he poured the drink. But stranger things have happened. The lab is running a check to see if the seal was steamed and reglued. There was cyanide in both the bottle and the highball glass, so it wasn't a question of slipping the stuff into the glass or freezing it into the ice cubes."

"How come nobody smelled the cyanide—especially the bartender? The body reeked of it."

"Both the whiskey and cyanide have a nutlike smell. According to the coroner some people don't have the physical capacity to smell cyanide. The bartender could have poisoned the bottle himself, of course, but he hadn't any motive. None that we know of.

"We're putting the bit about the bottle out to the newspapers. If it was a gift the sender might come forward. In the meantime we're checking the folks in the bar. There's the bartender and you, the Club's golf pro— the guy you hit—and the rest are all lawyers and doctors, mostly retired."

"And rich as hell."

"Mostly. The bartender says Johnson was a fanatic about good scotch, and this stuff was something special. Care to guess how much it cost?"

"Two thousand dollars. It was in a crystal decanter, twenty-five-year-old scotch. I saw it advertised in *The New Yorker* last Christmas. Stuck in my mind."

"Yeah—I read *The New Yorker* myself. If it weren't for that I might peg this as a random killing, one of those political things, aimed at the rich folks. But I can't see a nut or political fanatic spending two thousand bucks on a bottle of scotch."

"Depends on the class of nut or fanatic you're talking about, Lieutenant. But they can't sell many of those bottles."

"Sold nine hundred cases last winter. Lots of wealth in this great country of ours. All of them had to be bought by special order, and we might get something from local shopkeepers. It's a long shot, but that's what we've got. There's the cyanide too."

"Nothing else?"

"Not much. When Johnson came off the course he was in a good mood and wanted to try the whiskey. Lucky nobody joined him. Scotch is a tough drink at noontime. Death was instantaneous according to the coroner, who happened to be Johnson's golfing partner. He's the guy you saw bent over the body. Doctor Florian."

"Should have been an historian. What do you think about the wife?"

"Nothing specific. We're told she doesn't inherit much from Johnson's estate, everything's tied up in trusts that go to the daughter."

"Maybe the killer was after the wife, or both of them."

"She says she's allergic to scotch and most everybody knew it. She got some at a party recently, by mistake, and had to be taken to the hospital."

"I didn't think they did any socializing. You know their marriage was a secret, at least from Mrs. Streeter. Which is another point—whoever wrapped that bottle knew about the wedding."

"Sure, though I don't see where it gets us. Christ, can you imagine what we'd have on our hands if Johnson'd poured a shot for everyone in the damned bar to toast his new wife?"

"That expensive a scotch, he'd be less likely to give it away."

"True." We were both silent a few moments, thinking, then Mangenello said, "Maybe it was a weirdo after all, and the bottle was stolen. That's something else we might get a line on. Or maybe Johnson took this way to commit suicide."

"With a brand-new wife and pots of money? And would he have wrapped the bottle and sent it to himself in the mail?"

"Stranger things have happened."

"Right. Are we finished here? I've got a dinner date."

"I guess so. I've shelved that assault charge, but it's still on the books."

"Thanks." I stood and picked up my credentials and the Gertrude Stein book. "I'll be working on this," I said.

"Join the crowd. It does bug you that it happened right under your nose, doesn't it?"

"Sure, but it's not just that. Whoever did this was a real asshole. Poison's bad enough, but like you say, this stuff could have nabbed anybody."

He nodded. "By the way, did you really drop that golf pro with one shot? He's a big boy."

"I carry little green pills in my pockets, made of spinach."

The big trooper laughed, but Mangenello had stopped him with an incredulous stare by the time I went out the door.

CHAPTER FIVE

A Rose is
a Rose

THE RAMBLER HAD been impounded, but after going through the requisite red tape I got the attendant to open the gate to the parking lot and set me free. It was commuter traffic time, but going south into the city wouldn't be too bad. Driving out to the highway I stopped at a Rexall drugstore and called Morgan Streeter. Phoebe answered. I told her I was just leaving the police and I knew about Mr. Johnson. She said Mrs. Streeter couldn't come to the phone but would I visit tomorrow, at ten?

I got to the office a little past six that night. The third floor was quiet; by that time the guy who makes dentures had left and the young lawyer who works the late shift in the Combat Zone hadn't arrived. There are only us three rent-paying tenants—we're a sideline for the owner of the club, and she rents to people she likes and keeps half the offices empty.

The red light on Della was blinking. I sat at the desk by the front window and watched the evening traffic on Charles Street and played back the messages. Julie said she'd meet me at my office as planned and we could walk to her place and she'd cook dinner. Phoebe came on and said I should make tomorrow eleven instead of ten. Then there were two long-playing dial tones.

With luck Julie would show in the next hour, and calling her would only distract her from whatever she had to get finished. I picked up *The Autobiography of Alice*

B. Toklas. About ten minutes later I turned off the lights, pulled the heavy drapes across the window onto the street, and sat looking at the lit green water of the pool in the darkened area below my office. A few swimmers making laps threw shadows up onto the walls and ceiling around me.

I was wondering whether I had time or energy for a swim when Edgar the masseur stuck his bald head into the office.

"Jimmy, what ya doin' in the dark? There's a taxi downstairs for ya with a beautiful chick in it."

"Julie?"

"Naw, it's a blonde." He winked and disappeared out the door.

I went after him and then through the lobby to the street. A white suburban cab was at the curb, with Susan Johnson in the back behind the driver. I pulled open the door. She hadn't changed her clothing since I'd last seen her. The pupils of her eyes were widely dilated.

"I wanted to talk," she said.

"Come upstairs."

"No. But I want to talk."

I got in and closed the door. "What are you doing in Boston?"

"Going to friends' house. Want to talk."

"Where are your friends? They know you're coming?"

"Yes. They said I shouldn't be alone."

"Where are they?"

"Church Court Condos."

"That's close to where I live. I'll drive with you and we'll talk. Wait."

I went back into the Trojan and made a call to Julie from the front desk. Somebody answered after the tenth ring and said they'd leave a message. I told them she should wait at work for me or go home and I'd call her there. I went back out to the cab, climbed in, and gave the driver the address of my apartment.

I watched Susan Johnson as we started up. I wondered why the cops had let her take off alone and on tranquilizers.

"I want to hire you," she said. "You said you were a private investigator."

"Hire me for what?"

The cabby spun around a car that hesitated too long at the intersection of Stuart with Charles, and I reached out to steady Susan. She said, carefully enunciating each of the words, "To find who killed my husband. Of course. You should not trust Morgan."

"Trust her to do what?"

She smiled. "Tried to call you. Got your answering machine. Who is that girl?"

We rattled over the construction site at the new Four Seasons Hotel on Boylston. She said, "Morgan was in love with Caleb." Her eyes focused briefly on mine. "Morgan married an older man, you know."

I almost felt like laughing. "You're not thinking clearly," I said. "They've got you on tranquilizers. You married an older man yourself. It doesn't mean anything."

She gave me a wan smile. "I was in love with my father too."

Her head rolled when the cab turned at the Public Garden to go up Beacon. The garden looked nice in the evening light, with well-ordered flower beds under big trees and the old-fashioned black street lamps and wrought-iron fence. Susan Johnson passed out and I caught her as she fell across the seat.

I told the driver to take us directly to Church Court Condos. It's on the river by the Mass. Ave. bridge and it's becoming a landmark—an artsy reconstruction of a burned-out church that was vacant for years until a clever architect got the idea to turn the walls and nave into a courtyard and build around it. Some people think of it as a monument to sacrilege, but I like it.

The cab needed shocks and made a lot of noise cruising down Beacon, missing the red lights through a system of continuous acceleration. It was interesting to see that even suburban cabbies drove that way when they got into Boston. We pulled up at the entrance to the condos on the intersection of Mass. Ave. and Beacon. I shook Susan awake and she mumbled the name of her friends.

The meter showed a hefty tab, but I paid, wondering if I should charge this one to Mrs. Streeter. I lifted Susan out and walked her to the door, then stood her up and rang the bell next to the friends' name. Through the glass of the door I saw a preppy fellow in a plaid shirt come down the stairs. He was expecting her. He wanted to know who I was and I told him not to worry about it. I left them together in the lobby.

My apartment is on the fourth floor of a building in the last block of Marlborough Street, by Charlesgate and the small park of locust trees at the Muddy River. I'd left the window shades open in the front room and I could see across the street into the lit-up apartments of my neighbors. I've got two rooms, plus the small kitchen and bath. The living room has a working fireplace and lots of photographs and art produced by friends.

I called Julie and got her at work. I told her I'd walk to her place. She didn't expect to be much longer, but I should feel free to go up and make myself at home. She'd given me a key a week before, almost exactly one month after our first dinner together. At the time I'd supposed that meant we were beginning a more serious relationship, and I'd hesitated about the key, but decided it was difficult enough seeing a corporate attorney without complicating things with principles. It still made me a little uncomfortable. Better I should pick the lock when I needed to get into the place.

I went to my small bedroom and changed into a pair of blue jeans and a light blue T-shirt and sneakers, then went out and down the three flights to Marlborough Street and started into the city.

It had cooled off after the hot day and it was pleasant walking between the old brownstone and brick townhouses, each of which fits the pattern of the street, four stories with bay windows, but each of which is also unique.

They built them at a time when people sat down with an architect and designed their own places, and the designers all had a love of detail and ornamentation. At least I imagine it happened that way—hundreds of townhouses raised one at a time by newly prosperous families marching across the long flat of the reclaimed Back Bay, glorifying life, art, and progress.

Thus encumbered with nineteenth-century nostalgia, I turned right at Fairfield Street to Commonwealth and the mall, then to Newbury Street to pick up a bottle of wine at DeLucca's Market. DeLucca's looks like it should be a restaurant or café, with its glassed-in front extending out from the brick building behind it. It sells good fresh fruit and groceries and deli items among a scattering of plaster statues of naked goddesses. There's a nice wine selection in the basement. I had a lot of cash from the check Phoebe'd given me, and I bought a good bottle of St. Julien and a bottle of Mumm's and stopped on the way out to pick up a jar of beluga caviar and white bread for making toast.

Julie owns all of the fourth floor of a building on Commonwealth Avenue. I rang the buzzer and got no answer, so I used the key and walked up three flights to let myself in. It was cool and dark in the front room. There was a Steinway grand in one corner of bay windows, an oriental rug that glowed in the half-light, and a scattering of antiques and wing chairs. I hit the switch to light a big reading lamp in one corner of the room beside a treacherously comfortable blue sofa, and turned down a corridor to the back of the house and the kitchen.

The kitchen is almost as large as the front room, but lined with cedar paneling, and it looks out through three windows to the alley and the backs of the houses that front on Newbury Street. There are three ovens, including the microwave, lots of wooden cabinets, wood chopping-block counters, an oversized refrigerator and freezer standing side by side, and a dozen efficient-looking appliances lined up on the work counters. There's also an old butcher block table Julie got from a defunct meat shop in the North End, in the middle of the polished hardwood floor, lit by a single red, conical ceiling lamp.

I put the caviar and wine onto the counter and went to the refrigerator for eggs, which I covered with water in a saucepan and set to boil on one of the six commercial-type gas burners. I got out a heavy silver ice bucket, packed the bottle of champagne with ice from the ice maker in the freezer, and left it in the center of the butcher-block table. The water with the eggs was boiling and I turned down the flame and went to a wooden bin beside the refrigerator for a Bermuda onion.

I decided it would be simpler not to use the Cuisinart and instead got out a sharp knife and a big round cutting board, peeled and cut the onion, then carried the board and the chopped onion to the butcher block.

I figured we could eat the caviar in the kitchen while Julie cooked, and dine in the front room, so I went out to the front and moved two of the big wing chairs into a half-circle beside the piano, looking out onto the mall and the statue of Alexander Hamilton. I went back to the kitchen for place mats, silverware, and wineglasses and set up a small table at the windows. When I had finished, it looked cozy. I wished it was cool enough to build a fire.

In the kitchen I made toast, cut up the boiled eggs, spooned the caviar into a blue china dish, and arranged everything on the cutting board in the center of the butcher block.

I was thirsty and I didn't want to open the wine, so I got an Amstel from the refrigerator and sat down at the table by the back windows and watched the lights of the Hancock tower and the Pru where they showed over the tops of the buildings across the alley. People were still working up there. It had been a long day for me. I was tired.

She showed up thirty minutes and two beers later. She was gorgeous. She wore a gray linen suit, and her long hair, like a Polynesian's, was down in wings at each side of her wide face and the bright blue eyes.

"I'm sorry to be late," she said. "Do you mind?"

"You're always late, sweetheart," but I kissed her to show I didn't mind. She smelled of perfumed shampoo.

"I do it to keep you in line, you lousy ruffian private eye. So how was your day? Nice place you got here, what an income you must have. What kind of wine is that?"

"It's good wine. Get some glasses."

I opened the champagne and we sat at the table and touched the glasses.

"I started a new job," I said. "Someone was murdered."

"How romantic. My clients never kill each other. All that stuff I learned in law school about degrees of homicide, intent, malice aforethought—all down the tubes."

"It's because corporations never die. This one was tough, though. He was on our side, and they poisoned him while my back was turned."

She took my hand. "Are you all right?"

"I'll tell you about it."

"Let me change first."

While she was in the other room I sat and sipped the champagne. I watched two cats meeting in the alley below, a tiger and a big black, and I thought about Genoa where they have real alley cats and where I'd seen old ladies feeding them the way people feed the pigeons here.

Julie came out wearing blue jeans and a faded green t-shirt and gave me another hug and kiss. I stood at the butcher block and spooned out chopped onion, egg, and caviar onto pieces of the toast, and handed them across to her as she cooked. In between bites I told her about my day at the Bombay.

"You should join," I said. "It's a swell place."

"They don't let Jews into places like that, do they?"

She had cut up the chicken breasts the night before and now she stir-fried them in butter and spices, made a red wine sauce, and stirred in hearts of artichoke. Artichokes are not supposed to mix well with wine, but the recipe was based on a dish served at Felicia's in the North End, and the smell of the tarragon and fresh lemon and the rice steaming in chicken stock almost made me forget how good Julie smelled as I stood beside her at the stove.

When it was finished I helped her dish it into bowls over the rice and we took them with the red wine out to the front room and the chairs I'd arranged at the bay windows. She poured wine into two glasses between us on the small table.

I sat and watched as she looked down at the lights of the cars on the street below. The profile of her face showed the strain of a long day.

"I started *The Autobiography of Alice B. Toklas* today," I said. "I like it."

She turned back to smile at me. "Didn't you tell me you liked Ernest Hemingway?"

"Nobody likes Hemingway anymore."

"Including Gertrude Stein."

"And besides, the wench is dead," I said.

"Hemingway said that, right?"

We ate some more in silence and drank the wine. I asked her about her day at the office and she said she didn't want to talk about it. We didn't bother to clean up the dishes. The maid would be in the next day. We stood together by the piano and I held her and asked if I should get a cab since my car was parked in the lot by the Trojan.

She opened her eyes. "Why are you talking about cabs?"

"I'm suggesting you might not want me to stay the night. I didn't want to take you for granted."

"Let's not be formal, sweetheart."

So we went together into the big bedroom between the front room and the kitchen. We were both tired and we lay on the bed with our clothes off, talking and kissing. We were a new enough relationship so that we did a lot of kissing.

After a long silence she said, "Who do you think did it?"

"The murderer? Too soon to tell."

"Take a guess."

"Phoebe the private secretary."

"Why her?"

"Because there isn't any butler."

"Don't be stupid."

"Come on," I said. "It's been a long hard day."

"Speaking of long and hard," she said.

After we'd made love, while she was up to use the bathroom, I lay in the bed listening to the few street noises coming from the front room, and when she came back into bed we both lay together, listening.

"It's a weird life," I said.

"A rose is a rose is a rose," she said sleepily.

"You're silly," I said. "I suppose you want to become unconscious."

"And sometimes it doesn't smell as sweet," she said.

"And there you have it," I told her as her breathing slipped into a slower pattern of sleep. A few moments later I had joined her, but I started on a long, involved dream about almonds and golf carts and important messages that had to be carried to strange houses on strange shores. In the last part of the dream I caught sight of the solitary man who'd sailed past the house in Marblehead and waved, and just before the boat disappeared into the fog at the entrance to the harbor I saw that the man was Caleb Johnson, and he was dead.

CHAPTER SIX

Is a Rose?

I WALKED JULIE partway to work and kissed her good-bye on the bridge in the Public Garden. It was early, and the kids who pedal the swan boats around the duck pond were just starting to get ready for the day's work. Most of the ducks were asleep, floating with heads turned behind shoulders and nestled into back feathers, or else squatting in clusters up on the grass of the bank. A half-dozen fed on Wonder Bread thrown out by an old woman in the shadow of the bridge.

"They really like this stuff," she said.

"Builds strong bodies twelve ways," I pointed out. I turned to watch Julie pass through the gates. Her long hair was pulled into a ponytail and she wore gym shoes and carried a brown leather briefcase. She looked stylish and serious disappearing toward the big downtown office buildings.

I turned back and walked around the pond on the Arlington Street side, under old willows that grow right into the water and make a cavern of shadow beyond the bank. At the far end there was a woman with very long auburn hair on a bench in shafts of sunlight, two sleeping collies stretched out at her feet. It looked good, but it was also good to be going to work. I had a lot ahead of me.

The Trojan is not far from the park and only a block from Park Plaza, where they're building the big new hotel by the statue of Abraham Lincoln emancipating a slave. Outside the front entrance of the club a blue, unmarked police car waited at the curb. Simon Mangenello got out. He moved well, considering his size. He held a Styrofoam coffee cup, which he finished and tossed into the back seat. He wore a heavy brown wool suit and had the jacket buttoned.

"Going to be hot," I said.

"I never notice."

"I didn't think the Commonwealth would stay involved in the Johnson case."

He shrugged. "Multiplicity of jurisdictions. The cyanide was delivered to Johnson through the mails, from Boston. We're lucky not to have the FBI involved. You saw Susan Johnson last night."

"Yes. You put a tail on her?"

"Not exactly. My man offered to drive her into town. The doctor had her on scopolamine, and he didn't think she should go off alone. The stuff takes away your judgment."

"I noticed."

He cocked an eye at me. "The girl insisted she had something to do and wanted a cab. So my guy got the number and checked on it afterward."

"Wondered why you let her go off alone. Come up to the office?"

"What kind of office you got, in a health club? Can you give it to me quick?"

"She wanted to hire me to solve her husband's murder."

"That all?"

"She thinks Morgan Streeter killed Johnson out of love. She was pretty zonked by the medication. I took her to the friends' house."

"You working for her?"

"I've already got a client. You get anything new?"

"Nothing, but we're just getting started. No apparent motives anywhere. Johnson didn't even owe his lawyers money."

"Can't be very good lawyers."

He smiled and turned abruptly and climbed into the car.

I put one hand on the roof over the open window. "You know, you could have called."

"I did. Got your damned answering machine. I hate those things." He started the car and drove off.

I walked up five stone steps into the Trojan. The brown-tiled lobby with empty trophy cases set in the walls on each side always makes me think of the entrance to my old public high school. It was dim and cool out of the sun. Harry sat behind the front desk on a stool with wheels. Harry has no legs. Behind him the cage overflowed with clean towels and sports equipment, and to the right and left stairs went down to locker rooms.

I said, "Edgar in?" I didn't feel like going up to my office to make coffee and deal with Della.

Harry dropped a cigarette and jerked a bony thumb over his left shoulder. "Downstairs."

I went down and caught the smell of Edgar's fresh coffee from his small office beside the space where his leather massage table sits. The office was crowded with barbells, two big console radios, two ratty armchairs, and a desk cluttered with tools and playing cards and magazines next to a small daybed. There was a dart board over the bed and a lot of old centerfolds taped up, the kind that look like paintings instead of photographs, and among them was a reproduction of one of Picasso's sleeping women.

Edgar came from around the corner behind me, carrying a broom.

"Jimmy," he said. "Wanna massage?"

"Nope, just coffee."

He leaned the broom against the wall and went in. "Guess that blonde took all the kinks outta ya last night." He poured himself a cup from a percolator and sat in one of the armchairs. I followed, poured coffee, took a plain donut, and put two quarters into a brightly colored cigar box. I sat across the room and put the cup onto the exposed wooden arm of the chair. There was a battered brass reading lamp slung over the back of each of the armchairs—at one time it had all been a matching set.

Edgar said, "Anything happenin'?"

"Working on a case. Guy got murdered."

"Nothin' but the high-class stuff for you, Jimmy."

He picked up a copy of *Playboy*. I dipped my donut into coffee, then picked up an old copy of *Time* magazine and read "Milestones." Heinrich Böll and Diego Giacometti had both died. I looked up and saw Edgar's eyes had gone unfocused and he was flexing the stringy muscles of his forearms.

"Who you fighting now?"

He grinned. "Joe Louis."

"Never saw Louis fight."

I looked at the big green school clock, finished my coffee, and stood up. "I'm off. Go easy on old Joe."

Edgar got up and walked me to the door of the locker room. I went on through, past battered green lockers stacked like crushed soup cans, and up to the office to get into appropriate clothing. I ignored Della, went down to the back entrance and the Rambler, and drove it to Brookline.

Phoebe met me at the door. She wore another plain brown dress—maybe it was a uniform. She led me back into the house, into the formal study I'd noticed two days before. The floor was stained dark and was mostly covered by a beige oriental. There were bookcases filled with leather-bound books, a big mahogany table and couch, and two straight-backed reading chairs by a fireplace across the room. Both the couch and the chairs were upholstered in what looked like an ancient French wall tapestry. The drapes over the windows were closed but lit behind by the morning sun, and they filtered in a burgundy light. It was stuffy in the room.

I asked, "How are they holding up?"

She frowned and said, "It's not my place to discuss it, Mr. Mallory. I'll let Mrs. Streeter know you're here." She turned and left.

I went over to the marble fireplace set with logs and kindling for the next chilly night. There was a big cut-glass mirror on the wall above the mantel and small objects arranged below the mirror. My eyes went to an antique paperweight beside the china figure of a young woman on horseback. The paperweight was clear crystal filled with twisted ribbons of color, like the center of a cat's eye marble. I felt a brush of sadness. It took me a moment to recall a hospital waiting room years before, and a complex jigsaw puzzle made from a photograph of a similar old glass weight. I realized that I'd come to associate them with death. At the time I'd neurotically thought that if I could finish that puzzle I would somehow keep death from coming.

I saw Mrs. Streeter come in and turned to take her hand. She looked a few years older. "I understand you were there yesterday," she said. "The police came to question me. Tell how it happened."

"There isn't much to tell. He was dead before I got to him." Melissa came in and sat on the couch behind Mrs. Streeter. The mother dropped my hand.

"Will the police discover his murderer?"

"There's a good chance in this kind of case. It must have been someone who knew his habits. That narrows it."

She sighed heavily and sat down beside her daughter on the couch, smoothing her black silk dress out over her knees.

"Will you continue to represent me in this matter, Mr. Mallory? To investigate his murder?"

"Yes. And I will find whoever did this."

She didn't seem to hear me. "Now that the risks appear greater," she said, "I assume your fee will be higher. I will entrust Phoebe to handle those details, and in general you may report to her. I'm not up to it at the moment. Is there anything we can do to assist you?"

"It would be a great help if you could think of anybody who might have wanted to hurt your stepfather. Anybody who'd have had a motive to kill him—whether from jealousy, greed, an old grudge?"

"I'm not sure I understand."

"Was he involved in any unusual business ventures, did he gamble, play the horses and not pay his gambling debts? Anything like that."

The two women sat side by side on the couch. The only place to sit opposite them was the edge of the mahogany table, and I leaned back against it.

Mrs. Streeter said, "I can think of nothing of that sort. Father was not a thug."

"You said Wednesday he had a tendency to get into bad situations."

"I was talking about Susan Winston and women of her sort. She actually married him, didn't she? I suppose that makes her my stepmother. Which is absurd."

"What about other women? Perhaps somebody was jealous because of his marriage to Susan."

"There were others, but I really don't know anything about them, except the one I mentioned, the one we paid. I understood she was well satisfied. I want you to focus on Susan Winston, Mr. Mallory. I feel certain she murdered Father. I can't imagine anyone else who would do such a thing."

"I don't know if that's true. But I plan to visit Choate & Masterson to get details on her background, and also to ask about your mother's estate. For that I'll need you to authorize the lawyers to discuss confidential information."

"I'll call John Masterson this afternoon. He's the senior partner in the firm and also an old friend of the family."

"You should look through your papers for whatever information you have on that woman from five years ago.

It's going back a long way, but I'd like to locate her. Do you remember the name?"

"I don't, but I'll look for it."

"I'm going to go back out to the Bombay, and at this point there's no need for secrecy, so I'd prefer to use that entrée you mentioned on Wednesday. I think that's the best place for me to begin. Will you have Phoebe call after you've spoken to Mr. Masterson?"

"Of course. Is there anything else?"

"Not for now."

Mrs. Streeter nodded and looked sideways. She reached over and began to stroke her daughter's hair. Melissa had not spoken a word. She looked up at me then and smiled.

CHAPTER SEVEN

Tennis, Anyone?

I COULDN'T GET in to see Mrs. Streeter's attorneys until Monday at the earliest, and that left me two days to get to the Bombay. We'd planned to take the cruise boat to Provincetown on Saturday, and since it's hard for Julie to make plans, we did that. We spent the day wandering around the town, ate a good meal in a restaurant looking out over the ocean, and got back into Boston Saturday night. But I had been distracted most of the day, little things kept kicking me back into the problem of Caleb Johnson.

Sunday morning looked like another beautiful day after a week of good weather. I called Morgan Streeter's number and let it ring seven times before Melissa answered.

"Hello. What happened to Phoebe?" I said.

"It's her day off. Is this Mallory? I'll get Mother."

"Hang on, I want to talk with you. I want to take you up on that offer of tennis at the Bombay."

"I'd love to play sometime."

"Just put on your whites and I'll pick you up in half an hour."

There was a long silence, and I thought perhaps I'd offended her.

"Listen," I said, "it's soon after your grandfather's death, but this has to do with getting me out to the Bombay. And it might make you feel better."

"Make it forty-five minutes," she said, and hung up.

I went to the bedroom and dug out tennis shorts from the bureau and an old racket from the closet. I hadn't played the sport for years, but the Bombay would be a good place to start again.

In Brookline, Melissa was standing at the curb dressed in white, holding a big canvas bag with the handle of a tennis racket sticking out of it. She hesitated only a moment before climbing into the Rambler—the seats were clean, if not fully intact—and dumped the bag between us. She looked very blonde, tanned, and young.

I had to reach across her to reclose the door—it never shuts completely unless you give it just the right lift. She smiled and said, "So what's the big secret? Why didn't you want Mother to know we were going to the Club?"

"What makes you think I don't want her to know?"

She made a face and said, "Never mind." It seemed rather playful for a mourning granddaughter.

She didn't say anything more until we were out on Storrow Drive and she noticed me looking at her tennis racket. It was made from graphite. I'd always thought of graphite as something they put into pencils and never have been sure how they get the stuff into a tennis racket. It had the oversized head people were using since somebody realized there were no rules saying how big a tennis racket could be.

Melissa took a look in the back seat at the scarred wood of my old Wilson, autographed by Pancho Gonzales and clamped tightly into a press. She picked it up and started plucking the strings.

"Do you really play with this?"

"When I can't find my badminton racket. What's wrong with it?"

"It's heavy."

"I like it that way. I know when I've hit the ball, and I like the feel of the wood and leather."

She made another face. "You're old-fashioned."

"Not really. And stop making faces at me."

She plucked again at the strings and said, "This is an antique."

We were climbing the ramp off Storrow Drive to Route 95, and I cut across the oncoming traffic from the Expressway and started the approach up the bridge, passing over City Square in Charlestown. I could see the harbor on my right, and I felt excited by the early morning and the beautiful young woman beside me. "My father gave me that racket when I was fourteen years old," I said. "I was four the first time he took me out on the courts."

"That must've been nice."

"It was. By the time I was fourteen we were the best doubles team in town. Tell me something about your folks."

"My folks?"

"Yes. What about your father?"

Her hands jerked slightly on the handle of the racket and it struck against the dashboard. "He's as old as Grandpa Johnson. He lives at the Cromwell Club."

"Do you see him?"

"No. He's separated from Mother, has been for years, and he doesn't like me. He's like Grandmother Johnson, she never liked me either."

We'd come off the bridge and passed the exits for Revere and then the new indoor cinema where eight different movies are shown simultaneously. When I was a kid there was an outdoor theater on the same spot with a screen you could see from the highway going into the city.

I said, "Why didn't she like you?"

"She was jealous. Maybe because I was Grandpa's favorite. He called me his little girl. She cringed whenever he said that."

"Did you see him much?"

"Grandpa Johnson? All the time. He used to live at the house in Brookline."

"You'll miss him." It occurred to me that I was talking

to her the way I would a teenager. I had to look at her to remember she was twenty-six.

"Did you ever think of marrying a rich girl?" she said.

"All the time. Why?"

"Melissa Mallory would be a nice name."

I smiled. We came up over the hill by Brown's Steakhouse, with its plastic life-sized cattle grazing out front and the lunchtime crowd already forming up lines in the long glass corridor that runs down the façade of the restaurant.

"Do you think Susan killed him?" I asked.

"Mother hates her, you know. Especially because of the marriage."

"What do you think?"

"I think it was an accident. Like those Tylenol capsules somebody put cyanide into. Just an accident."

I didn't point out that the Tylenol capsules hadn't been poisoned by accident.

She was quiet for a few moments and stroked the handle of the tennis racket thoughtfully.

"You know," she said. "I think I know what you mean about this old thing."

At the Bombay I changed in the men's locker-room and we walked together to the old clay courts. At that time of day on a Sunday it was busy and we had to wait almost an hour for a chance to play. The crowd, on the whole, was younger than it had been on Thursday. There was a smaller clubhouse by the courts where they served beer from coolers, and I sat on the porch with Melissa and drank two cold Heinekens. We watched a doubles game in the first court. The players were all very fit-looking men in their sixties, playing crafty tennis and moving with the quiet efficiency of people operating under familiar and private rules, and I thought again about my father.

When we got onto a court I played like somebody who hadn't held a racket in years and Melissa hit everything with the steadiness that spoke of lessons since childhood. She beat me six games to four, even after we'd changed rackets halfway through the set.

I left her at the entrance to the women's locker-room and went, still sweaty, into the men's bar. The same bartender was there polishing glasses and I was his only customer. I ordered a gin and tonic. He made it the way I'd asked for it on Thursday.

"You've got a good memory."

"Thanks, but Thursday's not a day I'm likely to forget. Can I get you something else?"

"I'm interested in hearing your story about what happened that day."

"Why?"

"I'm a private investigator. That means that, unlike the cops, I can put you on my expense account." I put a fifty onto the bar, and he smiled.

"This is a high-class club, you can't bribe the bartender." But he picked up the bill and tucked it into his shirt pocket.

"I've told this to the cops three times, so I've got it down pretty good. Mr. Johnson came into the bar Thursday morning. I'm open early for some of the members who like to start with a Bloody Mary, and I also serve coffee. He had a plain box with a few bits of tape and gold wrapping paper stuck to it, and he said 'look what I've got, Peter, a wedding present,' and pulled out the bottle and put it on the bar. It was a pretty impressive bottle, not something we'd stock here."

"Did he say who'd given it to him?"

Peter picked up a cloth and began to polish a glass.

"Nope. I don't think he knew."

"Why do you say that?"

"Because the police don't seem to know. Mr. Johnson wouldn't have told me that anyway. He wanted to keep the bottle under the bar and try some when he came off the course."

"Was that unusual?"

"Unusual? I guess so. I don't deal with cash here, everybody signs a chit, like you signed Mr. Garrison's name Thursday and I see you signed Mrs. Streeter's name today. You know some nice people. Normally I wouldn't pour from a member's own bottle, but I guess Mr. Johnson was a special customer. He was a real nice guy."

"So what happened after that?"

"He went out to play golf and came back a couple hours later looking happy. He asked for some of the scotch over ice. I gave him the drink and next thing I know he's on the floor."

"Just like that? He didn't talk to anybody in the bar?"

"Not after he took that drink. When he first came in I was pouring for other people and I heard him with Doc Florian talking over a chip shot he'd made on the ninth hole. He might have said something to somebody else, but I didn't notice. When I pulled the bottle out I cracked the seal and poured it for him. I watched him drink because it was the special bottle and I wanted to see what he thought of it."

"Did he smell the scotch before he drank it—like you do with a brandy?"

"No. Just looked at the whiskey in the light, raised it, and took a long slow drink. And that was that."

"Listen, it's important to know whether somebody could have gotten something into the bottle when it was here at the Club. Were you interrupted at all after you opened it, before you poured?"

"Absolutely not. I know that was important to the cops, but I'm positive. I cracked the tax seal right here on the bar and poured it all in one motion."

"You're sure? No way it could have happened otherwise?"

"No way. I'm sorry, but I wouldn't forget that. When he keeled over his glass broke and I saw an ice cube skid across the floor. Doc knelt down to help him, and that's when you came in."

"What happened after I left?"

"David ran off to catch you. Doc wanted everyone in the room to stay put and not touch anything until the cops showed up. Nobody was happy about that, not with Mr. Johnson lying dead on the floor, and a few men went out. Doc got me to write their names on a chit. When the cops came they sealed off the bar and took us into the dining room one at a time to ask questions."

"You gave the list of names to the police?"

"Sure. But I can remember them, if you'd like."

"Just tell me, was there anyone you think might have had it in for Johnson? Not necessarily somebody in the bar at the time he was killed."

"Nobody I can think of. People liked Mr. Johnson." He shrugged and looked down at my half-empty drink. "Can I freshen that for you? The management committee made me throw out everything we had in stock last Thursday, so I can guarantee the booze is okay."

I declined. Some men came in talking about thoroughbred horses and I finished the drink and thanked Peter. He tapped the shirt pocket and said, "Anytime." I went out to the veranda.

And ran into David the golf pro. He lifted his arms and growled, "I thought they'd arrested you."

I grinned and moved back to get ready for him. He didn't waste time but came at me like a bulldog, swinging a right up at my jaw.

I hoped for his professional sake he was better at swinging golf clubs than he was at swinging his fists. I stepped away from the blow and, while he was off balance, caught his left arm and brought it up behind his back, using his own momentum to run him up against the wall of the clubhouse.

The next step was going to be more difficult—how to avoid causing a scene? I didn't want it to get around that Morgan had hired a thug. Someone behind us cleared his throat.

I let go and moved to bring the new person into the

triangle. It was the lawyer, Stephen Littman, and he was smirking at us. He had a pale, pinched face and black hair just beginning to recede from a waxy forehead.

I kept one eye on David, but he'd given up trying to batter me. He just pointed a finger and said, "It's the guy that murdered Mr. Johnson."

Littman put his hand out to shake and said, "Pleased to meet you." He raised the other hand to indicate my adversary and said, "I know you've met, but this is David, an employee of the Club. And I'm Stephen Littman."

"Mallory," I said. I didn't take the extended hand, but kept my eyes on David.

"Oh yes," Littman said, then turned to the golf pro. "I don't understand your rudeness to a guest of the Club, and I'm certainly going to mention it to Mr. Franklin. I don't think you'll be working here much longer."

David looked like he wanted to hit Littman now instead of me.

I said, "I'd just as soon keep this among ourselves. David owed me one from Thursday." I still had my eye on him and said, "That was a cheap shot I gave you in the parking lot. Why don't we shake and forget it?" It was hokey, but given the man, I was willing to bet it could turn an enemy into a friend. He hesitated, then took my extended hand and looked to Littman.

"Very well," Littman said. "Run along and polish your clubs, or whatever you do."

David gave me one last look, not exactly friendly, and disappeared into the clubhouse. Littman said, "You really shouldn't interfere with our disciplining the employees."

"You're not a member, are you?"

"No, but I was glad to help you out. I'm practically a member, Mr. Mallory. I'm under consideration, and I spend a lot of time out here with my sponsor. I understand you're investigating Caleb's death?"

"What makes you think that?"

"Oh, you haven't blown your cover. Melissa told me. And here she comes now."

Melissa came out of the women's locker-room in a black bikini bathing suit. She looked very good in a bikini. Littman put an arm around her waist and said, "How are you? You're looking tired."

"I'm okay. You guys meet?"

"More or less."

Melissa smiled at me and said, "This is good. Mr. Mallory wanted to meet with you, Steve, to ask about grandfather's estate."

"John Masterson mentioned something about that. No sense spoiling a beautiful day with business. I could see you Tuesday in the office at four o'clock."

"Tomorrow would be better."

"I'm afraid I'm going to be out of town."

Melissa said, "I wanted to have a swim. Do you mind waiting, Mr. Mallory? You and Steve could have a drink and talk now."

Littman said, "I'd be glad to drive you into town later, Melissa. I said I don't feel like talking business. No need for Mr. Mallory to wait."

"I'm sorry. Let's do that," she said.

I didn't like it, but from the suddenly united look of them, it was apparent that unless I wanted to beat them up, I wasn't going to get anything useful until Tuesday. I'd had enough violence for the day. I bowed slightly and said, "Fine." Then to Littman, "I'll see you Tuesday?"

"Four o'clock. If you'll have Morgan give me a call to verify," then he put his arm back around Melissa's waist. There was something about the way his hand rested on her flesh above the bikini bottoms that made me like him even less than I had a moment before. But Melissa didn't seem to mind.

I told her I'd see her sometime soon, and went into the locker rooms to change. When I came back out they'd gone over to the swimming pool. I waved my racket at

Melissa, walked out to the Rambler, and drove back into Boston alone.

As I drove I tried to sort out my impressions. One thing was clear—the special bottle of scotch had been poisoned before it was sent to Caleb, and that made questions about who was at the Club at the time of his death irrelevant. Stephen and Melissa seemed to have more than just an attorney-client relationship, but that was probably also irrelevant. The bartender had liked Caleb, and the golf pro thought I was the murderer.

It wasn't much to start with, but I'd at least got some good exercise, and tomorrow was another day.

CHAPTER EIGHT

People Are Funny

ON MONDAY I cleaned up some small matters I'd been working on, then spent the rest of the day and part of Tuesday tracking down Caleb Johnson's mistress from five years back. Phoebe had called with the name and address—a condominium development just outside Harvard Square. She'd sold the condo. I managed to trace her through three subsequent changes in residence, each reflecting a decline in economic status, and finally came up with an old roommate who gave me her married name and an address in Malden.

The woman who'd blackmailed out a piece of the Johnson fortune was now an unhappy-looking housewife with a one-year-old. She lived in a small tract house with a bare, sandy front lawn and an unfinished carport put together with weathered plywood. I had a hard time convincing her that I myself was not a blackmailer. She said her husband didn't know anything about Caleb and that the money was long gone and forgotten. I believed her. I didn't notice any two-thousand-dollar bottles of scotch lying around. So that was a dead end.

Tuesday afternoon at 3:55 P.M. I rode the elevator in a large downtown office building on my way up to Choate & Masterson. My reflection in the highly polished brass walls of the elevator looked old-fashioned and respectable, like a sepia-tint portrait from the nineteenth century. Mrs. Streeter had confirmed my bona fides to Stephen

Littman and also set up an appointment with John Masterson.

I got off the elevator on the twenty-third floor and stepped onto a thick oriental rug. To my right was a teak reception desk, empty except for a vase of yellow roses, a beige telephone, and a blonde receptionist. I told her I had an appointment with Stephen Littman and she pointed me to a leather couch and offered a cup of coffee before she made the call.

Littman came out looking paler and less healthy than he had in the sunlight at the Bombay, wearing a tight-fitting blue pin-striped suit that emphasized his shortness. I found it hard to imagine him with Susan Johnson and I was willing to believe they'd been only friends and not lovers. We exchanged polite greetings and he led me down a wide corridor to a good-sized office with a view out of a floor-to-ceiling window to the airport, the harbor islands, and halfway across the ocean to France.

"Nice view," I said.

"Isn't it." He sat facing the opposite wall and a half-dozen diplomas and honor certificates hung in narrow black wooden frames. They made me think of my friend Frank Burger, who keeps a second-grade penmanship award next to his law degree from Yale. Littman said, "I was number-one in my class at Harvard." I sat in one of the Swedish-style chairs and glanced out at the horizon of sea and sky and a 747 rising painfully out of Logan. Before I could respond, Littman's phone made a chirruping noise and he pushed a button to shut it off and said, "What can I do for you, Mr. Mallory? As you see, I'm a busy man."

I said, "What if that phone call was from your mother?"

He looked so startled I grinned and added quickly, "Just kidding. I want to talk about how the Johnson estate is affected by Caleb Johnson's death."

"And just how do you think that will help your investigation?"

"Every little bit helps. I'd also like to talk about Susan Johnson. I understand you two are friends."

He leaned forward and castled fingers. "I see." He pulled a folder from a larger file he had on his desk. The folder must not have been relevant to my inquiry, because he put it aside and didn't refer to it again.

"It's my understanding that Susan won't be getting much from Caleb's estate," I prompted him.

"Oh, that's not entirely true. Caleb had money of his own, nothing significant for a family like the Johnsons, but several hundred thousands. All of that will go to Susan, and also the house in Marblehead, which she takes free of encumbrances. So she won't do too badly. That's under Caleb's estate, of course. The real money is in the family trust set up by Katherine's will. That reverts to Morgan. Before Caleb's death Morgan was a beneficiary and nominal trustee. Now she's sole beneficiary."

"What's the life of the trust now that Caleb's dead? Does the cash revert directly to Morgan?"

"Oh no. Morgan has a life interest."

"And then?"

"Then the funds revert to a perpetual, charitable trust, for the benefit of art and literature."

"I'm not sure I understand. Melissa gets nothing?"

"Nothing."

"Why?"

"I have no idea what Katherine Johnson's motives were, Mr. Mallory. I am somewhat shocked myself to think that Caleb's line of the Johnsons will be virtually penniless in another generation. The plan was conceived in the late nineteen fifties when attorneys were not as sophisticated as we are today, or perhaps people had different notions about personal property. Maybe Katherine thought the new generation should fend for itself."

"Who drew up the will?"

"John Masterson. You might ask him. I hope you're not suggesting that Katherine was non compos mentis?"

"I'm not suggesting anything. Who administers the charitable trust after Morgan's death?"

"Choate & Masterson, but please don't draw any conclusions from that. A firm of our size administers family trusts more as a service to clients than a money-making venture. We place almost all of the funds in the hands of professional investment advisors. We wouldn't be qualified to do any investing ourselves."

"And the choice of charities?"

"Will be made by John Masterson, as trustee, and then his designated successors."

A woman appeared at the door carrying two mugs of coffee on a small tray. My order had followed me from the receptionist. When she'd gone out I tasted the coffee, then asked, "Why were you arguing with Susan on Thursday?"

Littman smirked at me. "Is this cross-examination, Mr. Mallory? Because if it is, litigation is not my field, and you'll have me at a disadvantage when it comes to trick questions. I don't believe we were arguing. We were discussing dinner plans."

"For the three of you?"

"Yes. Caleb was also a friend. Speaking of plans, I hate to cut you short, but I'm extremely busy. And every minute you spend with me is being billed to Mrs. Streeter at a rate of one hundred twenty dollars per hour. It might be more cost efficient for you to move your investigation into a more productive arena. Unless you have an urgent question—shall I ring John Masterson for you?"

"I have a few more questions. I'd also like to talk with one or two people who were friends with Susan Johnson."

"I don't know of anybody else who was particularly intimate with Susan. A few of her friends left the firm before she did, or shortly after her. Not many people have the stuff to last under the pressures of the kind of practice we maintain at Choate & Masterson, and people like Susan don't really fit in."

A light came on at Littman's phone and this time he picked it up. He asked the party to hold and grimaced across at me. "I really have to take this. The receptionist outside will ring John Masterson for you and point you in the right direction."

I reached across and pushed a button to disconnect the caller. "At two dollars a minute I'd like to have your undivided attention."

His face went red. "Are you going to hit me now, like you did poor David at the Club? I thought I was being cooperative, Mr. Mallory. Morgan Streeter is a valued client of this firm."

I sighed, got my wallet, dropped two twenties on his desk, and went out to find the receptionist. I wasn't being paid enough to listen to him any longer than was absolutely necessary. I was already at the front desk before it occurred to me that I should have asked for a receipt.

John Masterson was as different from Littman as mahogany is from plastic. He was a frail old man who looked about ninety and had probably bounced Caleb Johnson on his knee. He was one of those old people who have a sense of humor about their great age. He didn't get up from behind his desk, but reached to shake my hand and gave me a smile. His hand was cold, and as wrinkled and soft as an infant's.

His office was two floors above and four times the size of Stephen Littman's. It was furnished in the same spirit as the study in Morgan Streeter's house, with a blue oriental rug, a set of four leather chairs ranged before a solid oak desk, and a big brass telescope on a tripod in the corner looking out to sea. I hadn't had to wait at all to get in to see him.

"I hope that our Mr. Littman was able to provide you with the information you require."

I sat down across from him. "There was at least one question, Mr. Masterson, he wasn't able to answer fully. I wanted to know how it is that, upon Morgan Streeter's death, the family's estate will go to a charitable trust and not to Mrs. Streeter's daughter. Mr. Littman did suggest that was an unusual provision." I realized I was speaking softly and with great respect, and that it would have been close to impossible to do otherwise. Assuming he wasn't senile, I'd bet he got a lot of mileage out of that gray hair and frail body.

Masterson smiled slightly and reached for a large cigar that had stopped burning in a heavy glass and leather ashtray by his right hand. "These are bad for your health, but would you like one?" I smiled and shook my head no.

He took a moment to get the cigar slowly burning. "Stephen undoubtedly suggested that the unusual aspects of the estate were the result of the great age of its author. It's hard to imagine such a man someday being my partner, but I now have more than fifty partners, some of whom I don't know by name. Ours used to be a more gentlemanly practice."

He must have noticed a hint of skepticism from me, because he smiled mildly and said, "Oh, I don't deny we were quite nasty in our own way. But what was the question Stephen was unable to answer?"

"Why Katherine Johnson set up her estate in such a way that, when Morgan Streeter dies, everything goes to a charitable trust and not to Morgan's child."

"Ah yes. There is a very complicated answer to that question, but I'm afraid I'm not at liberty to give it to you. I have loyalties not only to Morgan, but to her mother."

"A man has been killed."

"Yes, and the information I hold may be of some help to you. But we lawyers are forever having to do things that don't make a lot of sense. It's part of our code, you know, the code of unbreakable rules that often leads to practical absurdity. 'Every man is innocent until proven guilty' is a good example. The law is arbitrary because it has to be, in order to pretend that complicated things can be made simple."

"I wish you would change your mind. Perhaps if you could speak with Morgan again?"

"It's something that Morgan doesn't know." His phone rang, he reached across for it, listened a few moments, and returned it to its cradle without saying a word.

"And now I'm afraid I have another matter to deal with, Mr. Mallory." He gave his mildly self-deprecating smile again. "I'd walk you to the door, but it takes at least ten minutes for me to travel that far."

It seemed that a ringing telephone was the polite method of dismissing people at the firm of Choate & Masterson. Masterson was more of an expert than Stephen Littman. It also seemed evident that pushing him would get me nowhere. So I stood and shook his hand again, feeling the old bones give under my grip.

I went back out to the front feeling dissatisfied. There were secrets kicking around that place and I wasn't sure whether they were being kept from me deliberately or, as Masterson suggested, purely out of a sense of traditional reticence. But I certainly wasn't going to get anything by asking direct questions. I'd have to get sneaky.

It was after five, and although most of the offices were still occupied, there wasn't anybody in the reception room. I went on around the corner and down a hallway and came to an open door labeled file room. It was unattended.

There were five thick accordion files for the Johnson family, only one of which dealt with the family trust. I was looking for notes of conversations, but didn't find any. Most of the documents dealt with investment advisers and included financial statements, none of which made any sense to me—except the dollar amounts, which were very respectable. There was an extra Xerox each of Katherine's will and the trust, and I was pulling them from the file when a young guy in a suit came into the room.

He flashed me a smile, said, "Working late already, heh? You must be one of the new associates. I'm Mark Fenton," and he stuck out a hand to shake.

I closed the file door, took his hand, and gave a rueful smile. "Looks like an all-nighter."

"You'll get used to it," and he went past me to the

files. I wondered briefly if he was a sneak too, and was just throwing a bluff.

On my way down the twenty-five flights, watching myself in the reflecting brass doors of the elevator, I thought about the decision I'd made ten years earlier, after my father died, to drop out of law school and become an apprentice to old Jack Cahill at Cahill Inquiries.

I tried to imagine spending fifty or more years as a rich man's attorney in a place like Choate & Masterson. It was enough to make me feel sympathy for someone even as unappealing as Stephen Littman.

I was very glad to step out into the lobby downstairs and the evening bustle of people headed for home. I wanted a drink.

I called Frank Burger from a pay phone in the lobby. It was late, almost six, but that's early by law firm standards, and my only question was whether Frank would be able to get off. He sounded harassed, but when I offered free drinks at the Exchange he went for it.

A fat bald man in a three-piece suit waited behind me, keeping surveillance on his watch, and when I picked up the phone to dial a second number he shook his head in disgust and walked off.

I dialed Della and used the device that came with her and enables me to play back my messages from any phone booth in the known universe. A fellow with a shaky voice said he wanted to come by the office at four to discuss his wife, if that was okay, but he didn't leave a number. There was nothing else but dial tones. By then it was ten after six, and before I could leave the building the security guards made me sign out at the desk. I noticed that Littman had left a few minutes before me. So much for the busy young lawyer. Once outside I turned left toward the harbor.

The Exchange is my favorite downtown bar. It's next to the old Grain Exchange building on Liberty Square in

that lost area behind downtown proper that's being gradually incorporated into the cluster of new office towers.
It's a high-ceilinged place in an old brick building, with a
fireplace at the back, lots of plate glass windows, smoky
wood paneling, and inexpensive beer. The waitresses are
friendly and they get to know you. Every time I go there
I wonder how much longer it will last before they tear the
building down around it and put up a skyscraper, or one
of the new, high-gloss hotels like the Meridien where the
beers cost four dollars, but they give you a plate of paté
with every round.

Frank was waiting in one of the circular Naugahyde
booths along the wall. I slid in behind the table and tried
not to notice how old he was beginning to look.

"You look happy," he said.

"Yes."

He took a slug of his bourbon and water.

"Bad day at the office?"

"Those assholes are intolerable. I can't take it any
more."

"So quit."

"Oh no you don't! Don't start me thinking that way. I
swore I'd never be another young associate craving freedom and biting the bullet. It's a good job. So tell me why
you seduced me down to this disreputable place where I
never have to worry about running into partners from the
firm."

"I thought maybe you could help me with some legal
questions so I can write you off as a consultant. What do
you know about spouse's rights to estates, for example?"

"I know that when a question arises in that area I refer
it to the experts in the trust department and they give me
a lovely, concise opinion. Or maybe not so concise. That's
it."

"Can a wife tie up her estate so her husband has the
use of the money without being able to control it?"

"Sure, with something called a 'spendthrift trust.' People do it all the time to keep irresponsible types from

eating up their inheritances on fur coats and beluga caviar. So future generations can eat up the money on fur coats and beluga caviar."

"Would a wife who'd do that kind of thing be likely to have the whole estate revert to a charitable trust after the next generation, with no provision for grandchildren?" I told him about Katherine Johnson's will and my meeting with Morgan Streeter's lawyers, and I gave him the copies of the documents I'd borrowed.

"I'll take a look at these, but don't expect anything dramatic. You know you can get into trouble stealing things."

"It's okay, I know a good lawyer. But tell me what you think of this charitable trust thing. Why would she go to the trouble to protect the money for future generations, then give the money away to a bunch of unnamed charities?"

"Depends on her personality, I guess. I'm not an expert, you know, I do real estate development, not trusts."

"Then give me your layman's opinion."

"That's gone with the wind, sweetheart, a lawyer can't retrieve layman's status any easier than you could retrieve your lost virginity. But I'll tell you one thing, Art Linkletter was right. People are funny."

"For this I'm paying two bucks? Revisionist Linkletter?"

"Four bucks for two drinks. You were late."

"You're very quick."

"And you're sober." He waved to the waitress, and when she came I ordered a beer.

"I'll tell you another thing, I'm a little surprised this guy Littman told you that much about Susan Johnson's interest in Caleb's estate. He may have had Morgan Streeter's authorization to talk about the trusts, but strictly speaking her stepfather's estate plan is no business of hers or yours until they read the will."

"You know anything about Littman?"

"No, but I can ask around. I do know something about Susan Johnson, in the way of scuttlebutt. You interested?"

"If it's relevant."

"You're starting to sound like a lawyer. Gossip is always relevant, and with the buildup in the papers after Johnson died, there's been a lot about her. I was talking with a friend who went to law school with her. A few months back, just before the marriage, she joked with this guy about how she was marrying a rich client to get out of the rat race. From what Littman says, she's gonna make out pretty good, even though she doesn't get the family fortune."

"So she told a few bad jokes. Wouldn't you, under the circumstances?"

"Sometimes there's truth in them thar jokes. You used to say you were going to drop out of law school and become a private eye. We're still chuckling over that one. Of course you're right, it doesn't mean she killed the guy."

The waitress came with my beer and Frank ordered another bourbon. When that came he drank it very quickly and got up to leave.

"Would you believe it, I have to go back to work. I'll let you know if I hear anything."

"Thanks." After he'd left I sat on in the bar, ordered another beer, and tried to decide what Katherine Johnson'd had in mind when she cut Melissa out of her will, and whether it could have any bearing on Caleb Johnson's death. After a while I got restless and left without finishing my beer.

CHAPTER NINE

All Funerals Are the Same

THE NEXT DAY was Wednesday, the day of Caleb Johnson's funeral, and it rained. I decided to walk over late and sit in the back of the chapel to watch the people who'd come to see him off. I might find a clue tacked to the coffin. The services were around the block—at a funeral home on the corner of Commonwealth and Beacon in Kenmore Square—so I didn't have far to walk.

I wore a beat-up canvas hat against the rain and stuffed it into my coat pocket as I went through the gate and up the stone steps to the entrance. A tall man with mournful eyes gave me a sympathetic look, took my wet coat to hang in a cloakroom at the entrance, and led me back to the chapel.

I sat in the last row on the aisle, where I could see up front to the altar. There were twenty rows of pews running from back to front and most of the rows were full. It was a closed-casket funeral. The minister stood behind it talking about the triumph of life over death. In the two aisle seats at the front I spotted Melissa and Susan. Phoebe was near the back, also on the aisle. I couldn't recognize anyone else from the backs of their heads.

Soon after I came into the room the minister asked everyone to bow in prayer. When he'd finished he put his arms down in a final gesture and eight young men stood and walked to the casket, arranged themselves, lifted and turned it, adjusted their grips, and started down the aisle.

There was organ music now, coming from an organ down front that I wasn't able to see. As they went by I saw Stephen Littman among the pallbearers.

When the casket was out of the chapel people stood to follow it, beginning with the front rows. Morgan Streeter went by with the minister. Susan was behind her, beside a florid-faced man in a stylish black suit. I noticed that his hands were freshly manicured and decorated with three heavily jeweled rings. Melissa came next, walking alone and staring with fixed hatred at Susan and her escort. I wasn't sure whether the look was intended for Susan, the man, or the fact that the two of them were together.

Phoebe and I were the last out into the corridor where people moved about getting coats. We went to stand at the top of the steps outside. It was raining hard. A half dozen men in black stood on the steps and at the curb, handing out black umbrellas. We went down to the sidewalk under one umbrella, and Phoebe said, "Any progress, Mr. Mallory?"

"Nothing yet, Phoebe. But something will show up. Who is that man riding in the car with the Streeters?" and I nodded at the florid-faced guy climbing into the back of the limousine.

"That's Mr. Peter Streeter, Miss Streeter's father," she said.

It was an interesting designation—not Morgan's husband, but "Miss Streeter's father." I wondered if Melissa's hatred had been in fact directed at him.

I saw Susan's blonde head beside Morgan's in the back of the limousine. Knowing how they felt about each other I thought it took courage—or maybe just idiocy— for all of them to maintain the illusion of a family group. Maybe that's what's required of aristocrats, and if so Susan was holding her own with them.

Stephen Littman stood away from the curb and walked over to greet me. His petulance of the day before was apparently forgotten.

"Grim show, isn't it?" he said. "Makes a young man feel the mantle of responsibility settling down, when the old pass on."

I looked at him to see if he was serious, and he gave me a rueful smile, which changed quickly into the characteristic smirk.

"You must be busy with the probate of the will," I said. "How long does it take to get these things cleared up?"

"As I mentioned yesterday, it's a small estate. The trusts don't pass through the probate."

In line ahead of the hearse was a big, cut-down car, a kind of Cadillac sports wagon, loaded with bright, wet flowers. Behind the family's car a half dozen other black limousines waited with lights on and wipers going. People were getting into them in groups and other people were walking away to private cars, and the sidewalk was emptying. Two wet-looking Boston motorcycle cops sat on blue Harleys in front and another had parked across the Avenue.

Littman said, "Are you riding to the cemetery?"

"Is there room for me?"

"I think so. Come along." Phoebe excused herself, but I said, "Why don't we all ride together?" partly because Littman seemed to want to avoid her.

We went down the line to the very last black limousine, where an attendant held a bundle of wet umbrellas under one arm. Phoebe got into the front beside the driver, and Littman and I had the back to ourselves. I saw the cop across the street go into the avenue to stop oncoming traffic and the procession started. Looking behind I saw a few private cars following. Then I faced ahead and settled into the comfortable seat as we rode out through Kenmore Square.

The burial was at the family plot in Belmont where the late Katherine Johnson had been put to rest ten years earlier. At one point, riding out Route 2, I asked Littman why the trusts didn't have to go through probate.

"They're not really part of Caleb's estate, you know. The trusts are set up to descend automatically to the next beneficiary. I told you that yesterday."

"I suppose I didn't understand."

Beyond that there wasn't much conversation. The cemetery was on the Boston side of Belmont. We arrived through big gates opening from a high, wrought-iron fence at the perimeter, and drove down a narrow lane under trees to the burial site.

Littman excused himself to take his place with the pallbearers. Phoebe went to stand beside the Streeters and I walked through the steady drizzle, up a small hill, and stood a dozen yards back from the new grave.

There was a pile of fresh soil. The area around it was green with thick grass and the wet leaves of a big oak tree. The pallbearers came slowly up the hill with their burden, attendents holding black umbrellas over their heads. The crowd gathered at the grave, the minister and family standing apart at the front. I went to stand beside Littman, who'd somehow ended up at the back of the crowd.

I'd thought the minister would make the ceremony short because of the rain, but he went for the full show. He'd known the Johnson and Streeter families for years and he was impressed by their energy and zest for life. It was a great tragedy for Caleb to be cut down while still in his prime, but the Lord takes us according to his plan. Susan seemed to be crying, and I heard a sniffle or two from somebody else in the crowd. Littman stood craning his neck to see around the umbrellas in front. The florid-faced man was smiling.

"What's the story with Melissa's father?" I whispered to Littman.

He looked annoyed and spoke in a low, confidential voice. "He never sees them as a rule, but I think he's getting a kick out of this. He's a queer duck."

"They make a lovely family group."

The minister finished and started another prayer. The casket got lowered into the grave by means of a hydraulic device operated by one of the attendants who'd been standing in a line to one side of the family like a black screen against the surrounding countryside. When the casket was in place and the prayer ended, Susan and Morgan each took a shovelful of soil and dropped it into the grave. There was some confusion over whether Melissa was going to drop a shovelful, but she shook her head no, and that was the end of the ceremony.

The crowd dispersed. An attendent went to Morgan with a wreath of red flowers and said a few words, and she took the wreath and walked with it to a gravestone standing a few yards to the side. The stone was inscribed "Katherine Loring Johnson, 1912–1975." We stopped to watch as she placed the wreath against it, then started down the hill to the cars.

Peter Streeter was the last of the party to leave Caleb's grave. He seemed to be savoring the experience. I hung back a moment so that we ended up walking down the hill together. He glanced at me and smiled.

"I'd like to arrange to speak with you some time," I said.

"Me? What on earth for?"

"I'm a private investigator. Morgan hired me to investigate Caleb's death."

"My God, how like her! Not even this sordid affair could be left to the public authorities—dear Caleb must have the best that money can buy, even dead. I assume you are the best? But this is hardly the time or place, is it?"

He hadn't stopped walking. I said, "When?"

He reached into a breast pocket and produced an engraved card. "Do give me a call in the morning. We can have a nice chat."

I took the card. Peter Streeter went on to the family limousine and I ended up riding into Boston in a car with strangers. They all knew each other and talked about their favorite restaurants. I'd never heard of any of the restaurants, so I didn't join in the conversation.

Funerals, like weddings, are always the same. The limo dropped us in front of the funeral home. Walking back to my apartment I wondered if, having surveyed the crowd carefully, I'd at some point laid my eyes on Caleb Johnson's murderer. I looked forward to meeting with Peter Streeter the next day.

CHAPTER TEN

A Wise Child . . .

IT WAS STILL raining the next morning and I sat in my office in the Trojan watching it come down on the pavement of Charles Street. The water running in the gutters was heavy with mud from an excavation they'd started in front of the building, and passing cars threw up sheets of dirty water from puddles collecting in the new potholes.

After getting back from the funeral I'd spent the afternoon renewing old contacts in some of the higher-priced call girl operations around town and out in the suburbs. Nobody knew squat about Caleb Johnson. He'd apparently never taken that route to sexual gratification—or if he had he'd covered his tracks extremely well.

I needed facts, preferably sordid ones. Aside from John Masterson's hint of a dark secret related to the making of Katherine Johnson's will, and assorted bad behavior on the part of some of his close relations, I'd seen or heard nothing yet that indicated any reason for Caleb to have died a violent and ugly death—unless the Museum of Fine Arts had instituted a new and more aggressive program for obtaining bequests from wealthy Bostonians.

At 10:30 I dialed the number on the card Peter Streeter had given me. A man answered on the first ring and said I'd reached the Cromwell Club. He said he would speak with Mr. Streeter if I would hold the line, then waited for me to give an affirmative response. When he came back on he said Mr. Streeter would see me for a short interview that afternoon at one.

The Cromwell is a posh residential club on Beacon Hill overlooking Boston Common. In recent times Boston's venerable residential clubs have been mostly carved into apartments or condos, or, in decaying neighborhoods, flops and boarding houses. The Cromwell dates from the Civil War, when members split from the patriotic Union Club over the issue of running Lincoln's blockade of the South. They believed free enterprise was more important than the sanctity of the Union. It has survived to provide the Boston Brahmin with one last safe harbor, offering a margin of luxury for estranged husbands and other refugees from the mainstream of extreme wealth.

The weather was changing by the time I started my walk across the park to the big marble building on Beacon Street, and when I rang the bell the sun shone through remnants of the broken-up gray clouds. The buzzer sounded and I pushed open the heavy front door.

The lobby had an elaborate, sky-blue ceiling, a large crystal chandelier, and polished hardwood floors. A young man in a severe black suit came forward, and when I'd identified myself he took my coat to hang in a small anteroom beside the entrance. Across the lobby a carpeted staircase led upstairs, and beside the staircase a shallow, recessed alcove with a waist-high counter, like the front desk of a hotel lobby, held rows of wooden mail slots and a glass display case of expensive cigars offered for sale.

The young man didn't speak, but led me down a corridor to a private sitting room, past French doors hung with fine lace curtains looking into a courtyard. In the sitting room we found the recumbent and resplendent figure of Mr. Peter Streeter in a heavily embroidered red smoking jacket over velvet pants. He was in a green wing chair before a marble fireplace, feet up on a footstool and fanned out before the unlighted birch logs. The attendant announced my name and went out, closing the double doors behind him. My host started the conversation by putting out a hand to shake.

"I suppose you know I'm Peter Streeter. It's an odd name, isn't it? For some reason it brings to mind the oddest things—peter eater, peter beater, peter tweeter, that kind of thing—I hope you don't find that offensive? Thank God I was spared a public education. The ordinary student would've made mincemeat of me, though God knows my fellows at Choate put it to me well enough. So what can I do for you?"

I walked around him and sat in a second wing chair facing the fireplace. "I want to ask a few questions about Caleb Johnson."

"Poor Caleb. Can't say I'm sorry to see him gone. He despised the sight of me, you know, and quite a violent fellow.

"I tried to pump Morgan to find out about you, Mr. Mallory, in the car coming back from the funeral. A private eye must have such exciting times! She wouldn't answer me at all, only hissed at me to be quiet. Of course the sweet young wife was in the car, and I believe she thinks the girl did him in. Imagine Caleb marrying such a child. It was damned uncomfortable in the car.

"Morgan is so much like Caleb, and the odd thing is, there wasn't any blood tie between them. In case you didn't know it, he wasn't her actual father, even though she persists in calling him that. And God knows he never behaved like one."

"Yes I knew that. It's a matter of public record."

"Quite. But something there, you see. She always had a thing for older men, which is why she settled on me. Caleb was my contemporary, went back together as far as Choate. He bullied me through those years and I ended up his stepson-in-law for God's sake. In fact it was he that called on me to do the right thing by Morgan."

"How's that?"

"Everybody in the best of society knows about it, I'm

sure, but God knows a private eye might have been kept in the dark. No offense. It wasn't in the public records you see."

"You mean Morgan's being pregnant with Melissa when you married?"

"Quite. The child wasn't mine, of course. I was a poor choice for a husband, what with my reputation, but who else would've come forward? I needed the money. Dad cut me off years ago and gave every cent to bloody charity, the ballet, which I still think was a dig at me."

"Isn't this all a bit off the mark?"

"Well, Caleb would absolutely murder me for spilling the beans, but he's dead now, isn't he? That's what I find so amusing. Fortunately I don't believe in ghosts, or I'd be quaking in my slippers. You see, I'm quite certain Caleb was the father. I tried to hold it over his head once, in exchange for a small loan, and he actually struck me in the face. He knew my character, the bastard, and I never mentioned it again. Funny thing was, he disliked the child even more than I do. Beastly man."

I smiled at him. "Do you think Katherine knew there might have been something between her husband and her daughter?"

"Oh, I wouldn't say 'might have.' I'm really quite sure of it. And I always assumed that Katherine did know. She hated the child with a passion, especially as it got older. I took a good look at the girl, at the funeral, and there's definitely something about the eyes that speaks of Caleb. Must have driven the old bag quite mad. And yet the four of them lived together in that house in Brookline until Katherine died.

"She insisted on that. She was the matriarch type. Tight as a Scotchman, too. From what I hear she managed to tie things up even after she was killed. I used to think she was too mean to die. I called her 'mother' once, you know, just after the wedding ceremony, and she said, 'know your place,' and never spoke to me again. Fancy that. Really quite amusing."

"She was killed?"

"In a car crash. An accident, her car crossed the median strip and went into oncoming traffic. That was about ten years ago."

"No hint of foul play?"

"None whatsoever. A pity too, since she really deserved to be murdered."

"How long did you live with them in Brookline?"

"Less than a week after the wedding. Aside from my problems with Katherine, Morgan wanted me in her bed, even though she knew my reputation. That older men thing, you see. I've stayed on in the wings and occasionally I serve my patriarchal function in society. Funerals and such. And when young Melissa marries I'll give her away with a smile, just like any proud father."

"Does Melissa know about all this? That you're not her real father?"

"I doubt it, old man, but you never can tell. There's certainly no love lost between us."

I thought that, if Melissa did know, it would explain some of the things I'd noticed about her, including the look of hatred she'd worn coming out of the funeral home the day before.

The phone at Peter Streeter's elbow chimed softly. He picked up the receiver with an exaggerated "helloooo. . . ," giving me a wink.

He listened a moment, said "Yes, I'll see you then," and hung it up.

"I'll have to be running soon. Did you have any other questions? This is marvelous fun."

"I guess what I came to ask was whether Caleb had any enemies that you know of, or perhaps a woman he may have injured in some way, somebody who might have wanted to kill him."

"Enemies? How exciting. Aside from me I can't think of a single one, and I wouldn't hurt a fly. As for women, I'm afraid I don't move in those circles. I really couldn't say."

"You must have heard stories. I understand one woman was actually paid off."

"Is that true? I didn't know that. The damned thing is, Caleb was a personable chap. Very attractive and women after him all the time. As far as I knew he was always perfectly discreet. This is marvelous."

"He must have had other habits. Things that could have got him in trouble."

"Other than his wicked temper and his gambling, I can't think of a single thing."

He was very smooth about it, and I obliged by lifting my eyebrows. "Gambling?"

"Oh yes, did I mention that? He had a taste for low company in that respect. Nothing middle class, like Nevada or that place in New Jersey where the housewives go, but real aristocratic decadence. I was proud of him. Once he and I were out together and we ran into one of his poker chaps on the street, a hulking brute with piercing gray eyes. Quite made my stomach go silly."

"Where did he gamble?"

"I've no idea. Someplace in the suburbs. When you come down to it, I knew so little about old Caleb. I can't think of anything else that might help you. And now I must send you along. Sorry to be in such a bloody rush."

I stood from my chair and Peter touched a button set in the telephone. The attendant opened the double doors of the sitting room. He kept both eyes politely lowered and waited for me.

I turned at the door and said, "Thanks for the information, Mr. Streeter. If I think of any other questions I'll call you."

"Oh, please do," he said. "I do so love to talk."

CHAPTER ELEVEN

Raise You Ten

THAT NIGHT I had a date for dinner with Julie at the Maison Robert. I hadn't seen her since the weekend and she was going to start a new project the next day, so she'd arranged to get out of work early. That meant the sun was still shining when we got to the terrace of the restaurant and ordered our dinners and a bottle of red wine.

The Maison Robert is a classic French restaurant in the basement of a monumental granite building that was Boston City Hall until the city tore down Scollay Square and put up the ugly new fortress in Government Center. It's on School Street, across from the Parker House, and in the summer they have outdoor tables in the small park in front. In the center of the park a statue of Benjamin Franklin presides over the diners with a perpetual smile. The people sitting at the tables always look well dressed and happy.

Julie was dressed for work in a blue linen suit, but she'd taken her hair down. When the waiter left with our orders I said, "Tell me about your day. What's this new deal?"

"Just another public offering for a software company. I don't want to talk about it, really."

So we sat at the table watching the people and didn't say anything until the waiter came with our appetizers and the bottle of wine. He opened the wine and poured two big glasses, set the dishes onto the linen tablecloth, and went away. I'd ordered snails in garlic butter, and Julie had smoked salmon. I took a piece of the hard-crusted bread, soaked it in the garlic butter, and said, "I wish they made this stuff without the snails."

"Snails are slugs," she said. "Nothing but garden slugs. Your case must be going well."

"Why do you say that?"

"Because you look so damned happy."

"It's the night and the company. The case isn't going anyplace in particular. I'm just turning over stones, waiting to see what comes up."

"I bet it'll be slugs," she said. "Slugs in garlic butter."

I pulled a snail from its shell using the escargot fork, then took a drink of wine. The snail tasted bitter with the wine. "I do have a new suspect," I said, "who might be loosely categorized as a slug." I told her about my visit to the Cromwell Club and conversation with Peter Streeter.

"You're getting into some fancy, bigoted little places these days. I'm surprised this guy told you so much. You'd think he'd be ashamed of the whole mess."

"I think it was pure and simple revenge. He was dying to talk, especially since he thought I'd be too thick to get the whole picture on my own. Or he could have been throwing up a smoke screen. Mangenello, the state cop, is going to run a check on whether he bought or stole a dose of raw cyanide recently."

"Sounds like he could distill the stuff from his own blood."

"I personally think he'd be too chicken-shit to actually do it."

"Distill his own blood? If you ask me, I think it's the young widow. I've never met her, but she married for money, and killing hubby's the next step in that process."

"She's certainly the logical suspect. But it isn't that simple. She had access to more income when he was alive, unless he was shutting her off for some reason."

"Either way, alive he had access to her, and he was an old man."

"An attractive, virile man in his sixties."

"Huh."

"What does 'huh' mean?"

"You're not being objective. I think you've got a thing for the bitch." She lowered her eyes and cut a piece of the salmon.

"Bad mood, heh? You sound almost serious."

She made a face and swallowed the salmon. "Sorry. I'm tense about the new offering. The SEC's been putting the screws to us ever since that stupid client lied in its annual report and got caught. And there's something else." She took another strip of the pink salmon, laid it over a slice of onion. "I didn't tell you this, but Monday they let me know I'm going to make partner at the firm. Effective the first of the year."

"That's great."

"It should be great, shouldn't it? But I don't feel great. It's supposed to be a big moment, I've worked eight long years for that moment, eleven if you count law school. And you know what I did when I found out? I went into my office and cried."

I broke off another piece of bread. She was half leaning across the table.

"You know I have to work every day and night of this weekend, and every day and night of next week, and the weekend after that, and it won't stop there. I always thought it'd be better after I got to be partner, but it's going to stay just the same, and the extra money won't amount to much. In the first year I'll have to make a capital contribution to the firm, which means I'll actually make less."

"You want to finish this quickly and go back and get into bed? I could console you."

It was the wrong thing to say. She drew in a little and hunched her shoulders. "I thought you didn't want to take me for granted. I think I want to sleep alone tonight."

"Okay, then let's order another bottle and get stinking drunk. It'll work out, you know. You always feel let down after you've arrived at the place you've been headed for. I felt the same way when I moved into the third floor of the Trojan."

"I don't feel like being joked out of this. I don't like my job."

"Then don't accept the partnership offer. Quit."

"And do what?"

"Sell the condominium. Cut down on your expenses. Take a job where you'd work less hours."

"It's not that simple. You know that. It's not easy to take a step backward."

"It can be done. My father worked hard all his life at a job he never liked, waiting to retire. Then he died. People shouldn't do that. There's no point to it."

A waiter came by and I got his attention and ordered a second bottle of wine. We didn't say anything for a few moments. It was cool under the trees and I could see the sun setting in the reflecting glass of a high office tower two blocks behind the restaurant. Through the iron fence along one side of the terrace I saw the sunlight cutting across thick grass and oval shapes of gravestones in the old cemetery that fronts on Tremont Street. I thought about Caleb Johnson in the ground out in Belmont.

Julie looked across at me and said, "I'll be all right. Do you really think that guy Peter Streeter might have murdered Johnson?"

"I think it would be more likely that he'd kill his own mother, but I think it's possible."

I reached across the table and poured the rest of the wine from the first bottle into Julie's glass. Behind her I saw the waiter, with a tray over his right shoulder, bringing our dinners and the second bottle of wine.

I slept alone that night. Friday morning it was bright and cool with only a few white clouds and a strong wind blowing from the ocean. I went straight into the Trojan and downstairs to find Edgar. He was sweeping the long aisles between the men's lockers.

"Edgar, is Buddy Minasian still operating out in Arlington?"

He stood the broom against a locker and said, "Sure, been fine since you got him outta that jam with Bensen. He thinks you're tops, Jimmy."

Buddy is a small-time gambler. Frank Bensen is an upwardly mobile gangster who controls most of the gambling and vice in the suburbs west of Boston. Recently I've been hearing his name more often with regard to various sordid activities within the city itself. Buddy pays dues to Bensen, and years ago there'd been a misunderstanding over receipts. Buddy went underground. He emerged long enough to talk with me, and I managed to get evidence proving the misunderstanding was the work of a greedy courier on Bensen's payroll. Whereupon the courier went underground, and a grateful Buddy went back to work.

I asked Edgar for the number, and he found it on a crowded bulletin board in his office. "This is it, Jimmy. You ain't got the gambling bug?"

"Just working. Borrow your phone?"

"Sure." As I dialed he went back to the locker room.

Buddy answered and I said, "Jim Mallory here."

"Jimmy, my friend. How are tricks?"

"Not bad. I need to find out about a guy you might have done business with."

"I hate to talk on the telephone, Jimmy, and I've got business going on now. Why don't you drive out and I'll have George pick you up."

"Same place?"

"Right."

"Forty-five minutes."

I thanked Edgar, got the Rambler, and drove to Berkeley Street and down past all the major cross streets to the entrance to Storrow Drive. Storrow Drive runs along the Charles and becomes Soldier's Field Road, and from there I took the exit for Route 2 and Arlington.

As I drove I thought over what Peter Streeter had said

the day before about Melissa's paternity. If it was true, it certainly explained the grandmother cutting her out of the will. Littman had said the trusts were set up in the late fifties, about the time she was born. If revenge was Katherine's motivation, however, she apparently hadn't blamed Morgan—or even Caleb, for that matter. If she had, the trust money would have spent all of the last ten years paying for Monets or cancer research.

And I still didn't see how the information could help me, unless perhaps Melissa had murdered Caleb because he wouldn't acknowledge her. That was possible. She'd lied to me about being close to him, assuming, that is, that Peter Streeter was right about Caleb not getting along with her.

I took the Alewife Parkway toward Mass. Ave. and Arlington. I thought about Caleb as a gambler. Gamblers get hurt if they don't pay debts. According to Mangenello there hadn't been death threats before the murder, but Caleb could have kept them secret. It was a long shot, because organized criminals kill less often than people believe, and the cyanide in the crystal decanter was a bit artistic and chancy a weapon for the mob. But it was another stone to turn. I couldn't think of a better way to proceed.

At the north end of Arlington I pulled into a Stop & Shop and parked, then went over to stand in front of the entrance. A dark green Caddy pulled up to the curb. George hit the switch to unlock the door on the passenger's side and I got in. The front seat was as far back as it would go, and George filled the wide space between it and the steering wheel. Despite the cool day he had the windows closed and the air-conditioning set at sixty.

"Hello, Jimmy." He stuck out a big hand, and I shook it. He wore a bright blue Florida shirt decorated with pink flamingos, hanging loose over white pants. There were sweat stains in the armpits. He looked at me through one good eye and said, "Anything special bring you out?"

"Just need information, George. Still operating at the same house?"

"Naw, we got a better place."

He drove north up Mass. Ave. then turned left up a hill into a suburban neighborhood. We went through blocks of big houses in small, nicely landscaped yards, then pulled into the driveway of a blue ranch that was just like all the other houses. George hit the button of the transmitter clipped to the sun visor and the wide door of the two-car garage swung open.

Buddy was waiting and hit the switch to close the door behind us. He was a big man, gray eyes set in a face with a lot of bones bunched up close under the skin. There was scar tissue around the eyes. He wore a black short-sleeve shirt and narrow pink tie over off-white slacks and white loafers. I got out and walked around the front of the car while George pried himself from the driver's seat.

Buddy said, "Jimmy," and gave me a hug. "I've been waitin' a long time to do you a favor. Come on in, what can we do for you?" He led me into an immaculate suburban kitchen with avocado appliances and a green linoleum floor. We sat at the porcelain-topped table. Despite the cleanliness of the kitchen, the place smelled of booze and cigar smoke. The hallway leading to the rest of the house was dark, and I heard mumbling voices from the front room. It was eleven o'clock in the morning.

"A game?"

"Yeah, small potatoes. What's up?"

George got a beer from the refrigerator and a big can of sardines. He sat at the table, pried open both cans, and started eating. He held each sardine in two fingers and gave it a shake over the tin before popping it into his mouth.

I said to Buddy, "You know a guy named Caleb Johnson, might be a gambler?" I reached into a pocket and pulled out Caleb's picture.

Buddy's eyes narrowed. "I'm not sure."

"C'mon, Buddy. I thought you wanted to help."

"It depends. Seems I saw that guy in the papers the other day. Got himself killed."

"Right."

"So I know him, or anyway I've seen him around."

"And?"

Buddy got up and tore a green paper towel from a roll over the sink and came back to wipe sardine oil from a spot on the table. He sat down. "He was a player, if that's what you need to know, but not often. I'd say he was here five times the last year. Only the big games."

"What was he like?"

"Man-of-the-people type, in good shape, drank hard liquor, talked tough. Especially when he had a broad with him, usually some young thing. But not a bad sort. Rich, I think."

George looked up. "He drove a big Merc, Jimmy. Fifty grand at least." Olive oil from the sardines ran out the corner of his mouth and stained the head of a flamingo.

"I thought he might have made some of the wrong people unhappy," I said.

"I doubt it. He paid, and not like it was a hardship. And he was never a big loser. I'll ask around about him if you want, but don't look for no names from me if it looks like he got nailed for reasons."

"You said he brought women along. Was it always the same one? This one?" I handed over a picture of Susan I'd clipped from the *Herald* on Thursday. They'd run a photo of the family coming from the funeral parlor, and one of Susan up close, standing beside Peter Streeter.

"Naw, always different ones, and younger than that. I don't remember seein' her. I may have seen this guy sometime," and he tapped Peter Streeter's head with a thick finger.

"Where?"

"Probably with Johnson." He held the newsclip up for George to see, then handed it back to me. George shook his head and went back to the sardines.

Buddy said, "Johnson used to bring that lawyer of his sometimes. Littman's his name."

"Yeah? What about him? Was he a player?"

"Sure."

"Did he ever come on his own?"

"A few times. He hasn't been in for about a month. But the first time was with Johnson."

"Is he a winner or loser?"

"From me I'm ashamed to say he always picked up a thousand or so. But he's the type who gets cocky, you know? If they win too often they think they'll always win, and when they lose they can't believe it. Then you nail 'em bigger than you would if their luck hadn't run so good to start with. I'll get him someday."

"You don't seem to like the guy."

"He's a putz."

A short, hairy guy came into the kitchen wearing a blue cotton suit and a white shirt, with the shirt half-open over his potbelly. He got a beer and stopped to look me over.

"Who's that?" he said.

"Nobody, Frankie. Go back and lose some money."

The fat guy cranked off the bottle cap and tossed it into a corner before he left the room. Buddy got up and lifted the cap from the floor and deposited it into a green garbage pail under the sink. He said, "Fuckin' pigs," and sat down again. "You want me to ask about the lawyer too?"

"Sure. But the main thing is Johnson. I've got a problem figuring him as a murder victim."

"It surprised me too, Jimmy, but you never can tell. I'll do everything I can. Like I say, I owe you."

"You heard from Bensen lately?"

"Not a thing. I'm just hoping this thing, me asking questions, won't cause me any trouble."

"Do what you can, Buddy. And give me a call if you get anything."

I stood up. George finished his beer and we went back out to the Cadillac.

It was Friday afternoon and I wasn't sure where to go

from there. If you structure your life to have a lot of free time, it's important to learn not to feel guilty wasting it, so I stopped off in Harvard Square and wandered around bookshops. I had an early dinner in a German place that serves over fifty varieties of beer, tried a bottle of something called Sailer Pils, then switched to Amstel. After the dinner I sat on the terrace of Au Bon Pain and had a cup of cappuccino. I watched the students in the square and the people playing chess at the tables around me.

After the coffee I drove back to the Trojan, took a long swim in the pool, and worked in the weight room for an hour to compensate for the four beers I'd had with the sauerbraten at dinner. It was dark when I went down the back stairs and out to the parking lot, feeling relaxed and well exercised. The wide alley behind the club runs to Stuart Street, past the rear of the Bradford Hotel. The club's back door opens at a porch with a wooden railing, and the cars are in slots to the left, parked head-on into the brick wall of the club.

There was a Cadillac in the alley, its motor idling and lights out. My first thought was George, but it was too soon for Buddy to have information, and besides, the driver's window was wide open. George always drives sealed up tight, air-conditioned in summer, heated in winter. The door of the Trojan locked behind me and the driver spotted me and threw a half-smoked cigarette out into the alley.

I jumped over the railing onto the roof of the first car parked against the wall. A big guy with a gun stepped from behind the Rambler, two cars down, and said, "Freeze."

The gun looked like a .357 Magnum. I froze. He came another car width closer and stopped. He had a hat pulled close over both eyes and from where I stood all I could see of his face was a large nose sticking out from under the brim of the hat. The nose looked like it had been broken several times. He was wearing a business suit.

"We are not going to hurt you at this point, Mr. Mallory, but there are important people who'd like to see you discontinue certain activities in connection with the death of Caleb Johnson."

I said, "Sure. Who's Caleb Johnson?"

"That's very good," he said, "if it indicates you have forgotten the matter." As he spoke he started to move in a wide arc around the back of the car, keeping well out of range of any move from me. I must have made a lovely target up on the roof of that car. I started to turn with him but he raised the gun a notch and said, "Keep facing in the direction of your motor vehicle, Mr. Mallory."

He kept moving and went out of sight behind me. I said, "Who you working for?"

A hand yanked at my left ankle and I went down. He kept the grip on the ankle, giving it a little twist, and said, "Rest assured that we are professionals and that we will hurt you severely, even permanently, if you persist. Your question was evidence of persistence." He let go of the ankle, and when he spoke again his voice came from the direction of the Caddy. As far as I could tell, the driver hadn't bothered to get out of the car.

"Please do not turn around, Mr. Mallory. If you have any notion of following us in that relic of yours, you should know that I have released the air from its tires. Be smart and you won't see us again."

The car door shut and the Caddy's headlights lit up the alley. It darkened quickly as they backed away. I slid off the roof of the car and went to the Rambler. He hadn't lied about the tires. I used my key to get back into the Trojan, feeling angry, but also quite pleased. Things had crawled out from under one of my stones, and they weren't just snails, they were genuine, bona fide, high-priced escargots.

CHAPTER TWELVE

Midnight Madness

I CALLED BUDDY that night, but nobody answered at the house in Arlington. Saturday morning I called again and got him out of bed.

"What's going on, Buddy? I ask for discreet inquiries and next thing I know I've got a quarter ton of muscle at my back door. With large guns."

"Jimmy, what's the matter? I was asleep."

I told him about my visit from the thugs.

"Jimmy, I wouldn't give your name to nobody. What time did this happen?"

"About nine."

"It couldn't have been me. I didn't start asking until the game, and that was after midnight. It doesn't figure."

"They were talking about Johnson, Buddy."

"That doesn't mean it came from me, Jimmy. The only way I could figure it from here is maybe that slob Frankie listened in the hall and heard you asking about him."

"What does Frankie do?"

"He's small potatoes, drives a bus for the MBTA. Sometimes gets in on something not so kosher. But even if it was Frankie, they'd have had to work awful quick. He was here till after six, which would give them three hours tops to organize and get into town by nine. Who works that fast?"

"Maybe Bensen."

"It'd have to be something big."

"See what you can find out, Buddy. Ask around. Talk to Frankie. But this time drop my name all over the place."

"Jimmy, I told you I wouldn't do that."

"I'm serious. I want them to know I'm after them. If we can't find them, I want them to find me."

"You sure?"

"Do it for me, Buddy. If you run into heat, back off. But do what you can. Okay?"

"Whatever you say."

I cut the connection, then tried to reach Mangenello in Lynn. The cop at the switchboard told me he was based at state headquarters at 1010 Commonwealth Avenue in Boston, and gave me the number. Mangenello answered on the first ring.

"I didn't know you were central office," I said.

"I move around a lot. What's up?"

I told him. "I just thought you should know in case I turn up floating in Boston Harbor."

"What do you think it means?"

"For one thing Johnson must've been involved in something relatively complicated. Those boys in the parking lot were professionals. It could have been gambling debts. It could have been drugs, sex—who knows?"

"I'll put out some inquiries. You'd better lie low a few days."

"I don't think so. The only way to find out who paid those creeps is to have them come at me again. Next time I plan to be ready."

"You hope. Or maybe we'll be working up two murders instead of one. I'm not telling you how to run your life, Mallory, but you'd better let us handle this. They hesitate before they shoot a cop."

"I'll keep that in mind. You got anything new?"

"I got something on Susan Johnson. She saw a travel agent about a big trip to Greece."

"How'd you catch that?"

"She told me. Wants to know if it's okay."

"Tell her I think it's great. We should have the murderer in a few days anyway."

"Right. Be careful." He hung up.

That left me nothing to do but wait until Buddy stirred up some trouble. I called Della, but the only message was from Susan saying she'd call back. I decided I might as well finish my inquiry into Caleb Johnson's habits, so I tried Doc Florian's office number in Hamilton. I got his service, and they wouldn't give me his unlisted home number. I told them I was having a coronary and if I couldn't get the doctor I'd have to call my lawyer instead. I don't know if they believed me or just gave me points for effort, but they gave me the number.

The doctor said to come on out, and so I made the drive to the North Shore one more time. He had a big house in Hamilton where he fed me two Grolsch beers and told me Caleb Johnson was a prince among men and, as far as he knew, hadn't made an enemy in sixty-five years of life on the planet. He'd also been a fine physical specimen. I drove back into Boston wondering why people thought Grolsch was worth the price the shops charge for it.

That night I called Julie at work, but she didn't have time to talk and sounded exhausted. I offered to carry a champagne picnic up to her office and she said it would only make things worse. So I went alone to a Katharine Hepburn movie at the Brattle Theater in Cambridge and went home and to bed early.

Sunday was even more exciting. I spent it cleaning my apartment and waiting for a threatening telephone call or knock on the door. I wanted to be available if the thugs came looking for me. I called Buddy, but he had nothing to report, so I drank half a bottle of wine with dinner and watched a special on channel 2 about mating whales. I went to bed feeling envious of the whales.

Around midnight there was a storm that woke me. I'd been having a dream about a mountain range of jagged peaks, with a castle on each of the peaks. To get to the green parkland I had to crawl through a confining maze of wire fence, and at the end of the maze was a guard dog, which I befriended and made my constant companion.

I lay in bed, still half in the dream, watching the strobe-flashes of lightning through the open window. The lightning illuminated objects on the big table at the window—a Smith-Corona painted yellow by a former lover, a coffee mug showing the New York skyline that Julie'd bought in a rest area off the New Jersey Turnpike, some books, and a green metal toolbox. There were framed photos of people I cared about hung on each side of the table, but I couldn't make out their faces. Some of the people in the photos were dead. They made me think of being a kid, how when a summer storm struck we'd run out to the front porch to watch the bolts of lightning and feel the mist rising from the rain off the roof and the street.

The storm was suddenly right on my block with a flash and explosion up the street, then the sound of heavy rain. I got up to close windows in the living room and went into the kitchen for a glass of milk. I sat with it at the table in the bedroom looking out at the storm. The cool air felt good. The rain slowed, then stopped, the thunder going farther and farther to the west.

The telephone rang. At twelve-thirty I figured it was Julie, so I picked up the phone and said, "Nothing obscene, please."

Phoebe's accented voice said, "Mr. Mallory? I think you should come to the house. Something is wrong."

"What?"

"I don't know, but something. Please be quick," and she hung up.

It didn't seem to be what I was waiting for, but I couldn't be sure, and of course I had to go anyway. I put on a pair of jeans and a dark T-shirt and my black Converse sneakers over dark socks. The Rambler was parked on the street below. I drove out through Kenmore Square and was in Brookline ten minutes after Phoebe rang off.

The Streeter house was quiet. I drove past, beneath the dripping trees of the small park where ball-playing was not permitted. I wanted to come in on foot, so I drove on and stopped at the far corner of the park by a high brick wall. A sign said there was a center for the education of the blind behind the wall.

Outside I caught the smell of wood smoke. A car came up the street, but it stopped at the gate to the blind center and a person with a long cane got out. The car went past, and then I heard the sound of its disembarked passenger tapping.

At the corner of the Streeter property I heard another small sound. It came from the back terrace—breaking glass. I went down the dead-end private way at the west side of the house. The road had a heaved, broken surface. The clouds overhead were lit orange by light from the city, but the hedge along the border was thick. I stooped and went through, releasing a small shower from the wet leaves.

A dark figure stood outside the French windows. I dropped to one knee, but he saw me and jumped the terrace wall and ran straight back toward the fence at the far end of the lawn. I took off after him. He went over the fence about twenty yards ahead of me, I vaulted after him, and we were into the trees and thick shrubs of the woods. I knew there was a small private park back there, Hall's Pond Sanctuary, running to Beacon Street. I heard him going through the woods toward the pond.

He had short legs, and when we came out of the brush onto a gravel path by the pond I was only twenty feet behind. He heard me and turned abruptly onto a disused side trail. The path went out onto a rotting walkway at the beginning of a marsh. The boards were half obscured by weeds.

He stopped and turned at the end of the trail, framed against the slight luminescence of the pond, and I stopped to wait for him. His face was covered by a black ski mask. I saw him take a deep breath, and then he came at me running, his right foot coming up in a surprisingly quick roundhouse kick.

I was ready, but as I stepped to avoid the kick the rotted footboards gave way under me, the side of his heel caught my head, and I went down in the muck.

I managed to swing toward the path to grab one of his ankles, but my legs were trapped in the broken boards and I was fighting for leverage. He kicked and got the muscle of the arm holding the ankle, I lost my grip, and he was off. I levered up quickly, but it was no use. I could barely stand on my right ankle. I heard him on the gravel going in the direction of the Streeter house.

I stood and listened to him disappear up the hill. My head was raw and sore where the shoe had grazed me. I'd had the bastard in my hands and lost him because I hadn't checked my damned footing on the boards.

I limped back. When I got to the fence behind the house I heard the whine of a car going too fast in reverse, then the growl of a high-performance engine accelerating in the direction of Boston. He must have been parked on a side street, since I hadn't spotted any cars when I'd driven in. I went over the fence and up to the house.

Melissa opened the door after the first ring. She wore a pink robe, and when I said I hoped I hadn't woken the house she said they were all sleeping like dead people. Standing soaking wet in the hall I told her briefly what had happened. I didn't mention Phoebe's calling me, but said I'd had insomnia and driven past the house on an impulse.

She didn't seem to find that surprising. We went together to the back of the house and the double doors onto the terrace. The glass beside the latch had been shattered, and the doors stood slightly ajar. "I heard him break the glass," I said, "so if he got into the house it was only for a few seconds. Do you notice anything missing?"

She gave a cursory look around the hallway and shook her head "no." I didn't see any obvious clues. We both noticed I was dripping blood from my cut head, and I asked for a place to wash up. She pointed to the kitchen.

"Should I call the police?"

"Try to get Detective Mangenello." I gave her the number.

In the kitchen I bent my head at the sink and started water running down the back of my neck. She came in carrying a first aid kit.

"I got him," she said. "He sounds like a mean guy. He wanted to know what you were doing here."

"Just lucky, I guess. What about the Brookline cops? Isn't your alarm system tied to the station?"

"I think so. I'll check it." She went into the hall and came back a moment later. I'd found a high stool and was sitting in front of the sink. "The alarm wasn't on," she said. "Phoebe must've forgotten. I remember now, it was off when I answered the door." She came over to the sink and began to wet a cloth.

"This is kind of exciting," she said. "Is it always like this, being a detective?"

"Not if you're a good detective." Standing in front of me she pulled my hair up in back and began to wash the cut. She smelled nicely of perfume, or a perfumed shampoo. She looked down at me, then suddenly kissed me on the mouth, lightly, then kissed me again with her mouth open.

I was touched. She kissed the way she talked, like a young teenager. That is, the way I imagine a young teenager would kiss.

She stepped back and said, "I only did that because you look like such a pirate with that gash on your head. Actually I'm engaged to someone. You're not the type who'd mess around with the client's daughter anyway."

"Probably not. Who you engaged to?" I was starting to feel dizzy from the cut. "Is it Stephen Littman?"

She bent over the sink and washed my blood from the cloth.

"No. He's a lawyer, though, like Stephen."

"You're too nice for a lawyer."

She gave a tiny smirk over her left shoulder.

"Does your mother know?"

"No. She doesn't like him." She took a clean dish towel to dry my hair.

"You don't seem too concerned about somebody breaking in here tonight," I said.

She made a face. "We're rich. Did you see him before he hit you?"

"No. He was wearing a ski mask."

She reached for a bottle of iodine. "Probably some junkie."

"I heard him drive off. It didn't sound like a junkie's car."

She put a cotton swab soaked in iodine against the cut, and I winced with the sting. She smiled and began to apply a round contact bandage.

"You're very good at this," I said.

"Grandpa Johnson taught me. He used to take me hiking in the White Mountains and he said we should always be prepared for the worst."

"Tell me about him."

"He liked me a lot. Said I was the opposite of Grandmother. She was a real bitch."

"But what was he like?"

"Active. Real active. He beat me at tennis, even at his age. He used to beat all my boyfriends. They hated him, because he hated them. He didn't want to get old."

He won't be getting any older, I thought. I was very tired now. "You should check the rest of the house to see if anything's missing."

"I thought you said he didn't get into the house."

"Maybe I was wrong. I heard the glass break, but it could have been a piece that came loose when he was on his way out. Take a look. Is there a place I can sit down?"

"In the study."

But on my way out of the kitchen the doorbell rang. The cops had showed up. I went to the front door and opened it before the second ring. Simon Mangenello stood under the roof of the entranceway wearing the brown wool suit I'd last seen him in and holding a battered canvas rain hat. The rain was coming down hard behind him.

"Aha," I said. "The ever vigilant chief inspector."

CHAPTER THIRTEEN

Things That
Go Thump

THE BROOKLINE COPS showed up twenty minutes after Mangenello, and he spoke with them alone in the front hall. When he came back into the study I was sitting on the couch with Melissa. Mrs. Streeter and Phoebe were still upstairs. We'd lit the fire in the fireplace.

Melissa looked up and said, "Aren't they going to take fingerprints or anything?"

Mangenello sat in a chair he'd pulled up opposite her. In his brown suit, surrounded by the trappings of the English study, he looked like the headmaster of a school for young women sitting down to speak with a new student and her benefactor—except the student was in a pink robe and the benefactor was bloody and spattered with mud.

He smiled and said, "Mr. Mallory says the man was wearing gloves, Miss Streeter, so there wouldn't be any prints. If you're not too tired, I'd like to go on with my questions. You were saying you didn't hear anything at all until Mr. Mallory rang the doorbell. What were you doing before that?"

"Reading. I couldn't sleep because of the storm."

"I love a good book myself just before bed. What were you reading?"

"*Beowulf*."

"Really? It's been years since I picked up *Beowulf*. And when Mr. Mallory rang you were downstairs?"

"No. In my room reading."

"But he said you answered the door on the first ring."

"That's right. I guess I was coming down the stairs for hot milk."

"You're not sure?"

"Of course I'm sure."

"I see." He turned to me. "Anything you want to ask Miss Streeter? There's nothing missing from the house. I don't see any need to wake her mother."

"I'd like to speak with Phoebe," I said. "She might have heard something. Would you ask her to come down, Melissa?"

She turned to Mangenello and said, "No more questions for me?"

When he nodded she stood and went out. He raised an eyebrow at me. I said, "Wait."

Five minutes later Phoebe came downstairs alone, dressed in the brown uniform. She closed the door to the study and sat in the place Melissa had left vacant. She looked disapprovingly at my mud-spattered sneakers and blue jeans.

"You wanted to see me, sir?"

"You met Detective Mangenello the other day, didn't you?"

"Of course."

"I want you to know that Melissa doesn't know you called tonight."

She didn't say anything, but Mangenello raised the eyebrow again.

"Why did you call?" I asked.

"I'd heard a noise in the garden, sir, and I thought it was prowlers."

"Then why did you call me? Why not the police?"

She looked at Mangenello and he gave her an encouraging smile. "Begging your pardon, sir," she said, "but I haven't much faith in them."

She smiled at me, for the very first time.

"Was there a prowler, sir? Miss Streeter didn't say. You look like you've been hurt."

"Oh yes. I chased him, but he got away. When I got here tonight, Phoebe, the alarm system wasn't functioning. It hadn't been tampered with, it just wasn't turned on. Melissa says you must have forgotten it."

"If it wasn't on, then I must have forgotten. It's my duty to check it every night before going to bed."

"And you didn't think to check it even after you'd heard the noise in the garden?"

"I didn't."

"Did you see anything in the garden, or hear any voices?"

"To tell the truth, sir, after I called I went to sit with Mrs. Streeter. The doctor has given her sleeping pills, and I was worried for her. So I didn't see or hear anything until Miss Streeter came for me just now."

"I had the impression from your telephone call there was something more."

"Only that first noise in the garden, sir. It was just after the storm passed. I heard somebody walking in the gravel beneath the windows."

"But you didn't tell Melissa?"

"I didn't want to frighten her."

I looked at Mangenello. He said, "We're all very tired, Miss Goodrich, but I'd like to ask a few quick questions." He started on her, and after a couple of minutes I stopped listening. Phoebe had heard a noise, nothing more. Before the storm she'd been asleep in her room.

Ten minutes later she asked, "Will that be all, sir?"

Mangenello looked at me and I nodded. We all three stood and went out of the study. At the front door Mangenello got his rain hat from the rack and said, "When you let us out be certain to turn on the alarms."

"Of course, sir."

It was raining hard again, and we waited outside until the light of the alarm indicator went from green to red. Mangenello said, "You ever read *Beowulf*?"

"Sure. I've got a lot of sympathy for the agony of the grieving dragon."

"It seems an odd book for a young woman."

"She's an odd young woman."

"Well, come along and we'll take a ride. I'd like to talk. How's the head? Want to see a doctor?"

"It's fine."

I got into the passenger side of the official car he'd parked out front. I noticed a Brookline patrol car with its lights off in the narrow private way beside the house. Mangenello waved to them as he got in, and the cop at the wheel raised a thumb.

"You must have pulled some strings for that."

"Just for tonight. The chief owes me a million favors. Why didn't you want the Streeters to know about Phoebe calling?"

"I can't say for sure. Nothing about what happened tonight rings true."

"Well, something happened. Why keep it from the Streeters?"

"I got the feeling Phoebe's an ally of sorts, and it was better to speak with her privately."

"Ally against the Streeters?"

I shrugged. "Damned if I know. I guess I'm tired."

"Well, she's obviously no ally of mine."

He grunted, turned on the lights and started the car forward. At the next block we turned onto Carlton and down to Beacon, then headed toward Coolidge Corner. He drove slowly, the wipers pushing sheets of heavy water from the windshield, his brown, stocky figure bolt upright behind the wheel. He kept his hands at ten o'clock and two o'clock and his eyes fixed on the road.

"I take it the break-in and the thugs in the alley on Friday both have something to do with Johnson's murder," he said. "Any idea how they tie together?"

"They don't tie together well. That guy tonight wasn't any professional."

"Maybe it was just coincidence then. Maybe he was

some punk working his first B&E. Why would Johnson's murderer want to break into the Streeter house?"

"To take something that might be evidence against him? To hurt somebody?"

"You think Phoebe is on to something she's not telling us?"

"You talked with her. Hard to tell."

He frowned. "Damned British. How about this? The daughter was dressed like a man, she ditched you by the pond, then doubled back to the house and threw on a robe."

I looked at him. "It's late, Simon. Aside from the fact I can't imagine why she'd play such a trick, I heard the car drive away. You've got a point, though—I can't say for sure it wasn't a woman. It was a short person in loose clothing."

We didn't say anything for a while, and Mangenello turned the car at Saint Paul's to work back into the Streeters' neighborhood.

"Finally got the lab report on that bottle," he said. "The seal was steamed open and reglued with Elmer's glue. All we have to do is find somebody who uses Elmer's glue."

"And cyanide," I said. "Any luck on that?"

"Nothing on your friend Peter Streeter."

We came round through the one way streets and got onto Cottage Farm Road. Mangenello pulled up beside my car. "This yours?"

I nodded.

"Maybe we'll be thinking better tomorrow," he said. "Take care of that head."

I got out, climbed into the Rambler, and sat a few moments behind the wheel, watching the trees through the cascade of rain down the windshield. I started her and drove slowly around, past Mangenello's car, which had pulled up beside the patrol car.

I drove to Buswell Street through the heavy rain, turned on to Park Drive, then up Beacon. I'd put the

heater on, and the fan blew hot air at my feet. Going
through Kenmore Square I saw street people standing
out of the rain in the narrow shelter of a few doorways.
They looked cold and forlorn. I got to Marlborough
Street and spent ten minutes finding a parking space.

When I got upstairs I was exhausted but didn't feel like
sleeping. I took off the wet clothes, took a hot shower,
and put on a black terrycloth robe. I went into the front
room and made a fire of applewood logs left over from
the previous winter. I got a glass of orange juice and lay
with feet up on the sofa and read *The Autobiography of
Alice B. Toklas*. After a while I got up and filled the
half-full glass of orange juice with ice and vodka. By 3:30
I'd fallen asleep on the couch.

CHAPTER FOURTEEN

The Trojan Gym and Health Club

I WOKE THE NEXT morning with lots of sunlight leaking in from behind the window shades. My ankle had stiffened and the rest of me wasn't in such good shape after spending the night on the couch. I showered and dressed and left the apartment without bothering to make coffee.

I didn't use the front stairs. By then the thugs should know I was looking for them, which meant it was time for caution. I went down the narrow utility stairway from the kitchen and stopped at the ground floor to peer carefully into the lobby.

Nobody. The light at the head of the basement stairs was burned out, and I felt my way down the rough steps and out through the long corridor in back to the rear door and the alley. There were garbage cans in back of the building with the number 924 stenciled on them. I went out to Beacon and around the block to come down Marlborough from the far end. Still nothing. I went on down Marlborough toward the city.

At Exeter I crossed to Newbury and stopped at the Harvard Bookstore Café for coffee. They've got a nice collection of books in the front of the store and serve food in back. If you get there before noon the waitresses haven't started working and you can order cappuccino at the counter and take it to a table under the trees on the sidewalk in front.

My ankle felt better after the walk. I drank coffee and

read the newspaper until I came across an article that said the State Department advised American tourists not to sit in outdoor cafés in countries with a lot of terrorist activity. Being a good American, I finished the coffee, folded the paper, and continued down Newbury Street to Arlington and across Park Plaza to the Trojan.

In the lobby Harry was reading a wrestling magazine with two fat guys grimacing on the front cover. I asked when Barbi would be in and he said "noon," so I went down to the locker-room and got into trunks for a swim.

Barbi keeps the water warm and the pool lights low. I often do my best thinking there, but that day I just made the laps and kept my mind blank. From the pool I could look up two levels to the window of my office and the windows of three other offices down the width of the building. I did a mile, alternating between a crawl and an easy breast stroke, then dressed and went in for coffee and a donut with Edgar. At noon I finished the coffee and went up to the gym.

There was something I'd noticed the night before and needed to check against Barbi's knowledge of styles of self-defense. In any complicated sport, whether basketball, football, bullfighting, or fencing, a lot happens in a short time, and only the practiced eye can identify all the deliberate acts that make up the whole. That's especially true with unarmed combat. Barbi can not only see each separate move and countermove in a fight, she can watch a fighter on the mat and tell you what master he studied under. It was a long shot, so I hadn't mentioned it to Mangenello, but I was hoping Barbi could tell me where our Brookline prowler had learned to kick.

I opened the door to the gymnasium and spotted her sitting in semidarkness in the middle of tattered gray gym mats. There were parallel bars, uneven bars, vaults, and balance beams throwing shadows around her. Like the Trojan's lobby, the big gymnasium reminds me of my old high school—it's three stories high with brown tile walls and only a few narrow windows at the top to filter in natural light. I switched on the overhead fluorescents. The door swung to with a sharp crack and Barbi called out, "Mallory?"

"How'd you know it was me?"

"Harry said you were looking for me." She uncoiled and stood up from the mat, a tall, sinewy lady of no known age.

I'm always impressed by how solid and quick she looks, whether working out in the gym or sitting back in the big couch up in her office with coffee. When Edgar is being funny he calls her "da cat lady."

"I should get that door fixed," she said, and put her hands up to run through the short-cropped brown hair. The door to the gymnasium has probably swung unchecked since she bought the place twenty years ago.

I have no idea what she did before that. There are rumors, but nothing worth repeating. She stands and moves like a dancer, and I assume she danced. I know the Trojan was formerly an all-men's gym and bathhouse with a nasty reputation, and Barbi paid cash for it and shut down the old operation on one day's notice. In three weeks it reopened as a club for the people who work the Combat Zone—a place to come at any hour after a hard night and get a rubdown and maybe take a swim in the long, faded blue pool. Lately she gets a lot of young professionals from downtown, but the character of the place hasn't changed to accommodate them.

Coming across the mats she spotted the new scab at the side of my head.

"Not bad," she said. "Who nailed you?"

"Wouldn't I like to know."

"Tell me about it."

I told her briefly about the Streeters and Johnsons and she listened closely, as she always does, standing about two paces away with hands on her hips. When I got to the scene by the water she listened with particular attention.

"The kick was different in style from anything I've seen

before," I said. "It wasn't karate, but it wasn't just kicking either. There was method to it. What it made me think about was French kick-boxing. I once saw some pros working out at a club in Paris. I can't remember what they call it in French."

"Savate," she said. "Show me the kick as you remember it."

I stepped forward a pace and, moving with exaggerated slowness, lifted a high, sideswiping kick at her head.

She caught the foot at the apex of the upward swing. She held me balanced up on one foot and said, "In French kick-boxing they use their feet as well as fists to strike the opponent. From your position you can see the basic flaw in the system—with a quick opponent who's not playing by the rules you can end up standing on your toes. It's not much more effective than standard English boxing."

I said, "Ahem," and she said "sorry" and let my foot go.

I stretched the knee and said, "I wasn't very quick last night."

"You had bad luck. I studied savate years ago, in Marseilles. I quit after my teacher got himself knifed in the back in an alley."

"You just say that kind of thing to make me curious about your past. Is there any place in Boston where they teach it?"

"Only place I know is a center in Cambridge, at Kendall Square. Run by a guy named Hound Dog."

"Hound Dog?"

She grinned. "You'll see. He's a friend. Come upstairs and I'll get you the address."

I needed the Rambler to get out to Cambridge to see Barbi's friend, so I left the Trojan and walked down Charles Street, back through the construction at Park Plaza and right on to Hadassah Way to the Public Garden. The big trees were shining, roses were out, and crowds of children stood in line in the sun waiting to ride the swan boats. A pretty girl on the grass beside a Keep Off the Grass sign gave me a nice smile. I crossed to Arlington, past the two buildings of the Ritz, and up the long tree-lined mall in the center of Commonwealth Avenue.

I've made that walk so many times the individual buildings have become familiar landmarks and it seems to take no time at all to get halfway across town. It was early so I missed the usual after-work crowd—beautiful women in business suits and gym shoes threading their way back to luxury condominiums, past people walking relieved-looking scotties. Up by the International Center a group of oriental men stood in a rough circle, keeping a fat badminton birdie suspended over their heads, kicking it up with heels and knees.

I went on up the mall to Mass. Ave. and turned right past Bildner's, moving carefully now, and crossed the Avenue to the alley and the rear of my building.

What I am about to say may sound a little silly, but since I was a child I have on at least ten occasions, when I was in extreme danger, been warned of the danger by detecting a very strong odor of burning cigars. On no such occasion was anyone actually smoking a cigar. My British grandmother had the same gift, but it didn't manifest itself until late in life, when the family put her in the care of doctors. Everyone said she was senile, but I knew her nose was warning her, and in the end, of course, her nose was right. The doctors made short work of her.

In any event, I went into the building and down the long back corridor and stopped to look into the front room where the landlord stores cardboard boxes of useless miscellanea and old furniture from the days when he rented the apartments furnished. The room was dimly lit by two narrow street-level windows half obscured by the shrubs out front, and it was filled with the smell of cigar smoke.

A shaft of sunlight came down from the door at the top

of the stairs to the lobby, and up there against the wall were the wide, clear-cut shadows of a man's legs. From the light I figured he had the door into the lobby open a crack and was waiting for me to come in the front.

I went slowly past the piled-up junk and stood under the head of the stairs, picked up an old wrench from the cement dust at my feet, and threw it into the back of the room. It made a lot of noise. The door closed above and the man took a cautious step down. I saw the highly polished black shoes through the gap between the risers, then reached up and grabbed the ankles and yanked back hard.

He went head first down the stairs and I ran to meet him. He was very quick—as his shoulder hit the wall he was already bringing the .357 Magnum up to aim at my middle. I sliced with my arm and sent the gun flying, and he lunged off the wall and caught me in a bear hug that sent us back into the tumble of old furniture and boxes.

The fall broke his grip and I was up first and hit him two hard rights in the face and the throat as he got up off his knees. He was all rage and muscle now and swung at me wildly. I ducked under a roundhouse right and got him twice in the nerve center below the diaphragm. He went back over an end table, struck his head against a metal post, and stopped moving.

I found the gun. The air of the basement was full of dust lit up by the dim light from the windows, but the cigar smell had disappeared. It was the guy who'd threatened me in the alley behind the Trojan. I recognized his nose even though I'd broken it for him yet another time. He was choking on the blood, so I rolled him with my foot and took the opportunity to get his wallet. Five one-hundred-dollar bills, nothing smaller, and no identification. It was the kind of money you carried for bribing cops or paying for a hit. I stuffed it into my pocket and tossed the wallet down beside him.

If the two of them ran true to form the Cadillac and driver would be on the street somewhere waiting. I found rope and tied the thug's wrists and ankles and went back out into the bright sunlight in the alley. I'd pulled my shirttails out and tucked the .357 Magnum into the waist band at the back.

Sure enough, around the corner of Beacon and Mass. Ave. I spotted the Caddy, parked a few cars up on the south side. If I'd walked up Beacon instead of Common-wealth I'd have seen it on my way to the apartment. The driver had the engine idling. The street was empty. I moved up behind the side mirror and whistled, then stepped forward as he spotted me and got out of the car.

He wasn't nearly as good as his partner. Maybe he was only supposed to drive. By the time he got out I was in close. He reached into his jacket, and I levered my foot up and got him in the groin. He started down and I kicked him in the head, then bent and got the gun from his shoulder holster. I stepped back and pointed it at the middle of his face. I said, "Don't move."

He moaned back at me. He was young, with a thin face and a crewcut. He had a badly shaped head, and I thought he should have worn his hair longer to cover it. The radio in the Cadillac was playing a Madonna song.

The street was still empty. I bent down and put the gun against his nose. He tried to move back, but I cocked it and pushed it into his nose and he stopped moving. I said, "I am very angry and I want to know who you're working for."

He looked at me and at the gun and said, "Bensen."

"Why does Bensen want me to lay off the Johnson case?"

"I don't know, I swear. The word was just to roust you."

I pushed the gun hard against his nose and said, "One more chance."

His eyes rolled back into his head and he started to cry. "I just drive the fucking car. Nobody told us any-thing, I swear it."

I stepped back and uncocked the hammer. Up the

street a young couple had come out onto the sidewalk and stopped to watch us. The front door of the Cadillac was wide open. I told the punk to roll onto his belly and checked in case he had another gun. Then I got into the car and drove it away.

I drove to Charlesgate, circled back to Mass. Ave., and pulled up in front of the Harvard Club. I had three options—I could go back and try to pry something from the thug in the basement, I could call the cops, or I could continue to steal the Cadillac. Now that I knew Bensen was involved I didn't expect to get much from the hired gun, and I knew the cops couldn't hold them. It was the name I'd wanted anyway. I decided to steal the Cadillac.

As I adjusted the seat and mirrors and headed across to Cambridge, another old memory came back to me. I remembered that driving Cadillacs was fun.

CHAPTER FIFTEEN

Hound Dog

I HAD THE GOOD feeling that comes when a case starts breaking wide open—or maybe it was just an adrenaline rush from all the recent violence. But I now knew Johnson's death was definitely connected to the activities of Frank Bensen, big-time thug. The most obvious connection was the gambling, but whatever activity Johnson had been involved in, it was something I could trace. On the other hand, the Bensen connection didn't exactly fit the events of the previous evening, and I still had to follow up on Barbi's educated guess and visit the Center for Savate Training.

In short, at that point I had more clues than I needed. But I was able to stifle my chagrin.

I got off Memorial Drive at the exit for the Longfellow Bridge just as a Red Line train ran down the center of the bridge and disappeared into the tunnel before Kendall Square, then I made my way through the complicated pattern of new streets where they're tearing up everything to remodel the subway station. The place was jumping with the sound of jackhammers and pile drivers and heavy trucks. I parked in an alley and left the car unlocked, the keys still in the ignition. I'd taken the guns apart and, going down the street, I dropped them into two different storm drains. Then I stopped at a phone booth to call the Boston cops and report strange noises in the basement of my apartment building. I hung up when the 911 operator asked for my name.

I was in Cambridge and it didn't look at all like the Cambridge of Harvard Square. There were low-income housing projects, boarded-up brick factories, dozens of faceless new buildings of high tech industries, and the older brick structures housing branches of MIT. Somewhere in the neighborhood there's a small nuclear power plant. The new companies specialize in things like microtechnology and genetic engineering. It's here the first gopher with butterfly wings will be created—if it isn't already living in the dorm room of some MIT freshman.

Right in the Square there's an old diner under a sign that says "Eat," probably where the workers in the factories used to go for eggs and sausage after the graveyard shift. Now it's in the middle of all the noisy construction. I found the Center on the third floor of one of the brick buildings on a quiet street behind the diner.

There was a stairway up the front with a series of red arrows beside decals of men kicking. I followed the arrows to a big, airy loft with hardwood floors and white painted walls and a plate glass window looking down on the street. At the far end of the room gym mats had been spread on the floor in front of mirrors and a dozen people in gray sweatpants and white T-shirts were doing stretch exercises, led by a guy with a crewcut, a big head, and no neck.

The big guy did a leg stretch in my direction and saw me. He said something to a dark-haired woman and stood easily from the mat. She started the group in a different set of exercises. As he came across the room I noticed he was missing his left arm. The rest of him looked very fit and strong.

He stuck out his right hand and said with a mild southern accent—that calm, competent voice of astronauts and army lifers—"What can I do for you, friend?"

"Shouldn't you at least feign a French accent?" I said.

"How's that? Oh, I got you, buddy. I learned my trade from the French in Nam, but to be honest I don't care for them as a race. I'm Hound Dog. You here to join up, there's room in the evening class."

"I'm Jim Mallory. Barbi called about me."

"Oh right. You want information. Come on into the office." He gave a thumbs up to the woman leading the group, then led me to a small room opening from the big one. He went in and sat behind a big army surplus desk.

I'd stopped in the doorway. I don't know what I'd expected—I suppose the usual coffee maker and a few posters of French guys kicking each other. What I saw was Elvis Presley, full-size, in rhinestones, sitting across from Hound Dog at the desk. I looked at Hound Dog and he smiled.

"People get surprised sometimes. What do you think of it?" and he waved his hand at the mannequin and the rest of the room—shelves with Elvis Presley beer mugs, bourbon bottles, china dolls, an Elvis Presley gum machine, movie posters, including a big one covering the whole right-hand wall and showing a young, lean Elvis in *Jailhouse Rock*. Above Hound Dog's desk I spotted a black-and-white photo of Elvis with his arm around Hound Dog. I went in to read the inscription—"You ain't nothin' but a hound dog. Love, Elvis."

"That's why they call me Hound Dog. I once spent two weeks at Graceland teaching Elvis a few tricks. Greatest honor of my life."

"You could knock me over with a feather," I said. I sat. In the aquarium behind Hound Dog I noticed a miniature Elvis frogman with bubbles coming from his suit.

"Barbi said you wanted to see a list of my students? What's it all about?"

"I'm investigating a murder," I mumbled. I was still taking in the room.

"You know, fella, savate ain't like karate or kung fu. You don't kill people with savate, it's a sport, like boxing."

I looked at him. "I understand. But there's a chance one of your students poisoned a man. He's been identified as someone who knows savate."

"That so?" Hound Dog reached into a desk drawer

and pulled out a single sheet of bond paper. It was a neatly typed list of about twenty names with notations in pencil beside each name showing dates of enrollment and tuition paid. Hound Dog said, "I'm a one-finger typist, but I manage."

I read each of the names and none of them rang a bell. I put the list back onto the desk. "Do you have a list of former students?"

"Afraid not. I'm pretty good at remembering, though, if you've got a name you'd like to run by me."

I reached into my breast pocket and pulled out the newspaper photo of Susan Johnson. "How about this woman? Know her?"

He leaned forward. "Sure, nice gal. Came in once a week for a year. Don't tell me she got herself killed?"

I looked at him and said, "Tell me about her."

"She used to come with a guy named Littman."

"Stephen Littman?"

"Right. I think she came just to keep him company. Is that pretty little girl dead?"

"No, she's fine. Tell me about Littman. Was he any good at kick-boxing?"

"He got real proficient, stayed on after she quit. But I had to get rid of him, told him I didn't want him around any more. Refunded half a year's tuition."

"Why's that?"

"Three weeks ago, what he did was kick me in the back when I wasn't lookin'. Thought he was cute, can you imagine? Is that the guy you lookin' for?"

"Could be."

"Well, poison'd be his style."

I smiled. "I got to say, you're an expert on style, Hound Dog."

"Yeah, but now I better get back to work, Jim." We stood and shook hands, and I went back out to the street.

I walked to the phone booth and put my dimes out on the shelf and called Littman's office. He was out of town again. I tried the Streeters' number and got Phoebe and she said Mrs. Streeter was feeling ill and had gone to bed.

"Is it important for you to speak with her? I could wake her."

"It's important, but nothing that can't wait until to-morrow, Phoebe. I'll call in the morning."

"Have you discovered something?"

"I'll let you know in the morning."

I used my next dime to call Mangenello. He answered himself and I told him I had a line on the guys in the Cadillac. "Registration says it's owned by Richard Kitchen of Arlington, but the driver says he works for Frank Bensen. License number two eight four, dash, IJP, Irving Jessup Prendergast. It's parked in an alley west of Kendall Square, if it hasn't been stolen. I left the keys in it."

"How'd you get the car?"

"Long story. Check with the Boston cops on a call about a prowler in a basement on Marlborough Street. I left one of Bensen's men down there, but his buddy probably got him out before the patrol car arrived. Not that either of them would be much good to you. I per-suaded the driver to give me the name, but he didn't know why Bensen's interested in the Johnson case. The hired gun's not the type to talk."

"You've been busy."

"I've got something even better," and I told him about the savate center and Stephen Littman. When I'd fin-ished a recording told me to deposit a nickel.

Mangenello's voice came back on the line. "That's pretty thin," he said. "It'd never convince a jury even if it got to them, and let's face it, you're not a qualified expert in French kick boxing. Not enough to give a positive i.d. based on one kick. Defense counsel would murder you on voir dire."

"Come on, Simon, we're not lawyers. I'm not saying he killed Johnson—he could be just a peeping Tom who likes to wear ski masks and watch his clients undress—but let's at least take a look at him."

"What about motive?"

"Take your pick. He was in love with Susan Johnson, or stealing from the Johnson trust and got caught. Or maybe both."

"Aren't you forgetting Frank Bensen? How does he fit into all that?"

"Littman's a gambler, he'd have contact with Bensen's crowd. Maybe he hired them to take care of me."

"Bensen doesn't work for lawyers, lawyers work for Bensen. Why don't you set up a meeting with the big man?"

"Because my health insurance has expired. Don't worry, I'll handle the Bensen end. But if Littman's it and we nail him, we'll find out soon enough how Bensen's involved."

There was silence on the other end of the line and finally I said, "Come on, Simon, I'm not gonna waste another nickel on you."

"Okay," he said. "So I'll buy it. I thought that guy Littman was a prick the first time I laid eyes on him. I hope he did kill the old man. You talk to Morgan Streeter and I'll talk to the DA about getting a look at those trust accounts. But remember there's politics involved. This guy's a lawyer working for a very hotshot firm. So go easy. And take care of yourself. And keep in touch." He hung up.

It was 5:30 and there's a Legal Seafoods out at Kendall Square, so I called Julie to ask if she could cab out and join me for dinner.

"I can't, sweetheart, I'm busy. Some of us were talking about the Exchange for drinks after work. You could join us, but it'll be late."

"Kiddo, the firm won't collapse if you run out for a bite to eat. This is the kind of thing you wanted to get away from."

"Look, I haven't any choice. I'm going to be here all night and I just want to be left alone."

She hung up. Since I was at a pay phone and she couldn't reach me in case she wanted to apologize, I should have called back—but I decided to let it lie. I picked up another dime and called my own number to play back the messages on Della. There was a new one from Susan, telling me she'd call again. I got information for Boston and the number of her friends at the Church Court Condos. I used my last dime for the call and a woman answered and I asked for Susan.

"This is she. Mallory?"

"Yes. Still in town?"

"My friends are hiking in the Sierras and they've left me this place. You got my message? I wanted to apologize for acting like a goof the other night. I saw you at Caleb's funeral. Have you found out anything?"

"What are you doing now? Can you meet me?"

"At your office?"

"No, I'm in Cambridge and haven't got a car. I could take a cab to your apartment."

"I was going downtown for dinner. Is there a place we could meet down there?"

"You know the Exchange Bar, Liberty Square?"

"Sure. It's got junk food munchies and cheap beer. I used to drink there after work."

"That's the place. Can you meet me in about an hour?"

She said she'd be there. I walked back around the construction site to the Kendall subway station and caught the train into town. Crossing the Longfellow Bridge I looked out at the Charles and saw half a hundred sailboats on the river, lit up by the evening sun. Then the train ran into the side of Beacon Hill and continued underground into the city.

CHAPTER SIXTEEN

Honesty Is the Best Policy

I SAT AT THE bar and ordered a beer and Susan showed up twenty minutes later. She was wearing a light-blue sundress and had her blonde hair down over her shoulders. She walked into the bar and three men in business suits in the first booth stopped talking and stared at her. I stepped over and led her to an empty booth. She slid into the back and gave me a smile.

"Hello, Max. Thanks for getting me to my friends the other night. Sorry if I said anything crazy."

"You were cute."

She made a face. "What happened to your head?" The waitress came with the beer I'd left on the bar, and Susan ordered a Budweiser.

I touched the side of my head. "Hurt it jogging. Long story."

The Budweiser came and she took a long drink and set the glass onto the table. "What did you want to see me about?"

"I wanted to ask about Stephen Littman."

"Really?" She took another drink and looked at me closely. "You wanted to talk about him the day Caleb died, when you were at the house in Marblehead. I wouldn't give you his name."

"It keeps popping up now, whenever I talk to people about Caleb. I wondered why."

"They'd gotten to be friends, I guess. Stephen handled

all the family's estate planning. He's at the firm where I used to work."

"Are you two still friends?"

"Sure. We hung out together more back then, things like art and dance classes. We started work on the same day, and that made us close—that and the fact that we both hated the work so much. Although Steve seems to have adapted."

"Why did you leave the Bombay in such a hurry the day Caleb died? You and Stephen were arguing out in the parking lot, weren't you?"

"I guess so."

"Can you tell me what it was about?"

"Nothing important. Caleb stopped having Steve out to the house after I moved in. I think he was a little jealous—he always was of younger men. Steve was putting pressure on me to invite him to dinner, that kind of thing, so I just left. I guess I was angry."

"You think Stephen was jealous of Caleb?"

"We were never anything but friends, Max. I think he may have been a little jealous of me for marrying into money. Money means a lot to Steve. That's why I think he's adapted to the job finally, he got into trusts and estates, and all he does all day is play with people's money."

"Now that Caleb's dead, I suppose they'll open up the books on the trust he's managed for the family."

She looked at me again. "Not the way it's set up, there's an automatic change of beneficiary. That's the whole point, to save the estate time and money. What are you getting at?"

"Aren't the beneficiaries entitled to an accounting of their money?"

"If they ask for one. I'm not a beneficiary, by the way. If you're talking about Morgan I doubt if she'd bother. It costs money to do any kind of serious accounting, and people use a firm like Choate & Masterson so they don't have to worry about things like that. I'm sure Morgan has known the senior partner there, John Masterson, since she was a child."

"But what if somebody was stealing from the trusts? How would anyone find out?"

"You mean a lawyer? It couldn't happen, Max. For one thing, the money's farmed out to investment advisors, and they're about ten times more reliable and conservative than God. You'd have to have the unlikely situation where a respected lawyer and a respected investment advisor were working together to steal from a client—otherwise I think you'd have trouble prying subway fare out of a trust." She frowned. "You think Steve's been embezzling?"

Before I could answer Frank Burger appeared at the table.

"Well, well, a little tête-à-tête. Mind if I join you?"

He didn't wait for an answer, but turned to the bar and got a beer. Susan looked uncomfortable. Frank slid into the booth beside her.

"Dropped in to see what was happening at this dive. I'm a lonely soul. By the way, James, I was just asking around about that guy you're interested in. The jerk."

"Later, Frank."

Susan said she wanted to go to the women's room, so I slid out to let her by. When she'd gone Frank raised his eyebrows and said, "Bad timing?"

"That happens to be Susan Johnson, Caleb Johnson's widow."

"Aha."

"I assume you were talking about our Mr. Littman just now. What you get? Any hint of scandal?"

"Nothing from those documents you gave me. But I've got some lovely hearsay about Littman. Like, he spent weekends at law school kissing ass at the dean's country house in the Berkshires. He actually played lawn tennis with his contracts professor. Apparently he's just as charming to the partners at C & M, and he uses it to avoid overworking himself. The associates over there think he's an asshole."

"All you lawyers are assholes, Frank."

"The money does that."

"Lots of people with money are perfectly charming."

"That's because they have all they want. By the way, how's Julie?"

"We're fighting."

"I noticed the bruises. You obviously need another drink," and he waved down a waitress. The bar had gotten crowded and noisy and the waitress looked harassed. Frank swallowed his beer and ordered a bourbon, and I ordered another beer.

"I think I drink too much," he said. "Where was I when you interrupted me with your tales of domestic squabbles? Nothing serious with Julie, is it?"

"A lot of pressure on her at work. You were telling me what makes you an asshole."

"Lust for money. Lawyers sit in conference rooms all day and watch clients pass big bucks back and forth and then go home to two-bedroom condos in the Back Bay, and it just ain't good enough."

"Seventy thou a year would be good enough for most."

"Ah, but James, having lots of money never makes people happy if they have to work too hard for it. The clients have that and more without lifting a finger." The waitress came with our drinks. We were running a tab.

"People call us money-grubbing parasites," Frank said, "but that's not fair. We're just members of the salaried servant class. Overpaid and overworked. We're bloody cormorants. You know cormorants? Those big birds oriental fishermen use? I saw a show on channel 2 the other night. The oriental fisherman ties a string around the cormorant's throat and sends it down after a fish. The cormorant is good at catching fish, but it can't swallow anything because of the string around its throat. It comes up to the surface and the fisherman takes the fish away and sends it back down for another fish, and then another and another. Every once in awhile the guy unties the string and gives the cormorant a little fish to eat, just to keep it going. Then he ties the string up and sends the cormorant down again. That's us in a nutshell."

Frank took a slug of bourbon. I looked around for Susan.

"It's a tough life, believe me. Wouldn't you rather be the fisherman? It's amazing more of us don't steal from the clients."

I didn't see Susan, and I was beginning to wonder what had happened to her.

Frank looked around the bar to find out what I was looking for. "I'm sure there could be all kinds of scams," he said. "The one I like involves wire transfers. Are you listening? You're at a closing and someone gets paid six million dollars for something. They've got to give the money to this guy, but not in cash, and a check takes too long to clear, even a certified check.

"So they wire the money between banks and it takes about ten minutes. The client turns to the lawyer and says 'call the bank and authorize the transfer.' Everyone's in the conference room at the closing. The lawyer sets it up with the bank in advance—which account to send it to at which bank, etc.—so all he has to do at the closing is make a phone call. Now, what if the lawyer has the money sent to his own bank, to his personal account? Would anyone know? The lawyer makes his phone call and tells the bank 'make the transfer.' The clients trust him. They assume the money's going to the right account. Am I right?"

"Sure, and they'd find out eventually that it didn't."

"Eventually. But what if the lawyer walks out of that conference room, calls his bank again and tells it to wire the new deposit to a second bank, in Nassau. He gets on a plane and down there in a few hours. Banks in Nassau don't ask questions. The lawyer draws out six million dollars in cash, puts it in a briefcase, and flies to Switzerland. If he's done everything on Friday it gives him at least the weekend before anyone could catch on. Then he goes into hiding. Or buys himself a new identity."

"Would it work?"

"Who knows? It's a nice little fantasy. To tell the truth, I opened an account the last time I was down in the Bahamas."

"You're kidding."

"Nope. But I've never taken it any further because I'm chickenshit."

"You've just got a conscience, Frank."

"What conscience, ripping off a few lousy millions from a billion-dollar corporation? Those guys lose more to people pilfering ballpoints. I'm chickenshit. And I bet it would work. People are amazingly stupid. Banks lend millions of dollars on collateral they never see—they see a piece of paper that says the collateral's there. Nobody checks those things. You know why? They think the lawyers can protect them from anything. They trust us.

"Not the average schlep on the street, I'm talking the corporate giants of the business world, people who push money that isn't their own, those bastards are too lazy not to trust us. And we've got this code of ethics of which the primary directive is 'don't rip off your client.' We can represent people who commit terrible murders, we can withhold the truth from a judge if it serves the best interests of our clients, we can use every trick in the book to make sure corporations keep on poisoning workers with asbestos dust or that some poor widow doesn't get her insurance money, but we can't rip off our clients."

"But lawyers do it anyway?"

"Sure, we're human, aren't we? That's why we have the bar and the code, we come down on those people hard. We make them stop being lawyers, a punishment worse than death. But even if a lawyer never ends up breaking the rules, all that money and all the meanness that goes into protecting it does something dirty to people." He stopped talking and suddenly looked unhappy.

"So why do you do it, Frank?"

"Because I like the money." He grinned and looked around. "Where's Susan?"

I looked at the clock behind the bar and got up and walked through the crowd to the back. Susan wasn't there. I stopped a waitress and asked if she'd seen a blonde go into the women's room.

"She left the bar ten minutes ago. She ditch you, Jimmy?"

"Happens all the time." I went to the counter where they have munchies and collected a paper plate of cheese, crackers, raw vegetables, and onion dip, and went back to the table.

"Susan split," I said.

"Aha. Sorry about that."

"Not your fault."

We sat awhile. Frank said, "Remember back in high school when you were going to be a lawyer and I was going to be a beach bum. What the hell ever happened? How about another drink?"

"Frank, how did you manage to get drunk before you came here?"

"Had a cocktail party at the firm this afternoon. One of those solidarity sessions, 'the firm that drinks together, etc.' But they ran out of booze." He turned and waved to the waitress.

"My theory is," he said, "if you're going to drink too much, you might as well do it right."

So we stayed on at the bar and drank and ate the food I'd collected, and I told Frank what had been happening. He insisted that we celebrate and he drank a toast to the demise of Stephen Littman. Later I called Julie from the booth in the bar. It was after midnight, and she was ready to go home. I said good-bye to Frank, left some money at the table, and went out. He was talking to the waitress and hardly noticed me.

I picked up a cab from the stand in front of the Meridien and had it drive me around to the entrance to Julie's building. She was waiting by the security desk downstairs, and we went back to her place.

CHAPTER SEVENTEEN

We're Just Friends

I WOKE THE NEXT morning in Julie's bed. When she saw I was awake she leaned forward and kissed me. It was a long kiss, and she came closer so that her whole body was against mine, and then she came over on top of me. I was half-asleep, and making love fit into the dream I'd been having.

When we finished she got up to pull on a green T-shirt and went into the bathroom. She came back out and said, "I've got croissants I can heat up," and went off toward the kitchen.

I used the bathroom, then found the copy of *Paris Review* interviews I'd been reading and climbed back into bed. I was feeling a little hung over and still half asleep. I looked at the room. It was blue—blue walls and blue enameled bureau, a dressing table, two bedside tables with reading lamps. There was a small supply of makeup on the dressing table and a photograph of me in a heavy blue frame on the bureau. I couldn't remember where she'd taken the photograph. There were no windows and no paintings or photographs on the walls. The only disorder was my own clothing, scattered on the hardwood floor.

It was basically a room for sleeping and making love.

Julie came in carrying a tray with a pot of coffee, two blue mugs, and a half-dozen croissants. She was still naked below the T-shirt, and I felt like pulling her back

139

on top of me. But when she'd put the tray at the foot of the bed and climbed in, the body language said clearly, "Don't touch." I sat up higher on the pillows.

"I was glad to catch you at work last night," I said. "I'd been at the Exchange with Frank."

"So you said. I never got down there. Sorry."

"How's the public offering?"

"We go to the printers next week."

She picked up a thick, typewritten document from the bedside table and began to read. "I ran into some strange developments yesterday," I said. She didn't seem to hear, but she answered.

"You were drunk."

"Before that. I beat up two professional gunmen."

"I don't feel like talking now. Is that okay?"

"Sure." I leaned across the bed and poured two coffees and handed one to Julie. We sat under the covers, reading and drinking the coffee. I was on my first croissant when she sighed and put the document back onto the bedside table. "Maybe we're seeing too much of each other," she said.

I put my book down. "You think so?"

She looked unhappy. "It's my job," she said. "I can't take distractions like you pressuring me to have dinner last night."

"I'm sorry, but I was hungry."

"I've thought this over very carefully," and the unhappy look dissolved—she just looked determined. "The problem is, you don't understand about being a lawyer. Did you think I could walk away last night? Would you, in the middle of an investigation, once things got moving?"

"I might take an hour for dinner." Once again, she didn't seem to hear me.

"The point is, I'm doing what I'm doing, and as long as that's the case I have to do things the right way. Don't you understand?"

"Sure. It's your decision. I take it you want to keep being a lawyer."

"I couldn't live like you—in that tiny apartment, driving that beat-up car. Don't you ever feel embarrassed? I think you do and you cover it up by joking. You're awfully self-righteous, you know. But you'd love to make the kind of money I do."

"You're unhappy. What does that have to do with me? Are you unhappy with me?"

"You said I should sell the condo. You certainly enjoy everything I've got here—you're just lazy—too lazy to get it yourself."

"Maybe. I'm glad you have nice things. It's pleasant, but it should make you happy."

"That's bullshit."

It certainly sounded like bullshit, but that's what happens when you argue about things that can't be resolved.

She said, "You think I should change jobs, but I don't want to be pressured into anything, and that's what you've been doing. Being a partner in a big firm is quite an accomplishment. I don't need advice, I'm a responsible grown-up. I make decisions every day affecting millions of dollars. Maybe what I need is some time on my own."

The coffee and croissants were getting cold at the end of the bed. I said, "I suppose I've been too concentrated on my own work to realize how unhappy you've been, kiddo. But whatever you want is okay by me."

"I think you're wonderful, Mallory. But I don't have the energy to deal with it. Maybe in a month, when I've got things worked out."

I couldn't help smiling. "We've only been together six weeks, kiddo. We're not serious enough to be separated for a month."

"Jokes."

"I do it to hide my embarrassment. You seeing somebody else? Somebody from work?"

"When would I have time? Don't start playing detective."

"Playing detective?"

"Do you want to stay to finish the croissants?"

"I'll pick up something later." I got out of the bed and

started dressing. She watched me dress, and when I finished I wasn't sure what to say.

She said, "Before you go, I want my key."

I smiled and dug the key out of my pocket. It's good to have something to do in awkward moments. "Have fun, kiddo. Call me if you need anything."

"I will call."

I went out of the bedroom and through the living room and made sure the lock on the front door locked behind me. Outside it was sunny and cool and I didn't notice any particular reaction, only a hollow feeling in the gut which could have been hunger. It's amazing how quickly things can happen—death and getting dumped. I was still feeling the glow from making love.

I stopped on Newbury Street to pick up a half-dozen croissants, then crossed to Marlborough for a long look up to my building. At that point the lobby was probably my safest way, but I went in cautiously, peering around the front door. I almost gave my third-floor neighbor heart failure. She dropped her mail, and I bent to help gather it, then went up. It felt good to use the front door.

I had already started a pot of coffee when I decided to check in with Phoebe. It was time to get things moving with Littman. The phone rang seven times, then the maid answered. She said Phoebe had gone to the hospital in the ambulance with Mrs. Streeter.

Morgan was listed in critical condition at Beth Israel Hospital. I drove out there, parked on Brookline Avenue, and jogged across to the front entrance. It's one of those newer hospitals where they've painted the walls with bright blocks of primary colors to cheer people up. I wondered if in fifty years it would look as sad and dingy as most of the older hospitals in Boston. I asked the woman at the desk where I could find Morgan Streeter and she looked through a Rolodex and told me Morgan was in the intensive-care unit, no visitors permitted.

"Where would the family be waiting?"

"There's a visitors' room on the third floor, left after you come off the elevators."

I rode to the third floor and went into the visitors' room. It was sunny and cheerful, windows looking out to the green area behind the hospital. Melissa and Phoebe weren't in there. Out in the hall the duty nurse told me they'd gone home—the daughter had been extremely upset. I asked if I could speak with Morgan's doctor, and she said he'd be in surgery with another patient until the early afternoon.

I walked back to the elevator, intending to drive over to the Streeter house, and ran into a harassed-looking Mangenello. He took my arm and led me to a small examination room opposite the nurse's station. He closed the door and leaned against the table, putting one fat hand into a stirrup. I stood against the cabinet full of medicines, plastic gloves, and tongue depressors.

"What happened?" I asked.

"Poisoned. The secretary thinks it was in the tea she drinks. She'd been feeling sick since the break-in at the house, and it kept getting worse. We've got the lab boys over there now."

"It couldn't be cyanide. She'd be dead."

"The doctor says maybe rat poison. That punk the other night must've got in the house after all. Unless you figure the daughter or private secretary?"

"That punk was Stephen Littman, Simon. I'm sure of it."

"It's possible. But what about Susan Johnson? You said she studied savate too."

"I did say that. My question is, why not cyanide this time? Why something less certain?"

"Maybe he ran out. Maybe he threw it away after killing Johnson. Or maybe the old lady was trying to kill herself and used whatever came to hand. Go on the assumption that she'd never had any cyanide to begin with. That the whole thing just got to her."

"She didn't leave a note."

"Old Phoebe would have burned anything like that. She's the one who brought her into the hospital."

"Did you speak with Melissa?"

"She was as close to hysterical as you can get without screaming out loud. It could be an act, but either way, there's no help there. The doctor says two or three days before Morgan's conscious. If she wanted to die, she came very close."

"Or somebody came very close."

"So I'm posting a twenty-four-hour guard on her."

He frowned and beat the heel of his hand against the stirrup. "You get the feeling we've been here before? I hate poison. The damned stuff's got too long a fuse."

"It's cleaner than gunshot wounds, Simon. Why not grab Littman now? Hold him for questioning. For that matter, pull in Susan Johnson."

"Right. You ever try to pry information out of a lawyer? Even if one of them's it, we wouldn't get a scrap, and in five minutes there'd be ten soldiers with briefcases filing writs and maybe even a suit for false arrest. You know that. I'll wait for solid evidence."

"When can the DA go in with a court order on the trusts?"

"I'm not sure he will. Same problem, no hard evidence. And you can bet those hotshot lawyers will fight it every inch. I'm going with you a long way on this because I think you've got something, but for now I think we'd better wait till Morgan comes out of it and can ask for the damned accounting herself."

"There's got to be another approach to this thing, Simon. Somebody's out there trying to kill people, and we're talking fighting with lawyers."

"Half my job is fighting with lawyers. You get any line on Bensen?"

"I haven't tried."

"Don't bother. He's disappeared."

"Probably down in Miami taking advantage of the off-season rates. He knows I've got his name."

"And he's quaking in his boots, right?"

"He's got a certain respect for me, but it's you cops he really likes to avoid."

Somebody knocked on the door and we had to vacate the room. Mangenello told me to be patient and went off to arrange for security on the intensive-care ward. I went back down to the lobby and, coming off the elevator, spotted Susan at the front entrance. She came ahead and met me. She wore a blue linen suit very similar to the one Julie had for work, and her hair looked damp, like she'd just come from the shower. I liked the way the blue linen looked with her hair.

"How's Morgan?" she said.

"You turn up in the strangest places. She's going to make it. What are you doing here?"

"I called the house and Phoebe told me. I'd wanted to talk with Morgan about all this."

"She's in intensive care. No visitors. Why don't we get some coffee? Did you drive over?"

"I took a cab."

"Good. I'm parked in front. There's a place nearby that sells the best croissants in Boston. Let's get half a dozen and some coffee and sit in the car and talk. I've got a craving for croissants."

"Okay, Max."

I said, "Good," and we went out and crossed Brookline Avenue to the Rambler.

Driving around the corner to Park Drive I said, "Why'd you walk out on me last night?"

"I guess all that talk about Stephen made me nervous. I wanted to think. Besides, I had that dinner date."

"What did you think?"

"I think Stephen would be capable of stealing from the trusts if he found a way to do it—but I can't believe he'd kill Caleb."

"What if Caleb caught him stealing?"

"I don't know. You've got to remember he's my friend.

When you come down to it, I really can't believe anybody'd want to kill Caleb."

"That's not very productive thinking." I turned at Beacon Street and made an illegal U-turn at the next light to come around to the Savoy French Bakery. I double-parked in front and asked Susan how she liked her coffee.

"Black, no sugar."

"And the croissants? Anything fancy?"

"Just plain."

Inside the shop smelled of pastry and chocolate. I got two black coffees and six plain croissants and took them back to the car, handing them in through the window. I drove around the corner and stopped under the shade of the maple trees on St. Mary's Street, beside a small park.

Susan made small appreciative noises when she'd finished the first croissant. "That's better than anything I've had in Paris."

I said, "What do you know about Melissa Streeter?"

"She must be going crazy about now. I don't know a whole lot about her, Max, except that Caleb didn't like her. She was a disturbed child, and he never had much patience with weak people. The only time I've sat down with her was in the car at the funeral, and then she didn't say a word."

"She told me she and Caleb used to climb mountains in New Hampshire."

"Caleb never climbed a mountain in his life."

"That's what I figured." I dipped my second croissant into the coffee. "Mangenello tells me you're going off to Greece soon. You don't want to find out who killed Caleb before you go?"

"There doesn't seem to be any point to that. I know everyone thinks I should wait."

"Where you going in Greece?"

"I spent two weeks on Ios three years ago. I've always wanted to go back and spend two or three months. Caleb and I were going to take a cruise. Would it be corny to say he'd have wanted me to go?"

"Yes. You staying in Boston until you leave?"

"I'll go back to the house. It'll be strange, but I love the place."

"It's a nice house."

"Yes. Caleb bought it after his first wife died, when he moved out of the place in Brookline."

I got my third croissant from the bag and watched two children come through the gate at the opposite side of the park. Their mother came in after them, pushing a baby in a stroller. Maybe she was a governess.

"Do you think I killed Caleb, Max?"

"Not really. I'm just playing detective. For example, I'd like to find out who you had dinner with last night."

"I had dinner with Stephen."

"That's what I figured. Did he pledge you his undying love?"

"He mostly talked about how well he was doing at C & M, how much money he was making. I suppose for Stephen that could have been a pledge of love. I told him you'd questioned me about embezzling from the Johnson trust."

"How'd he react?"

"He was amused."

"Good for him. Tell me what would happen if he was stealing from the trust, but before there was any accounting he managed to put the money back in."

"He couldn't steal from the trust, Max. I explained that to you last night."

"Some of the assets must be held in cash. If he was taking small chunks from more than one client's cash accounts, it could add up to something. You're the lawyer, figure how he could get away with it. As a hypothetical."

She thought a minute and I finished my last croissant. "I suppose there would be the cash accounts," she said. "And when a fund changes to a new investment advisor there's always a period when more cash than usual is held in the accounts—the proceeds from stock sales that haven't been reinvested, that kind of thing. He could drain off some of that money. But he couldn't switch investment advisors very often without arousing suspicion."

"But it's a big estate and it wouldn't have to be often. Or maybe he did it too often, and Caleb caught on. But say now somebody's on to him. He decides to play it safe and puts all the stolen money back. What happens? Is he safe?"

"That kind of thing would show in any formal accounting, especially if people were looking for it. But he might get away with it if all you were looking for was total assets."

"He could just stick the money back in and be home free?"

"There'd be other factors. For example, to fully reimburse the assets he'd have to put in money of his own."

"How do you mean?"

"Well, he'd be depleting the accounts by more than just what he took out in cash. Say he takes fifty thousand. He'd put it into a safe deposit box or something, because if it starts earning interest in a personal account, the IRS would want to know where he got the capital. That means the stolen money wouldn't be making money, but he'd have to keep paying out the normal dividends to the beneficiaries, and to do that he'd have to start depleting the principal. If he wanted to make the trusts whole again, he'd have to pay back whatever he'd stolen, plus whatever principal he'd paid out as phony income."

"So if Caleb'd asked for an accounting, he might not have had enough to cover himself. Unless he borrowed the money."

"If I know Stephen, he'd already be living at the end of his credit rating. Not that I think he did it, Max. Steve is weird, but not that weird. I've always felt sorry for him—being the way he is, he never had any real friends. Except for me. He was very loyal to me."

"I think for a lawyer you're remarkably uncritical about people."

"Maybe that's why I quit. How about you? You're talking to me about all this. What if I killed Caleb?"

"Talking wouldn't hurt. Morgan's safe under twenty-four-hour guard. When she comes round we'll get an accounting, a full accounting."

"I won't tell Stephen what you've told me. I'm not going to see him again."

"Go ahead and tell him. He must have a hint by now anyway. Maybe he's not guilty. If he was, I'd expect him to be headed for Mexico by now."

"Steve's excessively self-confident. It's one of his endearing qualities."

"I don't remember detecting any others." We'd both finished our coffee. Susan said she should get back to her friends' place—somebody was coming to fix the garbage disposal.

I drove the Rambler out to Beacon and through Kenmore Square to Mass. Ave. and turned at Marlborough so I could circle back and come up Susan's block. I looked up Marlborough when I made the turn.

She said, "You live up there, don't you?"

"Yes."

"It's right around the corner. Invite me over some time?"

"Sure." I pulled up to the condos and she got out. Before she closed the door she leaned back in and said, "Call me. I want to know about Morgan. And you're right to trust me." I watched her go in the front door. She moved well, in a way that reminded me of Barbi. Then she was inside and I put the Rambler in gear and took off.

CHAPTER EIGHTEEN

Secrets of
the Heart

I DIDN'T GO home. I drove back to the Trojan, called Mangenello, and told him what Susan'd had to say.

"Sounds to me like she had it all worked out in advance."

"I think she's been thinking it over, but what does that mean? It could just mean she wants us to nail Littman. We've got to get that accounting of the trust funds before we know which way to go. If you can't budge the DA, that means making sure nothing happens to Morgan."

He said he had security on Morgan absolutely tight, and hung up.

I sat at the desk and looked out the window. Across Charles Street the Sack Cinema was showing two horror movies. Julie loved horror movies—I hate them. I hadn't let myself think about her. With that kind of thing there was a chance she'd call in a day or two, or she might never call.

I rang up Phoebe Goodrich. She sounded perfectly calm but said Melissa was on tranquilizers and couldn't talk. Did I have anything special to report?

I said I'd speak with her again after I'd had a chance to talk with Mrs. Streeter.

I sat some more and thought about my options. From what Mangenello had told me it would be Friday at the earliest before Morgan was up and around. The cops would be watching over her, but I could protect her indirectly. I decided to follow Stephen Littman.

*   *   *

Wednesday I woke at 5:00 A.M. with the alarm and
packed a working breakfast—half a dozen scones from
Warburton's, a quart of fat blueberries, and a thermos of
strong French roast coffee. At the last minute I filled a
pint flask with cherry brandy and stuck it into the basket
with the other things. Both the basket and the flask—a
pewter one with my initials cut into it—had been gifts
from Julie.

Outside the air was cool and damp, with a fresh breeze
from the ocean. I was hungry and looked forward to my
picnic breakfast. Mangenello'd given me Littman's address, halfway up Beacon Hill on Mount Vernon Street.
It was one of the oldest neighborhoods in Boston and a
very good address, even for somebody making a law firm
salary.

I'd thought about picking up a rental car to avoid the
risk that Littman would recognize the Rambler from the
two times he'd seen it at the Bombay, but decided if he
did spot me I'd just go to Plan B—confrontation. The
shock might be good for him. I hadn't been joking when
I told Susan I expected him to head for Mexico. If he did
take off, at least we'd know where we stood.

There were no parking spaces on Mount Vernon. I
cruised around the block until a couple carrying coolers
and beach equipment came out of one of the buildings
and headed for a big Mercedes. My waiting for them
made them hurry, and the guy looked back and scowled
at me. Once in the space I started dipping scones into
coffee and eating the blueberries.

The brick houses along the street were old and stately,
big shade trees in front and brick sidewalks going down
the steep incline of the hill. A book requires too much
concentration for a stakeout, so when I finished the scones
I read the paper and kept one eye on the door to Littman's
building. It was almost nine before he came out, crossed
the street, and started up the hill. He didn't spot me.

I got out and followed. Crossing the Common there

were lots of people dressed for work and going in the same direction, up the hill to Park Street Church and the beginning of downtown. We went down Winter Street, where delivery trucks lined both curbs. There was a nice early morning smell from the bakeries, and the crowd moved more purposefully, as if everyone was ready for work.

We went past Filene's and Woolworth's and down to the building in Post Office Square. Littman entered and went up in the brass elevator and I took a position in the small park in the Square where I could see the two main exits from the building. It wasn't the best situation, but if I'd tried to hang out in the lobby the security guards would've moved in on me.

I stayed there until noon, then circulated with the crowd in the lobby. Littman didn't come down. At two I bought a hot dog and went back to my bench. At five the crowds showed up again and I circulated. At six the security guards locked all exits except the one by their station, and at seven Littman came down and signed out. I followed him down to the marketplace at Faneuil Hall.

Faneuil Hall was once a small produce market between Scollay Square and the granite warehouses of the waterfront. Now the warehouses have been converted into shops and the marketplace is the hub of the city's tourist trade. Hundreds of people were milling about under young trees in the spaces between the three main buildings. Couples sat at tables outside cafés having a drink and watching the tourists. It looked very friendly and European. Littman went past the cafés and the outdoor flower shop and across the street and into the Bostonian Hotel. He met a tall man in a gray business suit with an oversized briefcase. The guy was as plainly a lawyer as a soldier in uniform is plainly a soldier. They got on the elevator to the rooftop restaurant.

I went around the corner to the old Italian market. On Wednesday night there are only a few pushcart vendors. I went directly to the shop of a meat seller who looks like a demented Burt Lancaster and stands on the sidewalk smiling diabolically and asking every passerby, "Want some meat?" I bought two hot Italian sausages on French rolls with lots of peppers and mustard, picked up a quart of orange juice from the shop next door, and took it all back to the bench outside the flower market.

Upstairs, I knew Littman was undoubtedly dining on trout served on a bed of cucumbers, avocados, and limes. The Bostonian specializes in nouvelle cuisine. It also has one of the best wine selections in town. I once had lunch there with friends and I'd called the day before to make reservations. When we arrived there were matchbooks at every place with "Mallory" engraved on them in gold. When the entrées came under silver covers three waiters stood behind us to lift the covers simultaneously, and we all said, "Ohhh!" The lunch for three cost as much as a one-way ticket to Europe on People's Express.

I took a bite of the hot sausage and washed it down with orange juice. It was very good. When I'd finished both sandwiches I went back and bought another. Then I watched the tourists eating. Someone once did a study showing that people who went into one end of the main market building behind Faneuil Hall bought food an average of 2.7 times before they escaped out the other side.

Just before ten-thirty Littman and the tall guy came out, and I followed Littman up the stairs to Government Center and over the hill to Mount Vernon Street. There were three parking tickets on the windshield of the Rambler. By midnight the flask of cherry brandy had been empty for an hour, the lights had been out in Littman's apartment for fifteen minutes, and I went home.

The next day we went through the same routine, but at noon Littman came out of his office building and walked down Milk Street toward the waterfront. We crossed Atlantic Avenue to the plaza at the Boston Aquarium, by the looming sculpture that's supposed to represent the movement of the waves and instead looks like a cooked lobster, and at Long Wharf Littman bought a ticket and went aboard a cruise boat.

I asked at the ticket booth and they told me the boat was going on a forty-five-minute lunch cruise of Boston Harbor. I moved away and watched Littman climb the stairs to the sundeck and lean against the opposite rail to survey the skyline.

I was debating whether to risk getting on the boat when I spotted a guy with a piece of medical tape across the bridge of his nose. He bought a ticket and went aboard and up to the sundeck. It was my friend, Bensen's thug. He leaned against the rail a few feet from Littman. I said, "Aha."

So I got a ticket and waited until the boat was crowded with tourists and office workers. I went aboard just before the deckhands closed the gate and started uncleating the heavy bow and stern lines. The captain turned her in the channel, sounded the air horn, and we went out past the Aquarium and the brightly colored sailboats at the moorings in front of Harbor Towers.

Littman and the thug were talking, leaning out over the rail. I knew that with the wind I wouldn't be able to hear any of their conversation. People had brought bag lunches onto the boat. I bought two dogs and a beer from the bar on the lower deck and stood against the rail and listened to the loudspeaker as the captain described the wharfs along the harborfront of South Boston.

I felt good. It was nice to see the skyline rising up out of the green, windblown water, the way sailors see it. It made me remember that Boston is still a commercial fishing port and that it got started only because of its good, deep harbor. Every once in a while I went over and checked on Littman and the thug, still deep in conversation. That was fine by me.

I stayed near the bow until we docked and the thug got off. Littman got off a minute later, looking unhappy, and I followed him back up Milk Street. When he was safely up the elevator I went to the phone booth and called Buddy Minasian. George answered and said he'd pull Buddy out of his game. A minute later Buddy's voice said, "Jimmy, I've been trying to reach you. Can you come out? I got something hot."

"Tell me on the phone, Buddy."

"For you I'll break a rule. But remember, I never told you this. The scoop is, Johnson was clean. Didn't owe anybody anything. This guy Littman, though, is another story. He went out to Vegas about a month ago and dropped a bundle playing craps and blackjack. My friends out there figure almost a hundred grand. He's been tooling out there pretty often ever since, including last weekend. And here's something even more interesting. Recently the guy has gone to our friend Frank Bensen, and took out a big loan. Another hundred grand."

"Why would Bensen loan money to Littman?"

"The guy's a gambler and Bensen knows him. And he's a hotshot lawyer, right? Bensen likes to get that type on the hook."

"When did he go to Bensen?"

"Not until sometime last week. I don't know the exact day, but it was before you talked with me. That could explain those heavies, Jimmy. If you were leaning on Littman, Bensen would want to protect his investment. I also hear Bensen's not too happy with you—you really steal one of his cars?"

"Something like that. Any word on what he plans to do about it?"

"I heard he was headed to Bermuda for a vacation. He's got a big house down there."

"That would be nice. Got anything else?"

"That's it. I better get back and bleed some more for these bastards. Let me know if you need anything more."

I didn't need anything more. The rest of the afternoon I sat in the park, sometimes going over to circulate through the lobby. At seven he came down again and walked to the Common and Mount Vernon. This time there were only two parking tickets on the Rambler, and Littman came out thirty minutes later. He'd changed into tan slacks and a blue polo shirt. He got into a new BMW parked across the street and started down the hill.

I followed. We went out past the Public Garden to Berkeley and the entrance onto Storrow Drive. I thought he might be headed for Arlington, but he got off at the exit for Kenmore Square. We went on up Beacon and then off at St. Mary's and up Ivy Street in Brookline.

That was a problem. It meant he was going to the Streeter house, and in that neighborhood it wouldn't be easy to keep the Rambler out of sight and still maintain a watch on the house. But I didn't want to duck it because I was afraid Melissa might be in danger. So I followed him in and stopped two blocks up from the small park of oak trees.

Melissa was waiting at the curb in front of the house, just as she'd waited for me almost two weeks earlier. I took a pair of binoculars from the glove compartment and watched the car. When she got in she kissed him.

It all made sense, of course. They drove past and I saw her recognize the Rambler and turn to say something to Littman. I U-turned and followed. He didn't make any attempt to lose me on the way back to Beacon Hill. He dropped Melissa at the door to his apartment building.

I got out and called to her, but she gave me one quick look and disappeared inside. Littman left the BMW idling on the hill and came back to stand in front of the Rambler.

"Why are you following us?"

I said, "First you steal Morgan's money, now you're stealing her daughter. You shouldn't be so greedy."

"What are you talking about?"

"I'm talking about Las Vegas and bright lights and free money."

He looked just a little surprised, then said, "It may interest you to know that Morgan Streeter requested an accounting of the funds in the Johnson trust last week, and I've just finished going over the accounts with John

Masterson. When she is well enough, I think he will confirm to her that the trusts are quite intact and have been earning a respectable income.''

"That won't stand up under a real accounting."

"There will be no 'real' accounting, as you so quaintly put it."

He went back to the BMW. A big Mercedes was waiting behind the Rambler, and I noticed it was the same couple who'd been going to the beach the day before.

I went straight to the Trojan and tried to reach Morgan Streeter at the hospital. The night nurse told me she was out of intensive care, but still heavily sedated and not able to speak with anyone. I managed to get the nurse to connect me with Morgan's doctor. The doctor sounded harassed, but told me his patient was resting well, and I should be able to speak with her late the next morning. But not that night. It was impossible.

I called Mangenello. He didn't have time to talk, but told me his men were keeping the vigil at Morgan's side, and not to worry. I told him I'd speak with him the next day, hung up, went out to the Rambler and drove back to Marlborough Street.

All I could do was wait. I couldn't even call Julie. I made myself a gin and tonic with Booth's gin and lime, got out *The Autobiography of Alice B. Toklas*, and waited.

CHAPTER NINETEEN

Partners in Crime

I MET WITH Morgan Streeter at Beth Israel the next day. I had to wait until after eleven when the doctors told me I could go in for fifteen minutes if I promised not to excite her. There was a short Brookline cop on a folding chair outside the private room. I was on the list of people permitted in to see her, but he looked doubtful anyway and stuck his head inside to ask, "You wanna see a Mallory, Mrs. Streeter?" The gruff voice coming out of the squat body made me think of a Honda Civic with a broken muffler. He waved me in with a suspicious look and I shut the door in his face.

It was a sunny, white room, with no flowers. It was hard to believe, but Morgan sat up in the bed drinking tea. Somehow the souvenir cup with Queen Elizabeth painted on the side had found its way to the hospital. Morgan was thin and gray, but her eyes were still bright, and her mouth was set in a grim line.

"I came to make a report," I said.

"Just tell me, Mr. Mallory. Do you know who killed my father?"

There was no place to sit, so I stayed upright in front of the bed. I could see out the window, down to the lawns in back of the hospital. I said, "You'll probably recognize the name. He works for John Masterson. Stephen Littman."

She set down her tea cup and looked away from me,

out the window. "I know Stephen Littman, Mr. Mallory. I had an interview with my daughter this morning and she informs me he is her fiancé. I doubt that he killed my father."

"I'm sorry, but the evidence suggests otherwise. He was embezzling money from the family trust accounts and Caleb caught him at it—or at least went to him with his suspicions. And Littman killed him. We need to talk about that and about Melissa."

She looked at me then. "I'm not interested in talking. If Stephen Littman murdered Father then why haven't the police arrested him? I'm ill and tired of the whole mess." She actually tried to smile at me. She said, "I'm confident that you've done your best, Mr. Mallory, but now I want your investigation to stop."

"That can't happen, Mrs. Streeter. You're sick and maybe you're not thinking too clearly. But that can't happen."

"I pay the bills and will determine what happens. I spoke with John Masterson this morning and he assures me the trust accounts are intact. Since depleted accounts is the basis of your accusation, I think his information proves your error. It's enough to satisfy me."

"Stephen recently borrowed a large sum of money from a person with underworld connections. If necessary we can prove that. He used the money to pay back the trust. He'd lost the original money gambling in Las Vegas. We can prove that too. When your father guessed what was happening Littman killed him."

"No." She closed her eyes, put a hand to her heart, and leaned back into the pillows.

"Closing your eyes won't make me go away. I know what's happening here. You think Melissa's involved in this. She is. That night of the break-in—they set that up to look like somebody came in from the outside, but she let Littman into the house. Or she planted the poison herself. The poison for you."

"She did not. It's he . . ."

"Right. And now Stephen will marry Melissa and the three of you will settle down to live happily ever after in the house in Brookline. Is that what you plan?"

"I will deal with Mr. Littman."

"What will you do, pay him off?"

She glared at me. "I'm asking you to leave me alone. The police will take care of the matter. Your investigation has done more harm than good. Look where I am now."

She saw it wasn't working, so she lay back another moment, then tried again.

"Mr. Mallory, nothing will bring back my father. If you won't consider my wishes, then consider Melissa. She has been in and out of institutions since her childhood—mental institutions, Mr. Mallory. A severe trauma now, just after Father's death, could be her ruin."

"You can't protect her by letting Stephen Littman get away with murder. And you can't take the risk of his trying to kill you. Get her back to the doctors. If what she's done is the result of mental illness, she won't be prosecuted—not if you use your influence to prevent it."

"You don't understand. Melissa has been very ill ever since my mother's death in an automobile accident. She was in the car at the time. She developed a fantasy that she had murdered her grandmother. Any suggestion that she was involved in Father's death would be disastrous. She's the important thing in my life—more important than anything. What if the police wanted to put her away? I can't let that happen. Even if I were to die."

She closed her eyes again. I said, "You've got to deal with this. It's not going to go away and it's not going to stay a secret."

She turned and began to fumble in a drawer of the table beside the bed. "I don't want to discuss it further. I asked Phoebe to prepare this for you." She held out a slip of blue paper she'd taken from the drawer, but I didn't take it. She dropped it on the side of the bed. It was a check.

"I'm going to continue with this," I said.

"I'm instructing you not to."

I still didn't look at the check. I said, "For your sake as well as Melissa's, I'm going to continue with this," and walked out of the room.

I brushed past the guard at the door, and I was twenty feet down the corridor when Melissa came around the corner from the visitors' room. I'd kept my temper up till then, but she shrank back from me instinctively, and for some reason that made me angry. I said, "What did you tell your mother about yourself and Littman?"

"What are you talking about?"

"Did you tell her you'd killed your grandfather? That you'd tried to kill her? I can't believe she's protecting you—she almost died, and she's protecting you. Can you live with that?"

"That's not true. The poison just made her sick."

"That's a lie, Melissa. You tell lies."

"What do you want from me?" And I finally realized she really was crazy. I could almost see her slipping over the edge, one push from me and I was sure she would be gone. I realized I was just one more asshole in a lifetime of assholes, and I was clubbing her.

The cop came toward us. Morgan had got out of bed and was standing outside her room, supporting herself against the doorframe. She looked old and vulnerable with the white hospital gown billowing around her thin legs. A nurse started down the hall after her.

I told the cop to back off and stalked down the corridor to the elevator.

Downstairs I sat on a bench and breathed deeply for a few minutes. Then I drove to the Trojan and put in a call to Mangenello. For once he wasn't in, and I left a message. Next I called Michael Garrison. He answered over the conference speakers and I said, "Michael, please turn off the speakers and shut the door. This is confidential."

"Hang on." I heard him walk across the room and shut

the door, then the static on the line stopped and his voice came back sounding normal. "What's up?"

I told him about the investigation into Caleb Johnson's death and Littman and the trust and Melissa. "I'd like the last part of what I told you, the part about Melissa Streeter's involvement, to go down under attorney-client privilege, Michael. I'll send you a check for your retainer later today."

"Sure, it's one dollar and other good and valuable consideration, including that time you saved my ass in Chelsea's Bar. What would you like me to do, Jimmy? Put some pressure on Masterson?"

"Exactly. You know him?"

"I know some of his partners. There's been talk over there about forcing the old guy into retirement. He makes mistakes. If what you say is true, this was the royal fuck-up. I might be able to raise some eyebrows, get the other partners interested in doing a full-scale accounting."

"If you can, anything I have is yours."

"Crew for me when I take the boat down to Newport in September."

"You got a date."

We hung up, and the phone rang almost immediately. It was Mangenello. I told him everything I'd learned since we last spoke—about Littman's trip to Vegas, the loan from Bensen to pay off the embezzled money, and finally Littman's meeting with Bensen's man. I left out all the parts that included Melissa. I figured the world owed her one protector. She'd helped to murder her father, and maybe did in her grandmother, but I wasn't ready to throw her to the lions. Besides, I was still working for her mother.

For the first time since I'd met him, Mangenello sounded excited. He said, "I just got something myself. A family in Brookline had a party about a month ago and afterward they discovered a bottle of scotch missing from the liquor cabinet—*the* bottle. At the time they didn't want the cops involved, they spoke to the caterers and then took off for the south of France. Supposed to be there till the end of summer, but the husband got sick and they rushed back to get him into an American hospital. That's when they heard about Johnson and the poisoned bottle. Littman was at the party, Mallory. So was Melissa Streeter. I've got men talking to everyone on the guest list."

I told him that was great, then sprang it on him. I said, "On the basis of the new evidence, Simon, do you think you can get the DA to go for a court-ordered accounting?" I told him I'd spoken with Morgan and she wasn't going to cooperate.

"What the hell's going on? We've come too far for bullshit like that. What we got is circumstantial evidence, hearsay, garbage. We need to pin him for embezzling. There's a chance the DA'd go in, but why not Morgan?"

"Who knows?"

"What do you mean 'who knows?' You keeping something from me? Is Melissa Streeter involved in this somehow?"

"If I was keeping something from you, Simon, would I tell you?"

"Don't give me that crap. I questioned that girl the night of the break-in at the house, and I've got my doubts about her."

"I'm interested in bringing Johnson's murderer to justice, Simon. I also want to make sure nobody innocent goes down with him."

"You asshole—you're no knight in shining armor and she's no fair maiden. If you've got evidence implicating Melissa Streeter, I want it. If the old lady's stonewalling us, I want to know why. We're on thin ice here. We're talking pushing around hotshot lawyers. One of them's the goddamned DA."

"Talk to him," I said. "Then we'll see what happens." I hung up, disconnected the phone, and switched off Della.

CHAPTER TWENTY

Two Heads Are Better Than One

SATURDAY MORNING I sat behind my desk at the Trojan and wrote out everything I knew and didn't know about Stephen Littman and his connection to Caleb Johnson. Sometimes it helps to make lists. I told myself that an accounting would be the easy way to go, but if for some reason the DA wouldn't go for it, I'd find another way.

I'd been at it for an hour and hadn't come up with anything brilliant, except maybe going to Bermuda to kidnap Frank Bensen and get him to talk, or kidnapping Littman and beating the truth out of him. Of the two ideas, I really only considered the second one seriously. I'd also plugged the phone back in and taken some crap from Mangenello, but nothing had come of that.

At ten o'clock Edgar knocked and stuck his head in. He half pulled Susan into the room, winked at me like he'd brought my favorite kind of donut, and scuttled out. She had her hair down and wore faded blue jeans and a green T-shirt. She was smiling and holding a paper sack from the Savoy French Bakery.

"I would have called first," she said, "but I was scared you'd tell me to get lost." She sat in the chair next to the desk. The light from the window caught her blonde hair and I noticed again the wedge of amber in the blue of the one eye. I thought it was something you would probably forget about and then remember again whenever you saw her.

She said, "How's Morgan?"

"Well enough to fire me."

She looked puzzled and I said, "I'll explain." Then I told her everything. I told her about the break-in at the Streeter house, the Center for Savate Training, Littman's trip to Vegas and his loan from Frank Bensen. I left out Peter Streeter's theory about Melissa's paternity, and I kept vague the parts about Melissa's involvement with Littman—only said that Morgan was afraid she might be involved—but otherwise I gave it all.

Susan was quiet for a moment, then said, "That's something. Thank you for telling me."

Edgar opened the door and came in with two mugs of steaming coffee. Susan looked startled, then gave him a smile. He brought the mugs to the desk, and I swear he half bowed to her. She offered him a croissant, but he waved her off and went out, smirking at me.

I said, "It's funny. Edgar usually doesn't like people. Can I have a croissant?"

"They're for you." She raised her mug and blew on the coffee to cool it.

"What are you going to do?"

"Keep working. I'm hoping Mangenello can get the DA to go for a court ordered accounting."

She reached across the desk for my list and started to read it. "And in the meantime," she said, "you're writing everything down, trying to make it come out right?"

"Without much luck. But I figure his whole structure rests on support from Morgan and Melissa. There's got to be a weak point there."

She read aloud an item from the list. " 'Cyanide source.' That would be a chemical manufacturer. Choate & Masterson represents chemical companies. When we first started work, there was a public offering for a company named IBC Corp. That was six years ago, but IBC manufactured a lot of chemicals with a cyanide base. I remember that because the environmental concerns connected with the waste cyanide were risk factors in the offering."

"Good memory. That was six years ago. Would Littman still have contact with anyone from the company?"

"For a long time he was great friends with the president. Stephen has a knack for getting close to important people. Like Caleb. He played racketball with this guy every Thursday night. I don't know if he still sees him."

"So we can check. And if he was at the plant recently and dipped into the cyanide tanks or whatever, people might have seen him. It'd be all we'd need."

"I can't believe this," she said. "A year ago Steve and I were working together at the law firm and I hadn't even met Caleb."

I started eating a croissant. "Weren't you and he working on the same stuff? Including the Johnson trusts?"

"No, I was a corporate attorney. I met Caleb at a party. Fell head over heels. He was a charmer."

"Some people I know wouldn't agree."

"Oh, he had a mean streak in him. He was married to a real bitch for close to twenty-five years, and that can sour a man. But I think I made a real difference to him."

"Why did you keep your marriage secret?"

"It wasn't secret, Max. He suddenly got the idea we should get things settled. Maybe he had a premonition. He felt financial security was one of the big things he could offer me, and that meant marriage. He was in love for the first time, you know—really, and he was sixty-five years old. We both knew he'd probably die while I was young. It bothered him that most of his money was tied up in trusts controlled by Morgan."

"Did you love him?"

"That's a rotten question, Max."

"You don't seem that touched by all this—not like you're grieving, and not like you're really in shock."

"I should be dressed in black and wailing, right? I'm a young widow, so that's the way I should be—that, or counting his money. Doesn't seem fair."

"Maybe I expected anger—when I told you about Littman."

"This is the way I am, Max. I can't change that. And

I'm trying to help." She took a drink of coffee and watched me carefully.

"A friend once told me you talked a lot about marrying a rich client to get out of the law firm."

"Stupid thing to say, wasn't it? It was my running joke just before I left the firm. It's what people were thinking anyway, so I guess I was throwing it back in their faces. You think I killed Caleb, Max?"

"No. Never have."

"Do you think Stephen's going to get away with it?"

"No. Not unless he poisons my croissants." I looked down at the croissants and then at the list and had an idea. "As the widow, aren't you entitled to a final accounting of the income from the trust? Wouldn't there be undistributed income that's attributable to the period before Caleb's death?"

"You'd have made a good lawyer, Max. Not as far as I know, unless maybe distributions hadn't been made on schedule. I suppose I could make an argument that an accounting's necessary to assure that the income prior to his death was distributed on a timely basis and properly credited to me. I could ask for an audit, just as verification. Normally I don't think anybody'd object to that, but I don't know about now. It would help if I had some favorable cases to show them. I could research it."

"How long would that take?"

"Could be just a few hours. I'm rusty, but BU's library is open all weekend."

"I'll fix it with Frank Burger to set you up in his firm's library. Frank's the guy you met at the Exchange—the rude one. I don't want you running into Stephen at a public library."

"Okay, Max. It might work."

I called Frank at home, he wasn't there so I tried work. He answered after the first ring. He sounded tired.

I said, "Hello, trooper. Been up all night?"

"What day is it?"

"Never mind that. Think a friend could come in on the sly to do some research? It's Susan Johnson."

"Attractive blonde female, very rich? Since when is she a friend? Didn't she murder someone? Send her over."

"Five minutes."

We finished our coffee and I ate the last croissant. Susan made me bring the empty mugs down to Edgar on the way out. I told him I was taking her downtown, then going home to Marlborough Street.

We drove through the maze of one-way streets to Frank's building. He'd cleared us past the security desk, and I went in with Susan as far as the elevator. Just before the door closed, she gave me a big grin and a high sign and said, "Wish me luck."

On my way out the two middle-aged security guards grinned at me wistfully and I said, "It's all right, guys, she's not mine." I took the Rambler back to Marlborough Street. Walking up the block I spotted Mangenello's car at the hydrant in front of my building. He was drinking coffee. I got into the passenger side and said, "Watching over me?"

"I stopped at the health club and they told me you were headed this way." He tossed the empty cup into the back seat.

"I'm getting too old for this work. Bad news from the DA. He's John Masterson's nephew, can you believe it? He spoke with Uncle Jack yesterday and got full assurances that everything was fine with the trust funds, that Morgan Streeter agrees one hundred percent, and that you and I are nuts. They were considering a suit for defamation, but the DA did you a favor and talked them out of it. He won't do anything now without ironclad evidence—like maybe a confession."

"Anything from the people at the party where the bottle was stolen?"

"Nothing yet. It was a big party, and who's gonna remember somebody going for a bottle of scotch? I was crazy to think that was anything."

"I got something, talking with Susan." I told him about IBC Corp.

"I'll get somebody on it. In the meantime, I've got my own tail on Littman. Gotta shut that barn door. You and Susan getting cozy?"

"Her husband just got killed, Simon."

"Stranger things have happened. She's cute."

"Forget it."

"Fine. Remember that discussion we had about Melissa Streeter? You got anything else to tell me?"

"Nope."

"Fine. If it's any consolation, I think Littman's goose is cooked for all practical purposes. They may be telling us we're crazy, but they'll be watching him carefully from now on. And I bet Bensen's on his back."

"We're on his back, Simon. He can't pull this off."

"We nail him, Mallory, I'm gonna buy you all the beer you can hold."

I smiled and put out my hand to shake.

I'd given Susan my number at home, and she called at five. She sounded excited. "Got some beautiful cases right on point. It was fun. I think if it ended in court I'd win."

"Let's hope it doesn't go that far. Is Frank still there?"

"Went home, poor dear. Said he couldn't stand the place any longer. Kept mumbling something about bloody cormorants. Listen, I went to Choate & Masterson. Used my old building pass. They don't ever lock the file room, because people are always working. I've been through Stephen's files and it turns out there've been two changes of investment advisors in the last six months. That's practically unheard of, Max. And more money than would be normal has been held in simple interest-bearing accounts. There wasn't anything overt, but that proves you could be right."

My stomach had gone all hollow. I said, "You shouldn't have done that. What if he'd showed up? He's a killer."

"Nobody saw me. When I signed in I checked the sheet to make sure he wasn't there. It was fun. Any word yet from the DA? I wish I could tell him what I'd found today."

"It's no soap. We're going to have to do this on our own. We'll push till we get some reaction."

"There's a party for Choate & Masterson people at the Museum of Fine Arts tomorrow night. I'm invited and I'm sure Stephen will be there. Let me spring this stuff on him."

"Not alone. I'll be there as your guest. And we've got to be absolutely careful about this. In fact, I should do it alone."

"You're not a lawyer, Max. And he's got to know I'm serious about this. I'll talk to people I know at C & M and set it up for the party."

I couldn't see how it could go bad, as long as I was there with her. I said, "Okay." Susan said, "Now that's settled, why don't you come down and join me for dinner in the North End? We can compare notes on being sneaks. My treat."

"I don't think that's such a good idea."

"My God, you're old-fashioned. Okay, you treat."

"It's not that. What if we ran into Stephen in the restaurant? I think we'd better wait and see each other tomorrow. Unless you need a ride?"

She didn't say anything for a few moments, then said, "I'll take a cab. See you tomorrow." She hung up. People were hanging up on me all over the place.

I slept badly that night, with a lot of disturbing dreams that I remembered only vaguely. By noon that Sunday Susan had arranged everything about the party and we'd discussed on the phone how to present things to Stephen. I was to pick her up at six.

At 5:30 Phoebe called again. Melissa Streeter had attempted suicide.

CHAPTER TWENTY-ONE

"I'm late, I'm late . . ."

I CALLED SUSAN and she said she'd take a cab and meet me at the museum.

"Don't talk to him alone," I said. "Things are coming down on this guy. Stay around people and don't take any lonely jaunts through the galleries."

"It's a party, remember? Just get there as soon as you can."

I went down the front steps two at a time and out to the street. The block was in shadow, with just the tops of the buildings lit up on the side facing west. I stopped short of the Rambler—I smelled cigar smoke again, then spotted a smoldering butt in the gutter.

But stopping made me notice the front door on the passenger side hadn't been properly closed. I remembered shutting it after Susan. Nobody had been in the car with me since.

So I went back up and dialed the number for City Line Taxi and Charlie Smith. Charlie's drivers are all ex-members of Vietnam Vets Against the War. Some drive special cabs because they're missing an arm or leg. Charlie's never forgotten my helping one of his drivers framed by a bad cop on a charge of selling dope to minors.

By the seventh ring I started worrying about the Rambler sitting out there—if she was booby-trapped I didn't want vandals setting her off. It would ruin my insurance rating. Then Charlie answered.

I said, "Jim Mallory. Emergency conditions. Can you send two cabbies to Marlborough Street."

"Five minutes, Jimmy." He hung up without asking questions.

When I heard the first cab pull up outside I called Mangenello. He answered and I told him there was a bomb in my car, on Marlborough Street.

He didn't ask questions either, just said, "We'll be there. Guess Bensen wasn't afraid of you after all."

"I'll be gone. Somebody'll be watching the car. Approach with caution." I hung up and went back down.

The cabbies were big men with long hair and beards. I pointed out the Rambler to the first and told him it was rigged to blow up and to guard it with his life until the cops got there. I gave him one of the hundreds I'd taken off Bensen's man and still had in my wallet. I got in the other cab and we headed to Brookline, twenty minutes after Phoebe's call.

The driver made it in double time. I handed him a hundred and told him to wait. He passed it back and said, "Charlie said to take care of you special. What goes on the meter is enough," and he picked up a book and started reading. The book was *Voltaire in Love*, by Nancy Mitford.

Phoebe was at the front door. She took me back into the study.

I said, "What about a doctor?"

"There's no need. I'm a trained nurse."

"What happened?"

"Her mother's sleeping pills. It's my day off, but I came back to the house to check on her. She was vomiting most of them up—the body will reject that many barbiturates. There wasn't much for me to do but make sure she got them all up and put her to bed. She's slept some since."

I sat in the familiar tapestried sofa. "Why call me?"

"She's confessed everything, Mr. Mallory. She helped that man, Stephen Littman, kill her grandfather, and also helped him in his attempt to kill her mother. She's very confused. I don't think she should go to the police."

"And you want me to protect her?"

"If you can do it without letting Mr. Littman go free."

"I don't see how, Phoebe. He's not likely to keep the silence of a gentleman. If anything, he's liable to try to pin the whole thing on her."

"Perhaps you can make use of this," and she brought out a sheaf of papers from a drawer in the mahogany table. The first was a handwritten note on pink stationery that said, "Mallory was right. I can't live with what we did to Mother. I'm sorry." It was attached to six neatly typewritten pages on heavy white bond, each page initialed, the last signed by Melissa and witnessed by Phoebe. I read the first paragraph, then looked up.

"It's her full confession," Phoebe said. "She dictated it after I'd gotten the pills out of her system. I typed it while she slept."

She said that as if it was what anyone would have done under the circumstances. Lord love the British.

It was an incredible document. It was stream-of-consciousness, sometimes incoherent, but Phoebe had taken it all down, verbatim. Melissa'd been seeing Stephen for several months before Caleb was killed. She knew he wasn't after her money because he made a point of revealing to her that she had none coming. She'd first learned that from him. Everything they'd done since had been done to rectify that injustice.

She still believed the embezzled money was waiting in Switzerland, that Stephen was going to take her there, and that Morgan had been made sick only as a delaying tactic—after she'd made a request for an accounting of the trusts. They'd planned the phony burglary to explain how Morgan could be poisoned. Melissa had thought Stephen was being excessively cautious when he'd insisted on donning a ski mask and actually making a forced entry into the house, but the caution paid off. Mallory showed up, and because of the mask Stephen escaped detection. They'd decided to go ahead with the plan.

And something went wrong again. They'd miscalculated the dose. Morgan almost died.

From there the narrative began to ramble. Her grandmother had hated her. Her grandfather used to make love to her girlfriends. Morgan threw him out of the house because of that, and he'd blamed Melissa. She'd loved him, though. Until she learned of his betrayal. The last words of the document were, "I want everybody to know I love my mother. Mallory was right. I couldn't live with the fact that we'd almost killed her."

Phoebe'd typed out, "I solemnly swear that the above is the truth and all the truth, and my free act and deed," and Melissa had signed it.

Phoebe said, "As the family's attorney, he knew her every weakness, Mr. Mallory. At her last hospitalization there was a confidential psychiatrist's report filed with the court."

"When did Morgan request an accounting?"

"I made the request. I'm her business manager. I acted after hearing Mr. Littman's comments to you the day of Mr. Johnson's funeral. I'm sorry, sir. I had suspicions, I even had a fair idea what was happening on the night I called you. But I wasn't sure which way my duty lay. And I thought you had thwarted him."

"Maybe we rattled him enough to make him use the wrong dose of poison, or forced him to rely on Melissa to do his dirty work. But you should have told me."

"Will you see Melissa now, Mr. Mallory?"

I folded the typed confession and put it in the pocket of my jacket. I didn't see how it was going to help—not Melissa, anyway. But I nodded and we went together up the stairs.

Her bedroom looked like it hadn't been redecorated since early childhood—like a room she'd come back to rather than one she'd grown up in. Pink lacy curtains let in light from the setting sun, dolls in dresses were propped up beside stuffed bears and rabbits. Everything was rose-colored in the light from outside. None of it fit the way

I'd thought of her, tanned and in the clean white tennis outfit.

She was different now. No more bright mischief and flirtation, only her head showed above the tightly drawn sheets, and her eyes looked very tired. She gave me the same wan smile she'd worn on the day after Caleb's death. I wanted to take her hand, but she kept her arms under the sheet, as if she were paralyzed. She said, "Is it okay now?"

"It's okay."

"And Stephen?"

"I don't think he'll be okay."

She nodded slightly. "You read it?"

"Yes."

"There's something else. Maybe you can stop him. He knows she was at his office yesterday. He saw where she'd signed out on the sheet, at the front desk."

I was in the hallway and halfway down the stairs when Phoebe called to me. I turned and shouted, "Call Mangenello. Tell him the museum." I went out on the run and jumped into the cab. The driver dropped his book, I told him where, and we were off. I kept telling myself, "They're at a party, it'll be all right." But I was scared.

CHAPTER TWENTY-TWO

A Secret Singing

THE DRIVER raced the old cab out to Park Drive, past the Sears building and the Gardner Museum. He held his radio handset up as he drove and said, "You need help, I can have ten cabs out there in two minutes."

I told him the cops were on the way and he frowned, dropped the handset, and made the last tight curve before the museum. We turned down the street running along the west side and pulled into the visitors' lot. I handed him a hundred, said, "Don't argue," and ran for the entrance.

I knew that somewhere in the area there'd be an undercover cop assigned to Littman, and when Mangenello got the call he'd send him in. I couldn't wait. I got out my investigator's license and the picture of Susan and showed them both to the guard inside the door.

"You see this woman tonight?"

He took the picture and examined it closely. "Yes, I did."

"Has she gone out?"

"I don't think so."

"The police will be here shortly. If she comes this way, tell her to wait for me. If she's with somebody who wants to force her to go, hit the guy, do whatever you have to, but don't let them get out of here. You got that?"

"What's it about?"

"Tell you later," and I went in. The new West Wing of

the museum was designed by I. M. Pei and looks like a shopping mall. There's a museum shop behind glass walls and a café open to the second floor and to a high, arched skylight running the length of the building. Glass doors connect the ground floor to the old museum, and tonight they were locked. The museum shop was closed. I tried the doors to the auditorium and they were locked.

I could hear the party in full swing on the next level up. There was a special exhibition of American pre-Raphaelites in the Gund Gallery, and Susan had said a client was a major contributor and arranged a special showing for Choate & Masterson.

I went to the gallery at the north end, still on the ground floor, where there was an exhibit of works by Sean Scully. There were only a few couples in the gallery, none of them Susan and Littman.

Before going upstairs I tried the basement. The glass doors of the cafeteria were closed and locked. I went into the men's room, then opened the door to the women's room and called Susan's name. Nobody answered, so I went in and looked. Nobody.

I went back up two flights to the second floor. The upper hall was crowded with people. There were two makeshift bars set up with dozens of bottles and white-coated bartenders and tables with linen cloths and serving dishes of fresh shrimp and fruit and small sandwiches. The guests, dressed in suits and gowns, stood at the tables eating and talking, and a number of women in aprons and white hats moved from table to table replenishing the buffet. I didn't see Susan or Littman, but there were too many people to be certain.

I went to the guard at the exit from the Gund Gallery. He wore a blue blazer with a round patch showing the museum logo. I stuck the picture of Susan under his nose and told him to have her wait for me if she came by. I had to repeat it and show him my badge. Then I started through the crowd. A few people gave me questioning looks, but I kept moving.

The serving women were set up in the kitchen of the second floor restaurant, and I stopped to ask if anyone had seen Susan. I went into the men's room and then got a woman to look in the women's room—nothing. I went on down past the tables and into the entrance to the Gund Gallery.

Almost nobody was looking at the art. I went half running through the exhibition to the exit at the opposite end. The guard hadn't seen Susan. I pushed my way through the crowd again. I was going back down to try the guard at the front entrance when, from the top of the escalator, I noticed a third guard by the glass doors to the second floor of the old museum. He stood under the huge painting of Washington crossing the Delaware. I went over and used the picture of Susan one last time. The doors on that level weren't locked, and he said they were kept unlocked as an emergency exit. He was stationed there to keep people from wandering into the old wing.

I said, "Have you left this door at any time in the last hour?"

"What do you mean by that?"

I said very carefully and slowly, "That young woman might have gone in there, and she is in great danger."

"I stepped away a minute to use the john. Nobody's supposed to go in there."

An alarm went off somewhere beyond the door. The guard reached for his walkie-talkie and I went through, down the Asian art gallery, past big stone heads of Buddha and brightly colored silkscreens of Chinese men and women, out to the central hall at the marble staircase coming up from the Huntington Avenue entrance. My stomach felt hollow. I stopped under the dome of the rotunda, at the top of the stairs by the marble statue of Orpheus and Cerberus. I looked down to the ground floor. A security guard looked up and shouted at me. I ran straight ahead, into the corridor marked "Egyptian and European Decorative Art."

I stopped under a high statue of a pharoah and listened. I could hear shouts of the guards and the steady burr of the alarm signal. The high-ceilinged room was dimly lit by night lights.

I moved silently over tile floors, into another room of stone reliefs, then across a corridor and into a room of towering carved pillars and statuary of gods with heads of lions and birds. There was a red stone sarcophagus in the center of the room. Stephen Littman was trying to lift Susan's body up into it. She had on a bright green party dress that was hitched up around her waist. He saw me and dropped her.

"She's alive," he said. "I only hit her."

"It's all over," I said. "Melissa's confessed and the police are on the way."

I started to move, but he lifted an ugly little .22 pistol and aimed it at my chest.

"No closer, Mr. Mallory. You're supposed to be dead."

"You made a lot of mistakes. Don't make another, put down the gun."

He laughed and said, "Mistakes. You know I'd really only just started taking from the trusts when Caleb got on to me. The crafty old bastard. And I'd lost it all in Vegas—couldn't do a thing about it. I'd thought with that old fool Masterson in charge I was home free. And then you, you bastard. And Bensen, he wants half of everything."

I'd started moving again. "The guards are coming," I said.

"Then there's no time for anything except an act of pure vindictiveness."

He smirked and lowered the pistol to Susan's head and I came on the last few yards and crashed into him. The gun skidded over the tiles and through a door. We got up and he swung a kick at me, I caught the foot and hurled him back against a limestone relief built into the wall. A security guard appeared at the exit and leveled a gun at us. He said "freeze," but Littman got up and stumbled into the room where the .22 had gone, and the guard didn't fire.

I was kneeling beside Susan. I shouted, "He's got a gun."

The guard kept his pistol leveled at the entrance to the room and said, "There's no exit from that room."

I heard the sharp snap of Littman's little .22 and the sound of shattering glass. The guard looked across at me. Another guard and a cop came in behind me. The first guard pointed with his gun, and they all went slowly in that direction. When they could see into the room they lowered guns and one of the guards started to speak into a radio. Susan woke up. She looked confused, but smiled up at me. I smiled back and said, "Give me a minute."

I went over and stood beside the cop at the door to the room Littman had run for. It held a collection of wooden Egyptian coffins in glass cases. One of the glass cases was shattered, and in a small pool of blood and glass at the base of it, Stephen Littman was lying dead.

Behind me the big cabby had showed up, and then Mangenello came in. The cabby had a tire-iron ready for action. Mangenello knelt beside Susan and I went back over. He said, "You okay?"

"Sure. Is the Rambler okay?"

"No worse than it was before."

I smiled, and sat on the cool tile floor.

Epilogue

TEN DAYS LATER I was at a small inn in Tamworth, New Hampshire. I was making day trips to hike in the mountains, and in the evenings I ate at the inn and twice caught a play at the local summer stock theater. Both times the play was *Arsenic and Old Lace*. I had spent a weekend at the inn with Julie at the beginning of the summer and the staff remembered me and seemed sympathetic about my coming there alone.

I didn't mind. The last time I'd called Julie's apartment a guy answered and said she was in the shower. He sounded like a lawyer.

I was coming down the stairs for breakfast on the tenth day when the owner stopped me and gave me a telephone message from Mangenello. I'd given him the name of the inn before I left Boston.

I used my credit card and called from the phone at the front desk. Somebody at the other end told me they'd find him, and a minute later Mangenello's voice came over the line.

"Mallory? I got a message from Mrs. Streeter. She needs to see you."

"What's it about?"

"I think she wants to pay you."

"Aha. Anything new down there?"

"Nope. Not too much pressure on me to pull you back, since Littman's dead and we've got your statement on his confession. I still haven't figured out how he thought he'd get away with it. Susan's out of the hospital now. So's Morgan.

"The DA doesn't think he can pin anything on Bensen—and he's properly apologetic about it too. If there's an arraignment, you'll have to come down for that. And we ought to have a talk sometime. I still owe you those beers."

"Sure, Simon. Thanks for calling."

I rang off and told the innkeeper I'd be leaving for Boston after breakfast. He tallied the bill, I settled up, and went into the big dining room for a double order of french toast with real maple syrup. Then up to pack. Before leaving the room I took a final look to see if I'd left anything. *The Autobiography of Alice B. Toklas* sat on the bedside table, and I hesitated, then went back to stuff it into my bag.

Three hours later I was in Brookline. I hadn't stopped at the office or home, and my suitcase was still in the back of the Rambler.

The front door got opened by the maid who'd served me pastries almost a month earlier. In the study Morgan stood to take my hand. She looked better than she had at the hospital, but still pale.

"Thank you for coming, Mr. Mallory."

"I heard from Detective Mangenello that you wanted to see me."

She nodded. She walked to the mahogany table, opened a small drawer in its side, and came back with a blue slip of paper. It was a check for twenty-five thousand dollars, written out by hand.

"Part of this is for your discretion in protecting Melissa from involvement in this horrid affair. Phoebe told me everything. I received the transcript of Melissa's confession in the mail, which I assume you sent to me. I thank you. I also feel you've earned the money by your efforts in general on behalf of our family."

I didn't argue, just took the check and put it into my wallet.

Mrs. Streeter went to the couch and sat, leaning forward with the palms of her hands flat on her knees. "You'll be interested to know that Melissa is now a patient at a very fine institution in Switzerland, where she will be treated by the best doctors available in the field of personality disorders. Phoebe insisted upon that before she returned to England, and I thought it was warranted. The doctors say the prognosis is very good, so your efforts were not without fruit."

"Do the doctors know about her father? I think that might have some bearing on her treatment."

"I don't understand you."

"I've spoken with Peter Streeter. He told me about the circumstances of Melissa's birth. About you and Caleb."

She nodded. "I'd always thought he suspected that. I won't deny it, but if Melissa doesn't know, Mr. Mallory, I fail to see how it would help to tell her doctors."

"I think she knows."

Morgan looked unhappy. She said, "If you feel it is important, I give you my promise that I will speak to the doctors. In return, I hope you will agree to keep that poor secret from going beyond these walls."

"My lips are sealed. No extra charge."

She nodded again. "And now I would like to offer you tea, but I feel so dreadfully tired."

I bowed to her slightly. "I understand. And I am sorry for your troubles."

She smiled up at me. "What an old-fashioned dear you are."

From Brookline I drove to my bank to deposit the check, then directly to the Trojan. Things had worked out well. I felt extremely wealthy and I wished there was somebody to celebrate with, or at least a secluded place where I could stop the Rambler and give a bellow of joy without sacrificing my dignity.

The red light on Della flashed at me when I got into the office. I rewound the tape to play it back. There was an old message from Morgan Streeter, two recorded dial tones, and then Susan's voice.

"Dear knight in shining armor, et al. You were certainly right about Stephen. Are you still avoiding me? I want to invite you to another party. I'm back in Marblehead. That's not where the party's going to be." She hung up.

I stopped the tape, found the number on the resumé for Caleb Johnson, and dialed. A woman's voice answered. She said she was house-sitting.

"Susan flew to Greece two days ago."

I realized the message on Della must be several days old. "Did she go alone?"

"I think so."

"Where?"

"I'm not sure. Are you a friend?"

"A very good friend."

"I'm not sure where. She flew to Athens and was going to take a boat to some island. That's all I know."

"Thank you." I hung up.

I stood by the window and looked out onto Charles Street. I sighed, started up the tape again. Somebody with a voice like a foghorn wanted me to find his brother and left a number in Maine. Then Frank came on. He sounded excited.

"Sorry you're not around, old buddy, but can't wait. The cormorant has cut the bloody string. Hallelujah."

That was it. I swore softly, switched the machine off, dialed.

The switchboard operator at Frank's office said to hold, then came back to ask if the call were business or personal.

"Personal. And urgent."

"One moment."

Another voice, male, came on the line. "This is Harold

Peters. I'm an agent of the Federal Bureau of Investigation. Are you a friend of Mr. Burger's?"

"Son of a gun," I said, and cut the connection. I gave a bellow of joy. I got out the yellow pages and found the number I wanted and dialed. A young woman with a happy voice said, "TWA, Linda speaking."

I said, "When is your next flight out of Logan to Athens, Greece?"

"One moment, sir."

I held the line and Edgar popped his head in. "What's all da racket for?"

Linda came back on and said the next flight out was at 9:47 P.M.

ABOUT THE AUTHOR

RICHARD C. SMITH, a graduate of Dartmouth and Boston University Law School, was a corporate attorney in Boston for several years. He now lives and practices law in Philadelphia, Pennsylvania. *A Secret Singing* is his first novel.